# A Faerie's Tale

S. R. Hollands

# DEDICATION

This book is dedicated to my wife Nina. I cannot thank you enough for your support throughout this project. All those times that I was *'away with the faeries'* have now all been worthwhile. Thank you for believing in me, for supporting me and for humouring me.

I shall love you always…

# CONTENTS

# 1

## MARCH 1993

*For the first time in her twenty four summers the young woman experienced the creeping anticipation of genuine terror. Bad enough that from the outset they had blindfolded her, bound her wrists and dragged her through the forest for a full day, but now that they had finally reached their destination she knew in her heart that her situation would only worsen. Blind beneath the hood they had forced her to wear she stood waiting for something dreadful to happen. Her mind played tricks on her as it predicted the agony of a flint or bronze blade across the soft flesh of her throat, causing her to swallow in fear.*

*She knew they had entered a building of some kind for her senses had detected the drop in temperature, the paved surface of the floor beneath her bare feet and the sudden loss of the familiar forest sounds. Behind her she heard the cultured voice. The voice she had known since her childhood, the voice she had once trusted…*

*'This is where we part. Do not attempt to return or you will be dead before the next sunset.' Then a question, directed towards another, 'You know what you have to do?'*

*'Aye,' a coarser voice replied.*

*'Then we shall begin.'*

*The cultured voice continued, but this time in the old language, uttering an incantation so ancient that it chilled her soul. She knew these words and at once she understood what they were going to do to her. Her dread expanded tenfold.*

*The blade she had first feared struck out, but it did not touch her flesh. Instead, it cut through the bonds about her wrists. Then before she could react, the thrust of a boot against her backside sent her violently forward, flinging her into her destiny. She fell upon the stone floor, striking her elbows as she went down. Simultaneously the warm humid heat of high summer rapidly plunged to cold biting winter. Sitting up and removing the blindfold she found herself alone within a cold stone chamber. Faint light filtered through the slit of an entrance telling her that daytime lay beyond. Timidly she rose and ventured outside and her worst fears were confirmed. This was not her world. As she suspected, they had sent her into the realm of the others, the outlanders...*

*Now she wished that they had simply killed her. She would have preferred that, for in her opinion it would have been the more merciful thing to have done...*

\*

Seventeen year old Alice Wilson shivered. It was five in the afternoon, but already dark. Snow flurries had been present all day and a thin, patchy layer covered the ground. A sharp wind blew across the flat Somerset landscape, rustling the yew hedge at the end of the garden. She cursed Rory's stubbornness, understanding why he'd wriggled out of bringing in the firewood. Moodily she tucked the log basket under her arm and hurried down the path, her cat Copper following loyally.

The shed door scuffed across the concrete as Alice pulled it open. Reaching in she flipped the light switch and a dull glow illuminated the front half of the shed from the low wattage bulb. She slammed the door behind her, shutting out the wind as the odour of well-seasoned logs assaulted her nostrils. She loved that tangy smell and paused, breathing in the heady aroma with her eyes closed. Inside, logs of all sizes were stacked from floor to ceiling.

Alice selected some heftier logs, for they would burn longer. A spider, disturbed by her actions ran across the floor making her jump. Copper chased after the escaping arachnid, but lost sight of it as it disappeared into the shadows. She wandered off, looking for mice instead. It didn't take long to fill the basket and Alice was ready to go indoors.

'Copper?' she said. 'Where are you?' Getting no response Alice went to find her. She called again. 'Come on Copper, it's too cold to hang around out here, what are…'

A sudden outburst of angry hissing came from the corner of the shed and Alice's heart sank. Don't say that Copper had found another rat. That proved horrible last year, resulting in Copper being bitten. Striding forward Alice caught sight of her pet spitting furiously, her ginger fur standing on end.

'Copper, come away!'

Her cat's safety her first thought Alice grabbed a log and lunged forward in a bid to frighten off any rodents. She stopped dead in her tracks. Beyond Copper between the stacked logs crouched a human shaped figure. Alice stood frozen to the spot, fear gripping her belly despite the silhouette being tiny, like that of a child. The shadows obscured all detail, but a pair of eyes reflected the glow of the light bulb. Brandishing the log before her Alice found her voice.

'Who are you?' she asked, fear causing her voice to tremble. 'And what the hell are you doing in our shed?'

No reaction came from the intruder. Still clutching the log and feeling her stomach tighten Alice moved backwards, never taking her eyes from the shadowy figure.

By the door on a hook hung an old bicycle lamp they used as a torch whenever they needed wood from the more remote corners. Alice continued to edge back, groping behind her for the lamp. Her hand struck plastic and her fingers closed around the familiar shape. She moved forward bringing the lamp with her. Copper still stood guard, hunched and ready to spring at any moment.

Alice clicked the bicycle light on and pandemonium broke out. She saw a glimpse of something brown before a high pitched screech burst from the shape which darted into a corner, seeking out more shadows. Copper howled and flew past Alice, heading for the closed door. Alice also screamed and in her panic dropped the light which went out, throwing the corner back into darkness. Terrified now, Alice bent and grabbed the light and shook it. It remained off. She struck it against her hand and sighed with relief as it flickered and came back on. She raised it slowly, gradually allowing the soft glow to reveal whatever lurked in the shed. Alice gasped.

At first glance, what indeed looked like a child of around ten or eleven years old cowered in the corner. On closer inspection Alice could see that this was no child, but an adult woman of the tiniest proportions. Even childlike in her behaviour the tiny woman peered back at Alice through her fingers, her hands held over her face in fear. Now she saw the perceived threat Alice relaxed a little and spoke again.

'What are you doing in our shed?'
The figure whimpered. Intrigued now Alice crept closer, kneeling down as she approached so as to appear less intimidating.

'I won't hurt you,' she said gently. The figure refused to move and Alice grew impatient. 'Look, I can't help you if you won't talk can I?' she blurted out.

The woman stirred, but instead of coming out of the shadows she appeared to be trying to get further into the corner away from the light. A nudge at Alice's ankles reminded her of Copper. Seeing her owner taking charge had emboldened the cat and she returned, curious as to what lurked in the shed. Alice took hold of her collar.

'Copper won't hurt you; she's just frightened that's all. Look, I've got hold of her; she can't come near you now.'

The figure slowly lowered her hands from her face. As they observed each other Alice took in the details of the mysterious woman. Although curled into a ball Alice judged her to be no more than around one point three metres tall. She was no dwarf, but a perfectly formed adult – just petite to the extreme. Her unusual attire caught Alice's attention too for she only wore one garment – a tiny dress that came a short way down her bare thighs. It was sleeveless and off the shoulder leaving her thin arms and upper chest exposed. A small leather bag hung over her shoulder on a strap whilst a pouch and a sheathed knife were attached to her belt. Her hair was piled high at the back of her head with a wild looking fringe at the front, whilst spiky dark brown tresses and a couple of small plaits on either side hung down to just below her shoulders. Alice couldn't believe her eyes.

Tears trickled down the woman's face. She wiped them away with the back of a grubby hand as a child would and a sob escaped her lips. Alice mellowed and edged forward.

'Don't cry,' she said. 'We can sort it out, but you have to tell me who you are.'

'I am called Willow.'

*'Progress at last!'* thought Alice.

'All right Willow, well... I'm Alice...where are you from?'

'From Eyedore.' Alice had never heard of the place, but that didn't matter for now.

'You're hardly wearing anything. You must be frozen.'

'I do not feel the cold the way that you do. Where I come from...'

A scraping noise announced the shed door being pulled open as Alice's elder brother called out loudly.

'What're you doing Alice? I've made tea – how long's it take to get some bloody logs? Get a flippin' move on!'

Willow cowered back behind her hands and Alice lowered the lamp.

'Rory don't move – don't even breathe.'

Ignoring her, Rory barged forward.

'What are you doing?' he asked impatiently.

Alice raised her hand and stopped him in his tracks. Placing a cautionary finger to her lips to signify silence she beckoned him over. Rory edged towards her, dropping into a crouch before saying,

'What?'

Alice whispered back.

'Don't say anything okay? Let me do the talking and I'll show you something.'

Rory nodded. Alice spoke into the darkened corner.

'Willow, this is my brother Rory. I'm going to put the light back on, okay?'

As before Alice shone the light onto the floor and slowly brought it up. Willow had vanished.

'Buggar!'

Rory laughed loudly and Alice turned angrily towards him.

'You've really frightened her.'

'Frightened who?'

'Just watch and don't butt in.'

Alice swept the light around the corner of the shed. After a few moments she let the beam hover in the darkest recess where a tiny patch of brown could just be seen.

'There!'

'Where?'

Alice decided to be a little bolder.

'Willow, come out,' she said tartly.

A rustling sound preceded Willow as she warily edged her way back into the dim light.

'BLOODY HELL!' said Rory loudly.

'*SHUT UP!*' Alice responded.

Luckily Willow remained in view, although at Rory's exclamation she visibly flinched. Now understanding Alice's caution Rory sat silently, allowing his sister to do the talking.

'Willow, we want to help. We were doing so well before Rory came in. You were telling me where you're from.'

'You would not understand.'

''P'raps not, but we still want to help.'

'You cannot help.'

'Yeah, you're right there. The longer you tell me nothing, the longer we'll sit here - and I'm cold. Come into the house with us.'

'Alice, we can't ask her in,' said Rory. 'She might be a murderer or something.'

'Does she look like a murderer you bloody moron?'

'I don't know – I've never met one…'

'If this is your idea of helping then just go back indoors or be quiet – I told you to let me talk to her!'

Pulling a face Rory fell silent, but remained beside Alice. She spoke again.

'Come on Sweetie, let's take you indoors. It's loads warmer in there.'

Willow shook her head.

'I belong to the forest…your house would do me harm…'

Alice looked bemused.

'I keep telling you we won't harm you. Are you hungry?'

Willow replied, agitation now in her voice.

'Entering your home would kill me and that is what he wants…'

'Who?'

'My uncle, Flint.'

'This is weird,' Rory muttered. Alice ignored him.

'And yes, I am very hungry.'

Alice turned to Rory. 'Go and get her some food.'

'Why me?'

'Just GO!'

Rory stood up and walked off muttering, the door banging behind him.

'It's just us now Sweetie. Why can't you come inside?'

'My realm is the natural world – the forest, the meadows…to step into your home would make me ill – I jest not…'

'But surely you live in a house?' Alice asked.

'I did, but in another world. Not here.'

Alice felt confused. She bit her lip thoughtfully and for a few minutes silence hung over them. Eventually she spoke.

'If you're not from our world…then where is yours?'

'My realm runs alongside your own. You cannot see it

or enter it unless one of us invites you to, but we can enter yours whenever we please. There are...gateways, portals – points where the two worlds cross over. We can use those to move between the two.'

Alice screwed up her face.

'What like a parallel universe?'

'You might call it that – they are the same world, the same places, but in different zones – different things happening, different people...'

'Can you take me there?'

'No, it is too dangerous, even for me now; I do not think I can ever go back there.'

Willow began to weep again and Alice sat watching her. This all seemed so odd...

Alice could bear it no more. Standing up she walked across the six feet or so that separated them and sat beside her new friend. Willow ceased her tears and observed Alice nervously, but she did not cower away.

Sitting beside Willow Alice detected an odd smell she would not have associated with any young woman. She smelt of damp earth, moss and bark and leaves. In fact as Alice looked closer she realised that the flimsy dress worn by Willow was fashioned entirely of leaves – hundreds of them, all held together by the tiniest of stitches. They rustled when Willow moved and reminded Alice of the sound she made when she went walking through the woods. There were also flowers stitched into the garment to decorate it. The belt worn around Willows waist was made entirely from woven wicker withies. Some of the willow strands were stripped of their bark, others left with it on, giving a two coloured, attractive look.

Willow had also been studying Alice. Looking older than her seventeen years Alice was tall, slim and rather appealing in a typical girl-next-door kind of way. She rarely wore make up, preferring a natural appearance. The look worked well for her. But it was Alice's glasses that really caught Willow's attention. She reached out and touched them. Now Alice shrank away, but steeling herself, she let Willow run her tiny fingers over the black, plastic frames.

'What is this thing on your face?'

'They're my glasses. I can't see properly so they correct my vision – try them.'

She handed them to Willow who held them up to her own face. Her reaction annoyed Alice as she flung the glasses across the shed.

*'You mock me! They took away my sight! What evil magic is that?'* she hissed.

Willow retreated back into the corner whilst Alice retrieved her glasses. Checking they were undamaged she put them back on saying,

'I'm not mocking you. They suit my eyes not yours. If your eyes work properly the glasses distort what you see. It's not magic anyway – why would you think that?'

Willow looked on distrustfully and remained in her corner.

'Well they stopped *me* from seeing – silly, silly things!'

Alice shook her head. One moment Willow appeared full of wisdom, yet at other times she reverted to behaving like a sulky child.

Whilst she pondered on this the door scraped open again and Rory and Copper re-entered with a tray of food. Rory placed the tray on the floor between Alice and where Willow sat sulking. She didn't stay there for long. The promise of a full belly outweighed her sulkiness and she crept forward, still watching Rory and Alice out of the corner of her eye. Like Alice, Rory also stood tall and slim. He sported a shock of brown hair based on a swept back fifties style and he was always smartly dressed. Girls adored him. He was eighteen years old.

Rory had provided a good selection. Buttered bread, a jar of peanut butter, an apple and a couple of cold sausages all sat there enticingly. Willow picked up the apple. She said nothing, but just sat crunching on it, even consuming the core and pips. Wiping her mouth she picked up a sausage and sniffed it.

'What is this?' she asked.

'A sausage,' Rory said, 'finest pork & herb.'

You'd have thought Willow had been stung for she flung the sausage into the corner, picked up the other and threw that too. Copper, not believing her luck jumped on them in an instant. Rory showed annoyance.

'Hey, I wanted those for my breakfast tomorrow, but I let you have them – how bloody ungrateful!'

Alice put out a restraining hand as Willow picked up a slice of the bread and sniffed suspiciously at the jar of peanut butter. Without looking up she responded to Rory's protest.

'I do not eat flesh – just fruit, berries, bread and such like. What is this?' Unable to open it she held up the jar. Alice replied before Rory could say anything stupid.

'Peanut butter - it's okay, there's no meat in there.'

Taking the jar from her, Alice unscrewed the lid and handed it back. Willow sniffed at it and poked a dirty finger inside before taking a cautionary taste. After a moment she said,

'This is good, very good.'

Whipping out the knife on her belt she dipped it into the jar. The look of sheer joy on her face at taking her first bite caused Alice and Rory to both smile broadly. She rapidly ate all three slices.

'I put a knife on the tray for you – why didn't you use it?' Rory asked.

'Because it is made of ferrum I cannot touch it. Even to look at it makes me feel sick – take it away!'

'Ferrum? No it's made of steel, look,' said Rory picking it up. With a horrified look on her face Willow shrank back as Alice leaned forward and took the knife from Rory.

'Listen to her Rory,' Alice scolded. 'She doesn't like it – why hold it in her face?'

'Sorry, didn't mean anything.'

'I know, but just listen to her and show some respect.'

Rory caught Willow glaring at him. He looked down, feeling a little ashamed under her hot gaze. Alice changed the subject.

'Well what are we going to do with you? We still don't know where you're from and you won't come into the house, that's clear.'

'Look,' Rory said. 'Mum won't be home for a few hours. We have plenty of time. I think if Willow is happy out here we should leave her be. We can give her a blanket and bring her some food in the morning.'

Their mother worked as a nurse at the hospital in Yoevil, her shifts often leaving her children at home together. At seventeen and eighteen respectively Alice and Rory were highly capable of looking after themselves. From an early age they'd had to. Their father left home when they were small, leaving their mother Liz to bring them up alone. He had never seen, nor contacted his children since. The siblings had matured quickly and became extremely independent and close to each other.

Rory spoke to Willow again.

'What would you want for breakfast?'

'More nut butter?' asked Willow, expectation spreading across her face.

'Maybe,' said Rory, 'but judging by the speed you ate that it won't last long. What about eggs, do you eat those?'

'Oh yes,' she said. 'Eggs are fine and so is cheese – I love cheese, and apples – like the one I ate earlier – or barley porridge, honey, bread, wild berries, plums and milk, I love to drink milk and...'

'Hold on Babe, it's not a hotel you know, some of those things might be off the menu.'

Alice interrupted.

'Rory don't be so bloody rude. She's just telling you what she likes. Leave her alone.'

Rory blushed.

'Sorry Willow,' he muttered.

Willow responded by flashing Rory a dazzling smile. Her entire face lit up and Rory was quite taken at how pretty she looked. Seeing the glint in his eye Alice cuffed him round the head.

'Don't get any ideas brother,' she said smirking. 'If we're staying in here I need a coat. Want one?' Rory nodded.

As Alice made to leave a look of consternation crossed Willow's face, but Alice reassured her.

'It's okay Willow I'll be back in a moment. Rory can look after you – just don't listen to any of his smooth talk.' Willow looked a little confused at the mention of 'smooth talk' but accepted being left alone with Rory.

With Alice gone Willow retreated into the corner and sat looking at the floor. Rory, not knowing what to say came out with the first thing that entered his head.

'Can I see that knife of yours? It's pretty cool.'

'Cool?'

'Yeah – you know, sort of trendy.'

'Trendy?'

'You're hard work aren't you? Can I see your knife? It looks *interesting…*'

For a few moments Willow didn't move then she drew the knife and warily passed it over, handle first. Rory studied it minutely. The blade was made of a dull brown metal, and razor sharp. The wooden handle depicted engravings of stars, the sun and the moon. Willow watched suspiciously as Rory examined it. When he handed it back she relaxed. All his banter gone now he spoke to reassure her.

'Look Willow, I mean you no harm. Like Alice said, I'm a bit loud sometimes. Anyway, why can't you touch our knife? And what's ferrum?'

Willow looked thoughtful.

'Ferrum is the hard, black metal. Thousands of summers ago my people lived alongside your people.

Then, men discovered ferrum – the black metal - and the world changed. Ferrum is harder than our brown metal. Some men chose to fight us and steal our land, and our weapons were no match for their ferrum ones. We withdrew from your world and entered the other realm. I explained some of this to Alice, but she does not understand. Since those ancient days, my people have feared ferrum and anything made from it. We are born with an aversion to it.'

The same idea that previously bothered Alice now manifested itself in Rory's head. Looking at Willows tiny stature, her clothing and taking in her words about her home and people he spoke with disbelief in his voice.

'If I didn't know better I'd say you were a Faerie...'

Willow leapt up, her face scarlet.

'How dare you!' she hissed. 'How *dare* you use that word to my face? Mark this Master Rory, call me that again and I shall blight you! I shall blight your home, your crops, your family name and your manhood – especially your manhood! I shall blight...I...I...'

Shocked at the outburst Rory backed off and stuttered an apology. Willow stood glaring and that was how Alice found them upon her return. She wore her own coat and passed Rory his. She also carried a blanket and cushion for Willow. Handing them over she looked at the pair of faces before her – one clearly angry, the other confused.

'Okay,' she asked, 'what's he done?'

'He used a word, a bad word!' Willow said.

'Oh Rory, why swear at her? What did you say?'

Confused, Rory began to bluster.

'I didn't swear! And I didn't think it insulting either...'

'WELL IT IS!' shouted Willow becoming angry again. She pointed a finger at Rory. 'Do not call me that again. Do not even let me hear that word - *ever!*'

Overawed by the tiny woman Rory nodded.

'I'm sorry, but I didn't know you hate that word. I won't use it again.'

For a moment Willow continued to scowl before nodding her assent. Confused by her mood swing, Alice looked at Rory.

'Tell me what happened later, but for now we should decide what to do with her.'

The trio sat down. Willow picked up the peanut butter jar and began scooping it out on her fingers and eating it noisily. Alice and Rory grinned at her appalling manners. Rory spoke.

'Tomorrow is Sunday and we have a week off college. We have plenty of time to help you. The difficulty will be mum. She'll want to go to the Police or something.'

'Police? What is that?' asked Willow looking up from her jar. Her tiny hand groped as far inside as possible to reach the last smears of peanut butter.

'Police are...well...they are people, who enforce our laws,' said Rory.

'You've never heard of the Police?' Alice asked, in disbelief. Rory responded.

'She isn't from around here Alice; she told you that earlier - she comes from another world...I get what she is, but I can't say it in front of her or I'll upset her again.'
Without looking up Willow interjected.

'Whisper that word to her if she is familiar with it – just do not let me hear it.' She went back to her peanut butter. Rory nodded and leaning over whispered in Alice's ear.

'WHAT? No way! Who are you kidding?'
Rory shook his head.

'Everything she said adds up. We covered Celtic folklore in history at college last year. I've read some books on it – some of it can be fascinating. What Willow said really makes sense – and I've just realised what ferrum is.'

'What is it?' asked Alice.

'Iron, or in modern terms steel, which is mostly iron anyway. Traditionally Faer...sorry Willow, *her* kind really fear it. I think she's genuinely not of our world. Look at

her size, her clothes - and she doesn't even feel the cold –
that's not normal. '

Alice nodded.

'It just seems too far-fetched though. Too...story
bookish... And if she is what you say, shouldn't she have
wings?'

Rory shook his head.

'No, that's a Victorian concept. The old stories never
mention them having wings.'

Alice took in her brother's words and then spoke to
Willow.

'Is what Rory told me correct? Is that what you meant
by from another realm?'

Willow put down the empty jar. With peanut butter all
over her face she looked like a child still learning to feed
itself. Alice wanted to clean her up, but ignored it.

'Yes,' Willow responded. 'Rory is correct although his
choice of word for my people needs revising. We are
called the Fae.' She glanced at Rory sarcastically and he
blushed. Willow continued. 'In your world we are just
regarded as some old folk tale or child's fantasy. It suits us
if you believe that for we get left alone, but when we do
genuinely need human assistance it can work against us.'

'You said someone wanted you dead. Why?' asked
Alice.

Willow looked downcast.

'My mother died when I was tiny and my father brought
me up. He owned a great deal of wealth and land. He was
kind – not at all like his younger brother Flint. *Flint!* His
name is of the earth and his kind are hard hearted. He
really lives up to his name too. My father became sick and
Flint came to treat him. I thought he did father and I a
service at the time - but no! Instead of getting better, my
father grew sicker and passed into The Summer Lands.
Flint did not act in our interests at all. When father
passed, Flint imprisoned me, spread a rumour that I had
died too and stole all of my father's land and property.

Two days ago he opened a gateway into your world and flung me out. I cannot go back because he will have the gateways watched. If I go through any of them I shall be dead before the next sunset – he told me this. He told me...'

Willow sobbed and Alice put her arms around her and cuddled her like a frightened child. When her tears ceased Willow sat up, once more rubbing her face with the back of her hand. She looked a mess. Her eyes were red and puffy, her hair dishevelled and peanut butter covered her face. Silent, she sat looking utterly dejected and Rory, feeling the pull on his heart edged closer to her. Taking her hands in his he said,

'I don't know how, but we will help you. I don't know what we can do, but Alice and I will get you home. Do you hear me?'

Still shaking, Willow managed a watery smile. Rory stroked her hair saying,

'I mean it Willow.'

Her reply came low and soft.

'Thank you. You have both been so good to me and nothing like the stories I have heard about your kind.' Leaning forward she kissed Rory on the cheek and said,

'I am tired and would like to sleep. I am grateful for your hospitality. Thank you.'

Rory and Alice stood up. They towered over Willow, but she no longer shied away. Alice spoke softly.

'We'd best let you sleep then. Come on Rory, let's go back indoors. Willow, we'll bring you something to eat in the morning.'

'Nut butter?'

Alice smiled.

'I think you ate it all Sweetie, but if there's none for the morning I'll go out and buy you some tomorrow alright?'

As they made to leave, Willow unexpectedly flung herself at Alice, leaping as she did so and wrapped her tiny arms around the girl's neck whilst entwining her bare legs about her body.

'Thank you.' She said. 'Thank you both.' Sliding down she scampered her way back to the darkened corner, shook out the blanket and slid beneath its folds.

Sleep did not come easily to Willow. Her mind remained active for many hours as she lay in the darkness. Memories of her childhood, of her father and of her once kindly uncle tormented her. But mostly her thoughts returned to something else. Something she had not told to Rory or Alice. Something that she knew her uncle would be prepared to risk all for…

\*\*\*

# 2

# The Second Day

Despite the fact that Alice and Rory barely slept all night they were both out of bed early the following morning. Seven o'clock found them dressed and eating breakfast whilst 'Young At Heart' by The Bluebells played on the kitchen radio. Their mother Liz walked in tying the belt of her animal print dressing gown around her ample waist. Copper, busy eating some cat biscuits took a moment to look up from her bowl and mewed loudly to attract her attention. Liz ignored her.

Big boned, big bosomed and big hearted was how Liz described herself. She looked like an older, plumper version of Alice as she ruffled her fingers through her own dark hair in the same way her daughter did, before adjusting her glasses saying,

'What happened? You two never get up early! Somewhere to go today?'

Rory shook his head and spoke through a mouthful of cornflakes.

'Not really Mum. How did work go last night?'

'What do you think? A&E on a Saturday night? Several drunks, two blokes who were involved in a fight and a three car pile-up on the motorway. What happened to you two when I came home? You normally wait up. And both of you out of bed so early today. What's going on?'

She clattered about with the kettle as she waited for a response. Alice answered.

'We were both tired last night so we went to bed early. Going for a walk in a bit. I need to think some stuff through. Exams soon. Rory helped me last night with my physics revision, so I asked him to come with me to test me.'

Liz beamed. She often encouraged Rory to help his sister with her homework, but usually to no avail. Hearing he had done so for once warmed her heart.

'Well, I think that's wonderful. Rory that's lovely of you to help your sister like that. Bit cold for a walk though – seen the snow out there?'

Rory grinned at his mother.

'Yeah well, you know me Mum, all heart. Anyway, the snow's not that bad. Looks worse than it is.'

'Mum,' asked Alice, 'can we take some sandwiches with us?' Liz laughed.

'You've just eaten breakfast! What would you like?'

'Peanut butter?' chipped in Rory.

Alice sniggered. Liz gave them an odd look and rummaged in the cupboard saying,

'I saw the peanut butter in here only yesterday. It can't have gone already, surely? Either of you two moved it?'

'Rory got hungry last night,' Alice blurted out. Liz scolded her son.

'That was a new jar! I only opened it recently. You can't have eaten it all!'

She watched Rory glare at his sister.

'Thanks Alice, thanks a lot!'

Liz turned on him.

'That's just plain greedy and you know we don't have much money. You can bloody well buy a new one yourself!'

Looking sheepish Rory nodded.

'Sorry Mum, I'll buy one later. But can we still have something to take with us?' Despite her frustration over the peanut butter Liz gave in.

'What is it with you two? Alright, but sort it yourselves, I'm not slaving for you.'

'Tell you what, we'll wash up – won't we Alice?' he said.

Alice agreed.

'Yeah, put your feet up mum, you deserve a break – I'll make your tea if you like.'

Shaking her head, Liz put down the dirty dishes that she had gathered.

'Something funny's going on here,' she said. 'Don't know what, but I'll get to the bottom of it…' She walked off to the lounge calling over her shoulder. 'A couple of slices of toast with that tea would be good!'

\*

Alice and Rory worked hard. They made tea and toast for their mother, cleared the kitchen and prepared Willow's breakfast. Remembering some of her fancies of the night before they made her a couple of cheese sandwiches, packed a pair of apples and for good measure threw in some celery, a raw carrot and rather strangely, an onion. By eight thirty they were ready to leave. Hearing their mother's bath running, they made their escape. Pulling on her Parka coat and snatching up the bag of food Alice headed for the back door with Rory at her heels. Copper mewed loudly and joined them. She always followed Alice everywhere.

A thin layer of snow still covered much of the garden. A few wispy snowflakes still swirled around on the easterly wind, but the forecast on the new breakfast show GMTV on Friday morning had promised sunny spells over the weekend too. Alice advanced down the path and opened the door to the woodshed. The pair slipped inside, pulling the door closed behind them. Flicking the light on Alice called out.

'Willow? *Willow!*'

Silence. They crossed the shed. In the corner lay the blanket and cushion, the empty peanut butter jar, but no Willow. Alice saw consternation spread across Rory's face as her own stomach turned over.

'Where's she gone?' she asked. Rory shook his head.

'I don't know,' he replied. 'I don't know.'

Dejected, they sat down and Alice's hand became entangled in the blanket.

'It's warm,' she said, 'it's still warm – she can't have gone far!'

She gaped as Rory leapt up and ran out of the shed. Encouraged by his action she followed.

'Where could she have gone?' she called. Seeing Rory beckoning her to keep up, she continued after him.

Rory raced down the garden, through the gate and into the farmland beyond. She watched as he stared at the ground. Noticing the trail of tiny foot prints in the snow her brother followed, Alice called out.

'Do you know where she is?'

'I think so.'

Alice felt her confidence in her brother expand and loyally followed.

*

The footprints led to the field corner. There, tucked into the hedgerow stood an ancient barrow, a prehistoric stone burial chamber. Entry to the site had always been free to the public. Rory and his friends used to play there as children, imagining it to be a World War II bunker. The footprints led inside. Together they entered the darkness and Rory called out.

'Willow? Where are you? Come out, we're here to help!' They heard nothing. He called again, this time a little louder.

'WILLOW! WILLOW!'

A few seconds passed and they heard a whimper from within. Rory groped in his pocket for his key ring which had a small light attached. The walls glistened with damp and the drip of water could be heard. There were puddles on the floor and the atmosphere felt cold. The barrow smelt dank and unwelcoming and Rory's breath formed clouds in front of him as he walked. The weak light in his hand revealed a stone chamber opening up before them and as Rory entered, there in a corner he saw Willow sitting on the wet floor hugging her knees to her chest. Her face rested upon them and she had been crying again. Copper bounded forward and nuzzled against her bare legs.

'Why did you leave the woodshed Willow, you really scared us?' asked Alice.

'I want to go home.'

'But why have you come to this awful place?'

Willow looked up, her tear stained and filthy face looking ghastly in the dim light.

'I told you last night about the gateways...well this is one of them. It is where Flint cast me out from. I have tried to get back through, but the way home is barred to me.'

'What do you mean – barred?' asked Alice. Willow tried to explain.

'It is my uncle. Although I suspected that he may have the gateways watched I thought I might try to slip through unobserved, but Flint has done better than that – he has put a charm on this one. I can open it, but I cannot pass through.'

Willow fell silent again and Rory, dropping to his knees hugged her. She felt tiny in his arms like a child.

'Can't we take you through?' he asked. 'You'd have to show us how, but we could try.' Willow shook her head.

'No,' she said. 'There is something in there that would harm me - I could feel it when I attempted to pass through – I am quite unable to do it.'

Rory sighed, not understanding.

'Well there must be a way through. In the meantime, sitting here in this cold barrow is no good for anyone. Come back to our shed and we'll give you something to eat. You might not feel the cold, but Alice and I do!'

'Thank you, but I cannot live in your outbuilding

forever.'

She stood up and holding her hand Rory led her back to the safety of their home.

Although a part of the local farmland, the field had always been a popular haunt for dog walkers and a public footpath gave access around the boundary. On the far side of the field Melissa Gleeson walked her German Shepherd Max whilst listening to Grunge music on her portable minidisc player. Melissa lived next door to Alice and Rory. In the same physics and English classes as Alice at the local sixth form, she held a raging crush on Rory. From the opposite path she watched, curious as to whom the child could be that she saw with her friends. She smiled to herself – she never missed an opportunity to call round and see Rory. Melissa had convinced herself that Rory really liked her. Switching off the throbbing music and calling out to Max, Melissa began striding across the field towards Alice and Rory's home. They were just passing through the gate and as she picked up her pace she saw them disappear into the woodshed.

*

Back inside the shed Willow sat down, staring at the bag that Alice carried.

'You said you would bring something for me to eat,' she said brazenly.

'Yes,' responded Alice. 'Cheese sandwich okay?'

'Okay? I do not know this word – you and Rory use it a lot,' Willow said screwing up her face. Alice laughed, already used to Willow's lack of modern phrases and abbreviations.

'It means is it alright?' she stated, 'you know, as in, is a cheese sandwich alright?'

'I told you yesterday that I like cheese,' said Willow rudely holding her hand out. Her grasp of manners clearly needed honing. Alice opened the bag and took out the sandwiches. A heavy layer of cheese poked out from between the bread. Willow's eyes lit up for she could detect the strong cheddar aroma and she squealed appreciatively.

'Ooh,' she whispered, 'that smells lovely!'

Taking the sandwiches from Alice she placed one under the cushion for later, then closing her eyes she bit into the other. A contented smile spread across her face.

'It is good,' she said, spitting crumbs over Alice. Wiping her face Alice grimaced, ignoring Willow's lack of manners.

Once she settled into eating, Rory took over the conversation and questioned her.

'You said that the gateway into your world is barred to you – how does that work then?'

Rolling her eyes upwards Willow looked thoughtful before answering in between bites.

'It is difficult to explain,' she said. 'The gateway can only be opened by the Fae.' She continued chewing and looking wistfully into space. Rory continued to probe with more questions.

'So how is the gateway blocked to you – can you even open it?'

'Yes I told you I can open it, do you not ever listen?' she said crossly. 'I just cannot pass through. There is something there, something stopping me from crossing the threshold. I tried, but it immediately made me feel very ill as soon as I put one foot across. My legs went weak and I could not breathe. It is a similar sensation to the one I felt last night when you waved that ferrum knife around, but more intense.'

Rory thought for a moment and continued.

'You don't suppose Flint's placed ferrum in the entrance do you?'

Willow chewed on her sandwich, taking in Rory's words.

'I know not,' she said. 'He could have, but that would place him at risk too.' She looked up suddenly. 'However, he is a very powerful Magus and as I told you last night – Flint is an earth Fae. Although ferrum is just as dangerous to him it may be possible that he could know a way to protect himself. It did not just feel like ferrum – it possessed some other power, a more malevolent force - what else is in that bag? The bread and cheese tasted good.'

Alice passed it across and Willow took out the onion.

'What is a Magus?' Alice asked.

Without even peeling the onion Willow bit into it and began to eat it like an apple. Alice and Rory grimaced, but said nothing. Willow, crunching on the smelly vegetable without a care in the world answered Alice's question.

'A Magus is someone who is a great adept at magic,' she said. 'And Flint is extremely skilled at performing magic.'

Alice and Rory glanced at each other, not sure how to take this talk of magic. They fell silent and needing a break Rory stood up.

'I need the loo,' He said. 'I'm cold. Be back in a minute.' With that he headed through the door leaving Alice and Willow together.

*

'Hey Rory, what are you doing in there? And who's the brat?'

Rory spun round to see Melissa from next door standing by the shed. Seeing her hand already on the door handle he swiftly walked back towards her. Melissa pulled the door open and ducked inside. His need for the toilet forgotten Rory darted after her.

*

Inside the shed Alice and Willow jumped when the door burst open. Alice, about to scold Rory for startling them gaped as her neighbour and class mate walked into the shed. Willow sat frozen to the spot like a rabbit caught in headlights. As Melissa strode forward Alice stood up swiftly and tried to stand in front of the tiny woman to shield her from Melissa's view. The door scraped a second time and Rory re-appeared.

'What the hell is that?' Melissa demanded rudely, pointing a finger at Willow.

Furiously, Alice stood her ground protecting Willow. Melissa stared asking,

'Well?'

Melissa was a force to be reckoned with if she wanted to be awkward. Alice decided to appease her.

'Sit down Mel,' she said.

Melissa did as Alice asked, never taking her eyes off of what she now recognised as a tiny adult. Alice took charge.

'This is a friend of ours. Her name is Willow and she is staying with us for a few days.' Melissa found her tongue and as usual it proved to be unpleasant.

'Bloody hell,' she laughed, 'is she a bleedin' dwarf or something?'

Furious now Willow leapt up and pointing her own finger at Melissa said menacingly,

'Do not call me dwarf again girl. Dwarves are another thing altogether and I am most certainly not one of those. Alice has given you an explanation, so now you can leave!'

Unperturbed, Melissa giggled.

'Well if you're not a dwarf then you must be a midget,' she said. 'You only just come up to Alice's shoulder so something isn't right is it?'

Alice was aghast.

'How dare you!' she spat. 'I've never heard anything so bloody rude!'

Both girls squared up to each other and Rory stepped in.

'Mel,' he said, 'you're out of order. Stop being rude and we'll talk to you, but carry on and I shall take great delight in throwing you out!'

Taken aback and wanting to be liked by Rory, Melissa backed down.

'Okay,' she said between gritted teeth, 'I'm sorry for being rude, but you have to tell me what's going on.'

'Sit down Mel,' Alice said. 'Don't interrupt and don't be rude or Rory and I will both chuck you out.'

Melissa smiled.

'Ooh, I wouldn't want that,' she said sarcastically, 'so who's your friend then?'

'Better,' said Rory. 'Alice?'

Alice told Melissa of finding Willow and of how she would be staying in the woodshed for a while. Melissa looked dumbfounded.

'I take it your mum doesn't know she's here – why can't she stay in your house?'

All through this verbal exchange Willow remained silent, but now spoke up.

'I have no need to enter their house. I am happy out here. Alice and Rory have been good to me and I will not intrude in their home.'

Melissa remained unconvinced.

'Well it all seems a bit odd to me. It's clear Liz doesn't know you're here 'cause she'd insist on you going inside instead of staying in this freezing hovel. I wonder what she'd say if she knew you were here? And I'm not being rude, but why are you so bloody small and...I mean, just look at your clothes. They're far from normal – downright *weird* I'd say.'

Willow stood her ground.

'My size and my clothes are no concern of yours girl. As for Alice and Rory's mother – she must not know I am here for I would be forced to leave.'

Melissa grinned evilly.

'Well,' she said, 'someone's holding something back here - spill the beans or I might be forced to say something…'

'Okay Mel, you win,' sighed Rory. 'I'll explain, but only

on the condition that you don't interrupt.'

He related the more fantastic details of Willow's story to Melissa. It took about half an hour and at the end Melissa looked bemused.

'Not sure I believe all this,' she said. 'Sounds a right load of old tosh to me. However – if it were true, how would you get her home Rory?'

'We don't know yet, but we intend to find a way. If you want to help you can, but if you don't want to get involved, all we ask is that you don't give Willow away to mum or anyone else.'

Mellissa mellowed a little.

'Okay,' she said, 'it's a deal. Count me in and I won't say anything.' Turning to Willow she said, 'If we help, what do we get in return?'

Willow frowned.

'If I can pay you back I will for that is my way, but do not press me as it is considered rude to ask such a thing where I come from.'

Melissa bristled, but Rory quickly spoke.

'It's okay Willow, we're not doing it for that; we genuinely want to help, but we need a plan here. Anyone got any ideas?'

Melissa spoke first.

'Seems obvious to me,' she said. 'First thing we need to do is get Willow to open this gateway thingy and if she can hold it open long enough, maybe we can find whatever is causing the blockage.'

Rory, Alice and Willow all conceded that although obvious, this did seem to be the logical first step. Willow joined in.

'Yes,' she said. 'I can hold it open, but not for long. It takes great skill and a lot of energy. You would have to be quick and if I were unable to maintain it you may become trapped on the other side.'

The discussion continued and Melissa brought up another point.

'Let's say you open the gateway and one of us finds what is blocking it. What then? You don't know what's waiting for you on the other side do you? I think that before we open the gateway we need some kind of plan about what we intend to do next.'

Alice agreed through gritted teeth, refusing to forgive Mel for her previous rude comments.

'That's really sensible Mel,' she said. 'You're the expert here Willow; any suggestions about what you want to do if you can get through?'

'I just want to go home,' she said. 'I really have no idea about what else Flint may have put in place. I can only assume that if some of his militia or spies see me that I will be flung out again – or killed...'

'We won't let them harm you Willow, we'll come with you,' piped up Rory.

Willow shook her head.

'You cannot, it is too dangerous for you.'

Rory looked puzzled.

'You said that last night, about it being dangerous. Why? What's the problem?'

Willow's answer took them all by surprise.

'If you enter my realm,' she began, 'the time there passes differently to the way it does here. You may only go there for what you think is a short time, but when you return to this world, many moons may have passed. The longer you stay there the worse it becomes. There have been examples of humans visiting us for just a couple of our moon cycles and on going home they find that decades have passed here – sometimes so many that all the people they once knew are long dead and the world has changed so much they do not recognise it. In such cases the unlucky humans have returned to us and never left.'

Rory, Alice and Melissa fell silent now. Willow's world seemed so full of contradictions, but fascinating all the same. All three believed that Willow spoke the truth and genuinely hailed from Faerie stock. This just made Rory want to find out more.

'If you open the gateway and hold it open like you suggested would there still be a time difference?' Willow shook her head.

'No,' she said. 'So long as the gateway remains open you are safe, but I told you I cannot hold it like that for very long. If you are going to look for anything hidden you would have to be really quick about it.'
Rory nodded.

'Okay,' he said. 'I'm up for it – what about you two?' he asked turning to Alice and Melissa.

'Count me in,' Alice responded, 'what about you Mel?'
Melissa looked concerned.

'What if it closed,' she queried. 'What then?

'Well I'm going to try it,' said Rory firmly, ignoring Mel's question. 'Willow, what do you say? If you can hold it open for a few minutes we might get lucky.'

'I will try,' said Willow, 'but if I tell you to come back you must do so immediately, do you understand?' Rory nodded.

'So when do we start?'
Alice joined in now.

'After mum goes to work. She leaves around five today, so if we meet back here at say half six that should give us plenty of time.'

'We still haven't decided what to do after we clear the gateway,' said Rory. 'Any ideas?'

No one seemed able to come up with any further course of action so Willow closed the gathering with a final plea.

'Holding that gate open will be very taxing. I need to sleep to prepare. Thank you all, you are very kind.'

There didn't seem much else to say or do at this point. The three young people all stood up and made for the shed door. As they departed Willow snuggled under the blankets to try to get some well needed rest. However, once alone she sat up and reached into the leather pouch hanging on her belt. Her tiny fingers closed over something within – something hard, cold and metallic - an object which caused her to both smile and shed a tear at the same time. Fingering the item one last time before replacing it and fastening the pouch she finally settled under the blanket, closed her eyes and fell into a troubled sleep.

\*\*\*

# 3

# The Gateway

'Do you think we should trust Mel?' Alice asked as she finished her dinner of fish fingers, mash and beans. Rory shook his head, watching his sister as she chased the last few baked beans around the plate with her fork, a frown on her face.

'Probably not,' he said through a similar mouthful, 'but we don't have a choice. Mel has seen Willow so we're going to have to accept it and hope for the best.'

Alice nodded glumly. Having Mel involved in anything never boded well. She possessed a loose tongue and could give Willow away at any time. Rory looked at his watch.

'It's half five,' he said. 'That gives us an hour to get ready. Mel better be organised, I'm not waiting for her!'

Alice stood up and began clearing the dirty plates away to the sink. The conversation became muted as each became absorbed by their own thoughts. Alice felt concerned over Mel. She racked her brains for any way to disentangle themselves from her, but she could not justify the risk. At the slightest opportunity Mel could betray them all. When Alice voiced her views Rory agreed. Mel, it seemed would have to be included from now on.

At a quarter past six a bang on the back door made them jump. Rory opened it. Grinning from ear to ear Mel stood in the doorway. Opting for the 'grunge' look which she knew Rory liked so much, she sported jeans, flannel shirt and beanie hat with a parka over the top. The outfit obtained the desired effect.

'Cool! Looking good Mel!' Rory said. Still smiling Mel stepped into the kitchen to be greeted by a frosty faced

Alice.

'It's not a fashion show Mel, we're probably going to get wet and dirty out there you know,' she stated sarcastically feeling a little self-conscious of her own dowdy jeans and old sweater. Mel pulled a face and snapped back.

'We'll see won't we,' she said. Rory took charge, dreading the thought of the two girls falling out before they even began.

'Come on you two – form a truce eh?'
Mel just gave a sickly smile and Alice found herself biting her lip. She pulled her glasses off and polished them furiously on the corner of her sweater, her feelings clearly written on her face. However, Rory's comment cooled the situation for the time being and the tension between the girls seemed to ease a little.

Within minutes they were ready to go and with a final 'So long,' to Copper the trio headed out into the cold and down the uneven path to the woodshed. On entering the shed they found the electric light already on. Willow sat eating the last of her cheese sandwich along with some celery. She looked rested although she did appear nervous and on edge, jumping as they opened the door. Alice broke the ice.

'Hi Willow,' she said breezily, 'all set and ready to go?'
Popping the last of her sandwich into her mouth Willow nodded, but she didn't look at all confident.

'You okay?' Rory asked.

'Okay... Yes thank you,' Willow said awkwardly, grinning at her own first use of the human word, causing herself much merriment in the process. 'Just a little frightened of what we might find.'

'Come on,' Rory said holding out his hand. 'Up you get and come with us.'

Checking her pouch and shoulder bag were secure Willow stood up and took Rory's hand. Once on her feet Rory held on to her a little longer than really necessary, also slipping his arm around her waist protectively as he did so. She didn't seem to mind at all as she snuggled into the crook of his arm. Not liking what she saw Mel cut in.

'What's in that bag and pouch?' she asked rudely. Willow's hand flew protectively to the pouch on her belt and her eyes narrowed.

'That is no business of yours,' she said. 'You told me earlier that you would help me. I am grateful for that, but do not pry into my private things.'

The atmosphere instantly became tense, so yet again Rory changed the subject to try to ease things between the females.

'Willow, are you sure you're not cold? Your arms and legs are bare and your dress is so thin. We all have loads of layers on and we're still close to shivering.'

Willow shook her head whilst Alice and Mel, taking the bait began quizzing Willow on her clothes, her home and her lifestyle. Rory, sighing with relief at defusing the volatile women yet again, took the lead and headed out of the shed and into the darkness.

The walk around the field to the barrow took around ten minutes. However, the grassy mound that surrounded the stone chamber eventually came into view and the mood lifted somewhat, although an air of apprehension still remained. Once inside out of the wind they all felt more comfortable and focussed.

Rory had also brought a camper's oil lamp with him and once alight the warm amber glow it gave off made them all feel better. Rory addressed Willow.

'Okay, what do we do now?'

Being offered the lead imbued the little woman with confidence. She immediately began to issue instructions.

'That cleft in the corner is where the entrance lies,' she said. 'Rory, you stand there. Alice and Mel give him a bit of space to get his tools out – oh, and Rory, I already know that you have Ferrum implements in that bag, I can feel them – just be sure to keep them away from me!'

Everyone took up their allotted positions and watched

as Rory opened his bag and spread the tools on the floor at his feet. Willow winced at the sight of the steel tools and moved back a little. After making his selection he looked at Willow and awaited her next instruction.

'I shall open the gate in a moment,' she said. 'Once I do, you will see the entrance appear in front of you. The floor is paved with cut stones. Once it is open you need to walk straight in. You will see a short passage in front of you and at the far end of it will be fields. I do not know whether it will be day or night on the other side – you never know that until you open it. Somewhere around the centre of the passage I suspect is where the problem lies. It could be in the floor, the roof or the walls – you shall have to examine them all, but you need to be swift. Look for loose stones as it is possible something may be concealed beneath one. If you find anything come back immediately and bring it with you. Do not forget, I cannot hold the passage open for long.'

'What happens if I don't get out before the gateway closes?' he asked, seeking reassurance. Willow answered with a serious look on her face.

'If the passage closes with you in there you will find yourself trapped on the other side. I may be too weak to reopen it again tonight, so whatever happens if I, or either of the girls here tell you to come back you must stop what you are doing immediately and do so.'

Rory nodded. Understandably, the threat of being trapped for any length of time in the Faerie realm did not appeal to him at all. Gritting his teeth he shoved a trowel and a screwdriver into his pocket and advanced into the corner, facing the cleft in the stones. 'I'm ready whenever you are,' he said.

Willow stood directly behind Rory and also faced the corner of the stone chamber. Alice and Mel looked on in expectant silence. Willow made no sound as she closed her eyes and breathed deeply to compose herself. Then quite suddenly she raised both her arms above her head, held her breath and after a few seconds dropped both of her arms in a great sweeping gesture. Her lips moved as she muttered something under her breath and quite suddenly it happened. The cleft in the corner melted away and in its place, just as Willow had predicted stood an archway leading into a narrow tunnel. For a second or two Rory stood gaping and then everything Willow has said to him came flooding back. Stepping forward he entered the short passage and swiftly walked through to the centre, running his hands over the walls as he advanced. Beyond, he could see bright daylight entering the far end and fields of what looked like golden wheat gently swaying in a light summer breeze. The temptation to stare and take in the amazing sight took over. However, remembering his instructions and Willow's repeated warnings he turned to the task in hand and began casting his eyes around the walls and ceiling in a much closer examination. Nothing seemed amiss and so he began to run his hands around the dressed stones in a bid to locate any loose ones. Acutely aware of the time he was taking he turned his attention to the floor. At first everything looked fine there too and with his heart racing he turned to speak to Willow. Then he felt a movement beneath his foot, barely perceptible, but enough to capture his attention. Dropping to his knees he began pushing and pressing on the floor stones. The fourth one shifted – again, only the tiniest of movements, but enough to be noticed. Swiftly he grabbed the small trowel from his pocket and slid the pointed end down the side of the loose stone. A few sharp wiggles and it popped free, landing a short distance away.

Beneath the stone lay a small depression and hidden there he found a single item. Rory picked it up. Roughly the size of a walnut, black, hard and irregular in shape, it resembled a stone. What astonished Rory on poking it with his trowel was that it proved to be magnetic. Pulling the black nugget free Rory offered it towards the trowel again and looked on in amazement as it leapt from his hand and reattached itself to the steel blade. Intrigued by this phenomenon he became oblivious to all else. He pulled the stone off for a third time when he became aware of Alice and Mel frantically calling his name. Suddenly aware of his vulnerability in the tunnel and remembering the dire warnings given by Willow Rory leapt to his feet and made for the entrance. At the same moment the tunnel began to dissolve around him. The last few feet were before him and Rory literally dived forward, throwing himself out of the passage and back into the barrow, the trowel clattering across the floor. He landed heavily, aware of Alice at his side.

'Rory,' she said, 'we thought you were trapped! Didn't you hear us calling you?'

Rory sat up. Mel stood in the corner white faced, but worst of all, Willow lay on the floor motionless. Crawling forward he touched Willow's arm and looked up at Alice.

'What happened to her?' he asked with real fear in his eyes.

Wiping her eyes and shaking visibly Alice responded.

'Willow did really well, but you just took so long. She started to tremble – we could see her fighting to hold the gateway open and that's when we started calling out to you - but you didn't come – you didn't come!'

'Tell me what happened to her.'

'She was really struggling. You only just made it Rory – as you threw yourself out of there she just collapsed on the floor. It really has taken all of her strength...'

Rory turned back to the crumpled figure. Willow still didn't move and he whispered in her ear, pleading for her to wake up. Lifting her hair away from her face he stroked her cheek. Willow had become very pale whilst her lips took on an ominous shade of blue. However, she responded with a feeble groan and Rory, Alice and Mel knew that she still lived.

Retrieving his dropped trowel he felt relieved to see the magnetic rock still attached to it. Passing the items to

Alice for safe keeping he bent down and gently lifted the still unconscious Willow in his arms.

'Come on Babe,' he whispered, 'please wake up. Let's get you back to the shed. It's over.' He lowered his head and kissed her gently, his cheeks reddening at the intimacy of the moment. Mel, looking on frowned, her cheeks flushing a hot red too. Sensibly for once she kept her mouth shut. Willow's soft breath against his face reassured Rory further. Turning to the two girls he said,

'Let's go. We'll get her back and then once we know she's safe we'll have a proper look at that stone.'

They walked home in silence, amazed by what they had witnessed. Once back in the relative safety of the shed Rory laid the little woman down on the blankets, but remained sitting beside her, refusing to release her hand. Alice broke the silence.

'What do you think this is?' she asked taking the trowel and magnetic stone from her pocket. Looking up, Rory frowned.

'Keep it over there well away from Willow,' he said protectively. 'I think it might be a lodestone.'

'A lodestone?' Alice said. 'What the hell is that?'

'It's a naturally occurring magnetic stone or rock,' Rory said sagely. 'I think it's also known as Magnetite. Ancient mariners used to suspend them on a cord and use them as a compass.'

'If that thing is as harmful as Willow claims, how come her uncle could handle it and place it in the tunnel?' Mel asked.

'Because Flint is of the earth and so is the stone. I also told you that he is a powerful magician and as such can weave charms and protections around himself.'

All three turned and looked at Willow, now sitting up with her eyes open. Alice let out an exclamation of relief at seeing her awake and Rory bent and kissed her vigorously on the top of her head.

'Willow,' he said. 'We were so worried about you!'

The little woman managed a weak smile.

'Thank you; so you found it?' At her question her eyes widened enquiringly. Rory nodded and gestured towards Alice who held up the piece of lodestone. 'Urggh!' muttered Willow. 'I can feel its power from here. It is horrible!'

Alice quickly put the stone in her pocket and Willow appeared to relax a little.

'Well what happens next?' asked Mel.

'I know not,' Willow said. I could probably get back home now, but I daresay that Flint will know his magic stone has gone and he will watch out for me.'

'Is there no way that one of us can go with you?' Rory asked.

As expected Willow shook her head.

'You would get caught in the time difference – I have told you of that already,' she said. Rory looked exasperated.

'But there must be a way we can help you Willow,' he said. 'You have to expose your uncle.'

'I know,' Willow said, 'but right now I cannot. Besides, that is none of your concern. You have all helped me so much already – I could not ask you to do more on my behalf. Anyway, if you do not mind, after that ordeal I really need to sleep. Perhaps we can decide what I should do in the morning.'

Rory didn't want to leave, but Alice saw sense in Willow's request. The tiny woman looked exhausted and in need of proper rest. Looking at her brother she supported Willow.

'Rory,' she said softly. 'She's completely shattered. Just let her sleep. We can discuss this with her tomorrow.'

With a sigh Rory agreed and leaving her tucked up in the shed they went back indoors. Alice, Rory and Mel sat at the kitchen table. Alice made tea and opened a packet of biscuits. Being indoors made them all feel a little better. Stuffing a whole biscuit into his mouth Rory held up the magnetic stone and looked at it closely.

'Do you think it's dangerous bringing it in here?' asked Alice.

'Why should it be?'

'What if it's cursed or something – it could bring us bad luck.'

Mel sneered.

'Cursed? That's a bit superstitious isn't it?'

Rory answered for his sister who he could see struggling to bite her tongue.

'Mel,' he said firmly, 'this whole situation is pretty weird. Until yesterday I would have laughed at anyone who suggested that Faeries genuinely existed. Now we have one living in our shed and after what we've all just witnessed I'm prepared to believe anything. Alice could have a point. Perhaps we should leave it outside.'

Mel laughed rudely.

'Well, listen to you Rory! The pair of you sound like you're out of the bloody Dark Ages. It's just a bit of rock. Don't be so bloody stupid!'

Alice was furious now.

'Stupid are we? Well I think you should go home now Mel,' she snapped. 'Surely you've seen enough today to realise that this is all very real. We have no idea of what we or Willow are dealing with here. Just go home you moron!'

Melissa leapt up blazing.

'How dare you call me a moron,' she hissed. 'And you Rory – I thought you might stick up for me, but NO! You're too taken with 'Little Miss Perfect' out in the shed aren't you! Holding her hand and fussing over her like that. She's a sodding midget and you should chuck her out! I'm off – you two can play at 'faerie land' if you want to, but I think she's just using you for her own ends. And I'll tell you something else. She's got something in that pouch she doesn't want you to know about. I bet if you look in there you'll get some proper answers. And YES!

I've had enough too… I'M BLOODY WELL GOING HOME!'

Mel flounced out of the back door and slammed it so hard that the glass panel shook dangerously. Alice burst into tears and it took Rory a good quarter of an hour to calm her down. Both of them felt real concern now that Melissa would reveal Willow's presence to whomever she felt could cause the most trouble. Their mother Liz would be a prime candidate.

'We have to think of something Alice,' Rory said miserably. 'Mel is sure to open her big mouth and tell people now - she's really gone into one and you know what she's like when someone annoys her.'

'I know,' said Alice still blinking back tears, 'but we still have to protect Willow, we just have to.'

Rory played with the lodestone as they spoke. 'I'm not keeping this thing in here. Come on, let's do something positive and hide it in the garden,' he decided.

They stood up from the table, put their coats on and went back outside. Rory decided to check on Willow one last time. Creeping into the shed he found her snuggled into the blanket and breathing deeply. A little colour had returned to her face and relieved, he kissed her cheek before returning to Alice.

Together they looked round the garden for a suitable location to hide the lodestone. Alice quickly hit upon the ideal spot. At the edge of a rather sad looking flower bed by the gate stood a concrete gnome. Present when they moved into the house fifteen years previously Liz decided that he should stay.

'He lived here before us so it would be unfair to throw him out,' she had said to Rory and Alice who were both young children at the time. 'He can look out for us and keep us safe.'

Ever since, Alice in particular always looked on the gnome as her 'guardian of the garden'. As a child she often used to talk to him if something troubled her. She had even given him a name.

'Let's hide it under Mr. Hollyhock,' she said to Rory. He's always looked out for me – perhaps he'll look after this thing too and help Willow.'

Rory grinned, liking the irony behind Alice's choice.

'He does seem rather appropriate,' he said. 'Okay, under Mr. Hollyhock it is then.'

Lifting the gnome he scooped out some earth from underneath with his fingers and dropped the lodestone into the cavity. Pressing Mr. Hollyhock back in place he brushed his hands on his jeans and stood back. Alice patted the gnome on the head.

'Please keep this safe for us Mr. Hollyhock,' she whispered, 'and keep Willow safe too.'

With the stone safely hidden they could do no more that night. Returning indoors Rory added some wood to the fire and sat in his favourite chair. Alice flopped onto the sofa and let out a sigh. Both sat quietly for a while deep in their own thoughts and then Alice broke the silence.

'Do you think we should tell mum – about Willow I mean?'

Rory shook his head.

'No way,' he said flatly. If mum finds out she'll get involved and then we won't be able to do anything.'

Another thought occurred to Alice.

'What do you think Mel meant when she said Willow could be hiding something in her pouch?'

'I don't know,' Rory answered, 'but Mel may actually have a point there. Willow never lets that bag or pouch out of her sight. What if she's done something wrong? What if she's been officially banished from her realm – as a punishment? We don't really know if she's telling the truth or not do we? Because everything we've seen is so fantastic we've just gone along with whatever she's told us without even questioning it.'

Alice looked hurt.

'Oh Rory,' she said. 'You don't believe that do you?'

'I don't know,' he said. 'I so want to believe her, but how do we really know we can trust her?'

'Well I trust her.' said Alice emphatically. 'Mel is twisting everything around as usual and she's already started messing with your head – it's her we can't trust, not Willow.'

Still not sure what to think Rory merely grunted as the pair fell into an awkward silence before heading off to bed, divided in their opinions. Mel and her spiteful attitude had succeeded in driving a wedge firmly between them. Rory, despite everything, now felt certain that Willow held a secret. Little did he know just how close to the truth he really was…

***

# 4

# Elf Bolts and Hidden Things

On Monday morning Alice and Rory laid in, having slept badly. They had remained awake for hours fretting over Willow, pondering how much truth her story contained and what mischief Mel might cause them. Consequently, when they did rise, both were bleary eyed and irritable.

By nine o'clock Liz had already embarked on mopping the kitchen floor when Rory came stumbling down the stairs.

'I knew it was too good to be true,' she said laughing. 'You might have got up early yesterday, but I didn't think you'd keep it up for long!'

She watched Rory making toast and continued to bustle around, knowing her cheerfulness would irritate him.

'So what did you get up to last night?' she asked.

'Not a lot,' he said evasively, 'just sat about chatting.'

Liz suspected there would be more to it than that. She tried a different approach.

'What are you doing today, anything planned? Revision with Alice?'

Before he could answer Alice walked in, still dressed in her pyjamas.

'Mornin' mum,' she yawned.

'Morning love, you look rough – bad night?'

'Thanks for that mum,' said Alice huffily. 'But yes, rotten night actually. I didn't sleep well – must be worried over my exams.'

Liz noticed that both her children were unresponsive and in teenage mode that morning. She disappeared into the lounge with a duster and a can of polish, leaving them together.

'Have you been out to the shed this morning?' asked Alice once they were alone.

'What, in my pyjama bottoms and a tee shirt?' Rory said sarcastically.

Alice just huffed and realising she felt tired too Rory answered again, forcing himself to use a friendlier tone.

'We'll go out there together when we've eaten. Look, you have this toast, I'll make some more.'

Whilst eating they discussed Mel and her dreadful behaviour in whispered tones. With Mel already proving to be a problem they needed to find a solution to end her reckless behaviour. Lost in their own thoughts, they finished breakfast, showered and dressed and met downstairs again at half past ten.

It was almost lunchtime by the time they were ready to visit Willow. Rory made peanut butter sandwiches from a new jar, bought the previous day. Luckily, Liz had gone into Glastonbury for the weekly food shop and would not be around to interrupt their activities. Picking up the sandwiches and a bottle of lemonade Rory headed for the back door with Alice behind him. They walked down the garden in silence. With the lodestone retrieved, the only course of action would be for Willow to enter her own world alone and attempt to expose her uncle by herself. Both Alice and Rory felt a deep sadness at the thought of seeing her leave, having become rather fond of her – Rory in particular.

Approaching the shed they stopped in their tracks. Alice put her hand to her mouth in surprise and Rory gaped. The shed door remained closed from the night before. However, the object impaled in the door itself caught their attention. A small arrow protruded from the wood, the tip embedded deeply into the grain as though fired at high velocity. Rory stepped forward and taking hold of the wooden shaft wiggled the arrow and pulled it free. Turning it over in his hand he and Alice studied it closely. The arrow showed poor craftsmanship with the shaft not smoothed or finished properly. The fletchings on the end were merely a few black crows feathers fastened to the wood by thread bindings, but the tip, the arrow head itself caused most concern. Unmistakeably crafted from a piece of flint, that part alone had been beautifully manufactured. Perfectly symmetrical and razor sharp, anyone struck by such a weapon would be seriously injured or killed. Pulling open the shed door Rory stepped inside and walked over to Willows empty blanket.

'Damn, where is she now?' he said. 'Willow? Are you here?'

A familiar whimper from the darkened corner gave away Willows location. Looking upset she crept out of the shadows and into view. Alice gave her a hug.

'Come on Sweetie,' she said. 'What on earth is the matter? It's only us!'

Alice led her to the blanket and made her sit. Taking a tissue from her pocket she wiped away the little Faerie's tears and cleaned her nose.

'Thank you,' Willow said. 'When I heard the door open I thought it may not be you.'

'What, or who are you so afraid of? What happened in the night?' asked Alice.

Willow trembled, her usual cheeky smile and mischievous personality clearly dented.

'When you left me,' she stated, 'I wanted nothing more than to sleep and regain my strength. I fell asleep straight away, but sometime in the middle of the night I woke up rather suddenly.' She gathered her thoughts for a few moments before continuing. 'Something felt wrong – I could sense it. There was evil in the air – *real* evil. I just sat here really scared and then heard a loud bang on the shed door. Eventually the bad feeling subsided, but I could not sleep for the rest of the night.'

Rory took the arrow from inside his jacket and showed

it to Willow.

'We found this stuck in the shed door. That probably explains the bang you heard. Does it mean anything to you?'

Willow looked as though she were about to be sick, her complexion ashen, and her blue eyes wide. Putting her hand over her mouth, she swallowed a couple of times, picked up the arrow and examined it closely. Eventually she handed it back to Rory and sat down, still looking shaken.

'It is a warning,' she said.

'A warning against what exactly?' asked Rory.

'A warning to me! It is an elf bolt. They are used by my people to bring down game or to deliver messages. They often have a note attached. No note suggests they are hunting me and want me dead.'

Rory let out a whistle of surprise.

'If they wanted you dead why didn't they just come in and kill you?' Alice asked.

'That's a good point,' Rory said. 'What do you think Willow?'

'I know not,' she said flatly. 'If they could have, they would, and you would have found me with that arrow through my heart. Flint has a troop of Woad Warriors to carry out his work. They are lethal, and if they shoot at you with one of these they never miss...'

Together they sat discussing why the night's assailants satisfied themselves with merely shooting an arrow at the door. Something occurred to Rory.

'Willow,' he said, 'would you come outside for a moment?'

Standing up, she followed Rory into the garden. Curious, Alice watched. Rory walked to the end of the garden, through the gate and out into the field, beckoning to Willow as he did so. Following behind she got as far as the gate and then froze. A look of sheer panic spread across her face and she stopped.

'I cannot go on,' she wailed. 'It is exactly the same as in the tunnel. Flint must have placed another magic stone in your gateway to keep me in. I feel sick!'

Turning around Willow fled back to where Alice stood a few yards away. Alice reached down and slid her arm around Willow's tiny frame. Rory walked back, a smile on his face. Alice scolded him.

'What are you grinning at you idiot? Can't you see how terrified she is? – it's not funny Rory!'
Rory held up his hands.

'Calm down sis, I'm not laughing at Willow,' he said triumphantly, 'but I think I know why the hit men couldn't get her.'

'Go on.'
Rory pointed towards the gate.

'What do you see?' he asked. Alice studied the garden boundary.

'The gate, the hedge... The field?'

'Look again.'

'Mr. Hollyhock? MR. HOLLYHOCK – OF COURSE!' she shouted.

'Who is Mr. Hollyhock?' Willow asked.

Alice and Rory both began trying to explain at once and talked over each other. Willow just stared, still unable to comprehend the source of her friend's excitement. Eventually they stopped and taking the lead, Rory explained.

'Mr. Hollyhock is just under the bush by the gate – look,' he said pointing.

'What, that statue of an old man?' asked Willow.

'Yes,' replied Rory. 'Last night Alice and I didn't like keeping that stone in our house. We brought it outside and hid it under Mr. Hollyhock – don't you see? That stone was hidden in your gateway to prevent you getting home, but it probably also stopped anyone else getting out. Because I removed it from the tunnel, it allowed your enemies to pass through and come after you. I hid it next to our gate last night and it prevented them from getting through. What I don't understand is why they didn't just force their way through the hedge.'

Willow agreed with Rory's explanation and provided the missing link to his theory.

'That hedge is made of yew,' she stated. 'My people hate yew. It is not as bad as Ferrum, but we would not be able to pass through it. That is why in your tradition, yew hedges were usually grown around your church yards – to keep us out.'

The simple act of hiding the stone in the garden had saved Willow. Discussing this further they made their way back inside the shed. They concluded that it effectively imprisoned Willow in the garden, but should she need to leave they could remove the stone at any time. The concern remained as how to keep her safe. However, with an explanation in place the mood lifted. Remembering the bag of food, Rory took out the sandwiches and handed them to Willow.

'Peanut butter,' he said.

Willow's face lit up. Pulling off the cling film she bit into the bread and sighed with pleasure. Alice and Rory watched in amusement as Willow tucked into the food. Peanut butter was clearly something she adored. Rory offered her some lemonade.

'Lemonade?' she asked, 'what is that?'

As Rory opened it the drink fizzed and erupted from the bottle and Willow leapt to her feet pointing animatedly.

'It boils in the bottle!' she squealed.

Rory and Alice laughed and Rory poured some into a glass and offered it to her. Willow took the glass cautiously, touching it carefully, expecting its surface to be hot. Puzzled, she sniffed at the drink and after seeing Alice begin to sip from her own glass, took a tentative taste. She found it difficult to comprehend. In her mind the bubbles signified a boiling liquid, but having been in the fridge the glass felt cold. However, it tasted good and after the first couple of sips she tipped up the glass, quaffed down the contents and held it out for more. As Rory filled it again Alice remembered something.

'Rory,' she said quietly, 'mum will be home soon. If she comes looking for us and finds us with Willow it's going to cause all kinds of problems.'

'Mum's working again tonight so we can come down then. Don't worry; the stone should keep Willow safe for now. You're right Alice, we don't want mum seeing her.'

Rory and Alice both gave Willow a hug and left the shed. Walking back up the path they caught sight of their own back door. A second arrow identical to the first protruded from the wooden frame. Attached to this one was a piece of parchment held in place with black thread. Rory reached up and took down the arrow. Alice let out a groan and Rory mistakenly took it to be a sign of fear or shock. The groan however, signified something else.

'What's that you've got?' a familiar voice asked cockily. Rory turned round and saw Melissa standing beside his sister. Inwardly, he groaned too.

'It's nothing – part of an experiment for college,' said Rory quickly. 'It's to do with ballistics and trajectory. I'm just a rotten shot that's all.'
Mel gave Rory an odd look and then said,

'So where's your bow? Presumably you made one?'

Rory didn't know what to say. Mel, catching him out left no option, but to tell the truth. Surprisingly Mellissa actually seemed interested.

'So if there's a note attached,' she asked breezily, 'what does it say?'

'We haven't read it yet Mel,' Alice said.

'So read it now. Come on Rory let's take a look – this is rather exciting!'

Melissa showed no guilt over her frightful outburst of the night before. Alice badly wanted to tell her to get lost, but knew that if she did Melissa would cause more trouble. Instead, she gave Mel a withering look and said to Rory,

'Perhaps we should look at the note at least.'

Rory conceded, and after fumbling with the knots in the thread, finally managed to free the piece of parchment. Viewing the text Rory realised at once they would be unable to read it. The angular lines and styling were totally unrecognisable to him and they would need Willow to interpret the words written there. He rolled it up again, and ignoring Melissa spoke to Alice.

'We can't do this now. Mum is likely to be home any time soon. This is going to have to wait until she goes in to work.'

Also ignoring Mel, Alice said,

'Give that to me.'

Rory handed her the note, unsure of what she wanted to do.

'You go indoors and put the kettle on,' Alice said. 'I'll nip back and give this to Willow – she can study it in advance and hopefully have some answers for us later on.'

Before Rory or Melissa could protest Alice turned and made for the woodshed. Rory shrugged and sensing Alice trying to keep Mel out of the way, he invited her in for tea.

Alice came back indoors to find Rory and Melissa already half way through a plate of digestives. The two girls were getting on well by blanking each other and so Rory did the talking.

'What did Willow have to say then?' he asked his sister.

Alice picked up her tea and took a sip.

'She said it would be some kind of a warning. She needs a little time to interpret it properly, but reckons she'll be able to read it for us later. We'll have to wait until then.'

Melissa cut in.

'So what's the story? Why didn't they just go and shoot her dead and be done with it. Would've saved us a lot of trouble!'

Alice turned puce and stopped breathing, but before she could explode Rory put Mel firmly in her place.

'That's not fair Mel,' he said. 'Willow's done us no harm and she needs help. If you don't want to be a part of it that's fine, but I would ask that you don't tell anyone about her. If you want to help, then great. If not, feel free to go home now, but if you do then you and I are through as friends, and I mean that; I really mean that.'

Horrified, Melissa deflated on the spot, all her pompous airs and graces gone. She answered in a trembling voice.

'Okay Rory, you win. Yes, I'll help and I won't tell anyone, provided you promise me one thing in return.'

'Promise you what?' he asked suspiciously.

'In a few months Alice and I finish our first year at sixth form. Come to our end of year party as my partner. Loads of girls fancy you Rory, and most of them hate me. All the lads in my year think I'm a bitch. Do that for me and I'll help you, Willow and anyone else.'

Rory agreed instantly, thinking it a small price to pay. One night of treating Melissa like a Princess wouldn't hurt and besides, despite everything he actually thought her an attractive girl. Alice said nothing. Mel bribing Rory was dishonest in her eyes, but she could see the advantages of a truce. All three sat looking at each other and then Rory broke the awkward silence.

'It's a deal,' he said shaking Mel by the hand.

Mel beamed at Rory and then seeing Alice's glare she glanced down. Perhaps, she decided, it may be prudent to stop antagonising Rory's sister.

Shortly after, Liz came home from her shopping. Seeing Mel in her kitchen never filled her with joy as she often caused problems. Today however, everyone appeared to be getting along and Liz chatted with them as she unpacked the shopping. Alice decided to do some studying for her exams for she seriously needed to get into her physics books. With Liz at home it made sense to do the much needed revision, so reluctantly Alice took her leave of Rory and Mel and disappeared upstairs. Mel, taking the hint from Alice decided to do the same and after a few minutes of talking with Rory about music, also slipped away.

The afternoon dragged and when Liz finally departed for work Rory raced upstairs to retrieve Alice from her books. The revision had gone badly. Understandably, her mind would not stay focussed on the subject. They went down to the kitchen and sat at the table.

'Do we call for Mel or go ahead without her?' Rory asked.

'I'm for keeping her out of things as much as possible,' Alice said. 'However, if we do she'll go back on her agreement and open her mouth to everyone. Besides you have a hot date set up and you wouldn't want to miss that would you?'

Rory sighed. He knew that Alice would never let him forget agreeing to accompany Mel to the college party. He ignored the jibe and carried on.

'Agreed,' he said. 'I'll call for her now. I want to see what that note says.'

It only took a few minutes for Rory to knock at Mel's door and bring her back. She appeared to have undergone a personality transplant, her behaviour transformed.

They approached the shed with trepidation. As usual Alice took some food for Willow and as they greeted her she handed it over. Willow took the offered fruit and hard boiled eggs and tucked in. They let her have a few minutes to eat and then broached the subject of the note. Willow retrieved it from under her blanket. Alice, Rory and Mel all leaned forward expectantly as she began to speak.

'It is a warning as I suspected,' she began. 'It took me a while to read – my skills at such things are not good. The text is an ancient one called Ogham. The note says that Flint has sent people to find me. It says that you are interfering and should remove the magic stone from your gate so that they may enter. If you do not, they will find a way to get in and come after me. They will then consider you their enemies too. That is as much as I can interpret.

This script is very difficult to read, even for a master – and I am no master...'

Mel asked a pertinent question.

'Why are they coming after you at all? You said they threw you out to die and placed the stone in the gateway to keep you out. Why now, all of a sudden are they coming after you? Surely they could just put another spell on the gateway and leave you out here?'

They waited for Willow to respond, but instead she went red and stared guiltily at the floor. Playing with her hair she mumbled under her breath and refused to look them in the eye. Rory moved beside her and spoke softly.

'Come on Willow, out with it,' he said. There's more going on here than you're saying. Mel has a good point. Have you done something you haven't told us about? We can only help you if you are totally honest. We've been good to you, but if you're going to keep secrets then we'll have to leave you to deal with Flint on your own.'

'RORY! You wouldn't?' Alice sounded shocked.

Rory held up his hand and Alice fell silent. Willow looked up, clearly terrified.

'Please do not abandon me now Rory,' she begged, 'please...'

Rory ignored her plea. It broke his heart to do so, but as Mel suggested the previous evening, he also suspected Willow of hiding something. His harsh approach paid off.

Reaching into the pouch on her belt Willow withdrew her clenched hand and on opening it revealed a beautiful gold ring. Rory drew in his breath.

'You stole that?' he asked seriously. 'Is that why they're after you?'

Willow answered defiantly.

'I am not a thief,' she stated through gritted teeth. 'I have never stolen anything in my life! This belongs to me. Well, my father anyway. When he died it became mine by right.'

'Can I see it?' Rory held out his hand.

Willow reluctantly passed the ring over. Rory held it to his face to examine it. The craftsmanship was exquisite. Swirling patterns in a Celtic style ran around the band of the ring. A circle of oak leaves surrounded the centre and supported the seating for a polished black stone. Carved into the stone were more of the strange symbols used to write the note. Alice and Mel came closer too for a more studied look at the piece of Faerie jewellery.

'Do you have anything else or is it just this?' Rory asked Willow.

'No, just that ring,' she said quietly. 'Flint showed me my father's body to gloat at my expense. Then he expelled me from Eyedore. He did not know of father's ring and did not search me. He did not see me take it from his finger as he was whispering with one of his men. I did not take anything that did not belong to me, but I now believe that without the ring Flint cannot claim my father's estate. The stone is my family's seal and Flint will need it to complete his claim. I just wanted something personal that would remind me of father. Since then I have realised that taking it would cause Flint problems.'

Rory handed the ring back to Willow and she placed it in her pouch. He sighed.

'We now have to decide what to do,' he said. 'It's all very well wanting to help you Willow, but we do have to think of our own safety. What is Flint actually capable of? And be honest.'

'Anything and everything,' replied Willow. 'He is dangerous. I think he will aim to regain the ring and have me killed. My people believe that I am already dead. He cannot risk me going back. If I am seen by anyone Flint would be unable to claim my father's estate. If I did get back and managed to gain an audience with our King I could possibly even get him banished. He will stop at nothing to make sure I cannot do that.'

'Well, we have to do something,' Alice said. 'Whatever happens, I'm not giving up on her Rory and I'm shocked

to hear you even suggested it. How could you?'
Surprisingly Mel agreed with Alice.

'I didn't say we wouldn't help her,' Rory said. 'I just needed to hear all the facts. Willow you can't afford to keep anything from us. Promise me there's nothing else.'

'I suppose you should know about the fauns,' she said mysteriously.

'Fauns?' asked Alice, 'what are they?'

'Fauns are most likely what Flint will send after me,' Willow responded. 'They are vile creatures. They are similar to my own people, but are smaller...oh, and they have the hind legs of a goat. They generally look very dirty and unkempt. They stink too and are utterly heartless. They would think nothing of tearing me apart with their bare hands.'

Alice shuddered.

'I imagine you are exaggerating when you say that,' she said nervously.

Willow shook her head.

'No. Fauns can and do literally tear their living victims to pieces. They are lethal and once they have your scent they never let you get away. Flint has a whole troop of them that he has trained for all kinds of frightful things.'

Rory cut in now.

'I think the obvious thing to do here is to move Willow and hide her somewhere else,' he said seriously. 'Any ideas where she could hide?'

'How about the island?' Mel instantly suggested.

The island was located in nearby fields where a small lake lay situated. Roughly in the centre of the lake sat the island to which Mel referred. A covering of thick vegetation provided plenty of places to hide and remain unseen.

'Fantastic idea Mel,' Rory said. 'Willow, what do you think of living on an island?'

Willow felt far from happy.

'I would not like it at all,' she said. 'I would hate it.'

'But why?' asked Alice.

Willow shook her head.

'There are things you have no idea about. My people are unable to cross running water in your world. On an island I would probably be in the safest place imaginable – Flint and his followers would not be able to reach me. Getting me there however would be completely out of the question.'

'But why?' repeated Alice. 'Why can't you cross water?'

Willow shrugged.

'They say it is something to do with the one that your folk call The White Christ,' she said, wincing as she spoke the Holy name. 'He is not one of our Gods. Being immersed in water is not one of our rituals, it is one of yours and it fills us with fear.'

'So you're just scared of water then?' Mel asked insensitively.

'Scared?' whispered Willow, 'no, not scared – *terrified!*'

'Hold on,' Rory said, 'You stated you can't cross *running* water. The island is in a lake.'

Willow shuddered, but her answer sounded promising.

'Even still water forms a magical barrier to us,' she said. 'However, if forced I could probably cross it. But once on the island I would be a prisoner and unable to leave...'

'What do you mean by forced?' Rory asked.

'You would have to make me go against my will'

'What would you suggest?' asked Alice. 'Tell us how to get you there, but we must do it tonight. If they're after you they'll come soon. Tell us how to help.'

Willow's answer surprised them all

'You have to bind me,' she said. 'Tie my wrists and arms, restrain my legs and cover my mouth to prevent me from biting you. Even then you would still have to hold me down. '

'What? That's a bit drastic isn't it?' Alice asked.

Willow shook her head.

'I said it is the only way and I meant it,' she said. 'If you do not and you try to get me across I will fight you. I will kick, punch, bite, scream and anything else that possesses me. The island is a good idea – thank you Mel, but you can only get me there if you do as I say. Do it quickly before I change my mind.'

'We don't have a boat,' said Alice suddenly. Without one there's no point in even continuing with the idea. We'll have to think of something else.'

Rory grinned back at his sister.

'We do have a boat,' he said. It's in here – look!'

Rory went to an old cupboard and pulled out a large green bag. Alice squealed.

'The dinghy!' she said, 'I'd forgotten about that old thing! Rory you're a genius!'

Rory dragged the old inflatable rubber dinghy from the bag. As children he and Alice often used it on family holidays at the beach. At the bottom of the bag sat an old foot pump. Satisfied, he pushed the dinghy back in the bag and addressed Willow.

'Final decision Willow,' he said. 'Still want to go to the island?'

She shook her head.

'No,' she said instantly, 'I do not want to go to any island, but I must…'

'Are you sure about this tying you up business?' Rory asked.

'Yes,' she said. 'It is the only way.'

Rory nodded and went indoors. He returned carrying a roll of duct tape and a pair of scissors.

'Do we need anything else?' he asked. Alice answered immediately.

'Yes,' she said. 'We need to get some food for Willow. It won't be so easy to just pop outside and feed her now and we need to think about shelter for her too. Your old ridge tent you used to use for fishing is in here as well – she could have that.'

Alice went indoors. She returned after a quarter of an

hour with a couple of bulging carrier bags. Rory and Mel had not remained idle either, the rubber boat and tent bag being stacked and ready to go. As luck would have it the old tent poles, being made from wood suited Willow perfectly. They were ready to set off. It took Rory only a moment to remove the lodestone from beneath Mr. Hollyhock and place it under a flower pot by the back door of the house. With that done they headed through the gate and into the field.

***

# 5

# The Island

The walk to the lake normally took around fifteen minutes. However, with the darkness, the uneven ground and the bulky items they carried between them, it took the group almost three quarters of an hour. Eventually, arms and backs aching they reached the edge of the darkened lake. Willow also delayed their progress. As they came closer to reaching their destination she had begun to hold back and drag her heels. Now, standing by the water's edge she openly quivered with fear.

'Let's get this boat set up,' Rory said, expecting her to flee at any moment. 'Alice, why don't you and Mel take her over there away from the water while I do this?'

The two girls sat with Willow between them on a fallen tree. Willow cuddled Alice, wrapping her tiny arms around the girl's neck. Left alone, Rory pulled the boat and foot-pump from the bag and set to work. In minutes he had the boat inflated and ready to go. Only one task remained, and reluctantly Rory approached Willow with the duct tape and scissors.

'Come on littl'un,' he said softly, 'let's do this quickly.'

Willow sat up and offered her shaking wrists to Rory. Remembering to keep the steel scissors away from her whilst cutting a strip of tape he wound it around her wrists as tightly as he dared. Next, he taped her ankles and for good measure, her knees too. Willow sat crying now. Real tears trickled down her crumpled face and frightened whimpers came from her lips. Looking up and momentarily suppressing her fear she gave Rory one last instruction.

'Put some of that over my mouth or I will bite you,' she whispered, 'and however I react, under no circumstances free me until we are out of the boat on the other side.'

He agreed to Willow's terms and his hands shaking, Rory placed a piece of the tape over her mouth, ensuring her nose remained clear. Cradling Willow to his chest Rory climbed into the dinghy and said,

'Alice, you and Mel drag the boat into the water.'
After a couple of pulls at the boat Alice shook her head.

'No way Rory. With you aboard, it's just too heavy. Let's put it in the water first.'

'Okay,' he responded, struggling to disembark under his load. With the boat afloat he tried again. 'This won't work either Alice. I can't climb in carrying Willow. Here, you take her.'
Alice took the tiny woman as Rory stepped into the swaying dinghy. Once settled he held his arms out.

'Okay, let's have her back. Easy now…'

Finally, and with the boat already dangerously overloaded by the tent and food bags, Alice and Mel took up their own seats, picked up a paddle each and began to attempt the crossing.

The girls focussed on steering the boat in a straight line. At first they worked against each other and the dinghy made little progress, but after a bit they got into a mutual rhythm and began to edge in the right direction. Rory however had the most difficult task. As they set off he felt Willow stiffen. Then, as the boat moved further away from the bank she went completely rigid, her legs pushing outwards into the already cramped space. Holding on to her proved to be easier said than done, but as the crossing continued it became impossible. Rory soon realised that Willow's self-inflicted rigor mortis was not that bad after all. In that state she had at least remained still, but after a minute or two that changed. In terror Willow began to thrash about and despite her tiny stature, threatened to tip the boat over. Rory could do no more than cling onto her tiny, but powerful body as she arched her back and began to violently thrust her taped legs backwards and forwards in a manic bid to escape. Alice called over her shoulder.

'RORY! Keep her still – water's coming into the boat!'

Rory directed his efforts to holding Willow down. Amazed by her sheer animal strength, he quickly tired holding onto her. The fight continued for some minutes with Rory ever mindful of Willow's warning not to free her. As her struggles looked like becoming too much even for him, in desperation he forced her into the bottom of the boat and lay on top of her. Defeated, Willow ceased struggling. Rory's weight proved far too much for her to contend with and mercifully for everyone her strength ran out too. Trapped beneath Rory, she could only whimper through the duct tape.

To Rory the crossing felt like it took forever, and when the bottom of the boat scraped on the edge of the island he realised just how long he had held his breath. With a gasp he let it out and sat up. Willow immediately began to kick out again and seeing the grassy bank of the island just a couple of feet away Rory took the only option. Thrusting his arms under the tiny woman he scooped her up, stepped into the last few inches of water and waded ashore. Moving away from the bank he set down his charge before collapsing exhausted beside her. A moment or two later a rustle in the grass announced Alice and Mel carrying the bags of food and the tent. Rory took out his torch and shone it onto Willow. She stared up at him with pleading eyes. Hating seeing her bound and frightened Rory whisked out the scissors and despite them being made of steel, used them to quickly cut the tape. Lastly he peeled the final piece from her mouth. Willow turned away and for a moment Rory thought her angry, but the choking sounds she made, her heaving shoulders and the sour stink of vomit made him realise the extent of her terror. Putting his hand on her shoulder he spoke gently to her.

'It's okay Babe, it's over. You're safe.' He kissed her head and instantly felt better as Willow turned around and snuggled into him.

'I am sorry,' she sobbed through more tears. 'So sorry for everything. I have caused you all such trouble – you must wish you never found me. Please forgive me…'

The trio sat alongside her, offering reassurance until eventually, she calmed down. Erecting the tent became the next objective. A little way up from the water's edge a clearing opened out beneath the trees. Despite not having set up the tent for years Rory remained familiar with its components, and although he worked by torchlight the tiny structure proved ready in less than thirty minutes.

With Willow secure for the night Alice, Rory and Mel decided to go home. The parting became emotional. Leaving their friend behind on the island caused distress for both Alice and Rory. Mel didn't seem too fussed at leaving her behind at all and even Willow herself seemed quite content at being left alone. Rory held her hand until the last possible moment as he climbed into the boat for the return journey. Not now having to enter the boat herself Willow felt quite happy to walk to the water's edge. At the final parting she expressed her thanks once more.

'Thank you all,' she said. 'Without you I would now be dead. When this is over I will never, ever forget you. Come back as soon as you can – I shall miss you all so much…'

With a final hug and kiss for Rory the trio set off back across the lake. As they watched the retreating bank, the image of Willow waving faded into the shadows of the night.

They walked home quickly. No one felt like talking as they retreated into their own thoughts. Rory left the boat inflated and hidden beneath some bushes. It certainly made the going home much easier. Halfway home the sound of a horn being blown floated through the air, sending a chill down everyone's spine. Alice actually shivered at the eerie notes.

'What was that?' she said breaking the long silence.

Rory shrugged as the sound unsettled him too.

'I don't know, but I have a feeling that it's not going to be good,' he said.

They continued the walk home and as they approached the garden Mel bid them goodnight and sauntered off to her own home. Rory and Alice entered their garden and were making their way up the path when Alice grabbed Rory's arm and exclaimed loudly,

'My God – the woodshed is open!'

'Are you sure you closed it when we left?' Rory sounded much calmer than he felt. Alice nodded.

'Yes, I remember closing it,' she said, frightened now. 'I had trouble getting it to shut – the wood has swollen again.'

Rory slipped his torch out.

'Keep behind me,' he warned.

Taking the bull by the horns Rory strode forward and flicked on the light switch in the woodshed. Simultaneously he swept the beam of the torch around the inside of the small building.

'Look!' she gasped, pointing at Willow's blanket.

The bedding had been flung untidily into a corner and the cushion ripped to pieces, the stuffing left scattered across the floor. Some of the logs were disturbed too, whilst the old cupboard door hung open. One or two of the gardening implements and tools also lay scattered on the floor. With one final look round Rory ushered Alice back to the doorway.

'Let's get indoors,' he said. 'I don't like this, come on!'

As they stepped outside Alice screamed causing Rory to jump violently. Lurking nearby in the shadows of the garden stood a figure similar in size and stature to Willow. Rory wrapped his arm protectively around Alice's shoulders and for a few seconds they were frozen in fear. The figure spoke.

'It is time to talk.' The words were short and clipped and came as an instruction rather than an invitation. The tone sounded smooth and educated. The figure stepped into the full beam of Rory's torch and stood looking at them, waiting for a response.

The owner of the voice obviously came from the same realm as Willow. In human terms he looked around forty five years old. He wore green breeches, buckled shoes and a long frock coat with gold braiding around the button holes. A wide leather belt adorned his waist and various pouches and draw string bags hung from it. He sported shoulder length greying hair tied back in a ponytail and a neatly clipped goatee beard. As he approached, his movements were fluid and feline like. Alice shrank away in fear. The figure spoke again.

'My name is Flint. I believe you have been helping someone I am looking for? Knowing her I suspect she has spun you some sympathy filled tale and gained your trust. The girl is a thief and has stolen something of great value. I need it back and to take her home with me to face our laws. Where is she?'
Rory naturally defended Willow.

'We have no idea where she is,' he said quickly before Alice could respond. 'She did stay in our woodshed as you are obviously aware, but this evening we found her gone. We've been out looking for her, but there's no sign of her anywhere. We've decided to give up looking and come home – she's clearly left.'
Flint looked thoughtful for a few moments, stroking his beard as he took in Rory's words.

'You genuinely have no idea where she is?' he asked suspiciously.

'None at all,' lied Rory smoothly, 'I told you, we found her gone and have spent the last couple of hours looking for her.'

'You seem to have gone to a lot of trouble on her behalf,' said Flint.

'Yes we have. We fed her and wanted to help her, but now she's gone, but like I said, I've no idea where.'
Flint pondered on this and then asked a question.

'I suppose you removed the magic stone that I placed in our gateway? She must have shown you how to do that?'
Rory saw no advantage in lying.

'Yes I did,' he said. 'We wanted to help her get home. But as you may have noticed, tonight I removed it from our own gateway as you requested in your note.'

'Ah yes my note,' said Flint. 'I may have made a mistake there. By using our own Ogham script I knew you would have to show her the message – I wanted her to fear me coming for her. That is obviously why she has now vanished. A lesson learned methinks.'

'Why did you want her to know you were coming,' piped up Alice. 'Surely you would have been better to not alert her? That's why she's legged it, surely?'
Flint bowed his head in acquiescence to Alice's question.

'As I said young lady – a mistake on my part. I wanted her to feel fear at knowing I hunted her. Call it professional pride if you like, nothing more than that.'
Flint changed the subject.

'How would you two like to do me a service?' he asked smoothly.

'What kind of a service?' asked Rory.
Flint reached down to his belt and opened one of his draw string bags. The clink of metal accompanied his movement. Opening his fist he revealed two gold coins. He offered them to Rory.

'Here,' he said. 'One for each of you as a good will gesture. If the girl returns, all I ask is that you alert me to her whereabouts and I'll give you another ten to share between the two of you.'
Rory whistled loudly.

'Is that real gold?' he asked enthusiastically.

'Of course it is real gold. Here, take them.' Flint gestured impatiently with his hand and a smile spread across his face as Rory reached out and took the payment. Alice was aghast.

'Rory...' she began, but Rory nudged her with his elbow.

'Okay, you have a deal,' he said to Flint in a brazen tone. 'How do we find you when we need to hand her over?'

Flint turned and gestured behind him. To Rory and Alice's astonishment a second figure stepped out of the shadows and stood beside Flint. This one appeared younger, but quite callous looking with a pock marked face. He wore a breastplate and helmet of what appeared to be bronze and in his left hand he carried a short lance.

'This is my Captain – Zircon is his name. Give them what they need Zircon.' The evil looking little man stepped forward and handed Rory a small ram's horn, the tapered end being tipped in silver. Rory suspected it may have been the horn they heard earlier on their way back from the lake. As he took it Flint gave his instructions.

'If the girl returns just stand out there in the field and blow it once. Someone will come quickly and take her away. You will be paid in full on delivery.'

Rory nodded.

'Anything else?'

'Take this.' From another of his pouches Flint took out a simple leather thong with a small polished piece of flint attached to it. 'Show this to whoever attends the horn blast,' he stated. 'They will recognise you as one of my knights and will pay you off. '

Slipping the thong around his neck Rory nodded. Flint looked on approvingly as the stone slid beneath Rory's shirt and then he spoke for the final time.

'Our business is concluded here,' he said sharply. 'Zircon, take the fauns home for the night and we will await our young knight's call.'

In a moment Zircon melted back into the darkness and a low whistle came from the shadows. The sound of snapping twigs and the rustle of undergrowth followed, as though a great many creatures were scuttling about, and then only Flint remained.

'Do not let me down,' he said. 'Those who help me will be rewarded, but those who fail…' The sentence remained unfinished and with that Flint vanished. They didn't see him leave. He just wasn't there anymore.

\*

The evening left Rory and Alice exhausted. Silently they went indoors where Alice turned on her brother.

'What on earth were you thinking!' she scolded. 'We've helped Willow all through this and at the first hint of gold you're willing to hand her over just like that!'
Rory shook his head.

'No,' he replied, 'I just thought that by misleading Flint we may gain some time to decide what to do next. If I didn't agree to his terms what then? He could have caused all kinds of trouble here, but now we can make out we're looking for Willow and just not bother to contact him again.'
Alice felt less confident.

'I don't think it's as simple as that,' she said. 'Flint will keep coming back until he gets what he wants – we can't let him harm her Rory, we just can't!'
Alice just glared and Rory put down his tea and moved beside her.

'Come on sis,' he whispered, 'it's not that bad. It's given us a bit of time, that's all – that's why I did it. Stop worrying and let's think how we might help Willow to get home.'

They spent the next hour trying to come up with some kind of plan. Nothing seemed suitable and eventually they had to concede that they were both dog tired and that Liz could be home any moment. With heavy hearts, and sick with worry they went up to bed.

'That was really foolish Rory,' Alice said as she opened her bedroom door. 'We haven't seen the last of Flint.

He'll come back for her and when he does I just hope that you can justify what you did tonight. He will do everything to take her. When he does I trust you'll be able to live with yourself…'

\*\*\*

# 6

# FLIGHT AND CAPTURE

Tuesday morning brought heavy rain in place of the snow flurries and driven by squally winds the torrent battered against the bedroom windows as Rory and Alice awoke. They would not be able to visit the island under such conditions, and even if they did make such an attempt their mother would have asked some very difficult questions. The poor weather continued throughout the day and into the evening and they both spent a miserable time fretting over Willow's welfare. However, no one could change the situation and they resigned themselves to the fact that they would not be seeing Willow any time soon. Alice just felt grateful at having given her a substantial amount of food. Rory comforted his sister by saying,

'Willow is a natural little creature – she knows how to fend for herself. She'd find something to eat without us feeding her, I'm sure'

His words calmed Alice and she didn't feel quite so bad. However, despite the reassurances on Willow's welfare Alice still felt extremely angry towards her brother after his acceptance of Flint's coins and his agreement to assist in finding Willow. She remained tight lipped much of the day, only mellowing when he volunteered to help with her revision once more.

Alice accepted Rory's help, but remained frosty faced all afternoon. Only after their mother left for work did she open up a little to discuss Willow and her plight. Debating over the encounter with Flint, neither found answers as to what they should do next. Much to Alice's chagrin, Rory remained obstinate on that particular subject, still defending his agreement with Flint. Alice strongly disagreed and the air of defiance continued between them. The tension persisted into late evening, and still being no closer to working out a solution they both conceded defeat and went to bed.

*

The weather on Wednesday proved to be much better. Although a few grey clouds still remained, the rain had stopped and the wind lessened. Alice awoke with a more positive attitude than on the previous morning, the weak sunshine instantly lifting her spirits. She could never stay angry with Rory for long and on-going down to the kitchen and finding him already there, she greeted him over his cornflakes with a smile. Rory grunted back, stuck his tongue out and continued eating.

This morning Liz did not appear, instead relishing a lengthy lie in. With breakfast and their chores out of the way Rory and Alice called for Mel quite early and the trio set off towards the lake. As they left, Copper appeared from the hedgerow and with a loud mewing followed them. Alice tried to shoo her away, but to no avail. She gave up and the cat joined their party, loping along behind, but always keeping them in sight.

On the way Alice and Rory were able to bring Mel up to date regarding their encounter with Flint. Mel complained at not being updated the previous day and when she heard of Flint actually paying them in gold coins she demanded to see them. However, the coins were at home, but Rory did show her the ram's horn which fitted snugly into the inner pocket of his jacket and the polished stone that he wore about his neck.

On reaching the lake it only took a few moments to get the dinghy from beneath the bushes and launched into the water. Rory sat with Copper on his lap as the girls paddled. A few minutes later and they were ashore. At the clearing they found the tent, but no Willow. Rory and Alice were getting used to this now and weren't too concerned. Instead they remained by the tent and called out for her. She couldn't have gone far, for the island could be explored within ten minutes. After calling and patiently waiting, Willow still remained elusive and an uneasy fear set in. Alice predicted the worst and even the usually optimistic Rory wavered a little. Only Mel seemed unconcerned, sneering at their doubts and secretly glad inside that Willow could not be found. She still refused to forgive Rory for showing the little woman so much affection. However, she kept her hostile opinions to herself.

Finally, after calling for their ethereal friend again they were rewarded by the sound of a silvery giggle. It sounded as though the person laughing wanted to suppress their mirth and when Rory spun around looking for the source, the bubbly laughter came a second time from another direction. Exasperated, he put his hands on his hips and said,

'Okay Willow, stop messing about – where are you?'

Amazingly Willow stood right next to Rory. One moment she wasn't there, but in the blink of an eye, just appeared. Rory jumped and the look of surprise on his face caused Willow, along with Alice and Mel to burst out into loud laughter.

'How the hell did you do that?' he asked. Willow grinned and said,

'Watch.'

She seemed to take a single step back and melted away, blending into the trees and vegetation about her. Smiling, she reappeared a moment later next to Alice and then showed off by vanishing and popping up in all different places. Copper found this behaviour very disconcerting and crouched down hissing whenever Willow re-appeared. Rory, Alice and Mel were highly impressed, but above all they noticed a huge change in Willow's personality as she demonstrated a more mischievous and playful side. Her clothes, so recently dishevelled were now neat and clean and her dark hair appeared beautifully combed and shining in the sun light. They also couldn't help noticing her big blue eyes which sparkled with fun, totally lighting up her pretty face. She literally glowed from within and skipped and bounced around the clearing like a spring lamb. Eventually, tiring of her game she sat down by the tent cross legged and without a word pulled out a tiny wooden flute from her shoulder bag and began to play. The music sounded beautiful, flowing like water and making everyone want to dance. Alice and Rory were up in a moment, and then shedding her inhibitions, Mel joined in too. All three danced to several tunes with Copper scampering about their feet until Willow ended her impromptu performance and sat back waiting for their reaction. Rory spoke for all of them.

'Nice one Willow. Where did that flute come from? You're well skilled – that sounded amazing.'

Willow basked in the praise. She answered smiling, and still with a hint of a giggle in her voice.

'Music is the best magic,' she said mysteriously. 'It can make you feel happy or sad or both at the same time. My preferred instrument is my fiddle. If you get me home – well, just you wait and hear me play that! And I play the harp too. As for my mood, being back out here amongst my beloved trees is the best form of healing I could ever have.'

Meeting Willow again made everyone feel good, but hearing her speak of trying to get home gave Rory the cue he needed.

'We have something to tell you Willow – some pretty big stuff really,' he said.

Sensing a change of mood, Willow waited patiently for Rory to begin.

'The other night,' he started, 'after we left you – we got

home and Alice noticed the shed door open. We checked inside and it was a mess.' Rory paused here, noticing Willow looking a little more serious, the fun gradually draining out of her. 'When we came out of the shed we saw him...'

'Who?'

'Your uncle Flint,' replied Rory. 'He asked us where you were, so we lied and said you'd been living in our shed, but had run off and that we'd been out looking for you.'

Willow seemed to sag at this bad news, all of her remaining fun and glee evaporating instantly. Rory continued. 'He offered us gold if we'd let him know when you returned...'

'GOLD!' Willow shrieked, 'tell me you didn't take it – please tell me you didn't...'

Suddenly feeling ashamed of what he wanted to say, Rory lowered his head.

'Yes,' he replied, 'I did take it, but only two coins, and I swear I'm not going to tell him anything. If he wants to give me his money that's up to him, but I'll tell him nothing...'

'YOU FOOL!'

Willow shouted the words at Rory. His face reddened and feeling angry himself he retaliated.

'I told you I won't tell him where you are!' he said. 'Don't have a go at me, I don't intend...'

Willow cut him short.

'Do you not see?' she asked. 'By accepting Flint's coin you have entered into a contract. You are now bound to giving him what he wants. He has completely misled you!'

Willow burst into tears now, her former fun extinguished. Rory hung his head and Alice turned on him.

'Why on earth did you do it Rory?' she scolded. 'I said at the time it would cause problems – I knew it!'

For a short time they fell silent, deep in their own thoughts until Willow took control.

'What is done is done,' she said philosophically as she blinked back her tears. 'Rory, I accept you meant no harm, but mark this - what I said is very real. If you betray Flint he will pursue you. Now is there anything else I should know about?'

Rory took out the ram's horn and showed it to Willow explaining to her about how he should signal Flint's followers. She nodded, not too perturbed at the sight of it, but when he drew out the polished stone that hung around his neck Willow recoiled in terror.

'By The Goddess!' she exclaimed. 'Get rid of it – GET RID OF IT NOW!'

So saying she grabbed at the cord around Rory's neck and tore the stone free. In one swift movement she tossed the item far into the air. Moments later they heard a splash as it hit the surface of the lake and disappeared beneath the surface – the ever widening ripples the only clue to its existence. Willow trembled now and wrapping her own arms around herself, rocked backwards and forwards. It made a heart breaking sight. Only minutes before the little woman sparkled with fun and mischief. Now she looked utterly broken and without hope.

'What is it?' Rory asked sheepishly. 'What's so bad about the stone? Flint said it would identify me to his followers so they wouldn't harm me.'

Willow nodded and then through her anguish revealed the reason for her fear.

'The stone marks you as one of his, that is true,' she said. 'What he did not tell you is that through the stone he would always know where you are – he can track you at any time. Do you not see? By coming to the island with that stone, you have shown him where I am hiding!'

Rory hung his head in shame.

'I'm so sorry,' he said. 'Willow, please forgive me, I just didn't realise…'

Willow pulled herself together and said,

'You are not to blame Rory for you have no idea of how

cunning Flint is. Let me show you something – look here – see?'

Willow slid her hand down the inside of the front of her dress. She pulled out a thin leather thong similar to the one that so recently adorned Rory's neck. A small cluster of willow leaves and catkins hung along its length. Unclipping it from around her neck she handed it to Rory.

'See?' she said again quizzically. 'We all wear a birth amulet like this as a personal talisman. Mine is of the woodland and is made from the very tree whose name I bear. Flint's, naturally is made of flint. Hold mine Rory. Feel it, sense its power and connection with me.'

Rory held the tiny necklace in one hand. Closing his eyes as she instructed him he could feel Willow close beside him and as he turned in her direction, could sense the pull in his hand as the amulet tried to reunite itself with its owner. Stunned he handed it back.

'You felt it?' she asked.

Rory nodded, mesmerised by the experience. It reminded him of a tiny compass that wanted to pull him towards Willow. He handed it back and watched the cluster of leaves slip back out of sight beneath Willows clothes.

'Now you understand?' she asked. 'About Flint I mean – tracking you. He is a powerful master of magic and having given you that stone he can always sense where it is. Well now he can go and look for it at the bottom of the lake!'

She turned away from Rory and addressed her friends collectively.

'We need to decide where I can go. I cannot stay here – in fact we should move right away. Flint's is probably already coming. You three know this area – is there any dense woodland nearby? If I can get into a proper forest realm then I have a chance of eluding them. That is my natural domain and you have seen how I can disappear at will amongst the trees – they will protect me; Flint and his followers are of the earth, they would find it much harder to track me there.'

Willow's sudden optimism and positive outlook gave them all a little hope.

'How about Ravens Wood?' Mel suggested.

'Ravens Wood? That's quite a trek from here Mel,' Alice said.

'It's not that far – only about half an hour,' Mel replied, 'but it's quite dense and pretty vast. If you wanted to hide in the woods it would be the ideal place.'

The discussion continued for some minutes and then Willow spoke.

'I think we should go for these woods. How easy is it to get there?'

Rory shrugged. Their choice of locations was limited, and he could think of nothing better.

'We'd have to head towards home,' he said. 'That field our house backs onto, – we need to cut across there and follow a footpath that should take us by the quickest route. Only trouble is it means we have to go towards the gateway, and if Flint is coming for you we may run into him on the way.'

Willow looked thoughtful, her puckish face twisting in all directions as she ran Rory's comments through her mind.

'I still wish to try for it,' she decided. 'If I can get into the woodland the trees will look after me. They will hide me well.'

With Willow adamant that woodland remained her best hope they collected up her few possessions, caught Copper and headed for the dinghy. After their original trip to the island Rory had left the roll of duct tape in the boat. With great reluctance he withdrew it and turned to Willow.

'Come on,' he said softly. 'I don't want to do this but...'

With equal reluctance Willow nodded and offered up her hands. Rory bound her in moments and carried her to the water's edge. They decided to leave the tent where it stood. It would be less weight in the dinghy and would save them a substantial amount of time. Rory could collect it another day. With Willow bound and gagged as before they endeavoured to make the crossing as quickly as possible. Just before Rory taped her mouth she made one last request.

'Please hold me tightly,' she whispered. 'Just hold me close - I trust you Rory, I really do.'

Rory saw something in her eyes that made his pulse race. The way Willow looked at him caused a stir in his belly each time she addressed him. As they settled in the boat, this time Willow didn't kick and thrash about, but instead, buried her face into Rory's neck and nuzzled there trustingly. But despite her not fighting Rory could still feel her trembling uncontrollably as the little boat moved out across the lake. She whimpered too and her tears were wet on his neck. Rory comforted her by hugging her close and repeatedly kissing her hair which smelled of wild flowers.

The return journey went well and they were ashore in less than five minutes. Willow managed not to vomit this time, although she did retch when Rory pulled the tape from her mouth. She also clung to Rory far longer than required, much to the disgust of Mel who now considered him to be paying Willow far too much attention again. She huffed as she watched Rory comforting his tiny friend, becoming increasingly annoyed at the affection Willow received.

With the crossing complete and the boat hidden under the bushes, the tension eased away. Alice and Mel fell behind, whilst Rory walked side by side with Willow and Copper. They said little, preferring to keep their wits about them in case of trouble. Rory felt quite optimistic that they would reach the woods unmolested, but three quarters of the way into their walk trouble found them. The sound of a horn being blown somewhere ahead dashed their hopes. Willow jumped and went pale, gripping Rory's arm and cuddling up to him as the eerie sound echoed across the field. Rory sensed her thinking of making a bolt for it and slid his arm around her waist to prevent her.

Rory and Willow stopped walking and the two girls were beside them in a moment. Rory glanced around desperately for somewhere to hide, but could see nowhere to go. In front, behind and to their right the field spread out, leaving them fully exposed. To their left the dry stone wall ran for a couple of miles. Behind it lay an impenetrable hedgerow with more fields beyond. For a moment Rory felt panic rising in his throat, but fought it back.

'Keep going,' he said defiantly.

'Wait.' Willow drew Rory aside from the girls. 'Despite you falling in with Flint's plans I know you meant no harm Rory,' she said.

He made to cut in, but Willow placed her finger over his lips and continued.

'There is not much time and I want to give you this.'

She reached into the pouch on her belt and withdrew her father's gold ring. Placing it in Rory's hand she folded his fingers over the precious object as she said,

'Please keep it safe. Should Flint's companions take me down, I do not want him to get hold of this. Without it his plans can be thwarted. It is why he is hunting me in the first place.'

Rory held back, not wanting to take the piece of Faerie jewellery and Alice saw his hesitation.

'Take it Rory,' she said. 'Willow is right. If we keep this away from Flint it may even prevent him from harming her.'

Rory took the ring and slid it inside his jacket pocket. It would be secure there, zipped up and unable to fall free. Satisfied, Willow nodded and as a gesture of gratitude she wrapped her little arms around Rory's body and hugged him close.

'Thank you,' she whispered. 'Whatever happens, please

promise me you will not give that up easily to Flint? I trust you completely Rory – thank you.'

Then Willow stretched up on her toes, pulled Rory forward and kissed him fully on the mouth. Long and passionate, the kiss gave Rory a stirring in his heart like never before. He blushed instantly, but a wave of pleasure also coursed through him, imbuing him with total resolve to protect Willow and her father's ring no matter what.

Seeing the look of pleasure on Rory's face at Willow's kiss Mel finally broke her silence.

'What is it with you two?' she demanded loudly. 'Rory, she's too old for you, that's disgusting – put her down you don't know where she's been!'

'Mel that's unkind,' Alice said. 'You know what you and Rory agreed. This really isn't the time or place is it? We've discussed this – if you want to help, then do so. If not, go home. Either way I think you should apologise to Rory and to Willow – your choice.'

Mel's outburst left Rory speechless, and when Alice took over he let her continue. Mel bit her lip, frustrated at not being able to tell Rory the truth of her feelings. For once, recognising the situation they were currently in and not wishing to alienate Rory any further she wiped the back of her hand over her face and mumbled an apology. Simmering with anger Rory answered drily.

'Mel, I've told you before, if you persist in being a bitch to Willow I'll have nothing to do with you – do you understand?'

Miserably, Mel nodded. She felt dejected at seeing Rory taking such an interest in Willow. However, she also recognised the reality of Rory disowning her as a friend. Whatever happened next, she knew that she would have to help Willow to the bitter end to retain Rory's friendship. Sniffing, she nodded.

'I'm sorry,' she said, 'but I find it hard watching the way you two… you know…'

Rory shook his head in disbelief.

'Alice is right Mel; this isn't the time or place. We need to get on – in every sense. Now let's move.'

Grabbing Willow by the hand Rory marched her along the field boundary at a pace whereby the girls struggled to keep up. Mel complained immediately and when she stepped in a boggy section of ground and covered her new trainers in mud she swore profusely. She was ignored. Rory knew now that if he could get Willow to the cover of the trees she would at least have a chance. Sadly, it didn't happen. With only a couple of hundred yards to go, and with the woodland entrance teasingly close, a group of tiny figures appeared from amongst the long grass and shrubs. Several carried bows and everyone could see the wicked, flint tipped arrows being pointed in their direction.

'Woad Warriors!' Willow squealed. 'Now we are in trouble.'

Rory decided to press on regardless. Changing his direction slightly meant he could go past the group without going through them. However, a second cluster of armed men swarmed around the entrance to the tree line and as they approached, the group parted and there stood Flint, his arms folded, a mocking smile on his face.

'Move aside and let us through,' Rory demanded still gripping Willow by the wrist. He could feel her shrinking away from Flint and on risking a quick glance in her direction saw the terror on her face.

Flint shook his head.

'I think not,' he hissed. He barked out an order over his shoulder. 'Take the girl.'

Two men stepped forward. Rory recognised Zircon at once. He pushed Willow behind him and spoke directly to Flint.

'Why are you so anxious to get hold of her? What harm has she done you? Can't you just leave her here with us and forget her?'

Flint responded angrily.

'I told you she has stolen something that belongs to me.

I need it back and she must face justice.'

Rory continued to fight Willow's corner.

'Well I'm not giving her to you,' he said. 'I don't know what you think you can do, but she's staying with me. Come on Willow, I'm taking you home.'

Rory spun around, pulling Willow with him, walking off in the opposite direction. Alice screamed.

'RORY STOP!'

Halting, Rory spun round to see half a dozen bows pointed straight at him. Angry, and left with no choice he surrendered. However, not giving up entirely, he addressed Flint once more.

'Is there anything we can do or say to stop you from harming her?' he asked. 'Can't you just search her or something and be done with it? We'll look after Willow – if you don't want her back in your world she can stay here with us.'

Flint smiled, stroking his chin.

'I suspect if I search her she will not have it. She knows what I am looking for and would have hidden it if she has any sense – and one thing I do know is that she is no fool. She comes with us. You have no business with her or me other than to settle our agreement.'

Flint gestured over his shoulder and Zircon came forward bearing a leather pouch. He handed it to Rory.

'Our agreement is settled,' Flint stated. 'It is there in full – despite the fact that you decided to hide her. Do not insult me by counting it. Do not follow us. If, and I do mean if, you were able to enter our world I will have you and your sister tried for breach of contract. You could easily get a hundred years in one of our jails. Zircon! Bind her.'

Zircon pulled Willow free from Rory's grasp, whipped out a length of wicker withy and wrapped it around her wrists, binding her tightly. With a jerk on the trailing end he brutally pulled her forward and in amongst the circle of Woad Warriors who now closed around her. Furious,

Rory lunged forward, but a dozen bronze tipped spears appeared before him, thrust out by some of the dark skinned, unsmiling little men around Flint. Alice and Mel were both crying and Flint sneered at them.

'Fools,' he hissed. 'Forget you ever saw her and enjoy your gold!'

Flint walked away. The Woad Warriors parted and he disappeared into their midst, Swiftly the little group moved across the field and the last glimpse they saw of Willow was of her frightened eyes as she twisted her head around in a futile bid to see her friends one last time.

Utterly distraught and feeling helpless Rory, Alice and Mel could only watch their friend being spirited away. Tears ran down Rory's face and Alice sobbed loudly. Initially Mel stood silent and then to the surprise of the other two, rounded on them angrily.

'Just look at you two!' she sneered. 'Willow has been dragged off and you stand there blubbing. Is that all you can do? Rory – I really thought you were sweet on her – are you just going to watch them drag her off like that or what? Making out how annoyed you were because I called her names? What sort of a man are you? More of a boy I'd say! Come on! Show me what you're made of!'

Mel stormed off across the field following the little group that could still be seen moving along the far hedgerow towards the ancient barrow. Shocked and spurred on by Mel's outburst Alice and Rory could only stumble after her, breaking into a jog to catch up. Rory felt as though his head would explode. Not only did the taking of Willow cause him great distress, but Mel's comments about him being sweet on her really hit home. He hadn't even admitted it to himself quite how much he really liked her, but now seeing her threatened with danger he felt awful. Seeing Mel actively doing something gave him hope. Despite the previous few minutes and with a great change of heart he suddenly felt immensely grateful to Mel. Without her reacting so feistily, he and Alice would probably both still be standing in the field, helpless. Perhaps after their heated exchange minutes before, Mel had actually come to her senses. He risked a glance at Alice. She still looked red faced, but he felt heartened to see the look of determination she wore as she followed him across the field. As they reached the opposite side they could see the group ahead of them, with Zircon cruelly pulling Willow along. The weak winter sun glinted every now and then off of the spear tips and helmets, and seething anger replaced Rory's distress, spurring him on. Gaining on Mel now, he saw her stop and pick something up. Exclaiming loudly, she held it out for the others to see. Rory and Alice gasped at the sight of the leather thong adorned with willow leaves and catkins.

'Willow's amulet!' Rory said. 'Give it here.'

'No – there isn't time!'

Mel stuffed the necklace into her pocket and continued running. Flint and his men were almost at the barrow now and they all knew that once they passed through the gateway they would never see Willow again. Rory however, seemed to have another idea.

'Keep going,' he shouted at the girls, 'I'll catch you up!'

Running off, he headed back towards their house. For a moment Alice and Mel just gaped, shouting at him to come back, but then as one they both turned and continued their pursuit across the field. The group ahead were entering the barrow. Mel, catching a momentary glimpse of Willow being dragged along raced on like an athlete and about a minute or so after the last of the little men disappeared into to stone chamber she reached it herself. Glancing around she saw Alice making ground behind her, and some way back, Rory, also racing along back towards them like a whirlwind. Breathing hard from her exertions Mel ducked into the darkened chamber. The small party clustered together in the corner and as she watched the gateway opened. As the wall opened into the tunnel, sunlight streamed through from the far side illuminating the barrow in a soft golden glow. Mel shouted.

'Flint – WAIT! WAIT, DAMN YOU!'

The bulk of the group filtered into the tunnel, but Flint remained behind, standing in the entrance looking at Mel mockingly.

'You have something to say girl?' he asked, his voice rasping and harsh.
Mel nodded.

'Yes,' she gasped breathlessly. 'Please, can't we talk this through? There must be another solution. Whatever Willow has taken, can't we just find it and give it to you? I promise you won't hear from us or Willow again if you agree. Just give her to us and we'll talk some sense into her. Please don't take her...'
Flint shook his head.

'I cannot risk it,' he stated. 'I have far too much to lose. Go home girl and tell your friends to do the same!'
Flint walked into the tunnel. Simultaneously, Alice, closely followed by a heavily panting Rory and an excited Copper burst into the barrow.

'FLINT STOP!' roared Rory.
Flint disappeared from view, and a moment later blackness engulfed them as the gateway rolled shut.

The sudden loss of the streaming sunlight inside the barrow plunged the chamber into blackness. Rory cursed as he fumbled in his pocket for his key ring torch. Alice began to cry and as the weak light of the torch dimly lit the barrow once more all three spoke at once. Rory became vocal, cursing Flint and calling for Willow by name. Alice tried to calm her brother, but Mel rebuked him.

'Rory, why did you run back home? What the bloody hell were you thinking? If you'd stayed with us maybe we could have stopped them...' Her voice trailed away into an embarrassed silence. Rory rounded on Mel then and took out his frustration on her.

'Oh, so it's suddenly my fault is it?' he said. 'After all

your negative and snide comments you're now concerned? You don't even like Willow. Ever since we showed her to you you've done nothing but sneer at her or insult her. What do you care if she's been taken? You just didn't like her getting attention from me did you?'

Mel turned white. For a few moments she said nothing and Alice ceased weeping as the argument unfolded before her. Mel stepped forward until she stood inches from Rory and defended her corner.

'Yes, you're right Rory; I haven't liked watching you give all that attention to her. The reason for that is because I really like you! Willow is actually quite cute and despite everything, I do genuinely like her. But how do you think I've felt watching you fuss over her for the last few days? Only half an hour ago I stood watching while you practically kissed her face off! Okay, so I reacted when I saw that, but for heaven's sake Rory I bloody well love you! I have ever since Alice introduced you to me at school. Didn't you ever realise?'

Rory's jaw dropped. He felt hugely embarrassed. Despite her shortcomings, deep down he really did like Mel, but he had never thought of her in that way. Alice stepped in.

'Listen you two,' she said. 'Can't we sort this out later? Willow's been abducted and we're standing here arguing between ourselves. What the hell are we going to do? I don't know how to open that gateway – do either of you have any ideas?'

For a few moments Rory and Mel continued looking at each other and then Mel said,

'If you'd been here when I arrived you'd have seen me begging Flint to set her free. I'd have done anything Rory to help her, and not just for her sake either. I know you really like her and I'd have defended her to the end – for you! Now stop being so up yourself and let's find a way through this bloody gateway!'

Mel ran her hands over the wall finding solid,

impenetrable stone. The light from Rory's torch waned now, and miserably, he stepped forward to help Mel look for cracks or any other way through. He couldn't look her in the eye and his mind raced. With so much to think about his emotions were off the scale. But above all, Mel spoke the truth. He did genuinely care for Willow. Every time she smiled at him his heart bounded. The smell of her hair, the way she walked and the sound of her voice all caused his pulse to race and his face to flush hotly. When she played her flute earlier in the day Rory felt captivated and he now knew that Willow truly possessed his heart.

For the moment Mel seemed to have turned the other cheek, still frantically searching the wall for a way through. They spent half an hour scouring the stone work concluding that only magical means would get them through. Alice even convinced them all to hold hands with their eyes closed, concentrating on making the wall open. Nothing worked. Eventually all three, feeling dejected sat on the floor. Alice asked the question that so far remained unanswered.

'Rory,' she asked timidly, 'why did you run home? You never did say...'

Rory sniffed and slid his hand into his pocket and took out the lodestone. Holding it up he rotated it in the dim light and said,

'I went to get this. I thought I might use it as a weapon, but I failed. They still took her...'

His voice faltered and he blinked back tears. Alice stared helplessly, but Mel slid her arm around Rory's shoulders.

'Rory,' she said softly, 'I'm so sorry. I know I treated her badly, but at least you understand why. I'm so very sorry...'

Rory and Mel both sobbed and clung to each other. They remained that way for some minutes before Mel withdrew. Pulling away, she spoke from her heart.

'Listen Rory,' she said. 'I know I screwed up, but I promise you that I'll do anything to make amends.

Whatever it takes, I will do it to get Willow back – okay?'
Mel stood up and approached the wall again.

'There must be a way through,' she said, 'There must
be!'
Rory watched Mel for a few moments and then finally
snapped.

'FORGET IT MEL!' he shouted. 'WE CAN'T GET
THROUGH – I'VE LOST HER...'

At his outburst Mel tried to pacify him, but to no avail.
Still continuing to curse, Rory pulled the lodestone from
his pocket for a second time and waved it dramatically at
the girls.

'IF I HADN'T GONE BACK FOR THIS BLOODY
THING I MIGHT HAVE ACTUALLY BEEN ABLE
TO HELP HER!' he yelled.

As he shouted the words he flung the lodestone directly
at the corner of the chamber where the gateway lay hidden.
As it hit the wall and clattered to the floor a distant
rumbling sound entered the chamber, and for a moment it
felt as though the floor rocked sideways. Rory actually fell,
and stone fragments and dust from the roof dropped on
top of him. He sat up coughing. At the same moment
the wall rolled back and the entrance to the gateway
appeared. Sunlight streamed through once more and for a
few moments they all stared in disbelief at the field of
wheat beyond.

'Rory – LOOK!' Alice practically screamed the words.
As Rory tried to rise, still coughing and spitting out grit he
saw a rapid movement in the dust cloud as Mel shot
forward. In a moment she snatched up the fallen
lodestone, and followed by Copper she ran headlong into
the tunnel. Alice called out frantically, 'MEL – NO –
WAIT!'

Rory got to his feet and ran forward. With Mel and
Copper gone, lost in the blinding sunlight, Rory and Alice
reached the entrance together, but were too late. With a
second rumble the wall rolled closed and brother and sister

found themselves staring at tightly fitting stone blocks once more. Falling back they could only console each other at having lost Willow, their friend and their cat, and with the lodestone gone too they really could see no way through...

\*\*\*

7

# Through The Gateway

Disorientated and feeling sick, Mel emerged into strong sunlight. Rubbing her eyes she turned around and peered back at the barrow. It looked identical to the one at home. Even the moss and lichen patterns on the ancient stones were the same as she remembered them. However, on looking at her immediate surroundings, although familiar, they were also very different indeed. The general topography of the area remained the same as at home, but she could hear no traffic noise from the nearby roads – in fact there were no paved roads. An eerie silence broken only by birdsong and the buzz of insects surrounded her. The flat landscape with the familiar hump of Glastonbury Tor in the distance lay just visible through a thin mist as it always did, although in this world, the ruined church tower at the top did not exist, replaced instead by a ring of standing stones. The houses that lay on the far side of the field where they all lived were also gone. In their place stood a never ending sea of wheat, softly waving in a light summer breeze. In fact that proved an anomaly too, for on entering the barrow with her friends it had been a cold March day. Now midsummer, a warm breeze wafted about her. Stunned, she gazed about in wonder. Something else struck her too; everything here seemed so much more intense – the colours, the smells and the feel of the sunshine.

She found herself to be standing on an ancient track which passed by the entrance to the barrow. Along its flank a dry stone wall stretched for miles, disappearing into the distance – identical to the wall at home. Confused, Mel sat on the wall to think about her predicament. Suddenly she felt terribly lonely. Re-entering the barrow she called out for Rory and Alice, but her only reply came in the form of mewing as Copper emerged into the sunlight.

'Oh Copper!' she exclaimed. 'You silly cat – you should never have followed me.'

Frightened now, she sat back on the wall and wept. Fear rose in her throat and the thought of being trapped in Willow's domain filled her with terror. Ironically, she understood how Willow must have felt on being cast out of her own realm and how finding a group of friendly faces made all the difference to her circumstances. Eventually however, common sense broke through and Mel ceased her tears and thought on what she should do next. She had entered the gateway with a view to helping Willow and with that in mind she stood up, brushed herself down and re-assessed her situation. Her winter coat already made her too hot, so she took it off and shoved it under some bushes by the barrow entrance. Next, she went through her jeans pockets to look for anything useful. In one lay the lodestone – that could be worth keeping she decided, but more importantly in her other pocket she found Willow's amulet. Other than being a little crumpled it appeared to be in good condition. Remembering how Willow taught Rory to feel the amulet's pull she gave it a try. Closing her eyes she concentrated her thoughts on the tiny Faerie woman. Nothing happened. Disheartened she tried again – and then again. On the third attempt she felt excitement at a tiny movement in her hand. The amulet, she decided wanted her go left along the road. With nothing else to go on, she clipped the amulet around her own neck and set off with Copper beside her.

The road went as far as Mel could see. The wheat field to her right also seemed to stretch into infinity. To her left were unbroken meadows dotted with clumps of woodland and copses. The afternoon passed and Mel became hot, tired and worst of all, dehydrated, but she soldiered on.

She expected to encounter someone, or find a village, but it seemed as though no other soul existed. Having come so far she could not justify turning back – and even if she did, what then? With no idea how to get home, she continued to walk. Finally, after what seemed hours Mel found herself at a junction on the track. A second path led off through a clump of trees to her right. Furthermore, she could smell wood smoke and hear a rhythmic clump, clump, clump which reminded her of Rory chopping logs. Her heart pounding with apprehension at finally meeting someone Mel took the new path and with Copper following she strode on.

The trees thinned out and Mel found herself on the edge of a forest clearing. Nestled on the far side of the clearing stood a strange house. It was a house like nothing Mel had ever seen before, being circular, with wattle and daub walls to the height of her head. On the top sat a beautiful, cone shaped roof of thatched reeds. Smoke filtered through the roof from within giving a mystical appearance. Outside the house stood a little man, similar in size to Willow. He had his back to Mel as he chopped wood with a bronze axe. All this Mel took in instantly. Nearby, a circular wall caught her eye, and perhaps more importantly, the bucket attached to a rope sitting on the top. A dipper lay beside the bucket and Mel noticed a fresh, wet patch on the stones. Her thirst getting the better of her, she edged forward. Not wishing to disturb the little man and find him hostile Mel decided to help herself. It took only a minute or two to creep close enough to be able to reach the dipper. Her hand stretched out to touch the handle when without turning around the man spoke.

'If there's one thing I 'ates, it's thievin',' he said loudly. 'Thievin' ain't right. If someone wants somethin' they only 'as to ask. I'm always 'appy to oblige folk, but I really don't like thieven'.'

Mel stood frozen to the spot, her hand hovering just centimetres from the dipper. Understanding the message in the words she withdrew her hand, stood up straight and cleared her throat loudly. The man continued cutting wood. Mel tried again and feeling bolder called out.

'Excuse me?'

This time he reacted. Slowly putting down the axe, he took out a large red handkerchief and mopped his bald head. Then he turned around and studied Mel. She could see he possessed a short greying beard. He wore old blue breeches with a baggy blue shirt and a sleeveless leather jerkin over the top. However, his face was kindly, causing her to feel hopeful.

'Well 'ooed 'ave believed it!' he said. 'An ooman – an ooman bein' astandin' right in front o' me!'

Embarrassed, Mel didn't know how to reply so for the moment she remained silent.

'Wassup girl? Cat got you tongue?' he enquired. Then he laughed loudly – right from his belly as Copper walked into view.

'And 'oos this?' he bellowed, clucking at the big ginger cat in a friendly manner.

'That's Copper,' Mel found herself saying. 'She belongs to my friend Alice.'

The little man guffawed.

'She speaks!' he boomed, 'the 'ooman speaks!'

Mel felt irritated at being called an 'ooman' and she replied frostily.

'Of course I speak. And if it's not too much trouble I would really like a drink of water. I've walked miles; I'm hot, thirsty and I have a terrible headache.'

The man's manner changed immediately and he became apologetic.

'Sorry me dear,' he said. 'Forgettin' me manners I am. Please 'scuse me, but we don't 'ave many visitors round 'ere.'

As he spoke he strode towards the bucket, filled the dipper and offered it to Mel. Gratefully she took it and in her haste spilled half the contents down her front as she drank. Holding out the empty dipper she asked boldly,

'Could I have another please?'

Refilling the dipper and holding it out he watched as Mel downed a second drink. When she held it out a third time he shook his head.

'No,' he said kindly. 'If you're that parched you should wait a bit – won't do you no good gulpin' it down like that. Besides, this one wants a drink too.'

Refilling the dipper again he turned and bent down, holding it out so that Copper could lap at the cold liquid. Mel, remembering her own manners for once responded gratefully.

'Thank you,' she said. 'We were both so thirsty and we've walked miles.'

The man smiled at her.

'What's your name girl,' he asked.

'Mel,' she said, 'and yours?'

'Barleycorn!' he almost shouted. Then he spat on his hand, rubbed it on his breeches and held it out. Dubiously Mel took it and he shook hers vigorously.

'So what you doin' round 'ere?' he enquired.

'I'm a bit lost. I saw the path leading off the road so hoped I'd find someone to help me. Thanks again for the water.'

'Don't mention it lass,' he replied. 'Pleasure it is, a real pleasure.'

When he smiled his whole face lit up in merriment. Mel relaxed a little.

'Can you tell me...' she asked, before being cut short by a second voice.

'Oo you talkin' to Barleycorn? They could probably 'ear you from the other side o' the woods you're so loud.'

A woman came out of the door of the house and seeing

Mel exclaimed,

'Stars and moon! An 'ooman! An 'ooman and a cat! Wa's she doin' 'ere?'

Smiling as much through mirth as being friendly Mel responded to the little woman.

'I'm sorry to be any bother to you, but your husband gave me some water. I should go now and leave you in peace.'

'GO? Go where?' demanded Barleycorn.

Mel shrugged.

'I'm not really sure...'

'Does she want feedin'?' asked the woman.

Mel, not realising her hunger, immediately felt famished at the hint of food, having not eaten since her breakfast. Shyly she spoke up.

'I am very hungry,' she said, 'but I really don't want to be any trouble to you.' The woman beamed.

''Ungry is it?' she said. 'Well you just come with me Dearie and I'll soon fix that. Nice mushroom stew on the go right now. Want some?'

Mel liked mushrooms and she nodded eagerly.

'Come you in then girl, come you in...'

Mel followed the couple into the roundhouse. Inside it reminded her of a living museum. Beaten earth provided the floor whilst in the centre lay an open hearth where a fire smouldered, the smoke filtering up through the roof. The walls were painted with what Mel would have called Celtic designs. Flowing swirls of bright colours wove their way around the internal wall giving a decorative look. To her right and all in a line were three tiny beds made from logs. All were adorned with embroidered blankets and pillows. Large sections of tree trunk draped with sheep skins were placed around the fire on three sides for seating. There were a couple of large wooden chests nearby and a small table. The lady opened one of the chests and took out three wooden bowls and spoons before going to the fire. A bronze cauldron hung there on a tripod. When she lifted the lid a wonderful smell came flooding out and Mel felt her stomach churn in sweet anticipation. Copper also stood transfixed at the aroma. Whilst the lady dished up the stew Barleycorn went to the other side of the room and took three wooden cups which he filled with a golden liquid from a cask. He offered one to Mel. Sniffing at it she smiled. It smelt mildly of honey.

'What is it,' she enquired meekly.

'Finest 'omemade mead,' said her host. 'The 'oney is from our own bees too.'

Barleycorn tipped up his cup and downed it in one. Mel gingerly sipped at hers and immediately liking the taste, took a more generous swig.

'It's lovely,' she said.

Barleycorn beamed and waved her over to one of the log seats. 'Sit yourself down lass. You're in for a right treat with 'er cookin' I can tell 'ee!'

Mel accepted the invitation gladly. Flopping onto one of the logs she held her hands out to receive a bowl of stew from Barleycorns wife.

'I'm sorry,' Mel said, 'I don't know your name.'

'Well, ain't it just like 'im not to introduce us? They calls me 'Azel. What's your name Dearie?'

'Mel.'

'Well tuck into that stew Mel. It'll do you the power o' good.'

Mel needed no reminding. Dipping her spoon into the thick gravy she pulled out a couple of mushrooms and cautiously popped them into her mouth. The stew tasted delicious. Hazel picked up a homemade loaf and tearing it into pieces, handed a substantial section to Mel. She ate hungrily whilst Barleycorn handed her a second cup of mead. Not forgotten, Copper lapped at a bowl of stew on the floor and Barleycorn and Hazel sat down to join them. With the meal over Barleycorn wiped his mouth with the back of his hand and said,

'All right girl – time to pay for your supper!'

Embarrassed she said,

'I'm really sorry... I... I have no money... I can't...'
Barleycorn laughed loudly.

'It ain't coin we want girl – we wants a good story. Tell us 'ow you got 'ere an' where you're agoin' an' that'll be payment enough!'

Mel relaxed a little. When she accepted the food she'd given no thought to payment. Telling her story would be easy and besides – maybe these two would be able to help. Sipping at her mead she began.

'It all started a few days ago – in my world,' she said. 'My friends Alice and Rory found a Faer...sorry – one of your people hiding in their woodshed. She couldn't get home so we decided to assist her. She told us that her uncle flung her out of your world. She couldn't get back as something blocked the gateway. With her help we removed the blockage, but her uncle then broke through and abducted her. My friend Rory managed to open the gateway and I ran through thinking they were following, but the gate closed behind me and now I'm trapped here.... I need to get home, but I also need to help *her*... I promised Rory I would...'

Mel's face crumpled then and Hazel slipped an arm around her and hugged her.

'Don' you go frettin' lass,' she said. 'Maybe we can all 'elp each other. There's lots o' bad things been 'appenin' around 'ere that needs fixin'. All kinds o' trouble. Young'uns goin' missin'...'

Then Hazel started to weep and Mel hugged her in return. Barleycorn, sitting nearby also cried, big tears rolling down his cheeks and Mel realised that despite the homely atmosphere something was seriously wrong here.

'What did you mean,' she asked, 'by young'uns going missing?'

Hazel pulled away and wiped her eyes. Gesturing to the three beds she said,

'One o' them belongs to our girl Tansy. A few moons

ago she went out to collect firewood. She never came 'ome. She ain't the only one either. A lad and a girl went missing from the village 'bout the same time as our Tansy. It coincided with poor ol' Lord Oak passin' away. Died of marsh fever 'e did – and 'is daughter too. She were a pretty little thing. Bein' a woodland sprite, she used to roam the woods all day playin' 'er music and dancin' about... Well, anyway Tansy used to meet 'er in the forest when she went wood collectin'. She brought 'er 'ome 'ere sometimes... Next thing we knew, they were both took sick and Oak's brother come to tend 'em - but they didn't make it – both of 'em died. The brother 'as took over as Lord and it's all changed. Tithes 'ave been increased to an unbearable level. Those 'oo can't pay get evicted. 'E sends 'is Woad Warriors to bully anyone 'oo stands up to 'im. Some of us 'ave thought about goin' to the King, but no one's brave enough. 'E finds out and we'll all be evicted – or worse.'

Their story resonated with Mel. There were too many coincidences and timidly she asked,

'This Lord Oak who died – you say he has a brother? Is he called Flint?'

Barleycorn rounded on Mel then.

'You know 'im? You ain't workin' for 'im are you? Don' tell us you works for 'im...'

Mel, shocked at the accusation answered angrily.

'NO!' she shouted back, 'I certainly do not work for him. Flint has taken our friend Willow. I suspect from what you have said that she is Oak's daughter? Well I'm telling you she's alive. I need to help her. That's why I'm here.'

Barleycorn, looking shocked flopped back down onto the log bench.

'Alive? Willow is alive? She can't be... She died with 'er father...'

Mel nodded triumphantly.

'She isn't dead,' she repeated. 'At least – not yet

anyway. But I believe that Flint will harm her if he doesn't get what he wants.'

Barleycorn and Hazel both became deflated. Mel, seeing their distress filled their cups with mead as a way to pacify them. Eventually Barleycorn spoke up – more meekly this time.

'Is she really alive lass – you ain't jestin' with us?'

Mel shook her head.

'No I'm not,' she replied gently. 'My friends found Willow hiding in their log store. She told us her father died of marsh fever and Flint stole his lands. He needed Willow out of the way to prevent her making a counter claim. Apparently she took something that Flint needs to secure his plans. I don't really know what it is, or where she may have hidden it – all I do know is that Willow's been abducted and is in danger. I really need to find her. Do you know anything at all that may help me locate her?'

Mel chose to lie about not knowing of the ring, for she still didn't really know whether to trust these people. Barleycorn glanced at Hazel and said,

'What you thinkin' woman?'

'Same as you I suspec'. We just needs to take a chance an' trust 'er…'

Mel could only sit back and watch as the pair whispered together, then something occurred to her. Pulling out Willow's amulet she showed it to Barleycorn.

'Willow dropped this when they took her,' she said. 'I think she dropped it on purpose as she'd only just shown my friend how it could be used to find her. Could we use it?'

Hazel drew in her breath and Barleycorn held out a shaking hand. Taking the amulet from Mel he held it reverently for a few moments before saying,

'It's 'ers alright! I can feel 'er. She's sick and very frightened somewhere, but the girl speaks the truth – Willow lives!' The amulet appeared a little yellow around the edges and Barleycorn pointed to it. 'Those leaves show she's sickenin' for somethin'. If the amulet ain't returned to' er soon, she'll die. The more the leaves go yellow - she'll worsen. If they start to crumble she'll die. She needs it back – and quickly.' Turning to Hazel, Barleycorn said, 'Go summon 'im Missus. Summon 'im now cos there ain't much time!'

Hazel stood up and walked outside leaving Mel sitting with Barleycorn. She felt frightened now and timidly she asked,

'What did you mean about summoning someone?'

'She's gone to fetch Cinder, 'e's the local Cunnin' Man from the village. If anyone knows what to do it'll be Cinder.'

Mel screwed up her face.

'Cunning Man?' she exclaimed. 'What does that mean?'

Barleycorns voice took on a mysterious air and dropped to a whisper.

'Cunnin' Folk are special folk. They 'eal the sick, they can bewitch or cast counter spells, they can scry the future and they can find lost or 'idden things. Cinder'll know 'ow to find Willow.' Something occurred to Mel then.

'If that's true,' she enquired, 'could he not have found Tansy when she went missing?' Barleycorn shrugged.

'We thought that too,' he said. 'But Cinder were a'travellin' round when Tansy got lost and by the time 'e came back the trail 'ad gone cold. Might 'elp find that little woodland sprite o' yours though.'

They sat talking a little longer and then Hazel walked in looking pleased with herself.

'It's done,' she said. ''e's on 'is way and so is Vetch. They'll be 'ere at first light'

Barleycorn nodded.

'Yes, Vetch should be 'ere too,' he agreed. 'In the meantime girl,' he said to Mel, 'it's gettin' late and bein' farmin' folk we goes to bed early an' we rises early.' Indicating the bed belonging to the missing Tansy he said, 'I think she'd be 'appy for you to use it. Get your 'ead down lass. It'll be a long day tomorra and I suspec' sleep ain't somethin' you're goin' to be seein' for a bit.'

Mel asked one last question.

'Who's Vetch?' she asked timidly. 'That's a weird name.'

Hazel answered with a smile on her face.

'Vetch is the Mayor from the local village of Flax In The Marsh,' she said softly. ''It's only right 'e should know what's 'appenin' 'ere. 'E might be able to offer some advice too. Now do as Barleycorn says an' get your 'ead down.'

Mel convinced herself that she would not sleep, but amazingly after lying down with Copper beside her she quickly fell into an exhausted slumber. Despite her busy mind and the bed being too short she slept soundly.

*

When Hazel roused her the following morning rush lamps lit the interior of the house. Hazel beckoned to her to follow and went outside where stars – far more that Mel could normally see - were studded all over the dark sky. Away to the east a smudge of light showed above the tree line and Mel realised that dawn approached. She followed Hazel around the back of the roundhouse and through a gap in the trees. The sound of running water suddenly came to her and Hazel led her down to the edge of a small, but fast flowing river. She indicated the water with a flourish saying,

'You can wash in there. Barleycorn and I 'ave already been in. Get yourself rinsed off and when you come back breakfast'll be waitin'.'

She handed Mel a handful of dried roots and indicated a hollowed out rock by the water's edge.

'Take this,' she said. 'It's soapwort. Pound it in that 'ollow with an 'efty stone and the sap will give you a lovely lather. It'll work wonders in your 'air.'

Without waiting for a reply Hazel turned around and walked off leaving Mel alone. Confused, she remembered Willow's terror at running water and wondered how her new friends were able to enter the river. She filed the thought away, deciding to ask about it another time. Kneeling down beside the flow she splashed cold water on her face. Suddenly Mel felt really dirty. She had walked miles the previous day in the full sun and sweated profusely. Ensuring no one lurked nearby she made a decision. In just a few moments she stripped off all her clothes and plunged into the water. She gasped at the stinging drop in temperature, but after a minute or so of splashing around, she quickly became accustomed to the cold. Reaching over for the roots she did as Hazel instructed her and in just a short time made a wonderful, soapy foam which she rubbed over her body and into her hair. It felt marvellous and Mel didn't want to come out. That done she grabbed her underwear and washed that too, then still dripping wet, she dressed. Running her fingers through her hair as she walked, Mel made her way back to the roundhouse admiring the glow of light now permeating the trees as the sun slid above the horizon. It promised to be another hot day.

Walking in through the door she immediately noticed two extra people sitting on the logs by the hearth. One reminded her of Barleycorn. Like him, this fellow sported a bald head and beard, but his attire spoke of a higher status. He wore a long frock coat, breeches and knee high leather boots. A green felt hat lay on the log beside him with two huge cock-pheasant tail feathers adorning it. She wanted to laugh for he reminded her of a pantomime character. On the old fellows lap sat a dish of porridge which he busily spooned into his mouth. The second visitor however proved far more striking. He sat wearing something that Mel could only think of as a pale grey monk's habit. With the hood pulled up over his head he leaned forward over another bowl of porridge. A leather belt adorned with various pouches and bags lay at his feet which were clad in soft looking leather boots. A whispered conversation between the elderly fellow whom Mel guessed would be Vetch and Barleycorn ceased when she walked in. The figure in the hood ignored her and continued eating.

Smiling, Hazel offered Mel a bowl of barley porridge sweetened with a generous helping of honey and indicated for her to sit. Next to the hearth Copper feasted on some of the left over stew from the previous evening. Mel sat as Barleycorn introduced her to his visitors.

'Miss Mel,' he said grandly, 'let me introduce you to Vetch our Mayor. Vetch, meet young Mel, a very sweet 'ooman indeed – nothin' like the stories we 'ears.'

Mel stood up and offered her hand to Vetch who took it and pumped it up and down vigorously. When he released her and sat back down he continued to stare at her in wonderment. Barleycorn continued.

'May I also introduce Cinder, our local Cunnin' Man 'oo is 'ere at your service.'

Mel again extended her hand in greeting, but Cinder didn't take it. He didn't even acknowledge her, but continued spooning porridge into his mouth. She said nothing and sat back down. Polite conversation seemed to go back and forth between Barleycorn, Vetch and Hazel. Every now and then one of them would briefly address Mel, but she still felt like an outsider. Cinder said nothing, just carrying on eating, and Mel thought him rude. So far no one thought to mention Willow, her predicament or any solution as to how they might be able to help her. With the porridge finished Mel expected the conversation to become more constructive, but instead Hazel brought out bread coated in a creamy looking cheese. Vetch and Barleycorn both tucked in heartily. Cinder quietly took a couple of pieces and silently ate them. Mel seethed inside and standing up she spoke her mind.

'Don't get me wrong,' she said, 'but Willow is

somewhere out there in trouble. Maybe I'm mistaken, but I thought we were supposed to be discussing looking for her. There seems to be a lot of talking going on here, but not much action regarding Willow. Barleycorn – you and Hazel have been wonderful since I came here yesterday and I'm very grateful, but last night when I showed you Willow's amulet you said she didn't have much time and could die! We're all sitting here eating and chatting! You said...'

Mel's voice trailed off as she realised everyone sat gaping at her. Barleycorn, Hazel and Vetch all looked rather sheepish. Cinder however reacted a differently. As words continued to spew from Mel's mouth Cinder slowly put down his bowl, stood up and advanced on her. With a flourish he raised both hands and flicked the cowl of his robes back. His appearance took her completely by surprise. Mel expected Cinder to be some wizened old man with white hair like some classic wizard. Instead he looked to be just a few years older than herself, with shoulder length dark, wavy hair and a chin covered in spiky stubble. The chin possessed a cleft and his eyes were as blue and piercing as Willow's. As her words faded away Cinder held out an open upturned hand and said,

'Where is it?'

She guessed at once what he wanted. Thrusting her hand down her top she pulled out the fading amulet. The edges were more yellow than the night before. She unclipped it and dropped it into Cinder's open palm. His blue eyes bored into Mel's as his fingers wrapped around the precious willow leaves. Then they closed and Cinder took a sharp intake of breath which he seemed to hold for an unfeasibly long time. Everyone fell silent and stared at Cinder, holding their own breath in expectation. Eventually Cinder's eyes flicked open and he exhaled loudly. Handing the amulet back to Mel he said,

'You should keep this. She meant for you or one of your friends to pick it up. Keep it safe.' Then he turned to the others and spoke authoritively.

'She's correct. We sit here dallying and one of ours is out there dying. Her amulet is fading. There's still time, but it's limited. We need to move quickly. The human girl will come with me. If we can snatch Willow back we shall. After that anything we can do to bring down that imposter Flint – well, we'll do that too.' Turning to Mel he addressed her directly. 'We travel light. Water, food and little else. Just the two of us. We go south – that's what the amulet is telling me. She's not far away either, so I'm guessing that she's being held at Lord Oak's old home – which is now Flint's stronghold. The hard part will be getting inside, but once in I shall find her and die trying to get her out if I have to. Flint needs to be stopped. The power he wields around here has become a strangle hold. Are you with me girl?'

Mel nodded for Cinders words greatly inspired her.

'I'll come, but only if Copper comes with us. She could be useful.'

Cinder shrugged and snorted rudely.

'If we have an infestation of mice. If that's your only condition – granted, but if she causes any problems we'll have to leave her behind.'

Mel nodded in agreement although she would never leave Copper anywhere. She turned to Barleycorn and Hazel.

'You two have been kind to me. Thank you so much, I'm really grateful. If there's any way I can repay you, then say so. Without you both I wouldn't even have any chance at all of finding Willow. Thank you and bless you both.'

She stepped forward and embracing Hazel kissed her on the cheek. When she did the same to Barleycorn his face went crimson with embarrassment and Hazel laughed aloud.

Vetch stepped up then. Having spoken little, he shook her hand again and said,

'You are the first human I've ever met. Thank you for

helping us and good luck to you both.' Mel's outburst seemed to have inspired everyone into a flurry of activity.

Hazel began packing food into a bag. Barleycorn, Vetch and Cinder discussed how they might gain access to Flint's stronghold and for the first time they actually included Mel. For the most part she just listened. Vetch didn't contribute much at all, but more than once he continued to thank Mel for trying to assist in finding Willow.

The final outcome of the discussion remained unresolved. The only real option would be for Mel and Cinder to make their way to the Lord's hall and try to find a way to gain entry. Mel felt dubious, for this sounded somewhat half-hearted to her and highly unorganised, but Cinder remained positive.

'We'll find a way in,' he said mysteriously.

Finally, after what seemed an age they were ready to move out. So much of the morning seemed wasted on trivial chatter, yet here they were saying their goodbyes and preparing to leave. Mel couldn't help feeling tearful. The last few hours she felt cosseted and thoroughly spoilt by Hazel and Barleycorn and now, only a day later they urged her to leave their protection with someone she didn't entirely trust or particularly like. However, it couldn't be put off any longer and before she knew it they were heading down the path to a frightening and unknown future...

\*\*\*

# 8

# JOURNEY THROUGH THE FOREST

Mel wanted nothing more than to stay within the safety of the roundhouse with Hazel and Barleycorn, but she knew such a scenario to be impossible. Willow still desperately needed help, and Mel had promised Rory that she'd do everything she could to assist her. To stay would have betrayed Rory's trust further.

Cinder noticed her sorrow, but offered no comfort. Instead he set a gruelling pace right from the start, trudging through the forest at a speed that Mel found astonishing. Copper scampered alongside, enjoying the open countryside. Cinder rarely spoke, but when he did, he either chastised her for falling behind, or asked for Willow's amulet that he might check his navigation. The march proved to be hard going. Once or twice the path they followed petered out and on more than one occasion they'd retraced their steps to find an alternative route. However, every time they encountered an obstacle Mel refused to complain. At first only sheer stubbornness prevented her from giving Cinder the satisfaction of calling her weak. However, as time went on she also realised that as much as she despised Cinder and his arrogant manner at the beginning, he did seem extremely focussed and determined to complete their task. That impressed her greatly, and her trust in him grew by the hour.

The greater part of the journey passed through dense woodland, but occasionally they cut across a meadow or around a field of crops. Mostly, these were of wheat, but sometimes they would encounter a field of leaf beet or cabbages and on one occasion rows and rows of beans.

Amongst all this arable activity the one missing element was people. Mel mentioned this to Cinder, but he merely dismissed her question with irritation.

The day turned out to be hot again and when Cinder finally suggested they stop for a drink Mel couldn't have been more relieved. He offered her a bag made from some unknown animal skin. It smelt suspiciously of goat and the water it contained tasted warm as blood, but Mel felt grateful none the less. She swallowed noisily, glad at the chance to stop and rest. Cinder carried a small dish in his bag, and setting it on the ground he filled it with water for Copper. Cinder drank more sedately than Mel, sipping rather than gulping down the welcome liquid. When they were done he held out his hand. Mel passed over Willow's amulet for the umpteenth time, bored now by Cinder's closed eyes and dreamy expression. After a few moments he came to life again, handed the amulet back to Mel and continued along the path. Becoming irritated by the silence between them Mel resolved to get some answers from the strange little man.

'So why are you doing this?' she asked.

'It pays well.'

Not satisfied with his reply Mel probed further.

'You must have more incentive than money. Didn't you say this morning that you would give your life for Willow?'

'I did.'

'So why? Why would you say that? How do know her.'

'Know her? I've met with her once or twice in the distant past, but I cannot claim to really know her.'

Mel found this statement contradictory and said so. Cinder remained tight lipped and fell silent again. After a bit she brought the subject up again, but however she dressed up the questions Cinder always avoided giving her any meaningful answers. By the time midday arrived Mel felt extremely frustrated. Despite her continuous probing she knew nothing at all. When Cinder finally suggested they sit and eat she couldn't have cared less. Huffily she sat down at the edge of the clearing and waited to be fed as her stomach rumbled loudly.

Cinder offered her a small piece of goat's cheese and a hunk of bread and she wolfed them down. An apple and a plum followed and they quenched their thirst on a bottle of Barleycorn's mead.

'Tell me about your world,' Cinder said.

Despite her earlier frustration with him, Mel found herself talking readily.

'It's similar to yours, but different,' she said. 'We have so many more houses, roads – and people... We still have trees and plants as you do too, but we rely on machines to do things for us, our food comes packaged and ready to eat... we...'

'I've heard much of your world, but never been there. Are the people kindly or are they spiteful and arrogant as our histories tell us?'

'Many are spiteful and arrogant, yes. But some are decent. I suspect you have both kinds here too... Hazel and Barleycorn – they took me in... I miss them already...'

For the first time Cinder smiled at her. She saw kindness in his eyes and felt a little safer in his presence. She opened up some more, telling him of her friends and her home life. When she spoke of Rory she became a little tearful and when he reached out and squeezed her hand it felt as though electricity passed through her fingers. She glanced up to find Cinders eyes upon her. For a moment she could see Willow in the sky blue stare of those eyes. At times his likeness to Willow was uncanny, but when she mentioned it, Cinder merely laughed and dismissed her suggestion.

Then, as they sat talking a curious thing happened. Cinder fell silent and Mel realised that he watched something behind her. Turning her head she saw nothing of significance. Cinder made a small gesture saying,

'There - just above and behind you.'

This time she saw what caught Cinder's attention. Perched just above her head and looking directly at her sat a robin. He remained on his perch for a few moments longer and then took flight, disappearing amongst the trees. Turning back to Cinder, Mel smiled.

'How come he is so tame?' she asked, wonder on her face.

'Robins hold a special significance for me, although I have never understood their meaning. In times of danger or if my spirits are low one always appears to me. I take him as an omen – we should be on our guard.'

'Against what?'

'I know not.'

'But…'

'Just remain alert young Mel, just remain alert…'

Falling silent once more they continued with their meal, Mel wondering what this talk of robins and omens could mean. Eventually she found her tongue again.

'Will we reach Oak Hall today?' she asked.

'We should be there before nightfall.'

'So have you formed a plan yet as to how we can get inside?'

'We? I'll be going inside. You and the cat will wait outside. You said Flint has spoken with you. That makes you a liability.'

'That's nice - thanks!'

Mel fumed. Being called a liability felt far from flattering and not for the first time she wondered why Cinder even wanted her there. She began to complain.

'Why exactly am I here? She demanded. 'You've dragged me along, hardly spoken to me, and now I'm a bloody liability! You've got some cheek! I've a good mind to…'

Cinder stopped her mid-sentence. Not with his own outburst, but by raising the palm of his left hand and placing the fore finger of his right to his lips. His expression caught her attention. His eyes, although looking at her, were unfocussed, and alarm registered across his rugged features. Sensing danger Mel fell silent.

'Woad Warriors!' he whispered. 'Four of them, coming our way. YOU! Into the trees – NOW!'

Mel needed no further prompting. Like a startled hare she bounded across the clearing and into the undergrowth. Cinder held some branches back while she squeezed into a small gap and he made her lie down. Swiftly he bundled leaves and twigs over her and whispered instructions.

'See? The robin didn't lie. I'll fetch you when it's safe to come out. Do you understand?'

'Yes, but where will you be?'

'In the clearing waiting for them. If they kill me or take me away, wait until they're gone and go back to Barleycorn and Hazel. They'll get you home. Swear on it.'

'Okay, okay, I swear – what about Copper?'

'Leave her with me.'

'But...'

'Stay down – they're coming.'

Then a most curious thing happened. Before Mel could respond Cinder spoke a few words in an unknown language and passed his hand over her head. As he bounded away and resumed his seat on one of the logs Mel made to rise, but found herself completely paralysed. No matter how much she attempted to move she could not. She could only lay there, frozen to the spot and watch the drama unfold before her.

Four Woad Warriors trooped into the clearing. Cinder, sitting now, ignored them and chewed lazily on a piece of bread. All four Warriors were stripped to the waist and extremely muscular. On their lower bodies they sported brightly coloured, chequered breeches. Each wore his own obligatory birth amulet around his neck, but the one who clearly stood out as their commander also wore a large elaborate neck torc of twisted golden wires. A bright green cloak hung down his back, adding to his status. Each warrior boasted blue woad tattoos, but the leader again stood out with twisting blue serpents inked into his wrists and forearms. All were armed with a bronze sword and a shield and the three subordinates also carried bronze tipped spears. The leader addressed Cinder.

'So what have we here? Speak up peasant while you still have a tongue!'

'Just an honest man on the road. Who are you?'

'ME?' boomed the leader. 'Hear that lads? Who am I? Let's show 'im boys!'

The nearest of the warrior's stepped forward, picked up cinders bag and rummaged through it. Finding only food he slung the bag over his own shoulder and stated,

'Ours.'

Smiling broadly Cinder addressed the scowling commander who now stood sharpening his sword on a stone.

'Looking for anything in particular?' Cinder asked.

Glaring back the commander replied evilly,

'We'll know when we find it peasant. Your manner offends me and I'm just looking for an excuse to slit your throat or open your belly!'

As the conversation developed Mel could only look on and listen in abject horror. Part of her wanted desperately to leap up and confront the arrogant group of bullying warriors, but she could not move. Her arms and legs remained locked and she could only lie quivering, watching the drama unfold before her. As she continued looking on, one of the warriors let out a startled yelp.

'What in the Green Man's name is that?'

He pointed at Copper, who, having wandered off in search of mice had now returned. Amazingly all four Woad Warriors were somewhat perturbed by the sight of the cat. Seeing their fear, Cinder used it to his advantage by picking Copper up and stroking her. 'She's a cat,' he replied. 'I bought her off of a passing trader a couple of moons ago. A raiding party took her from the human world. Cost me a small fortune.'

'It's rather cute ain't it?' a weasley faced Warrior cooed.

'Shut up you imbecile.' barked the leader. 'I still haven't decided what to do with him yet. Any suggestions?'

Weasel face, anxious to redeem his image piped up instantly.

'Why don't we do to him what we did to that girl from the village – you remember the one?'

'How could we forget?'

'What did you do to the village girl?' Cinder asked.

A grin crossed the leaders face and coming up close to Cinder he whispered menacingly,

'We sent her into the woods and after half a day we hunted her.'

Weasel face, savouring the memory joined in.

'She didn't get far. When we caught her she provided a lot of entertainment.'

'Did you kill her?' Cinder enquired.

'Eventually,' whispered the leader. 'When we'd finished with her Spark there slit her throat.'

Weasel Face giggled hysterically.

'That I did. She bled like a stuck pig!'

The leader returned his attention to Cinder.

'If we choose to hunt you, you should feel privileged that we'll just kill you. What do you say boys?'

The other three gave their approval enthusiastically and in a moment the leader grabbed Cinder by the collar of his robe and pulled him to his feet.

Still unable to move a single muscle Mel, lying in the undergrowth yelped in fear, but fortunately in the general hubbub of things her cry became lost. But as she looked on, the situation changed.

The leader, one moment all curses and arrogance became servile and apologetic. The other three warriors fell into an uneasy silence.

'Hold on boys,' muttered their Captain, 'I think we may have been a bit hasty with this one.' So saying he released Cinder, brushed the creases from his garment and addressed the little man respectfully.

'Apologies. I'd no idea of your station. You should have said something.'

The leader addressed his men.

'He wears the symbol of the dried toad. Don't know about you three, but I'm not crossing a medicine man.' Turning back to Cinder he continued his apology. 'No offence meant. We have to be careful around here. His Lordship has charged us with scouring these woods for troublemakers. There's talk of an uprising in the village and it's our job to keep the peasants in their place.'

Cinder replied calmly.

'My bag of provisions? One of you men seems to have claimed it.'

Spark or 'Weasel Face' as Mel now thought of him handed back the bag without a word. Cinder addressed the leader again.

'What's your name?'

'Me? Cobalt. At your service. Like I said, we'd no idea you were a medicine man, no offence meant'

'None taken, we all have to earn a living. Did you really kill the village girl?'

'Can't lie and say we didn't. She caused a lot of trouble though. His Lordship needed some extra servants so we were sent out to find some. Got the girl along with a boy. Also picked up some farm wench too. She just does as she's told, but the other one kept trying to escape. We were told to make a proper example of her. Since then we've not heard so much as a peep out of any of the others.'

Cinder nodded.

'Well it's none of my business. Any work here for someone with my talents?'

'Not really. His Lordship, Master Flint, he's pretty skilled in your craft himself. Doubt he'd need you. Do you just generalise or do you specialise in anything?'

Cinder answered readily.

'I cover all the usual stuff – laying or lifting of curses, herbal healing, blighting of crops, scrying and suchlike, but I do pride myself on my skills at locating lost or stolen items. I've never failed at that yet and even if I say so myself, I've never met anyone who's as good at it as I am. If you need anything or anyone found – I'm your man.'
Cobalt, rubbing his chin replied,

'Hold on a moment.' He went into a huddle with his fellow Warriors and the four stood whispering together. Cobalt came back.

'It's like this. There may be some work after all. Someone stole something from his Lordship and he urgently needs it back. Yesterday he caught up with the culprit and brought her back here. So far she won't talk. Keeps saying she knows nothing about it. I reckon if you could make her speak he'd pay pretty well. Interested?'

'Might be. You said he possessed skill though. It can't be that hard making some girl talk? Tell her about the village girl. That should loosen her tongue!'
Cobalt took on a conspiratorial look.

'Well,' he said, lowering his voice. 'His Lordship rode out this morning on a bit of business and is due back tomorrow or the day after. Me and the boys here were thinking of visiting her in her cell tonight, just to give her a bit of company – you know what I mean? She's a right looker too. Threaten her with the same ending as the village girl and she's bound to open up. If I could tell his Lordship she's given up what he wants there could be a promotion in it for me. What do you reckon?'
Cinder shook his head.

'I really wouldn't advise that. It would be far better leaving it to me. On no account touch the girl. If you're serious about me finding whatever it is she's stolen then leave her be. What you do to her afterwards is up to you – I care not. But if you harm or distress her in any way now it sets up negative energy around her and it can make my job ten times more difficult – sometimes even impossible.

Let me sort it out – you can claim responsibility for hiring me if you like – Lord Flint should be happy enough with that.'

Cobalt looked crestfallen.

'We were looking forward to tonight. Maybe if you come back with us now and work your magic we could still have some fun with her later?'

Cinder shook his head.

'No. I have important business elsewhere that can't wait. I can make my way to the Lord's hall after dark. Where is it exactly?'

Cobalt pointed down the road in the direction that he and his men were travelling when they first came upon Cinder.

'About a mile that way you come to a fork in the path. Go left and it takes you to the village of Nettlebed – right will take you to Flint's hall. When can we expect you?'

'Like I said, not until after dark. Make sure you inform the guards.'

'We are the guards. Alright then – I agree, no one touches the girl – for now anyway, and when you've found the lost item you'll get paid. When you come later we'll parley and agree on the amount of coin.'

Cinder nodded.

'Shake on it?'

He spat on his hand and offered it to Cobalt. The big warrior accepted without hesitation, striking the bargain. Cinder took control.

'I have a few herbs and things to look for. I can't stand here talking with you all afternoon. Go back to the hall and I'll meet up with you after sunset – and remember what I said – it's vital that you don't touch the girl. I can work on her so much better if she feels less threatened or upset. If I get there and find she's been harmed in any way, then the deal is off. Clear?'

Cobalt nodded.

'You hear that boys? You might have to wait until tomorrow for your sport. Still, you'll have a keener appetite by then. Any of you scum touch her tonight and I'll personally nail your entrails to the nearest oak!'

The three warriors all nodded in acquiescence to Cobalt and after a few more conversational exchanges the group left the clearing and continued on their way. Cinder, looked directly at the spot where Mel still lay hidden, placed a finger to his lips and accompanied by Copper stealthily followed the warriors down the woodland track.

Mel, still hugging the ground just didn't know what to do. Even now her limbs remained firmly locked and she could only await Cinder coming back for her. However, she still couldn't decide whether to fully trust him or not. The conversation she'd overheard not only terrified her, but made her realise the differences between her own world and the one she now found herself in. Cinder appeared to be up to some double plot by agreeing to help Flint's men find the ring and the casual way he chatted about the murdered village girl appalled her. Her own safety seeming very fragile, Mel began to weep. She still sobbed into the leaves as strong arms took hold of her, pulled her to her feet and gently brushed the leaves and dirt from her hair and face. Miraculously, movement had returned to her muscles.

'What happened?' she blurted out. 'I couldn't move! What did you do to me back there…?'

'I put a charm on you to keep you from coming out of your hiding place. They would have killed you…'

'How dare you!'

'It kept you safe.'

Cinder's blue eyes bored into hers and Mel could immediately feel his genuine concern. She towered over him, but Cinder still pulled her close, stroked her hair and whispered soothing words. As her anger subsided he took her hand and led her back to the clearing and sat her on the log. Taking a little bottle from inside his robe he offered it to her. Sniffing it suspiciously she took a swig. Mel had never tasted brandy before and the burning liquid made her cough. However, as the warm glow spread down her chest and into her belly it instantly picked her up. Grimacing, she handed the bottle back to Cinder.

'Better?' he enquired in a caring tone.

'A little, yes.'

'You did well today. You didn't complain about the pace I set, and to stay silent like that with those four around took courage. Well done.'

'Thank you.'

Cinder knelt beside her and spoke gently.

'Look at me.'

Reluctantly Mel glanced upwards. Those blue eyes were really caring now and seeing his soulful gaze made her want to cry again.

'How much of that confrontation did you hear?'

'Everything.'

'Listen to me. Those warriors are lethal. At the slightest excuse they'd have killed me if they thought it worth their while. They only fear me because of my trade. To them, I have the ears of The Gods; I can perform magic and lay curses. Their kind are highly superstitious and for them to harm me would be extremely unlucky. That is why their attitude changed.'

'What did he mean about a toad?'

Cinder smiled and little lines appeared at the corner of his eyes. He squeezed her hand and then releasing it delved down the neck of his robe. Withdrawing it he brought out a leather thong adorned with the mummified body of a small toad.

'When Cobalt grabbed me he saw this. It's not my birthing amulet, but an emblem. All Cunning Folk wear one of these. It shows people we're tutored in the old ways and it's respected by all – even Woad Warriors.'

Mel screwed up her face.

'It's horrible,' she whispered.

'It saved my skin – and yours too.'

'Do you think they were serious about that girl?'

'Very serious.'

'The farm girl they spoke of – I think that's Barleycorn and Hazel's daughter Tansy.'

'I agree with you there.'

'We have to get her out too.'

'Mayhap. But not at the expense of Willow. Willow is of immense importance. We'll do what we can for the farm girl should we find her, but mark this – if helping her compromises saving Willow then we leave her behind. Understand?'

'But why, what makes Willow more important than another?'

'Mel, listen to me. Flint has taken over this whole area. He's causing havoc for the community around here with his inflated taxes and allowing his warriors to do as they please. We have to get Willow out and get her before the King. If we can do that we have a good chance of ousting Flint for good. Since her father passed into the Summer Land Willow is now the rightful heiress to Lord Oak's lands and tenants. She'd be a fair and beneficial Lady for the community she would serve. They'd welcome her and love her. Flint is evil and has spread a dark atmosphere around this countryside. This morning you asked me why there were no people around. They only go outside when they have to. To go outside is to be at the mercy of the likes of Cobalt and his thugs. Willow must come first. If we can save Tansy or anyone else then we shall. If need be we can always come back for them after Flint has been forced out. We can't allow him to stay here. It's not just Willow suffering here, it's everyone. Now do you understand?'

Mel nodded.

'It just seems so unfair,' she said. 'Hazel and Barleycorn were so good to me – how could I possibly turn my back on their daughter if I found her?'

Cinder could see this discussion going on for a long time so he ended it saying,

'Leave it for now. See what happens. We may not even find Tansy. If we locate her we'll make a decision then.'

Mel nodded again. However, inside she knew she would never leave Tansy behind should they be lucky enough to find her. Sensing victory Cinder stood up and stretched. With it now mid-afternoon he felt that they should be on their way. Gathering up the last of their possessions the two travellers and the cat continued along the forest path.

The trees were mostly oaks now and their large branches and leafy canopies towered over them. The familiar odour of damp earth and moss hung everywhere. Somehow it smelt comforting to Mel and she now understood Willow's fixation with the forest realm. Mel estimated they had walked for about twenty minutes when rounding a bend the path split into two separate tracks. Cinder cautiously took the right hand one, signalling to Mel to tread carefully and remain silent. They hadn't travelled far down this new track when Cinder came to an abrupt halt, at the edge of another clearing. On the far side lay the Lord's hall. It reminded Mel of depictions she'd seen in history books of Saxon great halls. Oblong in shape, it was timber framed with wattle and daub walls and crowned off with a pitched roof of thatch. Smaller buildings, some round, some oblong were scattered around it. A wooden palisade fence cordoned off the whole area. The hall stood on a high earthen mound within the compound and could be seen over the fence quite easily. Outside the palisade a deep ditch encircled the entire site. A wooden bridge gave access at the front whilst a watchtower overlooked the entrance. Two sentries manned the tower. Turning to Mel, Cinder whispered to her to go back into the woods. Once satisfied they could not be seen, Cinder ushered Mel off the path in amongst the trees and outlined his plan.

'I'm off to the village to buy a bottle of mead. I want you to stay here. It's nothing personal, but a human sighted this close to Flint's home may well alert him to our purpose.'

Mel frowned.

'Why do you want mead?' she asked.

'Because I want to get the guards drunk. More to the point I have a little something hidden about me that when added to the mead will make them sleep for days. If I can do that, then we have a good chance of getting Willow out.'

'What about Tansy?'

'Mel, we discussed this earlier. We don't know where she is. In the meantime I suggest you rest here for a bit. I could be a while in the village seeing what I can find out about Flint's set up. Knowing your enemy is half the battle. I'll come back and find you as soon as I've disabled the guards.'

Mel agreed to Cinder's suggestion. She felt put out at being left behind yet again, but the hint of being included in entering the fortress at all sounded highly attractive to her. She nodded enthusiastically. Cinder took her hand and once again took on his caring tone. It surprised Mel, for at the start of their journey that morning he had been cold and indifferent to her. Now coming to know him better, her trust grew and at his touch she felt that electric like shock for a second time.

'Take advantage of being on your own for a bit. Catch up on some sleep. There'll be precious little of that once we set Willow free. Oh, one last thing...'

Cinder held out his hand and Mel rummaged down her top once more for Willows amulet. Handing it over, she noticed the look of concern on Cinders face.

'She sickens further. See how the leaves are curling and turning yellow? If they begin to crumble it may well be too late.'

Cinder took his water skin and poured some over the dying amulet. It didn't appear to make any difference, but Mel supposed that the water may rehydrate the leaves a little and help to prolong Willows life too.

'Is it that serious?' she enquired.

Tight lipped Cinder nodded.

'If we don't get to her tonight she'll most likely die by sundown tomorrow. Those leaves are on the point of disintegrating. If I can reach her tonight and put this back around her neck she may still have a chance – but it must be done tonight.'

When Willow first bewitched Rory with her beauty Mel had been furious and felt nothing but contempt for the little Faerie woman. Now, having come so far to help her – all be it at the outset purely to impress Rory, she found herself so focussed on the task that the thought of Willow coming to any harm now mortified her. She voiced her thoughts to Cinder.

'Please don't let her die. I'll do anything it takes to help, just tell me what to do.'

'Thank you. Right now, sleep. I promise I'll come and get you when I can. Something tells me that you're going to be a great asset later on.'

Mel smiled although she didn't feel much like it. She found her hand reaching out and stroking Cinders cheek.

'Take care,' she whispered. 'Please come back.' Stooping, she kissed Cinders face. He nodded, squeezed her hand and walked away.

*

It took Cinder around twenty minutes or so to walk to the village. Not that he counted time in minutes or hours for that is the human way. To the Faerie folk of Eyedore time could only be measured by natural means – such as a heartbeat or the rising and setting of the sun or how long it might take for a man to drink a mug of mead.

When he walked down the main street, few people were about. A couple of small children were chasing each other around and outside a roundhouse a woman sat smoking a clay pipe and shelling peas. They stared at Cinder for he was known here...

Coming to an inn, he ignored two old men sitting outside playing a game similar to draughts. Its ancient timbers having distorted over the years gave the place a twisted, misshapen appearance. Strangely, the architecture of Eyedore was highly eclectic. Many of the rural folk such as Hazel and Barleycorn lived in roundhouses, which to the human eye were of iron or bronze-age origins. The inn would clearly have been quite at home in Tudor England, whilst the Lord's Hall had its roots firmly in the Saxon era. Cinder approached the building, and pushing open the door he went inside. There were only a few customers – an elderly couple sitting at a table sharing a large pie and three men drinking ale. In a corner a young man sat perched on a chair playing a stringed instrument not unlike a lute. He accompanied his tune with a strong voice and sang a farming song about the sowing of crops and the fertility of the fields. Everyone, including the musician fell silent and watched as Cinder advanced towards the bar, the last few notes of the song fading away. No one spoke. Cinder broke the silence and addressed the inn keeper.

'Mead.'

A bottle appeared in the inn keeper's hand. Trembling, he poured a mug of the golden liquid, the bottle clattering on the rim of the mug as his hand shook. Cinder ignored him, picked it up and downed the contents.

'Another.'

The inn keeper poured a second, which went the same way as the first. When done Cinder set down the mug.

'I want a bottle – a new bottle.'

The inn keeper obliged by producing a second bottle from under the counter in a flash. Cinder spoke again.

'You brew this here?'

'Aye.'

Taking the bottle in his hand Cinder broke the wax seal,

removed the cork and poured himself half a mug before setting down the bottle. Taking a small purple glass vessel from his pocket he opened it and poured half of the contents into the mead bottle. Replacing the cork he pushed the bottle back across the bar to the inn keeper.

'Reseal it.'

The inn keeper scurried away with the bottle and returned in a short time, a fresh wax seal enveloping the cork. The bottle disappeared into Cinders bag. Cinder turned around and addressed the customers.

'Some of you here may know me. Does anyone have need of my services today?'
Silence.

'You? Do you need a curse lifted or a lost item found?' This, to an old fellow sitting at the far end of the bar. He shook his head hurriedly. Another voice piped up.

'There's only one curse round 'ere that needs liftin'.'
Cinder turned and faced a small fat fellow dressed as a gentleman farmer and smiled.

'What curse would that be?'
The farmer hesitated. Cinder coaxed him to speak.

'If you don't tell me I can't help. I'm at your service and my rates are always reasonable.'
The farmer replied.

'We 'ave a new Lord. Old one and 'is daughter died of marsh fever a few moons back. The new one cripples us with taxes, takes our crops and 'is militia roam the countryside causing chaos wherever they go. Can you fix that?'

'Mayhap. Anyone else got problems with the new Lord?'

The farmer blanched, not knowing who Cinder worked for, regretting his openness. A couple of other customers were about to speak, but held back. Seeing their fear and hesitation and recognising it, Cinder decided that honesty would be the best approach.

'I'll tell you why I'm here then. I've never met your old

Lord, but I do know that his daughter Willow didn't die. She's alive and under Flint's watchful eye. Has anyone here been inside Flint's stronghold? I could do with some help here.'

A buzz of muted conversation ran around the bar. One old woman came forward.

'Begging your pardon sir, but I worked there under Lord Oak. I still have a key to a postern gate around the back of the compound.'

Cinder nodded gratefully.

'Now we're getting somewhere. You have this key with you?'

The woman hesitated and then delved into her pockets. She drew out a small bronze key which she handed to Cinder.

'The gate is about halfway along the rear wall below the palisade. A clump of hawthorn trees obscure it from the eye. You can open it with that from inside or out. Although the ditch runs all the way around, in the north eastern corner there's a set of steps cut into the bank either side, allowing a single person to cross. Gets wet in winter, but it's fine now.'

Thanking her Cinder pocketed the key.

'Anyone else offer me any advice?'

'Don't go in there,' someone called out from the back.

Cinder grinned. He felt sure that they exaggerated their fear, but none the less, he would observe caution in his task. His business at the inn concluded he pulled out a small draw string bag and addressed the inn keeper again.

'How much coin do I owe you?'

'There is no charge for you Sir.'

Cinder nodded his appreciation.

'Gratitude my friend. That is very generous of you, but we all need to earn a living.'

Pulling out a handful of coins he placed them on the bar.

'I also require a few provisions. Bread, cheese and fruit

would be good – enough for two. What do you have?'

Mumbling something under his breath the inn keeper disappeared out the back of the bar. Cinder just stood waiting whilst the customers continued to stare. He cared not. Their fear at his trade could always be used to his advantage. However, at other times showing compassion or decency could also work wonders as demonstrated here. Walking over to the woman who had given him the key he handed her a silver coin. Muttering her thanks she pocketed it in a moment as the inn keeper returned with some food supplies. His bag restocked with edibles he thanked them all graciously, pulled up his hood and headed back out into the gathering darkness and towards Oak Hall.

***

# 9

# INTO THE UNKNOWN

Walking back to the Lord's hall Cinder decided to leave Mel hidden in the woodland. He did not make the decision lightly for already, her tenacity and attitude impressed him greatly, and he wished to take her with him. However, the conversation at the inn reminded him of just how dangerous Flint and his men were. Cinder held no desire to involve Mel in anything that may put her at real risk, and so he chose to leave her behind.

Darkness preceded Cinder's arrival at Oak Hall and when he arrived at the entrance he banged loudly on the gate. A small opening slid aside and a hairy face peered out.

'What do you want peasant?'

Cinder answered with equal rudeness.

'Open the gate dog, before I put an infestation upon you. Go and tell Captain Cobalt that his Cunning Man is here. You delay me any further and you can answer to him.'

The voice replied with a little more courtesy.

'Why didn't you say? 'E told me to expect you. 'Old on a moment...'

A clatter announced the opening of the gate and the man beckoned Cinder inside. Cutting across the compound they came to a small square building. The hairy one knocked on the door which Weasel Face opened.

'What do you want scum?' the Warrior demanded.

'Tell your Captain his visitor has arrived.'

Cinder stepped out of the shadows. With the door held back he stepped across the threshold and into the guard house.

In the centre of the tiny room, Cobalt's men sat around a wooden table, playing cards. Bottles were scattered on the floor and Cinder sensed that they were already drunk. Cobalt, swaying on his feet stood up to greet him.

'You made it then. Concluded your other business?'

'Yes, but that is none of yours. Still want me to deal with this girl?'

Cobalt grinned and breathed alcohol fumes into Cinder's face.

'Will it take long? We're still anxious to have some fun with her.'

'It will take as long as it takes. Where is she?'

'Locked up at present. She's in one of the old wine cellars. You want her up here where we can watch, or in her cell?'

'In her cell. And I work alone. I don't need interruptions or anyone breathing down my neck and neither does she. I told you earlier, if I frighten her she'll be much harder to read'

Cobalt rubbed his chin.

'That could be a problem. If we left you alone with her we wouldn't be doing our job would we? Anyways, we want to watch. See how you get the information out of her. That's the deal.'

Cinder walked over to the table and sat down. A half full tankard of ale stood there and picking it up, he downed it. One of the Warriors complained.

'That's my ale! No one touches my ale! Pay up dog or...'

'Shut it Badger! Show the man some respect!'

'But you said...'

Cobalt struck Badger across the face.

'I said shut it! There's plenty more ale if you want it. That kitchen wench should bring us another jug soon!'

Turning back to Cinder Cobalt smiled ingratiatingly, saying,

'Sorry about this dogs manners. Let's discuss terms.'

'We've already settled terms. If you think you can change the contract just like that – think again. I'll come back when Lord Flint's in residence. We can see what he thinks.'

Cobalt placed a hand onto Cinders shoulder as he made to rise pressing him back into his seat.

'Don't be too hasty. Besides, I think Lord Flint should discuss terms with you. Take him down boys!'

In a moment all four Warriors fell upon Cinder and pulled him to his feet, the fear and respect they'd shown in the forest gone. Cinder found himself overpowered and dragged across the room to where a series of metal rings were attached to the wall. It took only seconds for the Warriors to hold and bind Cinder to the wall with a length of rope that lay ready. Something had gone very wrong. Cinder wondered if he should have been less open at the inn, but he dismissed the thought and awaited an explanation. Cobalt sat directly in front of the little Cunning Man and spoke.

'I knew something didn't add up when we spoke earlier.' He pointed at one of his men. 'Badger there took part in the raiding party that entered the human world to find the girl. Something troubled him about your story. After we left you he remembered it. Your cat? He recalled seeing it in the other world with the humans – which suggests that some of them have entered Eyedore – bringing that cat with them. Am I right?'

Cinder remained calm. Cobalt could prove nothing and he gambled upon that.

'I told you, I bought my cat from a passing trader. Cats are common in the human world. So Badger saw one similar to mine. It means nothing. When's Lord Flint coming back? You can rest assured that when I tell him about you he'll not be best pleased. As for myself, until he gets here I have plenty of time to decide which curse or bodily infestation to bring upon you – all of you!'

Cobalt felt confused. Part of him still worried that Cinder spoke the truth and the repercussions of his hasty actions would be severe, both from Cinder and his master. However, making the wrong decision now and allowing the girl to escape would be far more devastating. He chose the lesser of the two evils.

'All right. Let's say you speak the truth. If you are proven right, I will personally skin Badger alive and cast out what's left of him into the forest as prey to the wildlife. How does that sound? Fair?'

Badger, unnerved by this piped up.

'What? Listen, I might have been wrong, but....'

'Shut it!' Then back to Cinder, 'We'll honour your request not to touch the girl – for tonight anyway. You won't be harmed, just restrained until His Lordship returns tomorrow. In the meantime – Spark! See what might be in his bag.'

Spark, needing no further bidding to get up to mischief delved into Cinders bag. Grinning broadly he withdrew an unopened bottle of mead, the wax seal still fresh.

'Look at this Boss! That kitchen bitch hasn't brought our ale yet. This should keep us going.'

Cobalt nodded and addressed Cinder.

'I would ask you to join us in a toast, but I understand if you decline, your hands being tied as they are. Spark! Recharge the tankards. My mouth is as dry as a piece of salted meat!'

In a moment the contents of the bottle were shared out four ways. Cinder, despite being restrained couldn't believe his luck. It couldn't have worked better if he'd planned it this way. His heart in his mouth, he quietly watched as the mead disappeared down the four throats at record speed. Cobalt belched and resumed his seat.

'Well little man, anything else in that bag to keep us sweet?'

Cinder grinned.

'I think that mead will keep you all sweet enough.' He replied. 'Interesting little vintage that one.'

'Yes, but I prefer ale. Mead is for young girls. I'm surprised at you Cunning Man – I would have marked you down as an ale drinker any day.'

'I never turn down ale. But how about a well matured elderberry wine? On a winter's night that's a real gem. Warms the throat all the way down to your feet.'

The conversation went on like this for some time with Cinder and Cobalt comparing various beverages and their individual merits. After a bit Cinder noticed the conversation slowing down and Cobalt's speech beginning to slur until eventually, he could barely talk. Cobalt was a big and healthy warrior. However, the herbal extract that Cinder had added to the mead totally disregarded the fact. In less than ten human minutes the big man started snoring like a baby. The other three, all struggling to keep awake also succumbed. Cinder, tied to the wall just sat there and laughed aloud. There would be no waking up these four for some considerable time. However, despite this, Cinder remained completely incapacitated with his arms bound to the metal ring above his head. No matter how much he twisted his wrists or pulled on the bindings he could not work the rope loose. If he couldn't free himself soon and go and look for Willow things could still take a considerable turn for the worse. Having been so buoyed up at the incapacitation of Cobalt and his men Cinder's morale now plummeted. With no way of freeing himself he could only hope that somehow a solution would present itself.

\*

When Cinder left Mel in the forest she suffered mixed emotions. A part of her felt let down and excluded yet again, and strangely, another part, relieved. From amongst

the undergrowth she and Copper watched Cinder walk
down the path towards the village. With him gone Mel
sighed and sat wondering what she should do to pass the
time. It didn't take long and she realised just how tired she
actually felt. Cinder's suggestion that she should lie down
and sleep seemed very attractive and together, she and
Copper drifted into a contented and peaceful slumber.

Exactly how long she slept Mel did not know, but
something awoke her. She lay there for a few moments,
perfectly still, taking in the sounds and smells around her.
Then she heard it. Cautiously Mel sat up. The
undergrowth around her rustled a little, and the soft
sounds paused at her movement. After a moment or two
the sound resumed. Bolder now, Mel parted the branches
of the bushes and peered through them into a clearing.
Sitting on a fallen tree trunk in the diminishing light she
spied her quarry. A young Fae woman in peasant attire,
her face in her hands, wept. Mel thought her of a similar
age to Willow. Silently the human girl crept forward.
Mindful of her great height compared to that of the Faerie
folk Mel remained in a crouching position so as not to
cause any more alarm than she must. She spoke softly.

'Can I help you?'

The young woman sat up with a start. Seeing Mel so
close she made to rise and back away, but Mel placed a
reassuring hand on her arm.

'It's alright,' she whispered. 'I shan't hurt you – please,
sit and talk to me.'

As the woman tried to stand Mel noticed something
rather disturbing. A pair of bronze shackles with a small
length of chain connecting them adorned her ankles. The
woman could walk, but, if she tried to run it would be
impossible. Mel, concern etched on her face spoke again.

'Why do you cry? Can I help you?'

The woman's voice possessed a country lilt.

'Oo are you? Don't know about you 'elpin' me – don't
think anyone can do that.'

'Why are you chained up? Who did that to you?'

Wiping the tears from her face, the woman studied Mel.

'You ain't from round 'ere are you? Where you from? You look kind o' *long*...'

Grinning, Mel stood up. The woman looked staggered at her great height and shrank away in fear. Mel giggled at the expression on her face.

'You're right – I'm not from round here. I'm human. I found my way into your world yesterday. I'm helping someone with something... It's complicated really...' Mel sat back down and continued. 'So why are you crying?'

The woman's face took on a sombre look again as she replied.

'I'm missin' my 'ome and family. I was snatched and brought 'ere to work. Forced me they did... I wants to see my Ma and Pa...'

Feeling her distress Mel embraced her, offering comfort within her arms and speaking gently.

'Can't you just leave and go home? How can anyone force you to stay? And who put these chains on you?'

'If I try an' escape they'll 'unt me like they did to Amber. After she tried to escape they put these chains on me an' on a couple o' the other new servants. They 'unted 'er in the woods and... and…'

Mel stopped her there.

'Shhhh! Don't think about it. What's your name?'

'Tansy. What are you called?'

'Oh Tansy! I so wanted to find you...'

Now Mel wept. The relief at finding the missing farm girl hit her hard. Sobbing violently she clung to the little Faerie and let all her pent up emotions of the last few days come flooding out. Tansy, distracted from her own situation by Mel's grief asked her own questions.

'Why are you so sad? What did you mean by sayin' you wanted to find me? 'Oo are you? 'Ow do you know me?'

Pulling herself together, Mel related her story to Tansy. She kept it brief, omitting large chunks of detail, but when she came to the part of how she found herself in the world of Eyedore, and of how Barleycorn and Hazel protected and fed her, Tansy squealed.

'They's my folks! I was taken from 'em and brought 'ere. They must be so worried about me. I miss 'em so much...'

Mel interrupted her and continued her story. Having omitted the identity of the Faerie that she, Rory and Alice were helping, she filled in the gaps.

'The girl we were helping – I think you might know her?'

"Oo is she? Tell me what you know!'

'She's the daughter of Lord Oak. She...'

'Willow? But everyone 'round 'ere 'eard she died along with 'er Pa. You mean she still lives?'

'She does, but she's very sick. I'm with someone called Cinder and he's going to try to get her out tonight. He made me wait here as Flint's men may recognise me from my own world. He spoke sense, but I hated watching him walk away alone. Can you get me inside the hall? If I can get inside I may be of some use to him – and Copper too.'

Tansy looked startled. With her attention drawn to the big cat, she found herself fascinated.

'What *is* that?' she exclaimed in wonder.

Smiling now, Mel tried to explain.

'Copper is a cat,' she said breezily. 'Lots of people own them in my world as pets.'

'Pets? What are pets?'

'Don't worry. I'll explain it another day. There's not much time right now. We need to do something useful to help Cinder and Willow.'

Tansy nodded.

'I know Cinder. Everyone's a bit scared of 'im, but 'e's alright. If I get you inside, what then? I'm willin' to 'elp, but if we get caught we could both be in 'uge trouble. I'm pretty sure I can get you in though. There's a sentry on the gate this time o' day called Clay – 'e quite likes me. 'E keeps makin' eyes at me every time I go in or out and 'e tries sweet talkin' me at every opportunity. Let me do the talkin'. In fact – don't you talk at all. I'll tell 'im you can't speak or somethin'.

Mel agreed instantly. Fear crept up on her now, but she also felt excitement and relief at the chance to actually do something rather than just sit in the shadows. She knew that Cinder would be angry for disobeying his instructions to remain outside. However, a nagging feeling also told her that making some decisions of her own would be the right course of action. Cinder had been gone a long time and night time now surrounded her. Bats were flittering around, hunting moths and once or twice Mel heard unusual noises from deep within the forest. The thought of being inside the compound, although fraught with its own dangers somehow made her feel safer. Their minds made up, the two girls cautiously crept out from within the trees and back to the path. Tansy reiterated her instructions for Mel to remain silent. They walked the short distance to the gate, seeing little point in trying to be stealthy or quiet. For one thing, the chains around Tansy's ankles rattled at every step. Also, creeping about would look suspicious. A bold approach would appear far more natural. Outwardly confidant, the pair, one short, the other incongruously tall approached the gate.

Mel's heart pounded in her chest as Tansy rapped on the wood. A little door slid open and a pair of eyes peered out. After a moment it closed, the gate creaked open and a small guard stood observing them. Tansy spoke up.

'Thank you Clay. We've been out lookin' for 'erbs for the kitchen. No luck tonight though. 'Ow are you anyways?'

Clay, staring in disbelief at Mel, answered.

'All the better for seeing your pretty face. Who's this? Not seen you before darling. Bit long aren't you?'

Mel, remembering her instructions from Tansy stared blankly back at the sentry. Getting into the role she let her mouth hang open and took on a gormless air. Tansy responded.

'She's a mute. She's so tall 'cos she's an 'ooman. 'Is Lordship bought 'er recently. Apparently she's been in Eyedore for years – taken by a raiding party as a baby. She's a bit simple an' I'm in charge of 'er. Bit slow to learn, but we're gettin' there.'

Clay nodded and tickled Mel under the chin.

'Don't worry darling,' he cooed. 'Tansy here is a gooden. She'll look after you. Do as she says and you'll be alright.' To Tansy he said, 'Might be simple, but she's good looking. Nice shape too.'

He slapped Mel playfully across the backside. Mel just grinned and fluttered her eyelashes. Tansy scolded him.

'I thought you only 'ad eyes for me Clay. Bit much sweet talkin' another girl in front o' me – I might go off you!'

Clay, seizing on the thought that Tansy might actually be interested in him at all responded exactly how she wanted.

'No offence Miss Tansy. You know you're my favourite. I'd do anything for you – you know that...'

''Ow about getting these shackles off my ankles then? I ain't plannin' goin' nowhere. Do that for me an' I'd be so grateful...very grateful indeed...'

Clay, suddenly hopeful licked his lips.

'You know I'd do that if I could. Ol' Cobalt has the keys. Keeps them on his belt. Leave it with me and I'll speak with him...vouch for you like. What would I get in return?'

Flirting outrageously Tansy rolled her eyes and answered provocatively.

'Wait an' see, but I guarantee I'll make it worth your while...'

So saying, she leaned forward and kissed Clay on his cheek. Clay couldn't believe his luck.

Waving the two girls through the gate he winked at Tansy.

'I'll sort the chains – and by the way – she's not that pretty!'

Tansy blew Clay a kiss as they passed through the gate and walked into the compound. Mel seethed inside. For one thing, having her backside slapped certainly displeased her. Then, to hear Clay say she wasn't pretty felt like rubbing salt into an open wound. However, she kept her cool and remained silent until they were well away from the gate.

'Well how about that,' she said. 'Bloody cheek! One minute he slaps my butt and the next he's slagging me off!' Tansy gave Mel a curious look.

'Just ignore 'im, 'e's an idiot. Now listen. I'm goin' to go in the kitchen and get a jug of ale for the guard 'ouse. I'm already late. You wait 'ere in the shadows 'til I come back.'

Mel nodded. A small log shed stood nearby and she slid inside to wait for Tansy to return. She smiled to herself at the irony of hiding in there and thought of Willow. A lump formed in her throat at the memory of the dark haired little Fae woman and feeling a little disturbed, Mel sat down to wait for her new friend to return.

*

Tansy, having gone back to the kitchen filled a jug with ale from a cask and walked out into the compound. Her head reeled, and on her way to the guard house she reassessed her decision to help Mel. If caught assisting the human girl Tansy could expect no mercy. She knew she would probably be killed by Cobalt and his men, but at the same time, inside she felt hope. She decided to press on. With the guard house door before her, Tansy took a deep breath and pushed it open.

She gaped at the scene inside. Cobalt lay asleep on a chair snoring like a baby. Two of his men were curled up on the floor, also asleep with the third slumped across the table. On the far wall a figure sat with his arms raised, tied firmly to one of the bronze rings embedded there. Cinder broke the spell by speaking to her.

'Don't just stand there Tansy – do something useful and come over here and untie me. Look sharp girl!'

Tansy came to life. Glancing nervously at the sleeping Warriors she crossed the room and fumbled with the knots imprisoning Cinder.

'Cinder! We 'ave to be quick – what if they wakes up?' she whispered.

Cinder laughed loudly and Tansy squirmed at the sudden outburst, terrified that the violent little men would wake. As his arms were released Cinder stood up and strode over to Cobalt. In a moment he'd swung back his leg and kicked Cobalt as hard as he could in the shin. The Warrior neither moved nor cried out. Cinder laughed again and said to Tansy, 'These rogues won't wake up for at least another day. Not after what I've given them. Is that ale?'

Tansy nodded and watched, astonished as after taking a hefty swig Cinder upended the jug and poured the remaining contents over Cobalt and around his feet. He smashed the jug on the floor and scattered the pieces.

'Why did you do that?' Tansy asked.
Cinder grinned back at her.

'Might as well make it look like they're just drunk,' he said. 'If someone comes in here I don't want any suspicions aroused. Now listen to me – I don't have much time. I'm here to help someone – someone very important. They brought a girl in here recently. I need to find her – NOW! It's vital I get to her or she may be dead by morning. Do you know where she's being held?'

Tansy nodded her reply. Cinders sense of urgency and the mention that Willow may die completely unnerved her.

'Do you speak of Willow? Mel 'as already told me, she said...'

'Mel? You've seen Mel? Where is she now?'

''idin' out be'ind the kitchen block, she...'

'You mean she's inside the compound?'

'Yes.'

'Take me to her! Then we need to find Willow. Has anyone else seen Mel?

Tansy nodded looking sheepish.

'Yes,' she responded, 'one o' the sentries on the gate, but 'e shouldn't cause no trouble – 'e ain't very bright...'

'When does Flint return – do you know?'

'Tomorrow I think, why?'

'Because when he finds Willow gone, he'll be out looking for us. The sooner we get her out the better, now take me to Mel and then let's find Willow.'

'Wait!' she exclaimed.

In a moment she knelt at Cobalt's side and rummaged at his belt. With a look of triumph she pulled a set of keys free and began trying them in her leg shackles. The fourth key fitted. There were a couple of soft clicks and the chains fell away. Smiling, she stood up, free at last. Cinder nodded his approval.

'Give me those keys,' he instructed. 'They could prove useful in freeing Willow.'

Tansy handed them over and then threw her arms about Cinders neck.

'Can you get me out too?' she begged. 'Please? I just want to go 'ome.'

Cinder ruffled her hair.

'I think you've earned that,' he said. 'Come on, we'll go and find Mel.'

*

When Tansy left Mel hiding in the woodshed the young girl once again felt abandoned. Discontented at being left behind yet again, she decided to explore. Creeping out into the darkness she quickly searched the other small outbuildings. Most were empty or just contained old barrels, farming tools or pieces of broken furniture. Then she found herself at the door leading into the great hall. Cautiously she slipped inside. A couple of tallow candles burned dimly on wall mounted sconces. In the centre lay a fire pit, empty and cold. Benches ran around the edges, but in the corner another door beckoned. Fearlessly now Mel crept across and pushed it open. Weak candles lit this smaller room too, but provided enough light for Mel to take in the details. A table stood in the centre with a crystal ball on top. Charts of the night sky showing movements of the moon and stars hung on the walls, and a chest of drawers stood in the corner. In seconds Mel crossed the room and rifled through them, although for what, she knew not. Then she found a bag. A small, heavy bag made of leather with a draw string. Expecting to find gold she opened it with a shaking hand and tipped out the contents. A heavy object made a dull thud as it landed on top of the cabinet. Mel picked it up disappointed, and then smiled, grateful at her unexpected discovery. The 'object' turned out to be several items stuck together. Pulling one off Mel studied it close up. On letting it go it jumped back with a sharp click to its former position. Satisfied, Mel stuffed the clump of lodestones back into the bag and put it in her pocket, for something told her that these would be useful. A rapid search revealed nothing else of particular interest. There were a few large books, but they were all written in the same strange script used on the note attached to the arrow.

Finding nothing more, Mel thought it prudent to return to the wood shed and wait for Tansy. Creeping back to the door she pulled it ajar and peered through the crack. Annoyingly a servant stood raking out the central hearth. Cursing under her breath, Mel pushed the door shut. She'd given no thought to being trapped inside the building and with no other exit she could only hope that no one would enter Flint's study. Time passed as the fat serving woman took for ever to clear the spent ashes and prepare the hearth for the next fire. Eventually however, wiping her hands on her apron she stood up and waddled off into a corner where she began sorting through a small pile of logs. Taking a chance Mel pulled the door open, passed through and crept quickly across the hall. Unfortunately the door creaked and having only walked a few steps, she heard the woman call out.

'OI! Who are yous? Whats yous been doings in there?'

Running would only cause alarm so Mel adopted her role of a mute. Lolling her tongue out she rolled her eyes and grinned stupidly at the woman. Suspiciously the servant approached. She prodded Mel in the ribs with a fat finger and questioned her again.

'I asked yous who yous are! Outs with it!'

Mel dribbled and laughed foolishly. She pondered whether or not to bring out the lodestones to see what effect they might have on the woman when Clay walked in.

'Clay!' exclaimed the servant. 'I founds this...this... In 'is Lordship's study. Who the hecks is she?'
Clay grinned.

'It's alright Poppy, she's a new girl from the kitchen block. Tansy is supposed to be looking after her. She's a bit simple and can't talk – from the human world apparently, which is why she's so long. I'll take her back.'

Clay caught hold of Mel and pulled her towards the door and she breathed out in relief. She just needed to ditch Clay and she would be fine, but Clay had other ideas. Pulling Mel away from the main hall he steered her in the direction of one of the little storage sheds, pushed her into the shadows and against the wall.

'How about a kiss?' he cooed.

Mel, revolted at the idea did not know what to do. Clay gripped both her wrists in his hands and puckered up. Mel struggled, but Clay persisted.

'Come on, just a kiss or two. I'll look after you around here if you're nice to me.'

Mel wanted to cry out, but hesitated. For one thing she didn't want to give herself away and for another if she attracted attention she might have more of these creeps pulling her about. To her immense relief a soft voice spoke out from the darkness.

'There you are. What 'ave I told you about wanderin' off? Come back to the kitchen at once! Clay, thank you for finding 'er. I would be in big trouble if she escaped. Come on you!'

Tansy strode forward and grabbing Mel pulled her free. Before Clay could say anything Tansy marched off towards the kitchens dragging Mel behind her. Rounding a corner she placed a finger to her lips to keep Mel quiet and guided her back to the wood shed. Inside Cinder and Copper sat waiting. He scolded her immediately.

'I thought I asked you to wait outside?'

'You did, but I got fed up of being told what to do. Anyway, this is Tansy. I found her,' she said excitedly. 'Do you know where Willow is being held yet?'

'Possibly. And I already know who this is. Tansy? Can you get us to Willow?'

Tansy nodded.

'Under the great 'all is a series of cellars. There's a door roun' the back. I've been takin' food an' ale down to the sentry.'

'Sentry? How many are down there?'

'Just one as far as I knows.'

Cinder smiled.

'Go and get me a jug of ale,' he instructed.

'Do we seriously have time for drinking?' Mel demanded.

'It's not for me Mel – Tansy, do it. We need to get down there quickly.'

Tansy scuttled off leaving Mel and Cinder together. Cinder spoke gruffly.

'Don't disobey me again Mel. You don't know how dangerous it is here for you. If you're found by Flint's men they'll think nothing of killing you. I certainly don't want to see that happen.'

Confused, Mel didn't know how to respond. Touched by Cinders concern for her welfare, she still felt offended by the way he ordered her around. For the moment she bit her lip. Bending down, she played with Copper until Tansy returned with a mug of ale. Cinder took it from her, took a hefty swig and placed the mug down. Once again he took the little purple bottle from his belt and poured some of the contents into the ale. He handed the mug back to Tansy and said,

'Take this down and give it to the sentry. It's vital he drinks it – all of it.'

Tansy took the mug and headed for the door.

'I'll see 'e drinks it.'

'Good girl. We'll wait here.'

Tansy marched quickly around the rear of the great hall. She knew the way with her eyes shut and it only took a few moments to open the door and head down the steps into the corridor below. Moisture trickled down the walls and the air smelt of mould, rotting wood and decay. The usual tallow candles gave a soft glow to illuminate the way and Tansy found the sentry in no time. Bored, the Warrior by the heavy door smiled at the sight of Tansy and her ale mug. Smiling broadly she offered up the ale and looked on in gleeful satisfaction as the frothing liquid vanished down his throat. The sentry handed her back the mug and Tansy asked cheekily,

'Want another?'

'That would be good. Good brew you make here.'

Tansy nodded her agreement.

'It is. So 'oo's in there then?' she asked indicating the locked door.

The sentry grinned.

'Some woodland sprite that's upset His Lordship. No concern of yours though. Besides, she won't be here much longer.'

'No?'

'No.' Cupping his hand around his mouth the sentry bent forward and whispered in Tansy's ear.

'Word is his Lordship has stepped out to fetch a necromancer. The girl won't talk. A necromancer will find the truth don't you think?'

Tansy gasped. The talk of a necromancer disgusted her beyond belief. It couldn't have been any worse. Taking the ale mug she backed away, and with the sentry chuckling behind her she raced back to the wood shed. Breathless, Tansy burst into the building startling Cinder and Mel. Gasping with fear and struggling to get her words out she stood gaping like a stranded fish. Alarmed, Cinder asked,

'What's happened?'

Blinking back tears she took a deep breath and blurted out the dreadful news.

'I know where Flint 'as gone. 'E's gone to fetch a necromancer...'

Cinder visibly paled. He sat down and placed his face in his hands. Then looking up he spoke out boldly.

'We need to move all the more swiftly. Did the sentry drink the ale?'

'Aye. All of it.'

Cinder nodded.

'I'd prefer to give it a little more time, but we need to move. Come on.'

Confused, Mel asked Cinder the obvious question.

'What's a necromancer?'

'A necromancer is as bad as it gets Mel. A necromancer communicates with the dead. He can control spirits. He can cause evil spirits to invade a living body and take it over. He can use the spirits to cause a living body to give up its secrets and when that's done...'

'Do you mean it would kill her?'

'Worse. Not only would she die, but her own soul would be tormented and abused for all eternity. It would be the worst fate possible.'

'Can we stop it happening? I mean, if we get her out...' Cinder smiled.

'Yes, we can get her out. But Flint won't give up. They'll hunt us. If they catch us Willow won't be allowed to survive. Willow is the key to all of Flint's scheming. If she doesn't give up what he wants he will kill her. If she does give him what he wants – he'll kill her and take everything. I shan't let him do that easily. We need to move – now!'

With Tansy leading the way they made a trouble free run to the door leading below the great hall. Striding down the musty corridor Tansy felt relief when she saw the sentry stretched out upon the floor. They stopped by the solid looking door. It measured almost as tall as Mel herself with large, metal rivets studding its front. An ornamental bronze keyhole stared at them, almost defying them to enter. Swiftly kicking the sentry in the ribs satisfied Cinder he would not wake. He addressed Tansy.

'You're sure this is it?'

'Yes, certain. I've been bringin' food down for the prisoner. I 'ad no idea it were Willow though.'

Taking out Cobalt's keys Cinder selected one. It didn't fit the lock. He tried the other which also failed. Frowning, he addressed the two expectant girls.

'There are only two keys on this ring that are big enough for that lock. Neither of them work. Do you know where the key might be Tansy?'

She shook her head and then Mel made a suggestion.

'Search the guard,' she said. He's the one outside the door and has been opening it to feed her I presume?'

In a moment Cinder rifled through the sleeping sentry's pockets and came up with four large keys on a ring. He grinned at Mel and handed them to her.

'You open it,' he said. 'You thought of where to find them. Quick now!'

Mel needed no further bidding. Her hand shaking, she inserted the first key in the lock. They heard a loud 'clunk' as it turned, and pushing against the wood Mel felt elation as the door creaked inwards.

Cinder retrieved one of the candles from a nearby wall sconce and holding it aloft he followed Mel inside to reveal the old wine store. Tansy remained outside, keeping watch.

The weak candle provided just enough light to reveal the contents of the room. In a corner sat a wooden bucket and the stench emanating from it told of its purpose. An empty wine rack covered one wall and a couple of broken bottles lay on the floor.

Wrinkling her nose at the stink Mel advanced and stepped around a bundle of old rags. Confused now, she made to speak to Cinder, when out of the corner of her eye she saw the heap of rags move. In the blink of an eye Mel fell to her knees and pulled at the old rancid cloths. A tiny hand, pale in the candle light tried to pull the cover back and then slid from view. Mel, reaching out searched for the edge to the covering. As her fingers closed around the frayed hem she gently prised it back to reveal a tiny huddled figure beneath. Mel gasped. The face that greeted her beneath the old blanket shocked her. Gone was the glossy spiked and plaited hair, replaced by a matted and greasy tangle. Willow's normally flawless skin had suffered an outbreak of terrible acne, her lips were dried and cracked and her complexion, quite sallow. Most noticeable were her eyes. Always sparkling and full of life they were now dim and lack lustre, the vivid blue appearing grey and lifeless. Worse still, one of her eyes showed heavy bruising, blackened from being struck in the face with a fist whilst a thick scab protruded from her lower lip. Mel, deeply shocked put her hand over her mouth and backed away.

'Her amulet,' she hissed. 'Quickly, you must help her.'

In a moment Cinder knelt beside the dying Faerie woman, searching through his pockets for the precious amulet. He withdrew it carefully. The leaves were now yellowed and a couple were cracked, but despite this he still felt it pull towards its owner as it sensed her nearby. Cinder gestured to Mel.

'Sit her up. Be gentle with her she's very weak.'

Mel did as he bid. She watched as Cinder took his water skin and doused the amulet yet again, then reaching out he clipped the leather thong around Willows neck. Mel did not know what to expect. She had imagined some magical blaze of light and Willow making a miraculous recovery, but the reality proved far less dramatic. A soft sigh escaped Willows lips and just for a fleeting moment the ghost of a smile flickered across her face. Her eyes remained closed and nothing else happened.

'What now?' Mel asked lamely.

Cinder stood up.

'We need to get her out of here. Her amulet will be a great boost to her, even in its present sorry state. But she also needs fresh air and the forest around her to bring her back properly – oh, and love...'

The last comment came almost as an afterthought, but in a moment Mel knew what to do.

'I can give her love,' she said as tears ran down her face. She turned to Willow and supporting her head, whispered in her ear.

'Willow, Sweetie, it's Mel. I'm sure you can hear me. The others didn't make it through the gateway, but I know Rory would have wanted me to give you this...'

Leaning forward and turning Willow towards her Mel kissed her softly on the mouth. She drew out the kiss for as long as she dared and when she withdrew, let out a sob as she saw again that wisp of a smile cross the little woman's features. Best of all, Willow spoke.

'Rory... Thank you...'

Then she settled back in Mel's arms and fell silent once more. Mel glanced up at Cinder and smiled through her tears.

'That should help her,' she whispered. 'She clearly can't walk. I'll carry her. I'm bigger than you and Tansy; it'll be easier for me.'

Cinder nodded gratefully. For Mel, he thought, the burden should not be too great. Reaching down he assisted Mel in getting Willow up from the floor. They kept the old blankets around her and stooping beneath the low ceiling Mel made her way back into the corridor. Relieved to see them Tansy called out.

'You got 'er? 'Ow is she?'

Cinder explained Willows poor condition to Tansy and then reminded both girls of their haste. As he made to walk back down the corridor Tansy called out.

'There's an ol' door a bit further on. I've explored a bit down 'ere. I think it leads outside as you can feel a draught around it. Maybe some o' these keys might fit?'

'If it saves us time it is worth a try – you lead.' Cinder said.

Tansy took the candle from Cinder and set off. There were a couple more turns in the corridor and then Tansy stopped abruptly before another door. Cinder handed her Cobalt's keys. The second key fitted the lock and like Willows cell, the door gave easily. Cool air blew into the tunnel and Mel shivered at its touch. Somehow it signified a bad omen and for the first time she feared what lay ahead of them. Caught up in the excitement of her situation, and with no thoughts of danger she had felt invincible. Now, with that gust of air came unease and regret. Bitterly she remembered Willow's words of a few days before, warning them of the dangers of entering her realm – of the mysterious way that time shifted and turned in on itself and how anyone crossing that threshold could expect to return home years or even generations later. What if...

'Mel! We have to move!'

Cinders voice brought Mel back to the present. The weight of Willow in her arms, the cool night air and her empty belly reminded the young girl of the enormous responsibilities she now carried. Pursing her lips in determination she stepped out of the tunnel and followed Cinder and Tansy into the night.

\*\*\*

# 10

## FLIGHT

The door brought them out of the mound beneath Flint's hall to the west of the compound as the harsh light from a hunter's moon made them all feel exposed. Small snippets of conversation floated on the air accompanied by occasional bouts of muted laughter from a pair of Flint's militia men who hung about nearby, talking.

Cinder, taking advantage of the men's conversation took a chance. Warning Mel to remain hidden, he grasped Tansy by the hand and walked casually across the compound. The two militia men barely glanced in their direction and continued their conversation. Cinder and Tansy disappeared from view and Mel stood watching the two men out of the corner of her eye, praying for some kind of sign as to what she should do next. Her prayers were quickly answered. She heard what sounded like a faint 'swish' and a moment later a loud crash came from the direction of the kitchen block. As the two men bolted in the direction of the noise, Mel, with Copper at her heels and bending under Willow's weight, scuttled after her friends. As she reached the shadows she literally ran into Cinder in the darkness and almost cried out. Calmly, he pulled her over to foot of the earthen rampart that bordered the compound. High above them the palisade stood out against the night sky, and looking up at it in awe Mel asked,

'How on earth will we get over that?'
Cinder chuckled and replied breezily.

'Not over, young Mel – under!'
'Under? What...

Cinder brought out a key. Beckoning to the two females he moved off and Mel and Tansy followed. In the rampart lay a large black recess. Mel watched expectantly, but the shadows hid what lay beyond. Disappearing into the gloom Cinder returned moments later to usher the girls forward. Within the recess lay an open gate. They emerged on the other side onto a narrow track that bordered the rampart. Cinder pushed the gate shut behind them and relocked it.

'How did you know about that gate? And where did you find the key?' Mel asked.

Grinning broadly in the moonlight Cinder whispered his reply.

'An old servant told me about it when I went into the village. She gave me a key - and so here we are.'

'What happened back there? Something flew over my head just before that loud bang...'

Cinder pulled an item from his bag and held it aloft.

'My sling,' he said proudly. 'I flung a stone over by the kitchens. Did the trick, did it not?' Smiling at Mel he put the archaic weapon away.

The path ran left to right and after looking at the sky and studying the stars Cinder moved off to the left. After just a few paces he found the steps that led them down into the ditch and back up on the far side. Once across, he set his usual crippling pace. Mel, hugging Willow as close to her body as comfort would allow did her best and followed. Roots and branches were everywhere and Mel continually found herself tripping over them. Besides these obstacles the stinking blanket wrapped around Willow kept coming loose and snagging around her feet. She fell behind and every now and then Cinder and Tansy would have to stop and wait for her to catch up. Mel struggled, but refused to complain. Seeing her unable to keep up Cinder begrudgingly slackened his pace. His priority lay in distancing themselves from Flint as much as possible before daybreak, but it could not be helped. Mel, grateful for the opportunity to slow down, fully understood their predicament. Guilt tormented her at being the cause of their delay, but Willow grew increasingly heavy with every step, and now her arms, back and neck burned with severe pain.

The path, by good fortune became even once they travelled a short distance away from the hall, but after covering a few miles Mel reached breaking point. Setting Willow down, she collapsed beside her. Cinder and Tansy were at her side in a moment, rubbing her sore arms and massaging her shoulders. Mel sat weeping with the pain for some minutes, but eventually her tears stopped. Cinder made a difficult decision.

'We need to stop. Mel, you have done tremendously well, but you should have told me that you were struggling so much; we could have stopped earlier or taken a turn with Willow.' To Tansy he said, 'Stay with them. I'll find a suitable spot to rest.' He disappeared into the undergrowth, but returned almost immediately. 'There's a clearing just through here. Help bring Mel through Tansy.'

Bending down, Cinder scooped up the still sleeping Willow. He pushed his way back through the bushes while Tansy guided Mel. Exhausted, Mel sank down and leaned against a tree. She also suffered a blinding headache to go with her throbbing arms and back. As if in a dream she watched Cinder organise a plan.

'We need to keep watch,' he said. 'I 'll take the first duty. Tansy, Mel needs to sleep so it'll be down to us I'm afraid. I'll wake you later and you can listen out for trouble while I rest. As for now – we should eat.'

Opening his bag Cinder withdrew the provisions supplied by the innkeeper. Pulling aside the paper wrapping he found a small loaf, a whole goat's cheese, several strips of a mysterious looking dried fungus and a couple of apples. He tore the bread into four pieces, divided the cheese likewise and cut the two apples in half.

Re-wrapping one portion of each he replaced it in his bag saying,

'For Willow.'

He handed Mel and Tansy their share and they set to their meal with gusto. Cinder decided to hold back the dried fungus for the morning. Mel did not realise the extent of her hunger, having eaten nothing since the lunch she shared with Cinder around midday. She tucked in, not noticing as Cinder withdrew and disappeared off to the far end of the clearing.

As she ate, her condition improved and she felt sleepy until a friendly nudge roused her, and looking up she saw Cinder offering her the water skin. The contents were still warm, but it lifted her spirits. Smiling now for the first time in hours she handed it back gratefully.

'Thank you,' she said, wiping her mouth on her hand. Cinder sat beside her.

'How do you feel,' he asked concernedly.

'Exhausted. I have a headache and my arms feel as though they've been torn off. But thank you for the food and water. They've helped and I'm beginning to feel a little better.'

Cinder nodded and reaching out stroked her hair.

'You've been very brave today and extremely helpful. I'm glad I brought you along. Now, shall we see how Willow is?'

Mel blushed at Cinder's touch and kind words. That morning her feelings towards him were hostile, but already she enjoyed his company. Each time he smiled at her or complimented her Mel experienced a fluttering in her belly. His eyes mesmerised her too, and she glanced away, embarrassed in case he could read her thoughts. Cinder however turned his attentions to the still sleeping bundle beside her. Peeling back the blanket he peered down at Willow's slumbering form. Getting close to her in the dim light, he withdrew her amulet, examined its condition and gently replaced it. Satisfied, he turned to Mel and the still eating Tansy.

'She appears a little better. Her breathing seems easier and the leaves of her amulet feel a little more supple. They were dangerously dry earlier, but I think her essence has revived them a little. It'll take time, but she should be fine.'

Tansy, sitting nearby put down her apple and voiced her thoughts aloud.

'I really thought she were done for. She were so ill when we found 'er. Willow is like a sister to me. I grew up meetin' 'er in the forest and watching 'er dance and play 'er music. Are you certain she'll recover Cinder?'

Both Cinder and Mel could detect the tremble in Tansy's voice as she fought back tears. Despite having been through a great deal herself Tansy seemed more concerned for Willow. That touched Mel, and ignoring her throbbing head and limbs she rose up and sat beside the little country woman. Slipping an arm around her shoulders she reassured Tansy as best as she could.

'Don't worry Tansy,' she said. 'We've come this far. We'll get you home tomorrow and then we'll have to decide how we can best help Willow to stay out of Flint's clutches.' Mel turned to Cinder.

'Where exactly are we heading? We can't hide her at Hazel and Barleycorn's home - it would endanger them. Do you have a plan or are we just running until they catch us?'

Cinder gave an ambiguous answer.

'We travel towards the east. If we keep going and remain ahead of them for another day we should be safe.'

The response to her question gave no real answer, but Tansy appeared happy with that and Mel, feeling so utterly tired could not be bothered to ask him to elaborate further. Cinder seemed to think that they stood a good chance and Mel now trusted him entirely. Yawning loudly she asked for permission to lie down and sleep. Cinder gave it gladly. Like Mel, he'd resented his travelling companion earlier in the day. His own experience of humans was not good and he assumed she would be more of a hindrance than of any real use. Mel's plucky attitude and bravery changed that view. He even enjoyed her company now and he surprised her with his response. Holding out his hand he helped her to her feet.

'Come with me,' he said secretively.

Shivering with pleasure at his touch, Mel allowed herself to be led to a corner of the clearing. Cinder indicated a dry spot beneath a large oak tree.

'See here?' he pointed out. 'While you were eating I gathered some bracken together. It makes a soft bed. There's enough there for you and Willow to sleep on together. Settle yourself down whilst I fetch her over.'

Touched by this kindness Mel lay onto the springy bracken fronds gratefully. As she made herself comfortable Cinder returned carrying Willow. Discarding the old blanket he reverently placed the sleeping Faerie beside Mel and then surprised her once more. Leaning forward Cinder gently kissed Mel on the forehead, ran his fingers gently down her face and bid her to sleep well. Watching his back as he walked away, Mel's heart raced, for Cinder now excited her. He appeared to really care, and touched by his kindness, and cuddled up to Willow, Mel finally drifted into a deep and almost trouble free sleep. During the night a curious disturbance woke Mel. Beside her, and deep in her own slumber Willow cried out and briefly woke the human girl.

'Mama! The robin flied away… Where is robin gone?'

Her voice sounded childlike and the mention of the robin reminded Mel of Cinder's mysterious affinity to the tiny red breasted birds. Still sleepy, Mel resolved to ask Willow the following day of the significance of the robin in her dream. Holding that thought, Mel resumed sleeping.

*

'Wake up, we 'ave to move on.'

Tansy's voice, and her shoulder being roughly shaken, dragged Mel from the depths of a deep sleep. She sat up rubbing her eyes. Her arms and back were still stiff and painful from her efforts of the night before, but her head no longer throbbed. Stretching, she stood up and then realised that Willow no longer lay beside her. Anxious to find her little bedfellow Mel stood and followed Tansy. Coming into the centre of the clearing Mel's heart lifted as she saw Willow, awake now sitting with her back against a tree. Cinder knelt beside her, breaking up small pieces food and patiently popping them into her mouth one at a time.

'Willow! It's so lovely to see you awake. How are you feeling?'

Willow turned her head to Mel and attempted to smile. She still appeared very weak and barely moved. Cinder glanced up and flashed a big grin at Mel.

'You look much better too,' he said. 'I came to check on you both earlier and found this one awake. I brought her over here so as not to disturb you. I wanted to get some food inside her. She's still very sick, but much better than when we found her.'

Mel stroked Willows hair and reaching inside her pocket she pulled out a comb. As Cinder fed the little Faerie, Mel gently ran the comb through the tangled mess. Tansy, hovering nearby put a flat piece of bark with food upon it beside Mel.

'Breakfast Mel,' she said before sitting down herself.

The meal consisted of a portion of the dried fungus, but Tansy, ever the country lass had already been busy foraging. Alongside the dark leathery strips sat a handful of blackberries, some shelled hazelnuts and a large chunk of something soft and creamy looking that she didn't recognise at all. Mel tucked into the food. Although a little chewy, the fungus tasted good. The creamy item turned out to be a piece of the same substance, but fresh rather than dried. Tansy pointed out a tree with a massive colony of the stuff growing on it. Mel's stomach turned when she saw it growing, but not wishing to offend Tansy she smiled. Holding her breath she tried a small bite, finding the flavour like a peppery cheese and not unpleasant at all. When they finished eating Cinder ensured they cleared everything away. For one thing he did not want to alert anyone following of their presence here. Secondly, as he pointed out, the lore of the forest demanded it. To leave any kind of detritus behind would be disrespectful to the forest and the Gods who looked over it. The bracken bedding he walked some distance with and hid it beneath some thick bushes. Satisfied that no obvious trace of their presence remained, he declared them ready to be on their way.

Cinder insisted on carrying Willow. Cradling her in his arms with her hands clasped behind his neck proved far easier than carrying her sleeping form as a dead weight. Mel wanted desperately to talk with Willow, but for now she would have to wait. Besides, Willow still looked drowsy and as Cinder carried her, she drifted off in his arms into a contented sleep. Her overall appearance showed a stark improvement from when they found her the night before. Now, her cheeks were flushed, the bruising around her eye diminished and the acne receding. Cinder examined her amulet further in the daylight and happily announced that the yellowed leaves were beginning to turn green once more and ceasing to crumble. Willow was on the mend.

With full bellies and hope in their hearts they set off. Mel still knew nothing of any plans or objectives. Used to his secretive ways now she obediently followed Cinder along the path as they continued to trudge eastward. If it hadn't been for their plight Mel would have enjoyed the walk. With the forest path easy to follow, every now and then the trees would part to reveal more arable land abundant with crops. It seemed to be a feature everywhere. She asked Tansy about the extent of the farmland and the young girl explained that for the most part, everyone here in Eyedore grew their own food. Any abundance could be taken to markets and bought by the wealthier classes. The lifestyle here seemed idyllic save for the threat of Flint and his men. Tansy explained that it wasn't only Flint either. Sometimes raiding parties would come into the countryside from other far off places and pillage their way around. It didn't happen often, Tansy seeing it only twice in her lifetime. It appeared that Eyedore existed as a single country or kingdom within a realm of many such places. The raiders, Tansy went on to explain were foreigners from these other kingdoms, the most fearsome being from a place called Dunregal. That would be, in Tansy's opinion where Flint had recruited his Woad Warriors from.

Willow stirred in Cinders arms and he decided to stop for a break. Mel laughed at seeing the little Faerie slip from Cinders grasp and take a few tottering steps towards her. More importantly, for a moment her dazzling smile returned as she laughed at her own clumsiness. Mel caught her as she stumbled forward, about to fall to the ground.

'Careful you,' she said. 'We're just getting you better. Don't be too ambitious.'

Mel indicated a section of rocks and Willow seated herself gratefully, leaning her back against the outcrop for support. With Cinder looking for fresh water and Tansy foraging, Mel took the opportunity to speak with Willow at last.

'You look so much better. When we found you I thought you were dead...'

'I think if you did not find me I would have died by this morning. I am still very weak, but thank you – thank you so much for coming after me.'

Mel reached out for Willow's hand.

'The others didn't make it through the gateway,' she said. 'It only opened for a few moments before closing again. Copper and I were the only ones that were quick enough to pass through.'

Willow looked at Mel in silence, making Mel uncomfortable. Not liking Willow's change of mood Mel broke the awkward silence.

'What is it? Why are you looking at me like that?'

Her earlier grateful mood seemed to have evaporated and Willow became surly. Pointing a finger at Mel she spoke angrily.

'When Rory and Alice first found me they were kind. You on the other hand were rude, calling me dwarf and other such things. Why have you risked entering my world to help me? What has changed Mel?'

Mel found this course of questioning disconcerting, but secretly she agreed with Willow. Her behaviour, not only to the little Faerie, but also in general had altered a great deal in the last couple of days. Normally a selfish individual and often rude to others, Mel had transformed, becoming caring and thoughtful. She wondered herself at this and thought before she spoke.

'If I'm honest, when I ran through the gateway I assumed Alice and Rory were behind me. When it closed I realised I could find no way back. Having entered your world I could only go forward. And another thing... Just before the gateway opened Rory and I argued – over you.' Mel paused, but Willow remained silent, still icily awaiting an explanation. Having reached the point of no return Mel continued. 'Rory accused me of being horrible to you – and yes I was. The reason for that...' Tears welled up in Mel's eyes and she fought them back. 'Seeing you steal his heart – and you did you know – that hurt me so much…'

She sobbed again as she relived those awful emotions. Willow, understanding now dawning on her face turned to Mel. Slipping her arms around the sobbing human, Willow offered comfort as best she could.

'I never realised,' she whispered. 'I thought that you just did not like me. I am so sorry, for I never planned it that way. But you are right - I have stolen his heart – and he mine. I cannot help that and I cannot change my feelings. I love Rory with all my heart and will do everything I can to regain him. I mean you no harm Mel – you have been so very stout hearted in trying to help me. If I were you I would hate the sight of me and be glad at my misfortune. You could have stayed back there with Rory and left me here to die. Why did you still come?' Regaining control of her emotions Mel spoke once more.

'I came for Rory. He suffered so badly over you, and after me being such a bitch I needed to make amends – I *wanted* to make amends. I promised him I would do anything to help you, and I have kept that promise. It's weird you know… I can't forgive you for taking him from me, but in different circumstances I would be so proud to call you my friend... *Am* so proud… Please, if you get back to Rory, tell him I helped you. I'd like him to know that I kept my promise...'

Mel's tears flowed freely now and Willow continued to hug her. They remained that way when Cinder returned. He enquired over her tears immediately. Willow brushed it off, explaining that Mel felt home sick and wanted to return to her own world. Fortunately, he accepted the explanation and also offered Mel encouraging words. Having refilled the water skin, he now offered it to Mel, and gulping down the cold liquid made her feel better. Willow also swallowed a couple of mouthfuls as Tansy returned empty handed from her foraging trip. Ever the optimist she said breezily,

'We'll stop later. There's bound to be somethin' to eat further on.'

As they readied to continue Mel insisted on carrying Willow again. However this time, with Willow awake she tried a different technique. Turning her back she said,

'Jump up Willow, put your arms around my neck and wrap your legs around my waist.'

Willow appeared to have never heard of a 'piggyback' before being a little unsure of what Mel wanted. However, after a couple of failed attempts she found herself comfortably supported on Mel's back with her hands clasped at the front and Mel's own hands gripping the backs of her bare thighs. With a final shrug which bounced Willow a little higher Mel announced her satisfaction at the new arrangement and they set off.

Once underway Mel questioned Willow about her curious dream of the previous night.

'Last night,' she said, 'when you were sleeping you woke me. You were talking about a robin? I thought it a weird coincidence. Cinder told me only yesterday that robins hold a special significance for him. What are they to you?' Willow seemed embarrassed, but attempted to explain.

'I cannot say,' she said. 'Only that a robin often appears to me in my dreams and sometimes I see one that comes to me at a special place that I visit in the forest. When I do see him he always fills me with joy and sadness at the same time... And when he flies away I always feel abandoned, but I know not why...'

Clearly these tiny birds held a special significance here in Eyedore, but for now Mel did not have the time for a proper discussion. She decided to follow up this line of enquiry another time and so for now she fell silent. Midday passed and the little party grew optimistic about their chances of escaping Flint. Tansy mooted the point that perhaps Flint would just give up now, but Cinder shook his head.

'No,' he said seriously. 'That's the last thing he'll do. He has far too much to lose. They're following us, rest assured. Their progress depends upon Flint's return and how long they have been tracking us. Fauns or Woad Warriors could pick up our trail even after a week of rain!'

His words cast a gloomy air over the group. Noticing Mel getting tired again, Cinder offered to carry Willow. He still favoured carrying her in his arms with her head snuggled into his shoulder. Willow wanted to try walking, but after only a short distance she collapsed, exhausted. Everyone could see the result of the separation from her magical amulet to Willow's health, but they were all tired now. With little sleep and barely any food they were all close to breaking point.

As they continued on Mel, half asleep on her feet suddenly came to her senses with a jolt.

'Hey!' she said loudly. 'Isn't that the old barrow where the gateway is hidden?' They stopped to look.

'Indeed it is,' Cinder said. 'If we keep it to our right and continue along the path, we're heading in the right direction. A few more miles and we should be safe.'

Mel, still having no idea where they were even trying to reach asked once more,

'So far Cinder,' she intoned, 'you have just told me we are heading east. But where to? Where can we go that will be safe from Flint?'

Cinder stopped walking. Putting Willow down for a few moments rest he took a long draw on the water skin bag and handed it around. Wiping his mouth he finally gave Mel the answer she wanted.

'We're off to see the King,' he stated. 'If we can gain an audience with him then we have a good chance of seeing Flint ousted and of Willow being given her father's lands and property back. He needs to know the truth of what has happened here.

Cinder gave Mel a wink followed by a broad grin. She guessed that there was more going on than she could even begin to imagine, but finally realised that this was a part of Cinder's charm. The man enjoyed living surrounded by an air of mystery as a local wise or Cunning Man. Grinning back at him a shiver of pleasure coursed through her at the sight of his smile, and blushing profusely she looked away.

Changing the subject and hoping that Cinder could not hear her manically beating heart or notice her still reddening cheeks Mel spoke.

'Let me have another turn carrying Willow. You're looking a bit tired Cinder,' she said sarcastically.

Willow readily jumped up onto Mel's back and in a moment they were off again with Copper dashing alongside whilst Cinder and Tansy went on ahead.

The mood had been steadily lifting throughout the day, but only moments after they moved off their worst fears returned. A sound which sent shivers down the spine came floating on the breeze from somewhere behind them. All three stopped in their tracks simultaneously. Willow spoke first.

'A hunting horn! They are tracking us. We have no hope now…'

Mel looked enquiringly at Cinder and for the first time saw uncertainty in his eyes. He waved them forward.

'Keep moving,' he said quickly. 'The more distance we put between us now the better.'

'Is there nowhere we can hide?'

'No. If they're being led by Flint's Woad Warriors or Fauns they'll find us no matter where we hide. We must keep moving.'

Mel still didn't understand. They could keep moving, but eventually they would be overtaken. Sooner or later they would be caught and what might happen then didn't bear thinking about. Continuing to run, when you looked at it appeared to be their only option. However, they weren't actually doing much running. With Willow to carry it slowed them down immensely. Mel pursed her lips in frustration and gripping Willows thighs a little tighter she put down her head and began to jog. Under different circumstances the little Faerie would have loved this experience and would have cried out in joy. Now she just clung on tightly and did everything she could to fight back her fear. Willow knew in her heart that if recaptured she would be taken back to Flint's hall, her secret would be forced from her and then she would be horribly murdered – probably by being given to the Woad Warriors as a plaything until they grew bored with her. Her gratitude for what Mel, Cinder and Tansy risked on her behalf could not be imagined, but she hated having involved them in something so dangerous, particularly Mel who did not even belong here.

They continued to make progress. The pathway ran slightly downhill much to Mel's advantage, with the ground unbroken and even. The sun, although no longer at its zenith seemed to be at its hottest. Despite this Mel refused to give in and continued on her jog to who knew where. She was burning up now and she thought her heart would burst inside her chest, but pure anger drove her on. Every now and then Cinder or Tansy would run alongside her giving her encouraging words and she found herself in an almost hypnotic rhythm. They seemed to have been running now for what seemed a lifetime, but in reality probably only equated to around thirty minutes or so, when the sound of the hunting horn broke out behind them once more. This time however, it sounded dangerously close and Tansy, risking a glance over her shoulder squealed at the horrifying sight behind them.

'Oh Goddess!' she cried, 'Save us from them that would do us 'arm!'

Mel, coming out of her almost trance like state at the sound of Tansy's plea felt the full force of her exhaustion and stumbled. Tansy caught her arm and prevented her going over headlong in the road and together they went on, but Mel was nearing the end now. She could not continue at this pace and she began to slow down. Cinder, turning around encouraged them onward.

'Keep going Mel,' he shouted, 'keep going, they're not far behind and will catch us should we stop. We must keep Willow safe!'

Mel could not look behind, for with Willow around her neck any such manoeuvre would result in disaster. She felt physically sick and her chest hurt her terribly. Eventually, her pace dropped to a fast and then a slow walk. Cinder leapt to her aid then, taking Willow in his own arms and setting off ahead. Tansy, concerned for Mel stopped beside her and slipped a comforting arm over her shoulders.

'Can't you go a little further Miss Mel?' she pleaded. 'Come an' lean on me, I'll give you an 'and!'

Mel, grateful for Tansy's support waved her away.

'You keep going,' she managed to gasp. 'Don't worry about me – follow Cinder and Willow – I'll catch up in a bit.'

Tansy refused to go on and anxiously glanced behind her once more. The leading members of the hunting party were only a couple of hundred yards or so behind and moving swiftly. They consisted of two Woad Warriors who appeared to be in charge and half a dozen or so militia men. Behind this first group a larger gaggle of around thirty or forty helmeted men brandishing spears followed on. Grabbing Mel's elbow Tansy literally dragged the human girl along the road, babbling away in fear.

'Oh Goddess, 'elp us! Please 'elp us! CINDER, WAIT! WE CAN'T KEEP UP!'

Hearing her cry Cinder stopped running and turned around. One of the two Woad Warriors leading the hunting party was further ahead than the others. In a manner that could only be described as fluid he fell to one knee, swung a bow from his back and notched an arrow. As it flew from the bow Cinder remained speechless as it hissed through the air and found its target.

Mel, still coughing and wheezing and fighting back tears vaguely noticed Tansy at her side. Rendered speechless by her pounding heart and bursting lungs she could only stumble on, dragged forward by Tansy's helping hand. But through the blur of her tears and the general hubbub of their flight she still heard the thud of a flint arrow head finding its mark. Tansy's grip on Mel's elbow loosened. Turning her head Mel saw Tansy stumble and pitch forward as a cry burst from her lips. The little farm woman went face down on the road. For a moment Mel thought her to have tripped, and ceasing her own steps she reached down to pull Tansy to her feet. The arrow had gone deep. About half of the crude wooden shaft with its black feather fletching's still protruded from between Tansy's shoulder blades. For a moment Mel stared in disbelief before falling to her knees and pulling the little Faerie over. Tansy still lived, but only just. Bright red blood, frothing with bubbles ran from her mouth and nose. Her eyes rolled in her head, but somehow she still possessed the strength to clutch at Mel's arm. The human girl burst into tears and she cried out in anguish. Cradling the dying Faerie in her arms she hugged her close as Cinder, still carrying Willow knelt beside her. Weeping, Mel rocked her back and forth like a new-born baby. She could feel the hot blood soaking through her clothes as the precious life force oozed out of Tansy. It felt sticky on her hands and was already in her hair and on her face. Tansy coughed, spraying blood and mucus over Willow. Then she spoke.

'Tell my Ma and Pa I love 'em... Tell 'em it weren't your fault... You 'elped me get away ... Tell 'em...'

Tansy's words drifted away. She lay there for a few more moments in Mel's arms trying to smile one last time before she died. She made no dramatic cry or any sound at all. She simply closed her eyes as her tiny body relaxed and her spirit left her. She just quietly slipped away and Mel laid her gently to rest in the dust of the road.

\*\*\*

# 11

# SALVATION

Everyone could only stare at poor Tansy. Her death ended their run of good fortune as The Fates who had favoured them all the way through their journey now turned their backs and abandoned them. Sitting on the road, Willow wept, grieving for her friend and feeling all hope gone. Cinder, usually so stoic and always in control stood looking aimlessly at the advancing Woad Warriors. For the first time, Mel witnessed him at a loss as to know what to do. Cinder, always so positive and confidant now appeared crushed.

Still a couple of hundred metres away the leading pair of Warriors walked towards the trio who now huddled together in the road. Mel sat transfixed, staring at Tansy's still warm body in disbelief and continued to stroke her hair. Just moments ago the Faerie had been so full of life and running alongside her, encouraging Mel to keep up her pace. Now she lay broken and lifeless. It just wasn't right. Mel could feel her grief and anger turning into something more. As the rush of emotions rampaged through her head they combined and transformed into a blind and calculating fury. Seeing the others looking so helpless, Mel took control. She addressed Cinder in a matter of fact tone.

'Give me your sling – NOW!'

Cinder stared at her blankly not understanding her intent. Expectantly Mel held out her hand. Coming to life the little man reached into his bag and after a moment withdrew the weapon. Mel snatched it from his hand and delving into her pocket withdrew the leather drawstring pouch. Opening it she thrust her hand inside and pulled out a small black object. As the lodestone came into view Cinder recoiled in horror. Willow, still weeping cried out and threw up her hands to ward off the evil magnetic pulses as the full effect of the ferrum based rock spread towards her. Slipping the stone into the sling Mel glanced at Cinder.

'I've never used one of these before – how do I do it?' Gagging at the magic of the Ferrum stone Cinder advised Mel on the technique.

'Slip your finger in that loop at the end of one of the thongs... Hold the other end between finger and thumb, swing it and release it!'

Cinder backed away further as Mel began swinging the sling dangerously about her head. Building up the rhythm she judged what she thought to be the right moment and released the stone. It flew off harmlessly into the bushes. The approaching Woad Warriors, seeing her miserable effort laughed, and drawing their swords they quickened their advance. Mel withdrew a second stone and tried again. This one went high, soaring way above the intended targets in a wide arc before disappearing harmlessly somewhere behind them. Cursing, Mel turned to Cinder.

'Snap out of it!' she demanded. 'You'll have to shoot – I'm useless at it!'
Cinder shook his head.

'I can't touch those stones,' he said, 'I'm sorry Mel, but I simply can't!'
Keeping her eye on the rapidly advancing Woad Warriors who were now only about a hundred metres distant Mel hissed back.

'Don't be so bloody feeble! You just shoot – I'll load them for you!'

Thrusting the sling back at Cinder she watched as he took it from her and slipped his finger into the loop. Holding his arm out as far as he could Cinder grimaced as

Mel popped a third stone into the weapon. As she stood back he began his swing and after only two rotations released the lodestone. His haste to be rid of it caused him to fling harder than he normally would and the stone flew towards its target at an astonishing speed. The two laughing warriors were running now in a bid to intimidate their prey before making the kill. They were so close that Mel could see the tattoos across their chests and around their arms in detail. Despite this terrifying spectacle and the fact that the lodestone caused Cinder great discomfort his aim remained true.

Slightly ahead of his companion, the warrior to the left never even saw the stone coming. It tore into the centre of his face, spraying blood and fragments of bone in all directions, killing him before he hit the ground. His companion, seeing his accomplice fall hesitated, buying Mel and Cinder just enough time to reload. Seeing the danger presented by what he thought to be a harmless enemy, he raised his shield to cover his face and upper body, but Cinder prided himself as a master with the sling. As he released his second shot the warrior stood no chance. Seeing the lifted shield Cinder aimed low and the stone struck the target on the left knee, shattering the kneecap completely. Screaming in agony the second warrior tasted defeat and struck the road face first. Worse for him the magnetic missile lay on the road only inches from his face causing him to suffer the utmost distress. Mel whooped with joy. Being able to hit back restored her confidence and even brought Cinder back to life, and for one brief moment, focussing on their enemy relieved them of the grief of Tansy's death. Still cautious of the evil little bag in Mel's hand, Cinder still refused to go near her.

'Very good Mel,' he called out from a safe distance. 'Very good indeed. But it'll only delay them. Load me some more and I'll lay a few on the road!'

Mel nodded her agreement. The return of the immense pain at the loss of Tansy caused her to become tight lipped, for at that moment, despite the small victory that Mel and Cinder brought about, their situation could not have been worse. Silently she assisted Cinder by loading four more stones which he flung at various positions along the road between them and their pursuers. The remaining warriors and militia men all grouped together in a huddle further back and discussed their next move. Mel turned to Cinder.

'What do we do now?' she asked. 'We can't just leave Tansy in the road...'

Cinder shrugged.

'We may have to do just that. We can't just sit here and wait for them to outfox us – and they will. We need to move – now!'

'Wait! Something's happening – look!'

Mel pointed towards the hunting party and as Cinder followed her gaze his heart skipped a beat. The group were beginning to move. Initially they advanced towards their prey in a slow walk, but as they drew closer they separated and spread out. As they did so a single figure clad in green continued walking towards them in the centre of the road. As Flint advanced he simply walked up to the deadly lodestones spread across the road, picked them up and placed them in his own drawstring bag. Collecting the last one by the fallen Woad Warriors he walked the last fifty metres or so. Cinder, not taking his eyes off of Flint readied his sling and spoke to Mel.

'Give me another stone! I can take him down now!'

'I can't. We used them all.'

Mel's answer came in a monotone of defeat. Looking around Cinder could see nothing available lying nearby as ammunition and together they silently waited for Flint, cursing themselves for being so foolish at using up the precious stones so recklessly. He came within a metre of them before halting. Behind him his followers advanced as he cleared away the lodestones and they now stood a respectful, but useful distance behind. Two broke away from the main group and came and stood with their Lord, flanking him in a protective stance. Mel recognised Zircon immediately. For a few moments they observed each other and then Flint broke the silence.

'So here we are. The thief, the trickster and the burglar.' He indicated Willow, Cinder and Mel in turn at each of these titles. Mel spoke first.

'Burglar? Where did that come from you little creep?'

'No? So where did you get that bag of the magic stones from human? They look remarkably like the ones that went missing from my study last night.'

Mel fell silent. She couldn't deny taking the stones and agreed that yes – that most likely made her a burglar. Flint continued.

'You have all caused me an enormous amount of trouble. It ends here. *You!*' At this he indicated to Mel and continued. 'I warned you in your own world that this is none of your business, but you have persisted to interfere. I have to say that I admire your resourcefulness and tenacity – few would have dared or even been able to follow me. In different circumstances I would happily employ someone with your skills. If you would consider such an offer, walk over here now. We can discuss terms later, but be quick for my patience is short.'

'Bugger off! I hate bullies and crooks. I wouldn't work for you for all the tea in China! Stick your offer up your butt!'

Flint nodded.

'As I expected,' he said smoothly, 'so we shall waste no more time. Zircon – bind the thief and bring her over here. Your men can kill these two, but make it swift – not as some misguided show of mercy, but simply because I've wasted enough time on this.'

Zircon and his colleague moved forward and grabbing Willow by her wrists dragged her to her feet. Winding wicker withies about her arms he secured her as before, then pulling a rough sack cloth bag from under his jerkin he thrust it over her head. Together they dragged the now struggling woman back towards their Lord and Master.

Mel, indignant now and not caring one jot what happened to her stepped forward as a most curious development occurred. As Zircon and his accomplice dragged Willow away they heard an unexpected hissing sound. Lasting a millisecond it caught Mel's attention as two arrows struck each of the assailants in their backs sending them down into the dust alongside the fallen Tansy. Willow, totally blind under the hood just stood there shaking with fear. At the same moment that the arrows struck a trumpet blast rang out – not the deep discordant bellow like that of the hunting party's horn, but a sweet clear flurry of notes picking out a quite musical fanfare in the air. The arrows too were of a different nature. Not the crudely carved, flint tipped monstrosities that Flint's men used. These were slender, dead straight and fletched with white goose feathers and their razor sharp tips were crafted of the finest silver. As the two miscreants fell dead, both sides turned to stare down the road beyond Cinder and his party. A sea of tiny warriors advanced in great numbers. At first they were difficult to discern for they all wore clothing of greens and browns and blended into the landscape. As they came closer a most alarming figure could be seen marching at their head.

Clad in a shaggy deerskin robe of brown that almost reached his feet stood the King. He wore a great helmet crafted in the form of a stag's head from which a huge pair of antlers swept skyward giving him an unearthly and quite dreadful appearance. Around his neck hung a medallion of gold, fashioned in the likeness of a leering Green Man. Leaning on the shaft of a great spear he watched as his men bounded forward harrying Flint's now fleeing horde.

Cinder let out a yell of delight and cheered loudly. Mel, totally petrified could only stare at the advancing soldiers and wonder at their timely arrival. Coming to life and taking advantage of the changing situation Mel leapt forward and pulled the bag from Willows head, then freeing the tiny woman's hands hugged her close to protect her. A great swathe of arrows cut through the air above their heads and began falling amongst Flint's militia.

Many were still bunched together and the arrows slew a great number in seconds. Flint stood his ground however, fury crossing his features before receiving one last torment. Copper, during the calamity of Tansy's death and in the following moments had fled up a tree at the side of the road. Amongst the turmoil of events everyone forgot about the cat. In her own way she was a very perceptive and protective creature and seeing Mel and her friends being intimidated by Flint and his men, Copper took an instant dislike to them. Distracted by the falling arrows and cries of his followers Flint did not see the cat leap from the tree nor the lethal claws that struck out as she landed on top of him. Crying out he attempted to free himself of the stinging attack on his head. Then one of Copper's claws struck lower tearing through the surface of Flint's left eye. The searing pain caused the little man to strike out and finally he managed to rid himself of the hissing, spitting bundle of orange fur. Pointing at Mel with one outstretched hand and covering his injured eye with the other he shouted venom at her.

*'This is not over human. I will have what is mine and I shall personally make sure that you suffer for all the damage you have caused me!'*

In another moment Flint vanished; absorbed by the very earth itself. Copper, proud of herself paraded up and down for all to see. She sauntered over to Cinder and purred around his legs, but Cinder ignored her.

A pair of arms gently encircled Mel around her waist. Cinder pressed against her, and as she leaned forward to speak he placed his mouth to hers and kissed her passionately. After a brief moment Mel found herself willingly returning Cinders display of affection. For a few seconds thoughts of Rory ran through her mind, but she dismissed them almost immediately. She knew now that Rory was not for her. Instead, in that one moment she knew in her heart that she had fallen deeply in love with Cinder. The moment was sweet and perfect, but they found their kiss interrupted as a gaggle of the small, terrifying soldiers surrounded them. These though did not threaten or intimidate, but formed a defensive barrier around the group as their colleagues gave chase to Flint's retreating militia.

Cinder broke free from Mel and embraced a small man in a frock coat and feathered hat. Vetch returned the greeting and the two shook hands and clapped each other on the back for so long that Mel became bored with the sight. She also felt irritation at the way that Vetch's arrival interrupted their kiss. However, she still felt rather pleased to see the little Mayor again. Clearing her throat loudly she stepped forward and held out her own hand.

'Mistress Mel,' wheedled Vetch. 'A pleasure to make your acquaintance once more. A successful expedition I see. And my journey to see the King was not wasted either for here we are!'

'Successful in as much as we found and freed Willow, but that is all. We have dreadful news for Hazel and Barleycorn. We found their daughter Tansy and freed her too, but they've killed her with one of their horrible arrows – she's in the road over there...'

As the little man turned in the direction she indicated he burst into tears and ran over to view Tansy's corpse. He sat at the road side crying his heart out and screwing his hat up in his hands. Mel felt awful listening to his lament.

'I held her on her birthing day! My old friend's daughter! What a dreadful outcome! How shall I tell Barleycorn and Hazel that their child lies dead?'

Mel, already mortified at her friend's death broke down and together she and Vetch shared their grief until a firm hand on her shoulder brought her back to her surroundings. Looking up she saw Cinders deep blue eyes full of compassion looking into her own. He assisted her to her feet and for the first time Mel noticed the changes that had taken place around them. With the turmoil and clamour of the fighting over, the soldiers now stood around in small groups, their weapons safely sheathed. Mel now studied them properly. Like Willow's dress their tunics all appeared to be fashioned from leaves. Peering closer Mel realised that different units were clad in different leaves. Spearmen for example wore oak leaves whilst archers were covered with beech and so on. The men themselves were small and dark complexioned and every one of them sported either a moustache or beard. As they rested after the battle they dutifully cleaned and examined their weapons for damage or wear.

Those that pursued Flint's men were not yet returned, but already Willow's uncle suffered a serious defeat. Bodies were strewn along the road, arrows giving their corpses the look of giant pin cushions. The noise of battle had now been replaced with that of laughter, congratulation and victory. Only Mel, Cinder, Willow and Vetch remained dejected. As Mel looked around she noticed that a small group of elegantly dressed men were approaching. They were nothing like the soldiers and appeared to be of a different class altogether. The one who appeared the most senior wore a long velvet burgundy coat with a large floppy hat decorated with a tassel of golden thread. Striding up he spoke to them collectively.

'I am here to request that the Fae known as Willow, Cinder and Vetch and the outlander who goes by the name of Mel attend the Royal camp. The Stag King is most anxious to meet with you and discuss the terms relating to the claim of the wood nymph Willow. Your presence is requested forthwith.'

Not waiting for a reply, the Chamberlain turned his back and marched away. Mel suspected that although mooted as such, this came as no request, but a definite command. Her feelings were confirmed when without a word she saw Cinder assist Willow and Vetch to their feet and all three followed on meekly. Tears still ran down Vetch's face and he continually rubbed them away as he walked. Reluctantly, Mel walked after them, her feet feeling like lead. She couldn't have cared less now. With all the fight gone out of her, shock had set in. The hours of gruelling exertion and little food, the sight of her friend cut down by the arrow followed by the release of tension and fear had all taken their toll. All Mel now wanted was to go home.

The King waited about a quarter of a mile along the road. As they progressed, the elegantly dressed man continually beckoned at them to walk faster. Finally he stopped and when they caught up he spoke briefly.

'The Stag King awaits you through there.' At this he indicated off the road between two clumps of bushes where a narrow path led into the forest.

'When you go in,' he advised, 'do not speak until you are spoken to. Refer to the King as Lord or Highness and if he asks you anything just be truthful.'

Mel trembled and Cinder mistook it for her nervousness at meeting his King. Kindly he slipped his arm around her and held her close. It helped. Mel felt warm and protected. She wanted to nuzzle into his neck, but with the top of his head below her chin it was not a posture she could easily adopt. Craving reassurance she spoke her mind.

'Please kiss me Cinder – like you did earlier. It felt rather good and...'

Cinder reached up towards her. As he kissed her a second time Mel felt immediately comforted, but at the same moment even more tearful as her raging emotions went out of control. She broke away. Concerned, Cinder spoke softly to her.

'Was it that bad? I thought you wanted me to kiss you? Have I offended you Mel?'

Blinking back tears she attempted to smile.

'No. It felt perfect,' she whispered. 'I'm just feeling pretty bad right now – you know... Tansy and all...'

Cinder just held her close. He felt awful about Tansy too, but he knew that nothing could be done to bring her back. Sharing Mel's grief, Cinder in a rare moment shed his own tears too and they comforted each other. Willow and Vetch stood nearby looking downcast. They murmured between themselves and occasionally glanced at Cinder and Mel as they embraced, but made no comment. Willow still suffered from fatigue. She had managed the short walk, but felt very light headed again.

She sat down on the grass with Vetch beside her. Copper all the while paraded around them, brushing against their legs in that way that cats show their affection. She was feeling pretty pleased with herself after her attack on Flint and had been preening around ever since, lapping up the praise bestowed upon her. However, no one took any notice of her right now, so she simply curled up beside Willow and went to sleep as the little Faerie stroked her head.

\*\*\*

# 12

# A Royal Audience

The chamberlain beckoned them forward. Heads bowed they followed the gaudily dressed fellow amongst the trees. He continually urged them on saying,

'The Stag King will see you now. Do not dally – come along, quickly now!'

He left the road and slipped through the opening amongst the trees. The little group found themselves within a large clearing bordered by hazel trees. At its centre sat a figure so imposing that Cinder, Willow and Vetch all fell prostrate upon the forest floor. Seeing them so fearful, Mel judged it prudent to follow their lead and dropped down beside them.

Mel felt particularly uncomfortable at her dishevelled appearance. Filthy, and still with Tansy's blood on her clothes, face and hands she presented a frightful sight. Her companions were little better also being covered in mud, general dirt, blood and filth. Only Vetch remained clean.

The Stag King sat on a large chair in the centre of the clearing whilst beside him stood a trestle table. In place of his great antlered helmet he now wore a small mask of the type traditionally worn at masque balls. This one however reflected his sylvan origins. The mask itself was made of silver and ended by crossing the bridge of his nose leaving his mouth and chin exposed. Oak leaves decorated it with different hues, encompassing all of the seasons and an acorn sat upon the nose bridge. A smaller set of antlers topped the design adding to his height and importance. Bright green eyes shone out of the eye holes and Mel could feel his power as they flickered to each member of the group in turn.

As he observed Mel and her companions she couldn't help noticing that to the King's side stood a young Fae woman of a similar age to Willow. She wore no clothes other than a tiny pair of briefs made from leaves. She held her head bowed whilst her hands were clasped in front, just below her navel. Unusually for a Fae being her hair appeared a fiery red. She also possessed pale skin unlike the others Mel had met and her body sported a variety of tattoos of stars, suns and moons. She was slim, petite and small breasted. To the Kings right a wine jug stood on a small table along with a beautiful bronze drinking cup whilst atop the table lay a feast. A large water fowl of some sort sat in the centre - roasted to perfection and surrounded by an array of brightly coloured vegetables – some Mel recognised, whilst others were quite unusual. There were also bowls of fruit, cheeses and bread – lots of different breads. At the sight of all this food Mel realised she felt utterly famished and momentarily forgot her filthy and bloodied appearance. However, despite her great hunger the Stag King looked so terrifying that Mel could do no more than bury her face in her hands and remain rigid with fear where she lay. For a few moments only an occasional bird call or rustle of the trees could be heard. Then Mel sensed that he had risen and she could feel and hear each of his steps reverberate through the ground as he approached. The King spoke and the little group hugged the ground closer. His voice, when it boomed out sounded deep and authoritive, but at the same time refined with perfect diction.

'So you are the little band of heroes I have been asked to support in their cause? You do not look very much like heroes to me – and what is this? What is a girl of the race of men doing within our realm? Answer me human!'

Fear coursed through her veins. For a moment no one dared to look up and then just as Mel found her voice,

Copper broke the ice. Jumping up, she landed on the edge of the table and helped herself to some of the food. Horrified, Mel sat up and cried out,

'Copper – NO! Get down at once!'

She made to rise, but strong hands restrained her from behind and she realised that several of the little, dark soldiers were also present. The King, looking serious stepped to the table and grabbed Copper by the scruff of her neck, holding her before his face. Then a great grin spread across his features and he let out a bellow of a laugh. When he finished he sat back down on his chair and with Copper on his lap, beckoned to the near naked Fae girl. He whispered to her, and fetching some of the roasted water fowl from the table she handed it to the King. At last he spoke, whist feeding Copper the meat. It was the first time Mel had seen or heard of meat since arriving in Eyedore as everyone here appeared to be vegetarian.

'Well,' he stated matter-of-factly, 'I have never met a cat before. This one seems hungry. So who does she belong to? You?' At the question he pointed directly at Mel. Unsure how to react, she remained silent. He burst out laughing again and then gestured to Mel. 'Come here girl and take your cat!'

The soldiers released her and as Mel stood and approached, she bowed her head respectfully, scooping Copper out of the Kings hand. Copper mewed loudly and tried to get back on his lap, but Mel held on to her tightly. Being this close to the Fae King allowed Mel to take her first detailed appraisal of him. His skin matched the colour of bark with deep lines and wrinkles. A musty, damp woodland smell hung about him too – similar to that which often surrounded Willow, but far more potent. His eyes burned with a brightness she could only have imagined and she sensed as though she were in the presence of a being more ancient and wise than time itself. Terrified she found her voice.

'I'm so sorry,' she stammered weakly. 'I promise to keep Copper under control...'

The King stared suspiciously at Mel and then indicated that she should sit beside him. She sensed that he took in everything before him in extraordinary detail as he gestured to the remainder of his visitors.

'The rest of you may rise,' he boomed. 'And down to business – but first if you are hungry you may eat. Take whatever you wish.'

Mel, not wanting to look greedy or bad mannered held back as her companions reached out and took some of the food. Willow she noticed showed no regard for manners at all – not even for a King. Grabbing a sizeable piece of cheese she bit into it and before she'd finished the first mouthful she helped herself to some of the fruit too. The half-eaten cheese Willow tossed back onto the dish from whence it came. The King however appeared unperturbed and rising he picked up the discarded cheese and bit into it himself. Not feeling quite so shy now Mel stood and helped herself to a piece of bread and tore off a wing from the roasted waterfowl. Cinder also ate heartily and Mel came to the conclusion that table manners were somewhat more refined in her world than they were here. She didn't care. Her growling belly welcomed the food and for the first time since the death of Tansy she began to feel better. At first Mel enjoyed the food, but catching sight of Tansy's dried blood on her filthy hands she found she could eat no more. Sickened, she put down her meat and sat on the ground staring ahead. She felt terribly guilty. Her friend lay dead and here she sat stuffing her face. The King, noticing her change of mood challenged her.

'Is the food not to your liking girl?' he enquired. 'Does my hospitality disappoint you?' Mel shook her head. The others continued to eat and the King continued. 'I have little experience of humans. What I have seen in my lifetime has not been favourable. Gratitude is something your kind lack. But I have been told by that fellow Vetch that you are stout hearted and of an honest disposition. Do me the courtesy of being honest now. Speak of why you look so churlish at my generosity!'

Clearly aggravated at what he perceived to be Mel's change of heart his Highness awaited her reply. Her words were not what he expected to hear.

'Highness, it is not that I am ungrateful. In fact I am extremely grateful and in debt to you and your men. If it were not for you, I and my friends would be dead. It is simply this. Since coming here I have been shown great kindness by many of your people. I have been fed, cared for and trusted. However, I now find it difficult to join in with your festivities because my friend Tansy – one of your people was murdered just a short time ago. Her blood is still on me, her smell is still on me and I can't get her face out of my mind. Just a short time ago she died in my arms. I mean you no disrespect, but to see all of you laughing and feasting like this is just so wrong. What will happen to her? She is still lying out there now. I cannot be a part of this, I am sorry!'

Standing up Mel made to leave, but the King gripped her arm and forced her back onto the ground. His eyes bore into her own and she could feel him inside her head, searching for the truth of her words. Totally paralysed, Mel could only sit there as the King invaded her innermost thoughts. She could feel him probing her mind, seeking out her most recent memories and absorbing them into his own psyche. As the earthy aroma surrounded her Mel, thought of Cinder and how she felt whenever he kissed or touched her and she blushed hotly. At the same instant the King glanced at Cinder, a knowing and rakish smile on his face. Eventually he withdrew and Mel felt a release, her mind becoming her own property again. The King resumed his seat and turning to Mel addressed her once more, but this time she sensed a little more understanding in his tone.

'You are not afraid to speak your mind are you girl? Well at least I know you are sincere in your words. Forgive me if I frightened you, but I am gifted in the art of soul searching. You seem to have experienced a great deal in the last few days – much of which has been at your own expense and to the benefit of others. I do not generally trust humans for in the past your kind have caused the people of the Fae much heartache - but you have been given favourable references, and in your mind I can see you mean well, so in your case, I am willing to make an exception. I felt and understood your distress, but you should understand this. When one of the Fae passes to the next world although we may miss them, we rejoice at their glorious transcendence. Your friend Tansy has gone to the Summer Lands. If she so wishes, you may sometimes sense her around you. The world to which she has passed is where we all strive to go one day. Remember her and she will visit you in your dreams. Furthermore, have no worries about her lying in the road. My people have already retrieved her body and brought her here. She will be well taken care of.'

Hot tears trickled down Mel's cheeks, for her emotions were so mixed up. On the one hand she wanted so much to enjoy and embrace this experience of another world, but by the same token she feared it and hated the brutality here. Weary of it all she asked a question.

'When can I go home? Can I go home at all? Willow and Cinder have both told me how time passes differently between our worlds and that when I do go back nothing will be the same. Will my friends be dead? How far into the future will it have gone?'

The King, now knowing of their affectionate connection gestured to Cinder to make a reply. The little man chose his words carefully for he did not wish to appear heartless or merely interested in solving Willow's predicament. Mel sat silently, taking in his kind words.

'Mel,' he started, 'at the beginning of this, like his Highness here I have never trusted humans, and I suspect that my treatment of you when we first met made you aware of this. I felt little desire to speak to you when we were thrust together on this journey. But you came here and told us of Willow's dilemma. You risked everything by doing that. Along the way I realised what a kindly and loving soul you are and my view of you, sweet Mel has changed. I now know, thanks to you that there are some decent humans too. You wish to go home – and I will miss you with all my heart when you do. You *should* go home, but I have to ask one last thing of you. Willow has told me of who holds the ring for her. Without it she can't substantiate her claim on her property or land. She needs you to go home, to find the ring and to bring it back here. Afterwards you may stay here or return home as you wish. I can't say how much time will have passed when you go back – sometimes time can even go backwards. That is a mystery and always will be. You've risked so much for Willow that to not return the ring would be a complete waste of yours and Tansy's sacrifice. Help Willow one last time and I'll get you back here should you still wish to return – I promise you.'

Mel made to make her reply, but another spoke first. Willow, still looking very sickly came forward. She approached Mel and took her hands in her own. Looking directly into Mel's eyes Willow made her own entreaty.

'Mel, I owe you so much. Like Cinder, I have always been suspicious of humans – it is in our nature, and it is true that at first you and I were less than friends. But you and your companions have all shown me the greatest kindness. Without you, like our dear friend Tansy I would now be in the Summer Lands. Flint would have stolen my family estate and chaos would now govern the surrounding countryside. Many Fae owe you a great debt Mel. But Cinder is right. I need that ring. I will do anything for you in return. Name your price and if it is within my power to deliver it I will.'

As she finished speaking Willow stood on her toes and kissed Mel on the mouth. It was not a kiss of passion such as Cinder gave, but tender and caring. Mel could feel the love all around her and for the first time in her short life she actually loved herself. Squeezing Willow's trembling hands she replied.

'You are right, all of you. This is not over until Willow has her ring. I will do as you ask. I cannot say how I will feel afterwards and where I will want to stay. That depends on many things. But I will do it. My heart tells me that I must go back immediately for I believe that the longer I stay here the further into the future my own world will go. How soon can you get me home?'
The King made his own feelings known.

'Mistress Mel,' he started, 'you should return at once. The longer you stay here the further into the future your own world will travel. I charge Cinder to take you back to whichever gateway you entered by. The only mystery now is how we bring you back once you have located the ring. Cinder, what would you suggest?'

Cinder needed no further thought on the matter. For him the solution already lay to hand.

'In two days,' he stated, 'it will be our summer solstice. Mel, our worlds pass differently through time but there's always one constant in that the solstices will always coincide. We refer to it as 'the time of the twin suns'. I can send you through the gateway tonight. Upon your return whatever time of year it is in your own world you'll need to await your own summer solstice. On that magical day you should return to the gateway at sunrise. Two days from now, here in Eyedore I'll reopen the gateway at the moment that the sun appears on the horizon. If you're in place at the correct time you'll be able to come through. Here it'll be only two days from now. You may have to await several moons in your own world for that day, but do exactly as I bid and we'll get you safely back here.'

The King nodded sagely and gave his opinion on Cinder's proposal.

'Of course!' he boomed. 'It is auspicious is it not that we are about to enter the solstice?'

Mel gave her approval. The thought of going home filled her with deep joy. All she wanted now was her own bed and to be reunited with her friends. However, not knowing what her own world would be like on her return also filled her with apprehension. Cinder gave her one last instruction. Rummaging in his pocket he withdrew a tiny silver whistle strung on a leather thong. He placed it over Mel's neck.

'On the day of the solstice at the appointed time you'll need to stand by the gateway and blow this. Just one long blast and no more. It'll tell me that you're ready to return to us. Don't lose it and remember – just one long note.'

'Thank you, I will remember that. I do so want to go home,' she said. 'I'm afraid, but I know that I must go back.' Turning to Willow she said, 'I will get your ring. Is there anything else you need from my world?'
Willow replied with a tremor in her voice as she gave her answer.

'Rory. I want Rory. Bring him back with you Mel. I need the ring, but I want Rory more. And Alice of course. Please bring her with you too. And nut butter! Lots and lots of nut butter!'

Mel smiled. Willow had taken on her childish mood and as always it was rather endearing. From openly admitting how much she desired Rory and then including peanut butter in the same sentence gave Mel the much needed laughter she so badly craved. Her eyes moistening she laughed aloud and nodded her approval.

'Yes Willow. I will do my very best to get you those too. Now you need to rest I think. You are still very weak. Rory and Alice wouldn't like to see you like that I'm sure. Get yourself well and we'll meet in two of your days.'

The King, listening to this exchange cut in.

'Weak? What is wrong with her? She looks well enough to me? Speak up wood nymph! Come here and tell me what ails you!'

Shakily Willow stood up. She felt terrible. Slowly she advanced and stood before her King, shaking not through fear, but from total fatigue. She explained her malaise.

'Highness,' she said softly, 'when Flint and his men snatched me from the human world I left my birthing amulet behind that my human friends might have a means of following me. I spent several days parted from it and consequently I have paid a great price. Also, Flint kept me locked in a darkened cellar away from both sunlight and forest. They provided little food and Flint's warriors beat me in a bid to make me tell them where to find my father's ring. All of those things have left me sick. Mel and Cinder reunited me with my amulet and I am getting stronger, but right now I feel dreadful. With your permission Lord, I need to sleep. I ask to be excused that I may do so. I offer you no offence by my requested departure.'

Willow bowed her head and awaited an answer. The King, looking closely upon her throughout her plea saw for the first time the faded bruise on her face and the darkened circles under her eyes. He also noted her pale complexion and returning acne and after her grim story he felt pity for her. Reaching out a hand he spoke gravely.

'You have suffered as one of my people should not,' he stated. 'Furthermore it galls me that such an outrage should be inflicted upon you by one of our own. Come hither child and I shall heal you.'

Willow hesitated, but Cinder pushed her so that she stood directly in front of her King. Mel stared, curious as to what may happen. Unexpectedly the King removed his mask. Willow recoiled and Mel openly gasped. His face when fully revealed spoke of the wisdom of a thousand years. Something archaic lived in every line upon his countenance, something so powerful that it took the breath away. Before Willow could run the King took hold of her tired face in both of his hands and kissed her hard on the mouth. The kiss seemed to last a lifetime. Initially Willow went rigid and struggled in his grip, but after a few moments Mel saw her body relax and then she seemed to fill out with life and vitality. In a moment Willow herself reached up, wrapped her arms around her King's neck and with a little jump entwined her bare legs around his waist. They stayed that way for some time and it became evident to Mel that Willow found the experience rather agreeable. An age seemed to have passed, but eventually the King took his mouth from Willows and released her.

When she stood back a most remarkable transformation had taken place. Gone was the horrible spotted skin of her face along with the bruising and tired looking eyes. Her hair, mysteriously regaining its wild look literally shone in the dappled sunlight of the forest grove whilst the yellowed, curled leaves of her tiny dress took on a hue of the dark green of summer. Willow positively glowed with vitality and life.

'Thank you,' she sighed. Then she dropped to her knees, took her King's hand, kissed it and held it to her face. The King laughed his booming laugh and ruffled her hair, bidding her to stand. She stood and the King gave her leave to step away. Gratefully she walked backwards, her head bowed until she stood beside Cinder. Mel gaped. She did not remember ever witnessing anything so remarkable before and just sat there open mouthed until she realised the King directly addressed her. She focussed on his ancient face and tried to take in his words.

'Mistress Mel,' he said. 'You expressed a wish to go home. There is no time like the present. Cunning Man... You, I think should be the one to escort her!'

Cinder nodded graciously.

'Of course my King. The pleasure would be all mine.'

The King turned to Mel and offering her his hand assisted her to rise. She still felt confused. A very big part of her desperately wanted to go home – however, she felt equally drawn to staying in this other world. The King passed her to Cinder who took her hand in his own. The feelings that caused within her just complicated things further. His mere touch now sent flurries of desire through her belly and is seemed as though a small electric shock passed up her arm and into her heart. Cinder squeezed her hand playfully and a small gasp of excitement escaped her lips.

The King turned from them and beckoned to his flame haired servant for more wine. The whole scene felt totally surreal to Mel and she didn't want it to end. Cinder guided her back to where Willow sat and Mel found herself shaking off the warm cosy glow that spread through her. She felt a sense of loss and voiced her feelings.

'If we have to leave, can Willow come with us?'

The King glanced up from his wine.

'No, she cannot. Willow will be safer under my protection. Flint is still abroad and as yet we know not where. Some of his men may well still be roaming the forest and to bring her down would elevate them greatly in their master's eyes. I shall send some of my men to accompany you on your journey. They will keep you safe. Say your parting words with Willow now and be on your way before nightfall is upon us.'

Mel could see the wisdom in these words, but it still hurt her to know that Willow could not go with her. She nodded her agreement, comforted somewhat by Willow's own reaction. The tiny Fae woman bounded across the short distance that separated them and jumped up at Mel. The human girl caught hold of her and with Willow now wrapped around Mel they embraced one last time. Hugging the tiny woman tightly she kissed her repeatedly and they exchanged words of farewell. Cinder stood patiently nearby, but eventually he intervened. Prising the two females apart he wrapped his arm around Mel's waist and pulled her close.

'Willow will be here to greet you when you return,' he said. 'Don't fret. We need to go Mel – we need to get you back to the gateway before nightfall.'

Rubbing her eyes Mel responded.

'I know we have to go and despite being desperate to get home it's so hard leave! Hold me Cinder... Please?'

He took her in his arms and kissed her passionately.

'We have to go Mel – now...'

Sadly she nodded and turned to the King. He seemed oblivious to them sitting on his chair with the serving girl filling his wine cup yet again. Mel boldly interrupted his pleasure.

'Highness,' she said. 'Cinder is taking me home as you bid. I want to thank you for helping us today, for feeding us and lastly for trusting in me. I shall not let you down.'

The King, engrossed in his wine grunted and waved Mel away.

'Go girl and return as bid on the Solstice. Go before darkness comes.'

He returned to his drinking and Mel, sensing the dismissal returned to Cinder. Willow gave her one final embrace and then together, the human girl and the Fae Cunning Man set off on the road which would lead them back to the barrow...

\*\*\*

# 13

# The Return

They walked in silence as Mel marvelled over her experiences of the last few days. Who would ever believe that a world so beautiful, yet so brutal could exist just beyond the fringes of her own? She found that her mind would not dwell upon anything for long, but flitted from one thought to another and back again. She reflected upon Willow and her first introduction to the little Fae woman, of the conflict it caused her, of her arrival here in Eyedore, her experiences therein, of her meeting with the King and finally of Cinder – every few minutes her musings returned to Cinder...

With no need for food they were travelling light and they made swift progress. Copper scampered about, always a few metres ahead enjoying the freedom. The sun sank towards the horizon now, giving a warm orange glow to everything it touched. The air still felt comfortably warm and it had come to that time of day when the full heat has subsided, leaving a welcome coolness in the previously stifling air. They walked escorted by half a dozen soldiers and covered a good distance before Mel broke the silence. Since meeting the Stag King she wanted answers to a thousand questions which rampaged around her head. She knew that in the short time they would walk together that she could not ask them all, but one aroused her curiosity and continued to bother her.

'Cinder?' she said shyly, 'can I ask you something?'

'Of course. Ask away.'

Mel felt embarrassed by her question and her face flushed red. However, that could not be helped. Taking a deep breath she asked outright.

'The girl serving the King his wine... Why was she practically naked?'

Cinder laughed at her innocence.

'The girl is an elemental – a Fae who is connected directly to one of the four elements of earth, air, fire and water. Her name is Flame. She is, as her name and red hair suggest, a fire soul. Elementals are closely connected to nature and the world about them – hence they usually remain in a natural state and wear few clothes – sometimes none at all. They are benign folk and can be possessed of great magical skills or be guardians of some natural place or landmark. They also have the ability to love passionately and to cause others to fall in love with them within a very short space of time. When they do give their heart to another it is usually for all eternity. Willow is an elemental - she is a woodland sprite and at one with the forest realm. I think she may have worked her magic on your friend Rory from what I've heard. I too am born of that kind.'

Mel took in Cinders words, but something seemed out of place.

'If you and Willow are elemental,' she asked, 'then how come you both wears clothes? You said elementals prefer to be naked...'

Smiling, Cinder nodded.

'I did. Perhaps I didn't give you the full facts of the matter. Willow was born only half elemental, but that is enough to fit her into that branch of the Fae people. She does wear clothes, but very few – only that thin dress of leaves. And no doubt you've seen how she always embraces others, wrapping her arms and her legs around them? That is her way. She has traits of both elementals and normal Fae folk. Sometimes it can be hard being of mixed blood. Willow's father is... *was* Lord Oak. Her mother was a full blooded wood nymph named Rowan who used to spend her days roaming around the forest protecting the creatures that live there. They do say that she used to lay with Oak quite regularly amongst the trees and there is a legend that says she also gave birth to a son two summers after Willow. The story goes that during her son's birth Rowan died. They say that in his grief Oak wrongly blamed the child. No one knows what happened to that baby. Legend goes on to say that Flint had something to do with his disappearance, hence the animosity between the two brothers. It's been a local folktale ever since, but no one has ever questioned Oak on the validity of the story. As for Willow, on her mother's death she went to live at Oak Hall and Oak raised her there himself. That would have been unusual, for she should have remained with her mother in the natural environment to which she belonged. Being brought up in his home rather than living in the forest every day as she should have, she has grown accustomed to his ways – hence she wears clothes. Her first two summers she lived amongst the trees like her mother, but where her mother's passion was for song, as she grew Willow found that she possessed a natural talent for mastering any musical instrument. Music is her true magic.'

Mel was dumbfounded. These people and their culture became more bizarre with every new discovery. Something else struck her.

'Did you say that you are an elemental too?'

Cinder nodded.

'Aye. Like Willow I too am a half breed. My parents were travelling healers and I learned my basic skills from them. They raised me as a non-elemental and they never encouraged me to be wild in the same way as Willow, but my links with nature have enabled me to work with plants and herbs at a level few ever achieve. I'm happy with my lot. I always have a full belly and an equally full purse.'

Mel considered Cinder's comments. In her mind she reassessed her feelings for Cinder for the thousandth time. In just a couple of days her views changed from disliking him to feeling that she may even be in love with him. In fact when she thought of returning home without him her stomach churned and she felt physically sick. She voiced her thoughts.

'Will you be here when I return on the solstice?' she asked. Cinder nodded.

'Yes, I'll be here Mel. Even if you can't find Willow's ring, please promise me that you'll come back. I'll wait for you.'

He stopped walking and kissed her again. Mel felt wonderful. When Cinder held her it made everything good. As they parted she asked more questions.

'When we were on the run did you know that the King would meet us on the road?'

'No,' he replied. 'But I hoped he would send someone to meet us. I knew that Vetch would try to get word to him of Flint and what has been happening here in recent moons. Vetch has a cousin at court, but that gave no guarantee that the King would even speak to him, let alone come to our aid. Luck played a great part too.'

'Vetch did well. At first I thought him a silly little fellow, but now I freely admit to being wrong. I feel bad thinking of him in that way now...'

They continued talking all the way to the barrow. Mel estimated that the journey took them about an hour or so. When they came across the dry stone wall and began following it a sad thought crossed her mind.

'Who will tell Hazel and Barleycorn about Tansy? I feel so bad about her. She was such a kind hearted and brave little thing. They will be so distraught when they find out. I feel responsible for her being shot down like that. I had grown so tired... I held her back...'

Cinder held her close, offering her gentle words of comfort. Eventually she pulled away and rubbing her stinging eyes said,

'Come on, let's get this over. I need to get back and you need to return to the King before it gets dark.' She glanced at the sky and continued, 'The sun will set soon. Please don't get caught by Flint's men. You stay safe for me!'

Before they knew it they came upon the old barrow. It looked older and smaller than Mel remembered it. The gaping black hole of the entrance did not look inviting at all and Mel shuddered upon seeing it again. She felt glad that Cinder accompanied her. Copper however seemed positively pleased at seeing the ancient burial mound. Somehow she sensed it to be the way home and mewing loudly she bounded forward. Mel ran after her and caught hold of her just before she entered the inky black portal. Handing her to Cinder she said,

'Hold Copper a moment, I need to retrieve something.'

She ran past the barrow a few yards and rummaged around under some bushes. She returned a few moments later triumphantly holding her coat in the air. Slipping it on she fastened it all the way to the neck and grinned at the confused looking Cinder.

'When I came here it was winter in my world,' she explained. 'If it still is when I go back it will be cold and I have a bit of a walk before I'm home.'

Cinder nodded, smiling at her practicality. He admired the olive green Parka with its fur trim around the hood. He thought it made Mel look even more attractive. Giving her one more peck on the cheek he turned to the barrow and spoke over his shoulder.

'Let's do this Mel. Let's get you home that you might find the ring. Now you remember what I told you? Come back to the gateway at sunrise on your next summer solstice with or without the ring. I'll get you and your friends through. Now come on before you change your mind.'

Together they entered the barrow. As the darkness enveloped them Mel felt a shiver run down her spine. Once inside, save for a faint glow from the entrance the chamber was inky black. Mel sensed, rather than saw Cinder ahead of her. He moved slowly before stopping, facing the rear stone wall. His voice came from the gloom.

'When the gateway opens don't hesitate. It's difficult to hold it open for long. Just run through and you'll be fine. If there's anything you need to ask me, then ask me now.'

Mel did not hold back. She did not know if she would ever see Cinder again and so she voiced her innermost thoughts.

'I shall miss you terribly. Even the mere thought of being parted from you for a moment hurts me already. I have no idea how long I will have to wait in my world until I can return to you. How will I cope? What will I do...?'

Seeing her distress Cinder felt only compassion. He made her a vow.

'If you're at the depths of despair I'll send you a gift. When you're at your lowest then look around you and I'll send you a robin.'

'A robin?'

'Aye. I told you once before, robins are special to me. I know not why, but they always seem to appear to me at times of danger or distress. It is something that's happened throughout my life. Should you feel real despair while you're away a robin will be sent to visit you. When he does, then think of me and all will be well in your heart.'

'That is lovely, thank you. I so love you Cinder,' she blurted out. 'Just make sure you're here when I come back.'

Leaning forward she embraced the tiny Fae man and kissed him one last time. Cinder did not resist. He pulled her in to him and returned her kiss with ardour.

Eventually they parted and scooping up Copper, Mel spoke through gritted teeth.

'Do it!' she hissed. 'Open it before I change my mind!' Seeing her personal battle reflected in her watering eyes Cinder wasted no time. Raising his arms above his head as Mel had seen Willow do once before he uttered the ancient command and in moments the gateway opened. A cold wind blew through the barrow as Mel peered through into the gloomy chamber. Fighting against her instincts to stay, Mel took one last lingering look at Cinder before plunging forward.

Dimly she heard her feet pounding across the stone floor and then she found herself back in the barrow – her barrow in the human world. Whirling around on the spot she looked back and could still see Cinder silhouetted on the far side, his arms outstretched and head thrown back. Then she saw him relax and look directly into her eyes just before the stone wall rolled back before her.

Distraught, Mel sank to the floor and cried out as she ran her hands across the ancient stones. She battered them with her fists and called Cinder's name into the darkness. Ironically her mind recalled the image of Rory behaving in the same hysterical manner at the identical spot just a few days ago when Willow had first been snatched. Now she understood his pain. She could not say how long she sat there, but eventually she pulled herself together and stood up. Her hands throbbed and bled profusely, but she didn't care. Caked in mud and blood and accompanied by Copper she walked to the entrance and back into her own world...

\*\*\*

# 14

# HOMECOMING

As Mel emerged from the barrow into her own world the wind cut through her and she felt grateful for the protection of her coat. As she glanced around she immediately noticed many changes.

The greatest difference was the disappearance of the ploughed field in which the barrow stood. The old familiar footpath leading away from the entrance of the ancient chamber remained, along with the dry stone wall. However, the field itself no longer existed. In its place a huge housing estate of mock Tudor homes spread out as far as the eye could see. Mel gasped and put her hand to her mouth. She felt sick. How much time could have actually passed here she wondered? Grabbing at Copper she began a slow walk along the path, looking for some familiar landmark. A cluster of oak trees provided her with her bearings. To the left the undergrowth, trees and shrubs looked much the same as always, although a little more overgrown, but the houses to the right were just wrong. However, by following the path Mel knew that sooner or later she should find the back gate to her own home and to Alice and Rory's too. Her own home? For the first time in days Mel thought of her grandmother. She felt terribly guilty. The elderly woman had cared for Mel since the death of her parents in a road accident shortly after her birth. Judging by the amount of time that appeared to have passed Mel suspected that her grandmother may not even be alive. The thought filled her with horror, and with a rising dread she began to realise the full implications of her time away. Still following the path she eventually came to the rear entrance that bordered her home. In the garden an unfamiliar child's swing and climbing frame filled a corner. The house itself was smartly painted and a shining conservatory had been added to the rear aspect. Even as she continued to stare in disbelief the back door opened and a woman in her late twenties came out to put some rubbish into the bin. Thrusting her hands into her pockets Mel put her head down and walked further down the path. Tears ran silently down her face as she remembered her kind and loving Grandmother. It seemed so cruel to think of her dying in the space of what for Mel seemed only a few days - and worse still that there had been no opportunity to say goodbye or to offer any explanation for her disappearance. Mel began to feel very bitter. What at first seemed such an adventure now felt a hollow experience. She felt only shame. As she pondered on these black thoughts her eyes fell upon the gate and rear garden of the other property she sought.

Alice and Rory's old home also looked very different. The old wood shed where Willow once lived no longer stood. A modern ship-lapped structure with windows and a wooden veranda replaced it. Rustic looking flower beds filled with cottage plants and herbs bordered the garden. Most were dead or dormant for the winter and the grass needed cutting, but Mel cold tell that whoever lived here possessed a penchant for gardening with a natural and peaceful style. One new addition made Mel's heart skip a beat. A dwarf willow tree grew close to the rear gate. A set of wind chimes hung in its branches and tinkled merrily as Mel took in the scene. And then she saw him. The first familiar sight to remind her of her lost life. At the foot of the willow tree sat a very old garden ornament. Her eyes still brimming with tears Mel stepped through the gate and approached the little statue. Crouching down for a closer look she ran her fingers gently over the worn concrete.

For the first time since leaving the barrow a smile spread across Mel's face and excitedly she whispered his name.

'Mr Hollyhock!' She began to laugh, slowly at first, but then faster and louder. She still laughed as a voice behind her broke through her thoughts.

'What on earth do you think you are doing in my garden? Get out!'

Mel detected irritation in the voice, but at the very moment of its intrusion she recognised it at once. It sounded more mature and rather well-to-do, but there could be no mistaking the owner. Standing up slowly and wiping her face she turned around to face her old friend.

'Hello Alice…'

Mel's voice trembled and as the words came out she began to splutter with emotion. Through a fog of tears she saw the other woman properly now. At first glance Mel estimated her to be in her thirties. Alice's trademark long brown hair now hung to just below her shoulders. Gone too were her glasses, her vision now corrected by laser surgery. Dressed simply in jeans and a black sweater and with little make up, Mel thought her extremely attractive. As Mel turned around to face her Alice raised her hand to her mouth in disbelief and even as Mel stared at her the blood drained from her face. For a moment she looked as though she might faint, but managing to grope herself sideways Alice sat down heavily on a garden bench.

'Oh my God!' she started, 'Oh my good God! MEL! Is it really you? And look at you… You don't look…'

Mel ran forward and fell upon Alice. The two women hugged each other as though their lives depended upon it, but eventually Alice found her voice. Pulling away she gazed long and hard at her old friend.

'My God,' she exclaimed once more. 'It really is you! But you look identical to when you left us all those years ago… But what's this? You're filthy and… Is that blood?'

Her last question came out as a whisper. Staring at the filthy and bedraggled girl before her Alice could not even begin to comprehend the horrors of what may have taken place. Regaining her wits she stood up, gesturing for Mel to follow her into the kitchen, and then she saw Copper. The cat had been wandering around exploring the changes to her home with suspicion. Now, seeing Alice and recognising her owner, Copper bounded forward mewing loudly. Alice squealed.

'COPPER! OH COPPER!' Scooping her old cat up in her arms and without waiting to see if Mel followed her, Alice ran indoors. Setting the purring animal down she ran to the fridge and grabbed a bottle of milk, took a dish from the draining board and poured a generous amount before setting it down and watching Copper happily lapping it up. Her actions gave Mel the chance to observe the kitchen. The old nineteen seventies flat pack fittings were long gone. In their place a modern and professionally designed layout spoke of a comfortable standard of living. On the worktop a radio boomed out the rhythmic beat of a rap song and Alice hurried over to turn it off as Mel turned her nose up at the unfamiliar style. She waited for Alice to speak.

'I don't know what to say... My God look at you Mel! What has happened for you to get so messed up? And you still only look seventeen! You look exactly as you were the day you left us...'

'How long has it been... exactly?'

Alice rubbed the tears from her face, grabbed a tissue from a box and blew her nose. She handed a couple of them to Mel who accepted them gratefully.

'Twenty years,' she said, 'twenty long and painful years almost to the same date exactly. You disappeared on Wednesday the tenth of March nineteen ninety three and now you're back. Today is Saturday the ninth of March twenty thirteen! I just don't know what to say first. Is that really blood? Forgive me, are you hurt?'

Mel shook her head and tears began to flow as she replied.

'I'm fine. It's not mine... A friend... She...'

Mel began to sob and Alice embraced her. The two old friends went into the lounge and sat on Alice's sofa for some considerable time until their tears ceased. Gently wiping Mel's face Alice asked,

'Do you want to tell me about it?'

Mel nodded.

'Yes, but not now. There are things I need to ask you first. What of my Grandmother?'

Alice knew that she could not lie with her response. Feeling extremely uncomfortable Alice gathered her thoughts before answering.

'Your Grandmother passed away about a year after you left us. Your disappearance broke her heart and she never recovered from it. We couldn't tell her – tell anyone the truth. How could we have? Who would have believed us if we'd said that you'd gone through some kind of magical portal into another world looking for a kidnapped Faerie? We'd have been locked up! You can't imagine how difficult Rory and I found it...'

Looking at the floor Mel replied.

'It must have been awful, but it's so hard for me too. I feel I've only been gone a few days, but twenty years have passed here, my grandmother's dead, I have no home and you are now way older than me! I just don't know what to do... Where is my Grandmother buried?'

'At St Nicholas church in West Pennard. Rory and I can take you there if you'd like. That's the least we could do...'

Mel jumped at the mention of Rory. Her head reeled with thoughts of her longing for Cinder and her loyalty to her friends and Grandmother - not to mention her loss of twenty years of time in her own world. Timidly she asked,

'How is Rory? What happened after I followed Willow through the gateway?'

'Rory is fine now, but he suffered a nervous breakdown at the time. We were so concerned about you and Willow.

We lied terribly. To everybody. Our mum, your gran, the police... I still don't know how we got away with it.'

'What did you tell them?'

'That you and Rory argued and that you'd gone off in a huff and we hadn't seen you since then. We just stuck to that. The police searched for you for weeks. We didn't even know if you would ever come home. Even after twenty years things can still be a bit tricky. Every few years the local press bring up your disappearance and then people want to start asking questions again. Rory and I just refuse to get involved these days.'

Mel nodded and then asked,

'What about your mum? Does she still live here with you?'

Alice shook her head.

'Mum died ten years ago of cancer. Neither Rory nor I have ever married. A few years back I was with someone and we lived together for a bit, but it didn't work out. After mum died I moved back in here and bought Rory's share of the house. He now owns a small house on the edge of Glastonbury. I followed in mum's footsteps and trained as a nurse after leaving school. Eventually I specialised and became a midwife and have done that for the last ten years. Rory helps out as a volunteer at the library. He also writes books on folklore – Faeries mostly – no surprise there! He's become a leading figure right across Europe on that subject. After all that stuff with Willow he spent years researching stories of Faerie sightings, folklore and such like. He gets contacted by people from all over the world now. He does seminars, talks at universities, all sorts. He actually makes a reasonable living out of it. He's going to really freak out when he comes round and sees you. I think I'll ring him and ask him over for dinner.'

Alice pulled a slim white smartphone from her jeans pocket and called Rory. Mel stared open mouthed. The only people she knew of that possessed mobile phones were wealthy business people – and their phones were always huge, unlike the slim line, tiny piece of technology Alice now held to her ear. Goggle eyed she stared in wonder, trying to decipher the one sided conversation she could hear as Alice spoke with her brother.

'Hi Rory?' she began. 'Listen, something just came up. You really need to come over ASAP... Yes... No... Don't panic, it's nothing bad – in fact I think you'll rather like it... Can you come for dinner? Yes... Yes... Sooner the better... Now? Okay, see you in about thirty - bye.'
As she slid the phone back into the pocket of her jeans Alice made a decision.

'You - upstairs! You need a bath. I'll sort you out some clothes to wear. Come on.'

\*

Mel followed Alice obediently. Her eyes wandered around the familiar, but changed house as they traversed the hall and climbed the stairs. She wanted to ask so many questions, but for now they could wait. The thought of a hot bath really appealed to Mel and she eagerly stripped off her clothes as Alice ran the water. As she pulled her top over her head Alice saw the silver whistle around her neck.

'What's that?' she asked.

'My friend Cinder gave it to me – don't touch it!'
Mel sounded quite intimidating and Alice backed away.

'Okay,' she said meekly, 'I only asked, I promise I won't touch it.'

Mel nodded approvingly and still wearing Cinder's gift she slipped in amongst the bubbles, sighing with contentment. She could smell the forest in her own hair and see dirt and grime embedded in her skin and under her nails. She fingered the silver whistle as she lay there enjoying the sensation of the hot water against her bare skin. The water felt wonderful and Mel made the most of it by relaxing in the heat with her eyes closed. When she opened them, Alice and her filthy clothes were gone. Mel pondered on everything she had seen since returning. As she soaped herself down she considered how she might relate everything to her two friends. She also worried over Rory. When they last met, Mel had harboured a teenage crush on him. Now he would be in his thirties and she really didn't know what to expect. She considered Cinder too. He eclipsed Rory now and Mel could only wonder at the speed of her falling in love with him. She thought too of the conversation she held with Cinder regarding elementals and remembered his words of how they could cause anyone whom they may take a shine to, to fall in love with them. Is that how it happened?

'Penny for your thoughts?'

Mel didn't notice Alice returning. The older woman stood leaning in the doorway with a mug in her hand. She set it down next to Mel.

'I made you some tea,' she said. 'When you're done go into my room – I've laid some clothes out on the bed for you. Don't be too long – Rory will be here soon and we'll have so much to discuss. I'll start dinner in a bit. Chicken okay?'

'I don't eat flesh...'

Mel hadn't even thought of those words. They tumbled out of her mouth by their own volition. Alice glanced at her curiously as the sentence reawakened an old memory.

'Since when were you ever a veggie?' she asked. 'I've seen you tuck enough burgers away in your time to feed an army. When did that come about?'

Confused, Mel could not give a proper answer.

'I don't know why I said that,' she mumbled. 'I don't really know why, but the thought of meat just doesn't seem right... Sorry.'

Alice smiled.

'It doesn't matter,' she responded kindly. 'I'll rustle something veggie up if that's what you'd prefer...'

'Thank you.'

Alice left once more and Mel completed her bath. She felt restless now and desperately wanted to meet Rory so that she might tell both of her friends of her travels. Briskly she towelled herself down leaving her skin reddened and glowing. It felt so good to be really clean at last as she wandered off in search of Alice's room. Alice's clothes were a little large, but that didn't matter. Shyly she descended the stairs, aware of voices from within the lounge. The bottom step creaked loudly causing the talking to stop abruptly and Alice appeared in the hallway. Placing a finger to her lips the older woman grasped Mel's wrist and moved her beside the lounge door. With a conspiratorial wink Alice gestured for Mel to remain in the hall. Slipping back into the lounge Alice spoke immediately.

'Okay bro,' she started. 'Put your tea down a minute. I had a visitor today... We had a visitor today... You might want to... Oh God, this is so difficult...'

'What has happened Alice? If it's bad news just tell me...'

Alice shook her head.

'It's not bad – in fact you'll be delighted. It's just that... Mel came home...'

For a few moments Rory just stared at his sister as he processed the information. Then he leapt up, his words bursting from him.

'MEL! You mean our Mel? Are you joking me?'

Rory's voice rose in timbre and the excitement could be heard in his tone. Mel could stand it no longer. Stepping forward she pushed the lounge door open and walked in.

Rory looked as though he'd seen a ghost. For what seemed like an age the pair just stared at each other. Alice broke the ice.

'One of you say something,' she pleaded.

In a moment Mel rushed into the room and Rory held her in a bear hug.  Eventually they parted and Rory, holding her at arm's length broke his silence.

'MEL!  How wonderful!  My God... I didn't think... Jesus Christ...  Are you all right?'
A few moments passed and then the full enormity of Mel's appearance kicked in.

'You're still seventeen!  You haven't...'

'I know.  Only a few days have passed for me.  Alice tells me that I've missed twenty years here... It's been rather difficult to take in...'

Rory ushered Mel to the sofa and made her sit.  Taking the seat next to her he took her hand and looking her in the eye asked the question that she had been waiting for.

'I'm sorry Mel, but I have to ask this... Willow... Is she here?'
Mel shook her head.

'No.  I'm sorry she isn't, but she's quite safe and well. We rescued her from Flint and...'

Tears began to fill Mel's eyes and she blinked them back angrily.  Rory squeezed her hand and Alice sat beside her. Alice spoke softly.

'Take your time Mel.  You don't have to relive it all now.  Yes, we are both anxious to hear your story, but only in your own time.  I think we should eat first and get used to having you home.  Rory, lay the table and I'll dish up. Mel, you just sit tight and relax.  Don't worry about anything; it's over - just chill out...'

'Chill out?'

'It means relax – take it easy - a modern term...'

Looking at Rory, Alice gestured with her head towards the kitchen and giving Mel one last look he dutifully followed his sister.  In the kitchen Alice spoke quietly to him.

'Don't push her, she's really fragile.  I don't know what she's been through, but when she walked in here this afternoon she looked like she'd been in a war zone – and her clothes were covered in dried blood... just go easy on her...'

'Blood? Is she hurt?'

'No. She said it wasn't hers, it belonged to a friend. I still don't know what happened – she hasn't told me much and I didn't like to ask. I helped her into the bath. From what I saw I think she's pretty unscathed physically other than a few cuts and bruises on her knuckles, but God knows what's going on in her head right now. She's lost twenty years, her Grandmother and her previous life just like that in only a few days. Poor thing must be so bloody confused – I know I am...'

Rory nodded. He let out his breath sharply and rubbed his hands across his face. There were so many questions, but where to start? For Rory that was relatively simple. His first line of enquiry would be about Willow. After that, once he heard Mel's story he just couldn't wait to hear about the world of the Fae. Old memories and new questions ran around inside his head then and as Alice dished up dinner he saw a movement out of the corner of his eye - a hint of ginger fur and the swish of a tail. Rory couldn't believe his eyes.

'COPPER!' he exclaimed loudly. 'Oh my God! Alice why didn't you say!'

'I thought I'd save that one up,' she giggled. 'Isn't it magnificent? We must have the oldest cat ever!'

Rory fell to his knees now ruffling Copper's fur and tickling her behind the ears. Copper purred and rubbed around Rory's feet as he stood up. Alice felt moved at seeing tears pouring down his face. Putting down her serving spoon she embraced her brother and hugged him closely.

'Come on bro,' she said. 'It's a real shocker, I know. I didn't know how to react when I first saw her either. But she's back and we all need to deal with it – Mel included. Now come on, let's eat and then maybe she may feel ready to talk to us.'

Alice had made a Spanish omelette filled with chopped potatoes and vegetables. She served a large helping of salad alongside it with some buttered bread. Once or twice they all made to speak at once and then Rory began to laugh. Alice got the giggles too and a moment later to their great relief Mel joined in. By the time they regained their composure they all felt more relaxed and Rory chanced a simple question.

'How did you get home Mel? How did you open the gateway?'

Mel put down her bread and answered softly.

'A friend opened it for me. They sent me back.'

'Willow?' asked Rory predictably.

'No. His name is Cinder... Dear Cinder...'

Tears welled up in Mel's eyes and Alice scolded Rory.

'Leave her be Rory. She'll tell us when she's ready. At least have the decency to let her finish eating.'

Alice's words caused Mel to laugh. She pulled a tissue from her pocket and wiped her running nose.

'It's okay Alice,' she said. 'Rory has never been known for his manners or tact. No change there...'

Rory began to apologise, but Mel interrupted.

'I said it doesn't matter. You must both be bursting to know everything. I will tell you all of it, but it has to be in the right order or it'll make no sense – and I'll probably miss bits out if I'm not careful. This dinner is lovely Alice, thank you.'

The conversation turned a little in Mel's favour as she began to probe with questions of her own. There would be many changes over twenty years and she wanted to know everything she had missed. They spoke mainly of local matters like the new housing estate and people they used to know. With the meal and washing up completed, Alice opened a bottle of wine and they retired to the sofa.

'There you are,' she said, handing a glass to Mel, 'I think you've earned this.'

'Thank you, although I prefer ale or mead…'

Alice gave her a curious look, but said nothing.

All armed with a glass of Alice's favourite Chardonnay they sat in the lounge and momentarily the awkward silence returned. Mel sipped her wine once or twice and then setting the glass down she addressed Rory.

'Do you still have Willow's ring hidden away?'

The question caught Rory on the back foot. When he didn't answer Mel tried again.

'You haven't lost it have you? Please tell me you still have it...'

Rory nodded.

'Yes I still have it, although it's not here – but it's safe, no fear of that.'

'She needs it. That's why they sent me back. I'm not sure I'd have come otherwise...'

Alice interrupted.

'But why not? This is your home Mel! We've missed you terribly. We've talked about you every day since...' Her voice trailed off. She sounded hurt and Mel immediately felt bad.

'I'm sorry,' she stammered. 'I didn't mean... It's just... You don't know what I've seen, where I've been and who I was with…'

Alice put down her drink and slipping an arm around Mel's shoulder she spoke softly.

'I'm sorry too. But you're right – we shouldn't judge you. But you have to know that for us it's been a living nightmare for twenty years. I already told you how we ended up lying to everybody, about how you disappeared that day. The police wouldn't leave us alone for months. Our mother and your grandmother kept on asking us over and over again what happened that day. Rory and I almost ended up as recluses – we couldn't go out anywhere without people asking about you. Having you home is going to be equally challenging. If you go out someone may recognise you and then the questions will start up again. We just need to get used to you being back and working out how to deal with it...'

Mel understood what Alice said. However, it didn't make her experience or personal losses any easier either. She nodded and replied.

'It's wonderful to be back, but I can't stay. I have to return Willow's ring and...'

'And what?' Rory asked.

'She wants you two to go back with me. For good. To live there...'

Alice choked on her wine, but Rory whooped with joy. When the clamour subsided Mel said,

'I have to give her the ring back to confirm her claim on her father's property – you must understand that. But she wants you too Rory – I mean, she *really* wants you...'

'But I'm twenty years older. When she left I was six years her junior... she wouldn't want me now; would she?'

'Yes she does, very much so – and from what I've learned it's the norm there for men to marry women who are ten or twenty years younger than they are. I shouldn't worry on that account... Not unless you already have someone here...'

'No – there's no one...'

'Hold on Rory,' Alice said. 'How can you just go and live in another world? What about our home, our jobs, our friends...'

Rory became agitated now. The thought that Willow might still want him after all this time amazed him. When he spoke, both Alice and Mel knew that he meant every word.

'If Willow wants me in her world then I'm going. I've spent the last twenty years worrying about her and Mel, and now I know that she's out there, wanting me... I'm not losing an opportunity like that. No way - not in a million years...'

217

Alice sighed. She didn't know how she should deal with this, but it could wait for now. Shrugging her shoulders she decided not to fight this tonight. There would be another day for that. Trying to calm the situation down she spoke gently to Mel.

'Are you ready to tell us what happened...? What you saw and what you did?'

'Yes I'm ready,' she answered. 'It's a very long story so don't expect to go to bed early. Pour me some more wine and I'll tell you it all...'

\*\*\*

# 15

# PREPARATION

Mel slept for much of the following day. With exhaustion taking over her body, she badly needed to rest. At just after four in the afternoon she awoke. Her head felt thick and her temples throbbed mercilessly. Groaning she sat up and took in her surroundings. Mel did not recall going to bed although she did remember relating her story to her friends the night before. Throwing off the duvet she found herself in her underwear. Her hand flew to her throat and to her dismay she found the silver whistle gone. In a panic she leapt up and then sighed with relief as she saw the precious object lying on the bedside cabinet. She slipped it back around her neck and padded off to the bathroom. Having showered and dressed Mel felt much better and as a grumbling in her belly reminded her of her hunger she made her way downstairs.

Just like the old days Alice and Rory were sitting at the kitchen table drinking tea. Rory had chosen to stay the night and being self-employed it was not a problem to take a few days off of work. Luckily for Alice, her shifts as a midwife meant she was now on rest days and consequently she could spend some time with Mel. Alice greeted her cheerily, but Rory stood and hugged her.

'You okay?' he asked.

She nodded and pulling herself free from his embrace, sat on a chair. She watched as Rory began making her some tea.

'What time did I go to bed?' she asked blearily.

'Nearly three,' Alice responded. 'You finished telling your story and then you just fell asleep. Rory carried you upstairs and I put you to bed. You didn't even stir.'

'Did you believe it? My story I mean…'

'Of course we believed you,' cut in Rory. 'How could we not believe you after our own involvement?'

'You took the whistle from around my neck,' Mel said accusingly to Alice.

'Yes I did,' she answered. 'I put it on the cabinet by the bed – I felt worried that the thong may get twisted around your neck as you slept.'

'Okay,' Mel replied, 'but don't do it again – I asked you yesterday not to touch it.'

Alice looked at Mel curiously, but said nothing. Rory, sensing the old animosity between the two females beginning to resurface interrupted. He set the tea down and Mel gratefully sipped it, watching as her two friends began to argue.

'Okay,' Rory said. 'We have to decide what happens next. I'm all for going into Eyedore. I'm still a bit overwhelmed with all of this, but having wanted to see Willow for so long now, I don't see how I can just stay here…'

Alice shook her head.

'I disagree,' she said. 'Our lives, our homes and our friends are here. Do you think we could give them up just like that? What happens if we return? Twenty years passed for Mel. Our homes would be repossessed and we'd have nowhere to live…'

Rory disagreed.

'Think about this if you want to Alice, but I'm definitely going back with Mel. Willow needs her ring and I want to be with Willow – simple really… But I want you to come too. You're my sister and I'd miss you… Please say you'll come?'

'I can't Rory. Not just like that. It's such a huge step to take! You think about it yourself! You'd be walking into who knows what. You've heard from Mel how violent it can be there. Do you really want to live in a world like that?'

'It's just such a wonderful opportunity Alice. How many people ever get the chance to visit somewhere like Eyedore? Yes, it's a risk and our lives would change forever, but ultimately I would be with Willow – and you heard what Mel said - about how she still wants me...'
Alice frowned and fought her corner vehemently.

'I still think you're wrong. Mel, you've been there. For Heaven's sake talk some sense into him!' Mel, thinking of Cinder sided with Rory.

'I'm sorry Alice, but I'll be going there no matter what. There's little for me here now and I want to be with Cinder. I understand how Rory feels about Willow and whatever you both decide, I will return there – alone if I must. I'm sorry, but there it is...'

Alice knew she could never win this particular argument. She had spent twenty years watching Rory pining over Willow. True that in the last few years he had calmed down somewhat, but his passion remained for Faerie folklore. He spent all of his spare time pursuing this subject and Alice knew in her heart that she could not stop him if he really insisted on going. Mel too had now lost her heart to a Fae being and demonstrated a similar obstinate streak over Eyedore. But Alice just couldn't make her own mind up on what she wanted for herself and that sense of uncertainty fed mostly on her fear. In the early days, like Rory, Alice desperately wanted to find a way through the gateway and go after Mel, but as time passed she accepted their failure and moved on. Mel coming home reignited the issue and her frightening tale of treachery and death terrified the older woman. For Alice the jury still remained out and would do so for some time to come. She watched as Mel and Rory began to discuss going back and she felt like an outsider.

*

The planning and debating went on for weeks and the remains of winter turned towards spring. Rory and Alice both had their jobs to consider and for much of the time Mel was left alone in Alice's house. Rory in particular threw himself into his Faerie researches, studying as much as possible before he entered that other realm. Alice on the other hand possessed less enthusiasm. Still reluctant to just leave her own world and embrace the opportunity gave her many a sleepless night. Her work suffered too, as constantly tired and distracted by her private thoughts she soldiered on. Mel amused herself in catching up on what she had missed out on over the last twenty years. The internet proved to be a most useful tool and she spent hours devouring information from websites on a daily basis.

At first they all agreed that the best option for Mel would be to remain in the house at all times. However, it soon became apparent that living in Eyedore only for a short time had caused Mel to acquire some Faerie attributes. Not only did she become fully vegetarian, but keeping her indoors away from fresh air, sunlight and the comfort of the woodland quickly took its toll. Like Willow, Mel began to sicken as she craved the outdoors. One afternoon Alice and Rory gave in and took her for a walk. They went along the old track and cut past the new housing estate. Mel hated it. The sight of the bricks, fences and access roads sickened her and just felt wrong, but when they made it to the edge of the woodland and walked beneath the trees Mel felt as though she had been given a shot in the arm. Laughing, she ran ahead and skipped about in glee. She grabbed at the foliage and pressed the soft spring leaves to her nose, sniffing in their scent. She kicked her way through swathes of leaves left over from the autumn and she cavorted about as though on springs. Alice and Rory stared in amazement and both were instantly reminded of the day twenty years before, when returning to the island they found Willow behaving in a similar manner. After that walk Mel went out every day. One afternoon a neighbour questioned Alice about the girl staying with them. She lied, saying she was the daughter of a cousin and would be staying for a few of months whilst her parents worked abroad. After the drama of Mel's original disappearance, lying had become second nature to both Rory and Alice. Mel never went out alone. Either Alice or Rory would always accompany her. Sometimes all three went out together. One memorable afternoon they drove her to the cemetery to visit her grandmother's grave, something she had been asking to do since coming home. On their arrival Rory and Alice withdrew, leaving Mel alone at the graveside to make her peace. For a time Mel just sat there looking at the headstone and drawing on her memories. Then she began to speak.

'I'm so sorry,' she said. 'I never intended to disappear like that, but it just sort of happened... When the gateway closed behind me I couldn't come home... I miss you so much Nanna...' Tears trickled down her cheeks and she ran her fingers across the headstone. She sniffed, took a deep breath and continued. 'I'm sorry for all the hurt I caused you. I can't imagine how you must have felt, but I suffered too... I only thought a few days had gone by... I'll never forget you Nanna; I love you so much... I'm sorry. Since coming home I've realised what I've lost. You always cared for me Nanna; you loved me and protected me. I should have been here to do the same for you. All those good times we missed out on... birthdays, Christmases... days out... I feel so bad... I need you to forgive me. Please... send me a sign or something, just to let me know you can hear me...'

She broke down and sobbed for several minutes, emptiness and anger filling her soul. And then it happened. On the headstone sat a robin. He chattered his song at her and then to Mel's amazement he flew over and alighted on her shoulder. Mel turned her head and through her tears she spoke to the little bird.

'Did Nanna or Cinder send you? Do they feel my pain? I've lost my Nanna, but I want Cinder so much... Tell Cinder I love him with all my heart... And tell Nanna I will always love her too...'

The little bird bobbed up and down and flew back to the gravestone. Mel spoke again.

'Fly to them! Give them this!' She blew a kiss towards the robin. For a moment he chattered back and then in a moment he took flight and vanished. The encounter left Mel feeling warm inside. The emptiness she experienced talking to her grandmother had been replaced by something else. She now felt forgiveness. The robin reminded her of Cinder too and that took away some of her pain.

When Rory and Alice returned to collect her, Mel was at peace. She went home in silence, but with a feeling of wonderment and forgiveness. The experience of that afternoon would remain with Mel for the rest of her life. Although she could never think of her grandmother without feeling regret and guilt she now had closure. That, along with Cinder's wonderful gift of the robin made her feel good about herself once more.

*

Another day Mel accompanied Alice on a shopping trip which almost courted disaster. During a tour around the shopping mall they encountered a woman called Gwen. She stopped to chat with Alice, but couldn't help glancing at Mel every few seconds. Eventually her curiosity got the better of her.

'I have to ask,' she said, 'but who's this? She looks just like that girl that disappeared from our class all those years ago – what was her name... Mandy? No that's not right...'

'Melissa,' cut in Alice. 'This is my cousin's daughter Sarah,' she lied. 'She's staying with us and I'd thank you not to mention that unfortunate time again. Too many painful memories…'

Alice cut the conversation short and scuttled off dragging Mel with her. After the stress of that particular encounter, Alice and Rory both insisted on Mel cutting her hair and dying it a different colour. Mel chose post box red. She felt unsure at first, but once done she really loved the result. A pair of funky sunglasses also helped and after that she attracted no more trouble.

\*

Spring moved towards summer and before they knew it the beginning of June arrived. Only three weeks lay between now and the solstice and Mel became more and more agitated. Most evenings she walked to the barrow and sat outside the entrance. Sometimes she would venture inside and run her hands over the wall. For Mel midsummer could not come quickly enough. Alice however, dreaded it. She had slipped comfortably into the new routine of having someone staying in her home. The talk nearly always turned to Willow, Eyedore or Cinder and they all enjoyed discussing the other world and the beings that lived there. However, no matter how much they discussed it Alice still feared the thought of living in a different world where mediaeval standards seemed to be the norm. She hated the thought of the violence and harshness, but on the other hand the rural and natural way of life also seemed quite appealing. Rory played on this chink in her armour. Whenever alone together the pair often discussed Alice's feelings, sometimes at great length and he would always endeavour to keep the conversation centred on her love of nature and a self-sufficient life style. Rory felt torn. More than anything he wanted to go and find Willow, but if Alice refused to go he did not know if he could leave her behind. One evening at the beginning of June Mel had gone to bed early and so Rory took the opportunity to sit with Alice in the garden and discuss the issue over a glass of wine. Settling beside her on the bench he gently broached the subject.

'Not long now Alice. Only a few weeks to go…'

'Yes.' Her reticence made him all the more determined.

'Have you thought about it anymore…?'

'It's all I've thought of for months Rory. I still don't know what to do…'

'You know what I want. For us all to go and stay there for good. Is it that hard?'

'It is for me. You have Willow. She is what drives you Rory. Seriously, if it wasn't for her, would you really consider going there to live?'

'Maybe… I don't know… But I do know this… I love her with all my heart. I always have… To not go would be…' He fell silent. Alice sighed. Like Rory her loyalties were split. Inside, a part of her wanted to say yes, to just do something rash in her life for once, but Alice had always been cautious. She voiced her thoughts.

'It frightens me Rory. I mean it really frightens me. Where would we live? How would we live? What if Willow tired of you? It's a one way trip – that's what holds me back. Once we take that step there's no coming back – ever!'

'I know. I'm scared too you know… Like you say, there's no coming back. Yes, it could all go horribly wrong, but if I never do it I'll regret it for the rest of my life. You must see that!'

'Yes.'

'All I want is to see Willow again. But I can't leave you behind. Please come with me Alice… You're my only family… I love you and I'd miss you…'

'Stop trying to make me feel guilty Rory. I can't make a decision just like that. I need to think on it.'

'You've been thinking on it for weeks…'

'I know. It's all I bloody well think about! Do you know I forgot a woman in labour at work last week? I just left her alone in the delivery room and drifted off into this fantasy world of yours. When I finally remembered her and went back her baby was practically born! So far she doesn't seem to have made a complaint, but I really screwed up – because of this! Yes, I'll think about it, but don't press me. I'll decide in my own time, not with you breathing down my neck!'

For a time there was an awkward silence between them and then Rory spoke again.

'I'm sorry Alice, really I am. I know it's difficult for you…'

'Difficult? Yes it's bloody difficult alright!'

'Sorry…'

'Don't keep saying that. Look, I'll sort myself out okay? This whole situation terrifies me. But I do understand how much you want this… And if you left me behind I'd never forgive you…'

'Are you saying you'll come with me?' Alice could hear the hope in his voice.

'I never said that. I said I understand. Come here…'
Alice leaned across and wrapped her arm about Rory. She pulled him close in a hug and kissed his cheek. Rory sat there pressing his face against her neck.

'Oh buggar!'

Alice pulled away and stood up, wiping down her top where she had spilled the red wine. She poked her tongue out at her brother.

'That was your fault you bloody moron! Making me all emotional! I'll have to put it in soak before it stains.'
Rory made to speak, but Alice held up her hand.

'Not another word! I'll think on it. That's the best you're getting. Now come indoors and help me find something to clean this wine off with…'

\*

During the final weeks leading up to the solstice Mel discussed retrieving Willow's ring with Rory. He insisted it remain secure until needed, and he refused to reveal its whereabouts to her. They also discussed what they should take with them when they went.

Alice always joined in these conversations. Something inside her had changed. Ever since that night when she talked with Rory she sensed there could only be one outcome to her decision. She would not admit it to Rory yet, but every day she became more committed to joining him. It had been the look in his eyes that night that had finally swayed her. She knew that to prevent him from going would be wrong. Rory needed Willow and Alice could not watch him walk away, never to return. But she still couldn't bring herself to say it. Instead she just busied herself, checking lists and biding her time until finding the opportune moment to tell Rory the good news.

Everything could only be carried and so only essential items would be taken. When Mel told them that Willow had requested more 'nut butter' Alice and Rory laughed loudly. Rory agreed they could take a few jars, but the weight would limit just how many they could carry. When the notion of actually going to Eyedore and meeting Willow first became a reality Rory had decided to make her a special gift. His folklore researches suggested the perfect item. He spent much of his spare time over the last few months carving a 'lovespoon' for Willow from a piece of old seasoned oak. The design showed a heart carved on the end of the handle followed by a copy of Willow's ring, Rory and Alice's family coat of arms and a cluster of acorns and oak leaves. It took him weeks of patient carving, but Rory always excelled at wood work. On looking up similar items on the internet Alice and Mel were both amazed at the standard of his craftsmanship. He'd finished the spoon off by giving it several generous coats of beeswax and polished it until it shone. He hoped desperately that Willow would like it. Mel wanted to take Cinder some kind of gift too. She possessed few practical skills herself so Alice helped her make a drawstring bag from soft leather. His own bag she noticed looked old and worn and in danger of falling apart.

\*

During the final week Alice finally informed Rory and Mel of her decision. One evening as they ate their evening meal she broached the subject.

'You should both know that I have made my mind up. I shall be coming with you to Eyedore.' She set down her knife and fork and waited for the reaction. It was not what she expected. Mel just stared as Rory stood up, walked around the table and silently embraced his sister. As they parted she saw the tears in his eyes. 'That bad Rory? I thought you wanted me to go… What, no cheering? No gloating that you got your way? '
He laughed then.

'Want you to go? Of course I bloody want you to go! Alice, you've just made me so happy – thank you!' He kissed her on the cheek and then Mel was in their arms too, joining in the celebration. When they re-seated themselves Alice confirmed her commitment.

'The last thing I want is to leave here and go and live in a different realm. However, I do know that you will most likely go anyway. I can't sit back and watch you walk away Rory – and you too Mel, not a second time. I will come with you and share your futures. Just don't think we can ever come back…'

The mood was rather strange. Alice's cool acceptance rather than any outright desire to join the expedition into Eyedore tempered any real celebration. However, she knew that inside Rory and Mel would both be delighted and that made her happy too. She felt better now having said it out loud. She hoped with all her heart that it would be the right decision.

*

The solstice fell on Friday the twenty first of June and the sun would rise at precisely four minutes past five in the morning. The trio decided to go to bed early the night before, rise at around two o'clock and have a last breakfast in their old home. With everything pre-packed they would set off for the barrow at around four thirty and wait for the appointed time to arrive. Then Mel would use her whistle to summon Cinder. They had no real plan for failure other than to return home. Both Mel and Rory were terrified that the gateway would not open. If it didn't then there would be no way of getting through. Neither of them mentioned this fear, preferring to keep the notion to themselves and not to tempt the Fates. Between them, Alice and Rory composed a long and complicated letter explaining everything, including the truth of Mel's disappearance all those years before. They did not expect anyone who found it to believe a word of it, but it spoke the truth and gave them closure. They had taken several photographs of themselves with Mel on her return and these, along with some old ones of the trio back in the early nineties were included within the lengthy document to reinforce their written words.

The last day in their own world proved hectic and deadly serious. No one made any jokes as possessions were packed, letters written to friends and of course the retrieval of Willow's family ring. Finally, Rory revealed to Mel the whereabouts of the precious Fae jewellery. It lay hidden in a safety deposit box at the local bank. Rory had made an appointment to collect the ring at two o'clock in the afternoon. All three arrived at the bank in a state of trepidation. The process of collecting the ring turned out to be quite straight forward. After completing a small amount of paperwork Rory would be taken to a secured room, given a key and left alone. His hands shook as he opened the box. He always made regular checks a couple of times a year and felt confident that the ring would have come to no harm. He did however receive one surprise. Along with the ring Rory had also deposited the bag of gold coins given to him by Flint. He supposed that they may be useful and opening the bag tipped them out into his hand. For a few moments he stared in disbelief and then a knowing smile spread across his face. He knew of the legend of 'fool's gold' through many of his Faerie researches. It took the form of coin given over to humans by an untrustworthy member of the Fae as payment for some kindness or task. Legend said that after a time the coins would transform into something completely worthless. Instead of money in his hand, Rory held a pile of broken flint chips. Smiling, he returned them to the bag and placed them back in the box. The ring, he carefully wrapped in a piece of felt and placed it in the pocket of his jacket and zipped it up. All the way home Rory felt immensely vulnerable. Carrying the ring made him feel as though he were being watched and by the time they arrived home he felt completely paranoid. Alice and Mel did their best to calm his nerves by talking him into going over their plans for the night. They checked, repacked and checked again their bags. Finally, Mel bleached her hair and removed the bright red colour she had sported for several weeks. Cinder, she felt would not approve of the unnatural hue.

Alice prepared as much of their early morning breakfast in advance as she could. Mel and Rory made up packs of sandwiches and fruit to take with them along with a few packets of dried cat food for Copper. Each of them would carry a back pack laden down with their clothes, food, gifts and a few personal possessions. Their final dinner in the house became a rather sombre affair with everyone eating silently. Alice and Rory opted for a takeaway of southern fried chicken and chips, partly because no one felt much like cooking and partly because where they were going takeaway food would be a thing of the past. Mel refused the chicken and ate eggs instead. With the meal done and everything cleared away it was still only just after eight o'clock. However, with an early start ahead of them they wanted a decent sleep and so they went to bed.

The bleeping of the alarm woke Alice abruptly. Sitting up she rubbed her eyes and yawned. She couldn't believe what they all intended to do. However, an agreement had been struck and despite her earlier misgivings Alice held a secret longing to see the world from which Willow originated. She would never have confessed that particular piece of information to Rory in a million years, but curiosity really took a hold of her now. Climbing out of bed she washed, dressed and trotted downstairs to start cooking the last breakfast in her old home. She felt sad at that particular thought, but when Mel and Rory bounded down the stairs giggling together she couldn't feel melancholy for long. They made the meal a jolly affair, but whilst Rory and Alice opted for the full English variety Mel ate a simpler version. She shunned the sausage and bacon, but made short work of scrambled eggs, mushrooms and tomatoes. Strangely, when they were done Alice insisted on washing up and putting everything away neatly. She felt she could not leave her house looking a mess knowing that at some point strangers would enter here and begin a search for clues as to their whereabouts. Rory wanted to just leave it all. Not because he was lazy, but more to give an air of mystery like that of the legend of the Marie Celeste. Alice refused point blank and dutifully washed and cleared everything away on her own.

At a quarter past four they were ready to leave. They left the letters, bundles of photographs and a few items such as Flint's arrow with its written warning in the centre of the kitchen table. They did not expect anyone to ever believe their story, but no one really cared. Between them they took one final look around, put on their shoes and back packs, picked up Copper and walked outside. For all of them it didn't feel real. Only Mel knew what to expect and so Rory and Alice took their lead from her. She set off quickly, anxious not to waste a single second in case something should delay them along the way. She needn't have worried for with the first few streaks of daylight showing on the eastern horizon they soon found themselves outside the entrance to the barrow and on the threshold of a new life.

***

# 16

## The Time Of The Twinned Suns

Rory checked the time on his phone. It showed four fifty five, leaving them only nine minutes to wait. At five o'clock they entered the barrow by the light of a torch. Mel fumbled inside her top and retrieved the silver whistle. Rory looked at his phone again. Two minutes past five. The tension became unbearable and Mel began to tremble. Alice placed an arm around her shoulder and gave her a squeeze. Rory, holding Copper broke the silence.

'Four minutes past. Do it Mel!'

Alice released her hold on her friend and with a shaking hand Mel lifted the whistle to her lips. Taking a deep breath she closed her mouth around it and blew as hard and as long as she could. Only just audible, the note sounded discordant, filling the ancient chamber and bouncing off the walls. Mel blew until her breath ran out. Rory spoke.

'It hasn't worked. Do it again!'

Mel shook her head.

'No. Cinder said to blow only once, long and hard. Be patient, he'll come.'

'But where is he? I know what you said Mel, but...'

They all felt it. Just a tiny movement as though the floor shifted slightly, but it silenced Rory. Then, as they stared at each other in desperation it happened and the wall next to Alice rolled away just as it had twenty years before. Staring through the opening Mel shouted excitedly as she glimpsed the silhouette of her beloved Cinder with the wheat field behind him. Urging her friends into action

Mel pushed them forward into the tunnel and followed on behind.

'Quick!' she said. 'Before it closes!'

Passing through they all felt light headed and as they emerged into the daylight Rory dropped to his knees. Hands gripped his arm and pulled him up and a rough, but kindly voice welcomed him to this unknown place.

'Steady on your feet man. You must be the one they call Master Rory. I can't go delivering you to Mistress Willow covered in bruises now can I?'

Standing up and feeling rather foolish Rory found himself looking down upon a small grey robed figure with piercing blue eyes. Laughter lines bordered those eyes and a hand clapped Rory roughly on the shoulder. Embarrassed he could only stare back and Mel, sensing his awkwardness stepped in.

'Cinder, this is Rory and Alice.'

Pulling back the hood from his robe Cinder smiled.

'Pleased to meet you Mistress Alice,' he said politely. 'I've heard much about you, but young Mel there failed to tell me what a beauty you are!'

Alice blushed and stammered something unintelligible and then Mel, bursting with joy stole the moment. Unable to contain herself any longer she threw herself at Cinder, almost knocking him over. Hugging him to her she showered the top of his head with kisses and only stopped when he withdrew making mock gestures of defeat. Laughing they fell back into each other's arms whilst Alice and Rory watched patiently.

'I've dreamed of this moment for three moons!' Mel said, joyfully.

'Just two days for me my lovely, but it felt like three moons – welcome back.'

They stood kissing until Rory interrupted.

'Excuse me you two,' he began, 'but where's Willow? I thought she'd be here to meet us.'

Cinder broke free from Mel's affections and answered gravely.

'The Stag King won't let her leave his protection. Flint is still at large somewhere and some of his followers may be in the area. We've spent enough time tarrying here – we should move on.'

'So is it dangerous for us?' Rory enquired.

'It could be,' said Cinder, 'but I think not. It's Willow that they want – unless of course they realise that you have her ring – you do have it do you not?'

Rory nodded his response and Alice joined in.

'What do we do now?' she asked, 'walk somewhere?'

'Exactly that,' Cinder replied. 'We should get moving.'

To Mel he said,

'We're going to stay at Hazel and Barleycorn's tonight. Are you comfortable with that?'

'Well I am,' she responded, 'but how are they? Has anyone told them yet about poor Tansy?'

Cinder nodded, a shadow passing over his face.

'Yes, I told them straight after I sent you home. They were very distressed of course, but they don't blame you in any way. They were just as concerned about you. I told them you were safe and that you'd be coming back to us. That seemed to help them for they desperately want to see you again. And in addition to that the Stag King has been rather busy. Tansy was buried yesterday in the forest near to her home. At some point we'll visit her grave, but not today.'

'I should like to visit her soon. Thank you Cinder. It's good to know she's been treated with respect.' Wiping her face Mel attempted to smile and said, 'We should move on.'

They began walking. Cinder and Mel led the way and Alice and Rory followed behind. Neither of them said much, but preferred to listen and take in the details of their surroundings. Then Rory spotted a familiar shape in the landscape.

'Hey!' he said, 'that looks just like Glastonbury Tor, but without the church tower.'

'It is Glastonbury Tor,' Mel stated, 'but as it would have been centuries ago.'

'What is it called here?' Rory asked. Cinder replied.

'We call it 'The Isle of Apples,' my friend. It's named after the orchards which cover the lower slopes. In our world the Tor is on an island surrounded by a great lake. It's a magical place, being highly sacred to our Goddess – the Great Earth Mother. There's another gateway there where we can move between worlds. There are many gateways, although some have fallen into disuse over the years.'

Rory nodded. He knew of the legendary and mythological importance of Glastonbury in both the Pagan and Christian traditions. Being a gateway into the realm of the Faeries was just one small detail amongst a plethora of old folk tales.

The sun climbed rapidly as they walked. Copper ran alongside them free and happy. Once or twice they caught glimpses of Fae peasants working in the fields and at one point they noticed a small group of young men and women who wore nothing but a few garlands of summer flowers. They danced in a meadow whilst a tiny man played music on a pipe. Mel commented on this. She remembered her first journey here when she encountered no one along the way. Cinder explained that in the few days since Flint vanished, the population were already going back to their old routines. The scantily clad dancers were celebrating the solstice and acting out a fertility dance in a bid to ensure a bumper crop in the fields. Alice raised an eyebrow at their near nudity and looked at Rory, but he said nothing. Clearly, there would be much to learn here.

The journey proved uneventful and before midday they were at the fork in the road that led to Hazel and Barleycorns home. Mel felt uncomfortable. A part of her desperately wished to see the old couple again, but another part dreaded the meeting. Despite Cinders re-assurances she still blamed herself for delaying Tansy on the road and getting her killed. Just before they entered the clearing where the roundhouse stood Cinder, sensing her mood spoke gently to her.

'Listen to me. They don't blame you in any way. You didn't cause Tansy's death. I saw what happened. Never feel bad about facing them. By acknowledging their acceptance of what has happened will help them both immensely. Tansy played a part in this, but now she's gone. They know you helped her flee that place and for that they owe you a great debt. They cannot wait to see you Mel, so feel no shame in their presence.'

Cinder rarely said so much in one go and Mel appreciated his words and found some comfort within them. She nodded understandingly.

'Alright,' she responded meekly. 'I'm sure you're right, but it still hurts me just thinking about what happened. One moment she was beside me and the next...'

'I know, but you must let it go. You can change nothing. Remember her as full of life. As for now, she's travelled to the west and entered the Summerland. She's well cared for.'

'Thank you.'

Mel buried her face in Cinders neck for a few moments and then with a startling show of strength pulled away and said to Alice and Rory,

'Come on then. Let's go and introduce you to our friends.'

In a few moments they were in the clearing and Alice and Rory stared open mouthed at the circular dwelling. Rory let out a whistle of appreciation.

'It's an Iron Age round house! Bloody Hell – it's amazing! Can we go inside?'

Alice laughed.

'Iron Age?' she queried. 'I thought these people couldn't go near iron!'

Rory pulled a face at her as he made his way towards the door. As he approached, a small man with a bald head and short beard came out of the house. Seeing the group his face lit up in a smile and then he trotted down the path to meet them, shouting at the top of his voice.

''AZEL! 'azel! They're 'ere! Young Mel's back – Goddess, 'ow I missed that lass!'

He fell into Mel's arms and hugged her for all he was worth. A few moments later a woman came out of the door and together the pair almost smothered Mel in their desire to greet her.

Alice, Rory and Cinder stood back and allowed the old couple to fuss over their friend. When they finally withdrew Mel gestured towards her companions and introduced them properly. After what seemed an age of hand shaking, hugging and kissing, the four travellers were escorted into the roundhouse. Like Mel before them Rory and Alice were amazed at the warmth and homeliness of the place. They were offered seats on the log benches around the hearth and accepted gratefully. After being given mugs of mead an awkward moment of silence arose. Seeing everyone's embarrassment Hazel spoke to Mel. As she spoke she stared blankly into the hearth.

'Cinder told us 'ow you 'elped free our girl. May the Goddess bless you Dearie!'

Hazel wept and Mel and Barleycorn moved to comfort her. Rory and Alice felt great discomfort at this. Having never even met Tansy they were clearly outsiders to this discussion. They could only sit and wait patiently whilst Hazel, Barleycorn and Cinder along with Mel quietly discussed the tragedy. Eventually the melancholy conversation ended and after a few minutes of gloomy silence Hazel stood up, and putting on a brave face announced that they should eat. The meal was simple fayre, but good. Warm crusty bread, sheep's cheese, and a variety of salad items – some of which the humans had never seen before. A dish of some unknown stew appeared for Copper which she seemed to enjoy. Barleycorn offered a choice of home brewed mead or ale. Initially they ate in silence, but Rory, keen to learn about this world began to ask questions. It lifted the mood and in a short time they were all conversing with one another. Eventually, having resisted for some considerable time Rory asked the inevitable question.

'Where's Willow? When will I get to see her?'
They all looked to Cinder in anticipation of a reply. The little man put down his bread and spoke.

'I told you earlier Rory, Willow is being protected by the Stag King. She's not being held against her will, but for the moment it's safer for her to remain where she is. We're staying here tonight with these good people. In the morning we'll have almost a full day's journey ahead of us, but by this time tomorrow you should be able to hold her in your arms for she's just as keen as you for the two of you to be reunited.'

'I just want to hold her. I can't believe that twenty years have passed for me, but for her it is only a matter of days. It is difficult to get my head around it. Will she even be interested in me still? I've aged twenty years since she last saw me – now I'm thirty eight! How does that work?'
Cinder smiled and Rory thought he mocked him, but Cinder responded kindly.

'I wouldn't concern yourself too much with that thought my friend. Here in Eyedore it's traditional for women or girls to handfast with a man ten, fifteen or even twenty years their senior. That makes you very eligible to her. Also, I don't know if Mel has told you, but Willow – like me, is half elemental. That means that when she decides she wants someone then it's unlikely – highly unlikely that she'll ever change her mind. I think, Master Rory that like it or not, Willow has given you her heart to keep. Be sure that you look after it.'

Rory looked embarrassed, but inside he felt elated. Alice asked a question.

'Handfast? What's that?'

Rory answered her.

'It's a very old term sis. It means to conjoin with another – we'd say marry...'

'Marry! You're going to marry her?'

'No – I'm going to handfast her – if she'll have me. A handfasting is like a contract. Traditionally it can be for a year and a day, for life until one partner dies or it can be made for all eternity. I don't know all the details, but it is similar to a Christian wedding. Vows are taken and there is a ceremony.'

Alice looked curiously at Rory, but for now she said nothing. The talk of handfasting Willow appalled her. She made up her mind to discuss this with Rory when they were alone.

Sensing that Alice did not approve and wanting to avoid confrontation before their hosts, Rory subtly changed the subject. Turning to Cinder he asked,

'What are the plans from here on? We go to meet Willow tomorrow – then what? We have come here with Mel and have no idea of what we are getting into. Our own world is rapidly moving forward whilst we sit here talking – if we went back our old home would probably be owned by someone else – so putting it in simple terms we can't go back - ever. It would be far too difficult to explain our disappearance and return years later with no age difference. Mel got away with it because when she turned up at our home we knew where she had been and what happened to her. Alice and I don't have that luxury. Can we sensibly stay here?' Cinder nodded. He sounded very positive about the humans remaining in Eyedore.

'Yes,' he said. 'You may all stay. Much as our worlds are different and rare as it is, humans do settle here. Rory – Willow will undoubtedly want you to stay. Alice, as his sister you are very welcome too. Now, Mel, I believe Hazel has a proposition to put to you.'

They all turned to Hazel who looked dewy eyed and uncomfortable.

'Mel,' she said. 'When you stayed with us a few days back it were as though our lovely daughter were 'ome. You weren't 'er but you filled the gap she'd left be'ind. She won't be comin' 'ome now – we knows that. Barlcycorn an' I 'ave discussed this at length and we wants you to come 'ere an' live with us.'

Mel's jaw dropped. She had no idea that Hazel or Barleycorn thought so highly of her. She felt humbled, but at the same time confused. She assumed that she would spend all of her time with Cinder. Feeling betrayed she looked at him for guidance. Cinder knew her thoughts. The meal being over he spoke to the group collectively.

'I think Mel is a little overwhelmed with your offer Hazel,' he said. 'I think a walk with her may help clear her head. Would you excuse us?'

When they went outside an awkwardness had manifested itself. Mel spoke first.

'I thought when I came back I would be with you,' she said quietly. Cinder stopped and turned to face her. Taking both her hands in his he spoke softly.

'Dear sweet Mel. For now that just isn't possible. There are things about me you don't know or understand... My craft rules my life. In three moons from now I have to travel north to spend time studying some of the higher mysteries. I'll be gone for four seasons...'

'A year? NO! I've waited months to come back and be with you and now you're leaving? Please Cinder – that's too cruel... Please, please say you won't go...'

He shook his head.

'I cannot do that. It's the final part of my training as a healer and spellmaker. I've spent my whole life working towards this. It's only one year out of a lifetime. Hazel and Barleycorn would love to keep you safe for me until I return. It's a kind and generous offer. When I return we'll be together for good.'

Mel remained silent, but the tears running down her face spoke of her pain. Cinder embraced her and pulled her close. Reaching up he kissed her gently on the lips and continued.

'Remember what I told Rory about Willow. She and I are both elementals. I've given you my heart Mel – I *will* come back and claim you, have no fear of that.'

'But a year – a whole bloody year - can't I go with you?'

'No. The Gifted Ones would not allow it. Your presence would cause me too many distractions. When I return I'll truly be one of them. Then and only then will I be able to do as I please. My life since I was a boy has been bound to them. I've spent the last two years as you call them as a travelling healer and Cunning Man. Now I have to complete my training by learning the deeper mysteries and discovering and mastering the skills of Second Sight and Soul Searching. A year will pass quickly. I promise you Mel that I *will* come back for you.'

'It sounds as though I have no choice.' She said the words bitterly.

'Yes you have a choice. You could forget me and find someone more worthy of you and if that is what you want I'll give you my blessing.'

'NO! I want you Cinder! How could you even suggest that? I thought you loved me...'
Mel glared at Cinder defiantly and he embraced her once more.

'You silly, silly girl. I love you more than anything! That's why I give you that choice. I would never bind you to me if I thought it would make you unhappy. I have to go away, but if you're willing to wait for me – and it's only for four seasons, I promise to make you mine when I return. In the short time I've known you I've come to love you so much Mel...'

She gave in. Arguing would be futile and if Cinder insisted on leaving, she wanted to enjoy what time they had remaining together. Sniffing she replied in a small voice.

'I'll wait for you. I want no one else. But promise me something?'

'Anything.'

'Promise that when you leave you'll think of me every day. Promise me that at every opportunity you'll send me a robin and above all, promise that you'll never stop loving me...'

Cinder smiled and flashed his blue eyes at her.

'That is three promises, but I will honour all of them, for you.'

They kissed again, but this time it was not a simple peck on the cheek. This kiss held real passion that set both their hearts racing. Mel felt crushed by Cinder's news, but the kiss invigorated her. She felt a fluttering in her belly. She wanted him, but fear held her back. Her head buzzed with excitement and she could feel emotion building in her. When the kiss ended they held each other. Neither wanted to let go, but inevitably one of them had to. Cinder finally loosened his embrace and they parted. Mel still felt upset, but they now shared a clear understanding. She loved Cinder in a way she never thought possible before. She also knew in her heart that he felt the same way about her too. Life may not have been perfect at that moment, but it came very close. Together, contented and holding hands they returned to the comfort of the round house.

\*\*\*

# 17

# REUNITED

The following morning Barleycorn roused everyone. As before Mel slept in Tansy's old bed whilst everyone else made do with a pile of sheepskins on the floor. He scuttled about the roundhouse giving orders for them to rise and get washed and ready for breakfast. Mel led her friends outside and showed them the river. Alice loved it. Never one to be shy she promptly followed Mel's lead and stripped off to her underwear, washing herself down with the cold water as best as she could. In typical male fashion Rory made do with just splashing his face and neck. When they were done they re-entered the house to find breakfast ready. After the previous days long trek across the countryside they were all hungry, and when Hazel presented each of them with a generous helping of barley porridge they all voiced their gratitude. Thick slices of bread toasted over the open fire and spread heavily with homemade butter followed the porridge. When they were done with eating there were steaming mugs of a herbal tea that smelt strongly of lemons. Hazel made it by steeping a handful of leaves from a lemon balm shrub in hot water. It tasted subtle, but refreshing and Rory drank three mugs before deciding that asking for more would simply be bad manners. Whatever else may be strange here Rory decided, the food surpassed his expectations.

With breakfast done, the conversation inevitably turned to the journey ahead of them. Rory desperately wanted to get started. He remembered Cinder's comment of the night before that by the end of the following day he would be reunited with Willow. He intended to keep Cinder to his word. The more he thought of her the more desperate he became. In his mind he could see her sweet smile and he could smell her personal odour of earth and leaves and it became an image he returned to constantly.

Mel assumed they would meet Willow at the King's encampment in the forest, but Cinder corrected her on her assumption. The Stag King it seemed had gone back to his home and taken Willow with him. Detachments of his men still scoured the countryside for Flint and his followers whilst another group were despatched to Oak Hall to search the place for any sign of where Flint may have gone. Hazel and Barleycorn would also join them on their journey, for they wished to thank the King for treating their fallen daughter so reverently.

As the group set off, the humans watched in wonder as Hazel carried out a peculiar ritual. Just inside the doorway on a shelf sat a tiny hand carved figure made of stone. No one noticed it until Hazel took it down. The carving looked crude and represented the body of a heavily pregnant, large breasted woman. The head possessed no features and the arms and legs were mere stumps, but the fecund female form could clearly be seen. Taking the small figurine in her hand Hazel took it outside. Uttering a few unintelligible words to the carving she kissed it, bent down, scooped a small hollow in the earth in front of the door and placed the figure within it. She carefully covered it over, stood up and bowed her head and turning to the others announced herself ready to leave. Filled with curiosity Alice whispered to Rory.

'Why did she do that?'

Rory, drawing on his historical knowledge made an educated guess.

'I believe that carving is a representation of their Goddess – their Great Earth Mother. I think Hazel left Her there to protect their home while they are away – a sort of talisman. Let's hope She does Her work!'

The day promised to be a good one. There were virtually no clouds in the sky and a gentle breeze played about their faces. They found no shade as they began the journey, but Cinder promised that further along the track they would be under the cover and protection of light woodland. They soon passed the meadow where the day before the dancers had capered around singing. Today the field stood empty save for a few garlands of wilted flowers still scattered around to mark their former presence.

Rory and Alice were both still finding everything here a huge novelty. The sheer fact that this world actually existed at all boggled the mind to say the least. Like Mel before them they noticed the vividness of the colours, the enhanced sounds and smells and the sheer beauty that surrounded them. They were constantly turning their heads to look at this and that and commenting to each other on everything they saw. Mel and Cinder were walking ahead holding hands and talking together as though they were the only people on the road whilst Hazel and Barleycorn lagged behind. Finding herself walking side by side with Rory, Alice now deemed this the right moment to broach the subject of Willow.

'Do you really intend to marry Willow?' she asked bluntly.

Her question caught Rory unawares as he gawped at a small group of peasants in the distance working in the fields. Sensing conflict he let out a sigh.

'Alice, please don't presume to talk me out of this. I've spent the last twenty years waiting to be reunited with the woman of my dreams. I've tried a few relationships since Willow left, but they all failed because I never gave up on her. I could never commit to anyone else in case she ever came back. Now, after all that time I'm actually going to meet her – today! You can say what you like, but I won't change my mind. No way!'

'But she's not even human! How can you even consider it? And she's so small! What would happen if she fell pregnant by you? It could kill her! Could she even get pregnant by you? For God's sake Rory see some sense!'

Rory stopped walking. He didn't raise his voice, but turned to Alice and spoke firmly to her.

'I mean it. You will not talk me round Alice. You are my sister and I love and respect you dearly and I always value your opinions, but I'll tell you this – I love Willow more than I've ever loved anybody. I've never, ever felt this way about anyone. I've thought of her every single day since she left us. I sense her in my sleep and I smell and think of her every single day and I'm not giving her up now. Don't ever ask me this again Alice. I appreciate your concern, but please leave it there...'

Alice made to speak, but Rory shushed her by placing his finger over her lips. Blinking back tears she tasted defeat. She nodded sheepishly and turning away continued walking, her mind still reeling. Putting one foot in front of the other she did her best to accept Rory's love for Willow, but it would prove difficult to come to terms with. Up until now, in her own mind Alice still believed that at some point they would return home to Somerset. Now the reality of their situation struck home, filling her with fear. However, Alice remained a strong minded and resolute woman and whatever challenges she may encounter in the coming months she decided, she would meet them head on.

Before midday, Cinder's statement of the morning proved to be correct. Before the sun began to really beat down they thankfully found themselves beneath the welcome cover of the trees as promised. The heat and the damp woodland floor made for a powerful combination. The odours of moss, leaves, bark and a plethora of other unidentified smells continually assaulted their nostrils. Rory looked around hopefully, half expecting to see Willow come bounding out from amongst the trees. When Cinder called a halt at a small clearing and declared that they should eat, Rory tried to argue the point that they should continue on their way. For him, any delay in reaching Willow would be intolerable. Cinder talked him round. His big blue eyes bored into Rory's as he said,

'We need to eat. Hazel and Barleycorn need to rest. Don't be selfish. Willow will be there for you later. You should eat – and the sun is hot so you need to drink. The longer we stand here arguing about it the longer it is before we set off again. Sit and eat man.'

Hazel had done them proud with the packed lunches. Each package contained bread, cheese, sliced onion, nuts, berries and an apple. Barleycorn unexpectedly produced a couple of flasks of ale which also proved to be highly popular. Nearby, a small stream trickled past and around some of the rocks grew a large clump of watercress. Cinder pulled up a few handfuls and handed it around and it made a pleasant peppery addition to an already welcome lunch. They ate all of their food, but Cinder showed no concern. Before the end of the day they would be at the Stag King's home where food and drink were more than abundant. If the worst happened and they were delayed on the road he had no doubt that he could forage something to eat from within the woodland that they travelled through. Their meal complete they set off once more.

\*

*As they settled back into their march no one saw the single pair of eyes that followed their progress. Their stalker was well gifted in the art of concealment and tracking and had followed them ever since they left the roundhouse. Lowering the foliage he had lifted to view them he waited for a short time before resuming his silent pursuit. For now he felt content to merely observe. Information provided knowledge and in turn, knowledge gave power. The Master would be pleased with his report.*

\*

With the day progressing into late afternoon the small group emerged from the woods to find the road widening out. Amongst the trees they encountered no one, but almost as soon as they left the woods behind them and came out amongst open fields the peasant classes seemed to be everywhere. Everyone appeared friendly and curious at the sight of the humans. Often they were hailed and they returned the waves and smiles with relish. As they strode on along the edge of a field of crops they all noticed the workers here were both male and female of all ages. They were hoeing in amongst the crops which appeared to be turnips or swedes. It must have been thirsty work and even as Rory looked on, a busty young wench set down her hoe and picked up a large water skin and drank from its spout. She splashed water on her face and chest and waved cheerily at the group of travellers as they passed by. Rory found himself brought to his senses by a cuff around the ear.

'Stop ogling. Isn't Willow the woman of your dreams? Not that floozy!' Alice said.

She still smarted from her failed attempt to get Rory to see sense over his infatuation with Willow. Rory just grinned back at her.

'No harm in looking sis – just admiring a bit of local beauty.'

Alice remained tight lipped. She refused to be drawn into an argument any more. She continued to walk and decided that for the time being she preferred to ignore her brother.

Walking past the rural landscape they came upon their first clue that they may be nearing somewhere of special significance or of a higher status. Already they had seen a couple of well-maintained stone circles where the stones themselves were clean and cared for and the surrounding grass neat and well shorn, but as they rounded a bend, there before them stood a stone built, rectangular tower.

It thrust itself up amongst the surrounding trees in a way that could only be described as wondrous. The lower section was of dressed stone blocks covered in a layer of old flaking render, the only break in the stone work being a solid looking green door. There were no windows in the lower level at all. Higher up, the building widened out, giving the effect of a small house being perched on the top of a tall narrow plinth. A pitched roof of clay tiles topped off the structure whilst stone mullioned windows and window boxes of living flowers graced the walls. Again, old decaying render peeled from the walls giving the impression that the structure had been there for centuries. The smell of wood smoke also pervaded the area suggesting that someone lived within. Despite her irritated mood Alice passed comment.

'Oh how lovely!' she exclaimed. 'Cinder, what is that place? Do people live there?'

'They do,' he replied. 'That is one of the watch towers of the realm. There are four of them posted around the perimeter of the Kings home, looking out over the four cardinal points of the compass. That one is the watch tower of the south – hence the flowers representing summer. Those that live there are known as The Guardians. They use Second Sight and a network of spies to keep the kingdom safe from harm. When Vetch came here asking for help they already knew of Flint. Vetch filled in some of the gaps in their knowledge. He should be well rewarded by the Stag King for his loyalty.'

'Can we meet these Guardians?' asked Alice.

'Mayhap, but not today. I have no doubt that they already know we are here and we need to continue on to meet the Stag King – and of course Willow. It is not far now.'

He spoke the truth. It only took them about another thirty minutes or so of walking before they finally arrived at their destination. No one, not even Mel knew what to expect. What they saw and encountered literally took their breath away. The countryside became lightly wooded again with occasional clearings. As they moved along the path and rounded a bend they were greeted by the sight of a small open air market. People were milling around looking at stalls offering fresh produce, bread, trinkets, clothes, shoes and all manner of other things normally found in such places and as they passed through, the three humans could feel hundreds of eyes upon them. For the first time since arriving in Eyedore they felt like foreigners, which indeed they were. Alice quickly picked up Copper and shrank against Rory, and Cinder seeing her apprehension whispered to her.

'Do not be afraid of them Alice. Humans are a rarity these days around here. They are just curious at the sight of you, that is all.'

Alice wasn't so sure and when a couple of rough labourer looking types approached Mel, Alice held her breath.

'My you're a pretty one ain't ya!' leered one of the fellows.

They heard a flurry of coarse laughter and seeing the consternation on Mel's face, Cinder stepped in.

'These folk are with me and under the Stag King's personal protection. They're honoured guests. Leave them be and mind your manners!'

The man made to answer back, but seeing the toad denoting Cinders rank he backed away.

'Pardon me Sir, no offence. She's a comely looking wench and I thought...'

'I know exactly what you thought! Get away with you!'

For a moment it looked as though the scene could turn ugly as a small group of people began gathering around the young man. The word *'outlanders'* could clearly be heard several times over. However, at the crucial moment a small group of leaf-clad soldiers pushed their way through the gathering mob and one of them directly addressed Cinder.

'The Guardians have informed us of your arrival. The Stag King awaits his honoured guests.'

At the sight of the little men and at the mention of the Stag King the crowd dispersed. Cinder beckoned to his companions and they followed him and the soldiers through the throng of people and beyond the market place. Their final destination appeared to be beneath more trees as they entered another wooded area, but it quickly came to an end, opening out to reveal a building of astonishing style and beauty.

Before them stood a huge castle of stone. It appeared centuries old and like the guardians tower, peeling and crumbling on its outer surfaces. Cinder gestured towards it and spoke softly to his human followers.

'Once we go inside, don't under any circumstances consume any food or drink that's offered to you by any of the King's followers. In certain circumstances, if you do you'll be bound to this castle and be forced to stay within its walls for all of time. No one will be offended should you refuse their hospitality and you must abide by what I've said. I'll guide you on whether it's safe or not to partake of any food or drink offered you. It's fine for us Fae to partake of anything offered there, but any human who does, well...'

Alice, Rory and Mel all nodded their assent. They all resolved to remember what Cinder told them and in a few moments they stepped through a gateway and into the ancient building. Inside the atmosphere felt strange. It were as though they walked through treacle and Alice felt drunk. Then they were led through a door and into the main building itself.

The corridor was dimly lit, but warm and a pleasant smell of fresh flowers filled the air. No one spoke and they just followed their guides obediently. Eventually they found themselves before two huge bronze doors embossed with scenes of hunting. Stags seemed to feature quite prominently along with a man with antlers on his head and images of a large breasted, pregnant woman. Trees, ivy and mistletoe wove their way in and out of the depicted scenes giving an impression of real woodland and for a moment the scent of flowers vanished and all of the humans could smell the leaf mould, the sap and the dampness of the forest. Rory wanted to study the doors in closer detail, but without warning one of their guides reached out and pushed them open. As they passed inside, the scene that greeted them looked like something from a dream. Beyond the doors lay a vast hall – so vast that its outer walls could barely be seen. Great stone columns entwined with carvings of more trees and ivy thrust upwards towards the distant roof and although they were clearly inside a building, leaf mould and moss covered the floor. Trees grew out of the stone work whilst birds and butterflies flew about freely. However, the people carousing there really caught their attention. Scattered about randomly there appeared to be dozens of them – all small and dark haired. The age range here went from young adult up to wrinkled old men and women of many years. Whilst some lazed around drinking wine and eating fruit others were embracing and clearly enjoying each other's company. Several were dancing, either singly or in pairs or groups. Soft music filled the air although no musicians could be seen. Harps, pipes and the gentle beat of a drum set out the rhythm for the swaying bodies. As the travellers moved through the hall a young couple advanced upon them. The female approached Rory and slipping an arm around him she offered him her wine cup. Simultaneously the man came to Alice and pulled her towards him in an embrace. Strangely neither of the humans found the behaviour offensive nor distasteful and Alice began kissing the young man immediately. It wasn't until Cinder stepped in and pushed them apart making sure that the wine cup stayed well away from Rory that they came to their senses. Rory shrugged and shook his head and Alice felt her face flush red with embarrassment.

Fortunately Cinder, Hazel and Barleycorn each took charge of one of the humans. It simply would not do to have any of them trapped here.

Time seemed to have developed a life of its own in this place. No one could tell how long they lingered in the hall, but eventually they did pass through another doorway into a more sedate, but even grander chamber. The woodland theme continued, with tapestries and carvings of more forest deities around the walls. This room however was of more sensible proportions and here they were finally put before the Stag King.

The room contained just a couple of large elaborate chairs, two wooden benches, a wooden chest and a small table, all of which did not even come close to filling its dimensions. Their guides, who barely spoke to them bid them to kindly wait and in that mysterious way so specific to the Fae, simply vanished. They only waited for a short time with barely even time to start a conversation when Mel recognised the booming voice of the Stag King as he swept into the room. As before he wore his long brown cloak and the small antlered mask covered the upper portion of his face. At his side walked a woman with a voice equal in its shrillness to the Kings own boom - a woman who possessed all the regal bearings of a Queen. She appeared around forty years old, small and perfectly formed as all the Fae were. Unlike many of her people, their Queen possessed blonde hair, piled up in great tresses on her head and she wore a swathe of pale green, gossamer like material. The shape of her body could be seen through the thin fabric and her face shone with beauty. For the moment she stood silent, as the King spoke. He greeted them all directly.

'So these are the other humans who mean so much to the wood nymph Willow. You are all welcome here. Come my friends and be seated.' He gestured to the wooden benches. As they sat rather shyly, the King offered them refreshment.

'Would you like something to eat or drink after your journey? You must be hungry and thirsty – the sun is hot today.'

Collectively, the humans looked to Cinder for guidance. Remembering his instructions about not eating at the Royal household they all felt too embarrassed to refuse. Cinder, sensing their trepidation took the lead.

'We thank you Highness for your offered hospitality. A little food and plain water would be good for all of us.'

The King nodded. At the same instant a servant appeared carrying a platter of bread and honey, some apples and a jug of clear water. Cinder looked over the food for a moment and gestured to his friends.

'You may eat,' he said. 'Thank you Highness, this refreshment is most welcome.'

As they ate, the Royal couple seated themselves on the two grand looking chairs and watched silently as the small group of travellers took their fill. Copper, remembering the comfort of the Kings lap from her previous meeting bounded over and leapt up onto his knees. She turned around once or twice and then settled herself down and purring loudly promptly went to sleep. The Queen looked on in an amused fashion and stretched out her hand to tickle Copper behind the ears. When the group finished eating the Stag King addressed them once more.

'We have much business to discuss here. The first thing that you should all know is that whilst Cinder was on the road to greet you, Flint has been taken. My men found him skulking in woodland not far from where we intercepted you all on the road. Tomorrow he will be put on trial, and if found guilty - sentenced. You will all be required to attend.'

There was an outburst of exclamations and chatter and then Barleycorn spoke above the clamour.

'Sentenced is it? And what form will that take – with the greatest respect your 'ighness.'

The King turned his gaze upon Barleycorn and his wife and answered them kindly.

'Flint it charged with many wrongs here, one of which is causing the death of your daughter. Another is of conspiring with a necromancer. Whatever sentence I choose to pass will be fitting to his crimes. Flint is unlikely to be freed. The final decision is mine alone and already I have seen much evidence of his guilt.'

'Well we thanks you 'ighness, truly we does,' said Hazel. 'Pure evil, that's what 'e is, an' any punishment ain't never gonna be good enough for what 'e did to our girl.'

The King nodded and smiled at Hazel. Then he glanced around the little gathering and said,

'The trial will be short, but final. A guilty sentence will be carried out in the Forest of Shadows. A small contingent of villagers will also attend to see fair play and to give their own evidence.'

'Forest of Shadows? What's that?' asked Rory.

'A place of darkness. A place where few Fae folk ever go. It is riddled with decay, despair and fear. It is a place of ill luck and dark omens. There are some folk who reside there, but they would not welcome us. Anyone stranded there would never find their way back out. A place most fitting for Flint I think…'

The buzz of chatter broke out again, but the King silenced them by raising his hand.

'Talk of Flint is done. We have more business to conclude today. You Master Rory were summoned here for a purpose, a purpose for which I am sure you have been informed. I believe Willow entrusted you with something very precious to her. Do you have it with you?'

Still dwelling on thoughts of Flint's capture Rory momentarily found himself caught off guard.

'I'm sorry?' he queried. 'Could you…'

'The ring you dimwit!'

Alice's voice came as a muted hiss as she prodded Rory in the back. She smiled sweetly at the King as Rory hunted for the ring. Fumbling inside his jacket pocket he withdrew a small, crumpled package. He handed it to the King who unwrapped the ring and scrutinised it closely for a few moments. He passed it to his Queen who also examined it minutely and then she handed it straight back to Rory.

'No point in giving it back to him!' boomed the King as Rory re-pocketed the ring. 'Give it to *her*!'

Rory turned around and looked behind him to where the King gestured so testily. Standing behind his sister and friends were two figures. Still clad in her dress of leaves and wearing the most dazzling smile he had ever seen Rory recognised Willow instantly. Beside her and supported on her arm stood a frail looking Fae man who appeared to be around fifty years old. Wearing breeches and a tunic of brown he looked ill and drawn. Clean shaven, he stood just a touch taller than Willow and he leaned on an elaborately carved walking stick. For the moment Rory ignored the sick looking man and could only stare at Willow, then with the blood draining from his face her name burst from his lips.

'*WILLOW!*'

Simultaneously Willow bounded forward and in a single leap wound herself around Rory. His sobs were stifled as he buried his face into her neck, nuzzling against her and breathing in her unique scent. Emotion charged the moment. By the time Rory surfaced to take a fresh breath Alice, Mel, Hazel and Barleycorn were all around them and all pushing forward to hug and paw at Willow themselves. The reunion seemed to go on forever, and by the time they all took a turn in greeting the little wood nymph her dress and hair were both crumpled and wild looking. Some of the flowers were broken off and lay on the floor, but she seemed unconcerned. Strangely, only Cinder reserved at meeting her again. He stood nearby, quietly watching and holding back and made no move to take part. Mel, not understanding his attitude beckoned him forward.

'Come here Cinder. Don't be such a grump. You helped save her too!'

Reluctantly the little man came forward. As he greeted Willow he looked clumsy and awkward, his embrace minimal. Mel decided to ask him later why he looked so uncomfortable.

Through all of this the gentleman that accompanied Willow remained in the background silently watching everything. Now, Rory questioned Willow as to his identity.

'Who's this with you,' he asked. 'We haven't seen him before.'

The initial commotion of their reunion calmed down, but excitement and happiness remained. Overcome by it all and ignoring Rory's question Willow looked him up and down.

'You have changed a great deal since I last saw you,' she said.

Rory looked downcast.

'I've grown older. Twenty years older. You may not want me now...' Willow smiled and hugged him again.

'No,' she said. 'You are wrong. Here it is normal for men to be older than their women folk. It is perfectly natural to me. Before, although I wanted you so much you were too young. Now, you are not.'

Putting her arms around Rory's neck she kissed him firmly on the mouth and smiled sweetly.

'You are perfect Rory. Please do not ever leave me again. Promise me that.'

'I seem to think you left me behind...'

His response sounded indignant, but he couldn't keep up the pretence and began laughing. Giving Willow one last squeeze he gestured to the little man once more who still waited patiently in the background.

'Who is this?' he asked her again.

As if only just noticing the fellow, Willow gestured for him to come forward. He walked slowly and his use of the stick made it clear that he suffered from some illness. He stood just a little taller than Willow, but despite his fragility he still seemed to exude strength and confidence. He approached and faced Rory and when only a couple of steps away thrust out his hand in greeting saying,

'I am so glad to meet you at last Master Rory. Since being reunited with her, my daughter here has simply not stopped talking to me about you.'

'Your daughter?'

Rory looked sharply from the little man to Willow and back again. As he stared in disbelief the man nodded, but before he could speak again Willow cut in.

'Rory, Alice, Mel' she began as she looked at each in turn, 'meet my father...'

'But we thought... You told us...'

'I know. I believed him dead too. It was a sham – Flint threw a glamour over him, making him appear dead. After banishing me he kept father a prisoner in the cellars of his own hall. The King's men found him and freed him. Flint lied to me...'

Willow's father took over the conversation. He seemed mildly amused at their shocked faces, but related the missing part of the story in a kindly fashion.

'My brother is not a moral man. He believes in taking what he wants by any means – even if it does not belong to him. He would have taken my lands, seen my beautiful daughter die and thought nothing of it. You three people of The Race of Men have prevented that from happening. It is our custom, when a precious gift such as this is given to give something back. What would you have from me in return?'

All three stared at one another in disbelief. Mel found her voice first.

'I want nothing of gold or riches,' she stated. 'I simply want to be allowed to remain living here. I can't go home now. I don't want to go home. Let me stay here with Cinder.'

Lord Oak looked to the King for guidance. The King in turn looked to his Queen and together they whispered away for a few minutes. Eventually he glanced up.

'Granted!' he boomed in his loud voice. 'A sensible answer young Mel. You are welcome here, but for the time being you cannot dwell with Cinder. He is soon to be admitted to the College of the Inner Mysteries and will be gone for up to twelve moons. In the meantime we must find somewhere else for you to live. Perhaps we could build you a large house of your own somewhere of your choosing out in the forest?'

Mel shook her head.

'If it agrees with your Highness I should like to live with Hazel and Barleycorn and help them on their farm until Cinder returns. They have already made me such an offer. They'll need some assistance now that Tansy...'

Her voice trailed away and for a moment an eerie silence descended. The Stag King spoke quietly – a thing which took them all by surprise.

'You two peasants,' he whispered. 'Would you have this girl live with you as your daughter until this man returns for her?'

Everyone stared at Hazel and Barleycorn, seeing how the mention of Tansy's name distressed them. However, a look of deep satisfaction and relief graced their old eyes too as simultaneously they both nodded vigorously. Barleycorn skipped forward and throwing his arms around Mel gave a viable challenge to the King on the subject of vocal volume.

'Of course we'll 'ave you girl! It would be an 'onour, truly it would. 'Ighness, just you try and stop us takin' 'er in! You'd 'ave a battle on your 'ands if you did!'

Hazel joined in hugging Mel, demonstrating her own affection for the human girl. As they parted Mel moved closer to her new foster parents forming a little group.

The attention reverted to Rory and Lord Oak addressed him directly.

'And what of you Rory? What would you have? A house? Gold?'

Rory shook his head. He trembled all over for there could only be one thing he would ask for. Rejection would destroy him, but to not ask would be both cowardly and disrespectful. Taking a deep breath he spoke far more confidently than he actually felt.

'Your Highness, Lord Oak, I want Willow. I want to handfast her and make her mine. Can I have your blessing on that?'

A frown crossed Oak's brow and for a moment Rory really thought he would refuse. He countered the request with another question.

'What do you mean by making her yours? Willow is her own being. She cannot be owned. If she wants to handfast you as much as you seem to want her, then to that I give my blessing gladly, but make her yours? An unfortunate choice of words I think...'

Rory felt furious with himself. He desired Willow more than anything and he had almost lost her in one foolish request. He deferred to Oak's position.

'I am so sorry if I have offended you Lord Oak. As you say, my choice of words is at fault here. What I mean is that Willow means more to me than anything or anyone. I would defend her to my last breath if need be. I love her very much and would not want to be without her. Twenty years have passed in my world while I have waited for this moment. If I sounded flippant or if I have broken one of your customs then I am sorry for that. I meant no harm. I so desperately want her as my wife, but only,' and he glanced at Willow as he said this, 'only if she wants me in the same way.'

Oak looked thoughtful for a few moments. He glanced at the King who responded in his inimitable way.

'Do not think to look to me for help Oak – she is not my daughter! But if you want my opinion on the matter – well, he might be human, which of course definitely goes against him, but he does seem to have a few good points.' Turning to the Queen he addressed her. 'What do you think? Are they a fair match?'

The Queen, for the first time spoke up.

'I think that ultimately it is up to Oak, and Willow. If they are both happy to have an *outlander* in their family then that is their affair. Oak? Speak up man!' Oak rubbed his chin thoughtfully and looked at Willow.

'Daughter, I loved your mother so much that it hurt me at times. How do you feel about this man who stands before you asking for your heart?'

Willow looked from one to the other before giving her answer. When she did she walked over and stood directly in front of her father.

'If it were not for Rory, Alice and Mel - I would be dead. He makes me feel safe; he makes me feel cherished and loved. I want Rory more than anything father. If, as you say love hurts, then I am in constant agony. When Flint took me prisoner I constantly thought of Rory coming to find me. On that day he could not come, but that was no fault of his. I know in my heart that if he made it through the gateway he would have been equally as brave as Mel. My thoughts of Rory kept me alive. The answer is yes father. I do want him. More than anyone could know.'

Oak rubbed his chin a second time and looking at Rory said gravely,

'The maiden has spoken and you both have my blessing. I just needed to know her true wish, that is all. Rory, you are indeed a brave young man taking this one on. She has a wild streak in her that you will never tame. Do not even try to. But she comes with one condition.'

An expectant silence filled the room. Rory nodded. 'Anything.'

'If you ever strike her in any way you will find yourself
cast out of our world with no remorse. There will be no
second chance. It is an old tradition here when one of our
women handfasts a human. Promise me now that you will
honour that one condition and in your language – she is
yours!'

'I can promise that – I have no intention of ever
harming her in any way.'

'Then you both have my permission and my sincerest
blessing.'

Tears of joy were running down Willow's face, but she
still looked beautiful. An ethereal shimmer surrounded
her, a product of the Stag King's healing kiss that imbued
her with life and vitality. When caught in the peripheral
vision she actually appeared to be emitting a soft glow. It
was quite uncanny, but rather breath-taking too. Rory
took her in his arms once more and kissed her. Inwardly
he vowed never to let her out of his sight again.

Alice's emotions were in turmoil. She knew now that
whatever she said would never deter Rory from taking up
with Willow. Better to accept things as they were and not
fall out with her brother further she decided, but
apprehension still prickled at her mind. She felt left out
too. Mel loved Cinder and would be lodging with Hazel
and Barleycorn. Rory was now betrothed to Willow, but
Alice had no one. She bit her lip and blinked back her
own tears. She decided to wait. For the moment everyone
else seemed so happy and she did not want her negative
feelings to spoil that happiness. Stepping forward she
hugged Willow and Rory in turn – and she meant it too.
Perhaps it was just fear of the unknown, but something
told her that their battles with Flint were not yet over.

Oak spoke to Alice then.

'And you Mistress Alice, what would you like from me?'

Alice looked thoughtful for a moment before
responding.

'I don't know,' she said simply. 'I didn't help Willow for gain, but because of her plight. I can think of nothing.'

Oak smiled and approached her on his stick. Awkwardly he tried to embrace her saying,

'Well for now just accept my gratitude. Without you, your brother and your friend, my daughter would be dead. Thank you Alice, but if there is anything you desire in the future, do not hesitate to ask me.'

Alice bowed her head graciously, not really sure how she should react. She found herself mumbling her thanks and returned to her brother's side. Oak made one final statement on the matter.

'There is one other whom I believe took part in this. I believe that Vetch has already returned to the village of Nettlebed. He too shall know of my generosity. Without Vetch alerting His Highness, Flint would not have been intercepted on the road. He shall benefit from this too.'

Oak's gratitude having been shown, the Stag King took command of the conversation. In a sombre tone he addressed Hazel and Barleycorn.

'Your daughter was a fine young woman – a credit to you both. In the best Fae tradition she never gave in. You should always remember her in that way. She stood up to one of the Dark Ones. Few folk would do that. As you know, she now lies within the forest close to your home. At some point in the future a monument will be raised for her and a song composed that she may never be forgotten. In addition you will no longer pay any tithe on your home and land.' He held a hand up at that as a surprised look broke out on Oak's face. 'Do not fret Oak, I will pay it for them every moon until they are both gone. Your purse will not suffer.'

Oak responded smoothly.

'Highness that is gracious, but far from necessary. It is a generous and good offer, but I would happily accept no payment at all. Tansy aided my daughter and paid the ultimate price for doing so. Consider their tithe debt as fully paid.'

With these matters complete there still remained one more piece of business that needed to be concluded. Rory addressed the one matter that seemed to have been forgotten. With a flourish he withdrew the ring from his pocket for a second time and spoke directly to Willow's father.

'Sir,' he began. 'A long time ago in my world your daughter entrusted me to keep this ring safe. Up until today I always imagined giving it back to her. However, I now return it to your own safe keeping instead. I believe it rightfully belongs to you.'

Oak, leaning on his stick advanced to Rory and gratefully regained possession of his family ring.

'I thank you with all my heart. My daughter has chosen well. Welcome to my family.'

He embraced Rory and kissed him on both cheeks. Embarrassed, Rory changed the subject.

'Willow,' he exclaimed. 'I almost forgot – I have something for you too.'

Placing his bag on the floor Rory unzipped it and delving inside came out with a jar of peanut butter which he handed reverently to the little woman. Excited, she reacted predictably. Jumping up and down like a child she squealing in delight.

'Oh father! Look! This is the human delicacy I told you of! Nut butter! You must try it at once! Rory – how do I open it?'

Grinning Rory twisted the lid free and watched laughing as the jar passed amongst the Fae gathering. To hear peanut butter described as a delicacy caused the humans to laugh, but watching the Fae people tasting it was even better. Even the King complemented the gift. Grinning, Rory proudly told Willow that another five jars were in his pack and she rewarded him with a kiss. He decided at the last moment to keep the love spoon he had made for her well-hidden. He felt it would be more appropriate to give it to Willow on the day of their handfasting. His business complete he watched while Mel gave Cinder the new bag. Cinder, delighted with the gift hugged them all in turn.

All business, both formal and informal was now completed. With the protocols over, more food appeared and bellies were gratefully filled for a second time. After eating, the Stag King made one final gesture of hospitality. His guests were each given a chamber to sleep in and were shown to their respective beds by a serving woman. With true gratitude in their hearts and a weariness none of them had felt in a long time, they retired for a night of welcome rest.

***

# 18

# A TRIAL AND A CELEBRATION

Each of the guests awoke the following morning fully refreshed. Hazel and Barleycorn slept in a chamber together whilst Alice and Rory were given separate lodgings. Where Willow resided for the night no one knew and Rory had been rather disappointed when she bid him good night with a kiss, leaving with her father. Mel on the other hand insisted on spending the night with Cinder. Alice expressed concern at that, but Rory intervened on her behalf saying,

'She's been through so much and Cinder will soon be leaving her for a whole year. She's practically eighteen Alice; she's old enough to make up her own mind now.'

When presented with these facts Alice could only agree. However, she still felt somewhat responsible for Mel and still watched her and Cinder walk away hand in hand with misgivings in her heart. However, the look of joy and contentment on Mel's face that morning quickly dismissed her views of the night before.

There was no sign of the Stag King or his Queen. However, two small and smartly dressed fellows greeted them when they arose, informing them all that there would be a celebration for the fallen Tansy later that day after the conclusion of Flints trial and any sentence. Strangely, her parents no longer seemed so distraught over their loss, but spoke openly of their girl and of their memories of her. Willow joined them too, but Oak did not appear. Rory enquired after her father and Willow replied sadly,

'He is still rather ill. He suffered a great deal under Flint and may not even fully recover. He is very weak and it took a lot out of him merely by coming to meet you all yesterday. I tried to prevent him at the time, but he insisted. I have spent much of the night nursing him through nightmares.'

She looked a little downcast and Rory comforted her by holding her hand and whispering to her that whatever happened he would do what he could to assist in looking after Oak.

They broke their fast on a simple meal. The fare was rustic, but nourishing. There were hard boiled eggs, bread with honey, a selection of nuts, barley porridge and more of the cheese type fungus which seemed to be present at almost every mealtime. They ate ravenously and all chattered noisily. The men drank from a cask of good, dark ale and availed themselves of its contents generously. Alice frowned at the thought of ale with their breakfast, but this was a weak brew and quite normal here. Hazel and Willow both shared a jug of watered down elderberry wine and Alice and Mel joined them. It tasted delicious and diluted with plenty of water it seemed respectable enough.

They were in the same room as the one where they met the Stag King the previous evening, yet this morning it had been transformed. A great table ran down the centre with benches to either side. Trees and plants were literally growing from out of the stones where the night before no trees grew at all, whilst thick, fragrant leaf mould covered the floor. A gentle summer breeze caressed them every now and then whilst live birds fluttered about too. Had they not known better, all of them would have been convinced that they were outside. The smell of spring flowers pervaded the air again this morning and the soft notes of a harp from some unseen musician, and the tinkling of wind chimes gave a wonderful background to their meal. To the Fae seated at the table it all seemed perfectly normal, but to the humans the whole experience proved a sheer wonder.

The two races sat mixed together. Alice still felt a little left out and sensing her uncomfortable mood, Hazel made a point of talking to her. Her manners were worse than Willow's as she waved her bread around and spoke with her mouth full. 'Don't worry Alice, you'll get used to it 'ere soon enough. Young Mel there is one of us already! Just look at 'er with Cinder.'

Mel looked positively radiant. If Alice looked at her with her peripheral vision she could see the same glow about her that Willow possessed. She commented on it to Hazel.

'Aye,' the old woman responded, her mouth now stuffed with bread. 'She's taken to our world very well indeed. That glow around 'er shows 'er contentment. Few 'oomans take on that shimmerlin' quite as quick as she 'as. She belongs 'ere.'

Mel felt full of contentment and it showed in her face. Sitting beside Cinder she had never been happier. She and Cinder were speaking to each other in muted whispers and every now and then one would touch the others hand or arm in affection. As they chattered so happily Mel remembered Cinder's reluctance to embrace Willow the day before. She brought up the subject.

'Why did you seem so stand offish with Willow yesterday?' she asked quietly. Cinder fell silent for a few moments before answering her.

'I can't say,' he said mysteriously. 'Something about her presence unsettles me – but not in a bad way mind...' Mel looked confused at this for she could think of no reason why Willow should cause Cinder to feel uncomfortable. He continued his explanation. 'I rather like Willow,' he stated. 'She's a fine young woman, she has a good aura and one day when her father is gone she'll make a wonderful Lady for the estate and care for her tenants and farmers. But sometimes, particularly if I get close to her –

like yesterday when you bid me to hug her... I feel as though there is some hidden link between us... Almost as though I have known her all of my life, yet I am afraid to touch her lest I break some unspoken law or taboo... I can't explain it, but it both puzzles and unsettles me. I've met her once or twice before in the distant past, first when we were children and then as a young man, and it felt the same then. I enjoy her company, but sense some great unspeakable thing whenever I'm close to her. Perhaps given time I'll become accustomed to her presence...'

Mel found this statement even more confusing, but chose to drop the subject. Instead, she decided she would watch Cinder whenever Willow came near him. The little Fae woman had already stolen Rory from her and she would not let that happen a second time.

The meal seemed to go on for a long time, yet when they were done the sun still only just winked above the horizon. As they all rose from the table two tiny men dressed in fine clothes made one of those unnoticed appearances and strode boldly over.

'It is time,' one of them said. The man beckoned and walked behind a thicket. A wall and door lay behind the bushes and the small group followed their guides through. Miraculously they found themselves in another forest glade. This however looked like no forest they had ever seen before. The trees here were all long dead. The light was dusk-like, the air chilled and a stinking, stagnant lake lay silently nearby. The visitors stood and gaped at this new wonder. Alice, sensing the gravity of the place picked up Copper and carried her, afraid that the cat's inquisitive nature may cause her to become lost. She whispered to Cinder who stood nearby.

'Is this still inside the castle? It looks so real.' Cinder shook his head.

'No. The King's castle is very much a magical realm. It can act as a gateway to anywhere the King chooses. We now stand in the Forest of Shadows.'

271

Before Alice could ponder on this a trumpet blast sounded and a bitter wind blew eerily through the clearing. The humans all jumped, startled at the sudden sound, but the Fae merely shrugged and turned towards the direction from which the breeze came, almost as though they expected it. At the far end of the glade movement could be detected. A column of figures walked slowly in the direction of the small party and at the head marched the Stag King. He was dressed once more as if going to war in his great black cloak and antlered helm. Beside him walked his Queen. Today she wore a gown of dark green and black and with her hair piled high she looked rather intimidating. Behind the King and Queen a large group of soldiers surrounded another figure and a moment later they saw Flint in their midst, his hands bound. At the rear around twenty or so villagers completed the party. With the villagers, Willow's father Oak stood leaning on his stick. Willow went to his side at once.

The column halted and the Stag King removed his helmet. The soldiers deployed around the gathering, protecting them on all flanks. The Stag King spoke.

'We are gathered here today for the trial of Flint, brother of Lord Oak, son of Lord Hawthorn. The accused is charged with conspiring to incarcerate his own brother and to steal his property and lands. Also, to cast out his niece Willow, to die amongst the world of men. Furthermore there are separate charges of kidnap, accessory to murder and conspiring with a necromancer to further his own cause. Flint? How do you plead? Guilty or not guilty?'

Flint spoke loudly and clearly.

'Not guilty. I took nothing that was not mine. Do as you will.'

A low muttering rippled through the villagers and the King raised his hand for silence.

'I have already heard the evidence from those wronged. You still plead not guilty?'

'I do.'

The King nodded and addressed the gathering.

'I am gifted as a soul searcher. I know that those who have given evidence have spoken the truth. I also know that you Flint spin a web of lies, betrayal and evil. I find you guilty. You are sentenced to die.'

The only folk surprised at the rapidity of the trial were the humans. Rory made to speak, but Mel caught his arm and pulled him back.

'He knows what you are thinking,' she whispered. 'He got inside my head the first time I met him. I trust him. Anyway, we know the truth of it. Let justice be done.'
Rory nodded and relaxed, watching in anticipation as the King passed sentence.

'It is only fitting that you have time to ponder on your actions before you die. Therefore I find it fitting to sentence you to be sealed alive inside a hollow willow tree in the Forest of Shadows. There you may think on your crimes as you wither away. Take him!'

Four of the leaf clad soldiers took hold of Flint. In moments they marched him to a mouldering willow beside the lake and forced him inside a large split in the trunk. As they nailed a wicker panel over the opening and began to seal the split with wet clay Flint spoke out. His voice carried eerily across the darkened glade.

'You think it is over brother? Think again. *You*!' He raised his bound wrists and pointed to Mel. 'It is not over for you either girl! Nor my niece! Nor the cunning one! I shall…'

The last of Flint's words were lost as the opening was covered over with thick viscous clay. Mel shivered at the veiled threat and snuggled up to Cinder as a cheer arose from the assembled villagers.

\*

*No one noticed the figure standing to the edge of the group of villagers. His dowdy attire, unkempt look and cowed posture rendered him as faceless amongst the many. It had been a simple task to join their ranks and blend into the group. His eyes missed nothing. Silently he slunk away from the gathering, seeking cover behind some dead and rotting thorn bushes. He would bide his time. The Master would not die... Not today...*

\*

There had been a small clamour of satisfaction at Flint's incarceration. The representatives from the village were few and the humans did not feel comfortable enough in this new world to voice their own opinions. The applause were sparse, but heartfelt. Hazel and Barleycorn, delighted at seeing their daughter's tormentor meet justice accepted the verdict and subsequent punishment with a quiet satisfaction. With the formalities over, the King had one final speech to make.

'My people, it is always a sad day when one of our own leaves the path of peace and goodwill to follow their own twisted desires. Flint will torment this land no more. His day is done. To those of you that have been wronged, I would ask you to remember your loved ones as they were – vibrant and peaceable Fae beings. One such girl was taken from us. Tansy, daughter to Barleycorn and Hazel who stand with us today. In her honour I bid you all to return to my home where a celebration of her short life has been arranged for you all. She will never be forgotten, but will live on in our songs, our histories and our hearts. Go back through the gateway to feast, toast and dance to her memory!'

The Stag King gestured towards the open doorway through which they had entered the Forest of Shadows. At his bidding the people, with Barleycorn and Hazel at their head passed through the door and back into the castle. The King and his Queen departed in their own way by simply melting into the trees and vanishing from sight. Only one remained, hidden behind the undergrowth as he plotted his Master's return…

*

*He stood alone in the Forest of Shadows. The task would be simple, but he needed to move swiftly. Taking a small whistle from his pocket he blew a loud discordant note to summon the fauns. Four of them arrived silently and eerily, emerging from amongst the deadened forest to gather at his feet. They would do his bidding. He issued his instructions and the tiny horned beings set to work. Satisfaction crossed his face. He was done here. The fauns would complete this part of the plan. He left them to their work for he had more things to achieve before the Master could continue with his great scheme. Continue he would, and the result for all would be worth every effort. With one final glance at the progress of the fauns he set off. The walk back through this forbidden section of the forest would be long, but achievable before the days end. Anticipation spread through his veins as he thought of the pleasures to come in the days ahead…*

*

On passing through the portal opened by the King the humans found themselves outside of the great castle, but within the safety of its grounds. The royal party did not join them, but there appeared to be a considerable gathering of Fae folk all awaiting the arrival of the main group. Even as they joined the gathering a penny whistle struck up a gay tune and the Fae people began to dance. Amazingly, Hazel and Barleycorn were amongst the first to join in the revels and were soon dancing reels and jigs along with everyone. Ale, mead and wine all featured in this unexpected celebration of Tansy's life as the humans watched, amazed at the gaiety and enjoyment that was already in full swing. Alice, intrigued by the vast difference between this and a human wake asked Cinder why everyone appeared so joyous. He answered her matter-of-factly.

'It is a celebration of Tansy's life, not a time for sadness...'

Here lay another difference between the worlds. True, in some human cultures funerals involved drinking and feasting, but here in Eyedore there seemed to be very few tears indeed. Even as she looked on Alice stood goggle eyed as Willow, skipped forward, grabbed a fiddle and bow from one of the musicians and struck up her own tune.

The rhythm was fast and very upbeat and in a moment the dancing Fae were swaying and spinning to Willow's music. What amazed Alice more, Willow herself danced as she played. She spun and leapt in such a graceful way that all of the humans were totally transfixed. If anyone suggested that a violin could be played so beautifully whilst the musician pirouetted, leapt and swayed so wonderfully Alice would have laughed aloud. Seeing Willow perform like this mesmerised them all, and enchanted by her playing they soon forgot their sadness and found themselves joining in with the dancing. Willow played on and on and before they realised it the afternoon had flown by. Mel and Cinder danced non-stop whilst Rory accompanied Alice on and off. However, exhaustion eventually caught up with them. Alice and Rory could only watch now as they regained their breath and both stood shaking, only now able to look on. Seeing Rory motionless Willow finally ceased her playing. A great cheer rose from the whole assembly as she stood down and many begged her to continue, but smiling sweetly at them all she made her way back to Rory and falling into his arms she whispered softly,

'Would you walk with me?'

Rory, glad of a break from the festivities nodded his agreement immediately.

'Where too?'

'Just a walk in the forest.'

Overhearing them Alice looked on slyly. She watched as Rory squeezed Willow's hand as they headed for the door which led back into the castle.

Willow led the way. Just finding a route out of the building appeared to Rory to be quite a task. They passed down corridor after corridor, but when Rory questioned her Willow seemed to know exactly which way to go. Finally they came upon a doorway which took them back outside. They came out on the opposite side of the castle to the market they had passed through the day before and after only a short walk they were soon under the cover of the woods. The atmosphere here felt calm and serene. At first they walked in silence, broken only by the chatter of birds and the rustle of the leaves in the evening breeze. Willow led Rory down a narrow path which meandered gently between the trees. Nearby fast flowing water could be heard trickling away. They stopped briefly when Willow spotted a large clump of bramble bushes, and picking the large fat blackberries she shared them with Rory. Their fingers and lips were soon stained in purple berry juice and playfully Rory offered one up to Willow. She opened her mouth and he popped the fruit inside. Willow returned the compliment and passed Rory an equally large berry. They tasted wonderful and were so abundant that Rory could not remember ever having seen so many blackberries in one place. Willow looked thoughtful as Rory gently placed another berry on her tongue and she smiled mischievously as taking his hand she led him down another path. She stopped when they came to a flowing stream. It spanned about three or four metres across, but ran rapidly. Further upstream a small waterfall fed the deluge and the trees opened out into a small glade. Moss grew everywhere and a carpet of sweet smelling flowers clustered nearby. Rory commented on this natural beauty, but Willow merely shrugged and then placing her finger over his lips she whispered,

'Stop talking.'

For a moment Rory thought something was wrong and that maybe Willow might have heard some threat lurking close by. However, when she kissed him he understood.

The kiss was long and slow and Rory didn't want it to end. Comfortable in her embrace and with her scent in his nostrils he became totally lost in the moment. Somehow he found himself sitting on the forest floor with Willow beside him, his heart pounding. No woman had ever made Rory feel this way. He savoured the moment, looking at her and drinking in her beauty. He wanted to laugh, to cry and to shout her name all at the same time. He reached out to stroke her face and Willow, taking control of the situation slid into his arms...

\*

Rory couldn't have been more content. He didn't want to move, but the thought of Alice's voice scolding him for creeping away from Tansy's celebration crept into his daydreams. With a sigh he whispered to Willow.

'We should go. Alice...'

She stirred in his arms. She had been sleeping there with her head against his chest and looked so peaceful that it seemed a crime to disturb her. She sat up yawning and looking at the sinking sun through the trees she said groggily,

'We still have time for a swim – come on.'

Standing up Willow scampered down towards the stream. Rory called out to her.

'I thought you were afraid of water?'

'Only in your world. In that place it is a sign of baptism to your God. There, it would do me harm to fall in. Here, our own water poses me no threat at all.'

He followed her down to the edge and admired her beauty as she entered the water, squealing loudly at its cold touch on her bare skin. Rory ran in after her and splashed her profusely, laughing as she shrieked in torment. They played for a time like that, both naked and throwing water back and forth and swimming around in the icy flow, their love for each other keeping them both warm.

*

*Nearby that other pair of eyes looked on. His progress at leaving the Forest of Shadows proved to be swift and he had stalked them ever since they left the safety of the castle. He watched them share the berries, looked on as they lay together on the forest floor and then as they frolicked in the water, but he chose to remain unseen. It would have been so easy to kill them both, but this was not the time. Neither of them he noticed wore the ring. To slay them now would be premature. He withdrew and left them enjoying themselves. The Master would appreciate the new information that he held. It would add to his personal credibility and enable him to further his own cause. Just a little more surveillance remained to be done and then he could report back with everything he had learned. His own star was in the ascendant...*

***

# 19

# PLANS AND ACTIONS

When Rory and Willow returned to the celebration the party remained well underway. Alice glowered disapprovingly and grumbled under her breath when her brother and Willow returned. Coldly she said,

'Where have you two been for so long? No! Don't answer that, I don't think I want to know! Look at you Rory! You look like the cat that got the cream!'

Rory made no reply. Willow however responded confidently.

'I wanted some time with Rory on my own. We have waited so long to be together - Alice please do not chastise us like that for we have done nothing wrong.'

Still feeling annoyed Alice aired her feelings.

'This is a celebration for poor Tansy. Couldn't you two have waited just a little longer? Barleycorn and Hazel have both left whilst you were...were...well, doing whatever you were doing... They asked me where you'd gone! How do you think that made me feel?'

'I'm sorry Alice, really I am, but Willow is right, we've done nothing wrong. Don't take it out on her. She's suffered in this too you know. She just needed to get away from everyone for a bit and be shown a little TLC.'

Momentarily Alice felt awkward. She had forgotten how Willow almost died at the hands of her uncle, but she still thought of their sneaking off as inappropriately timed. She backed down a little, but not completely.

'Look, I didn't mean to offend you Willow. It's just bad timing that's all... I'm sorry, but it's alright for you... You have each other and Mel has Cinder...'

She fell silent then and Willow sensing what went through Alice's mind embraced her.

'I am sorry too Alice. I asked Rory to come with me, the fault is mine. I have no wish to fall out with you. Without you finding me in your shed I would have died in your world. I owe you everything – please do not think badly of me, but Rory is right. I just really needed a little time with him.'

Alice nodded although she still maintained that the pair could have waited a little longer. She decided not to push the point home any further. The hour grew late and despite the celebration for Tansy continuing on into the night the human contingent were all exhausted. Alice, glad to have resolved their spat rubbed her hand wearily across her face and said,

'I think I'm ready for my bed. Don't know about you two, but I'm done in. Would you show me the way back please Willow?'

The little Fae woman nodded, her face breaking into a smile.

'Of course,' she said sweetly. 'This way. Rory, I think Alice is right. We should leave these people to continue their dancing. Cinder and Mel can make their own minds up on what they want to do. They don't need us now, come...'

Turning on her heel Willow walked back towards the door with Rory. Following on, Alice couldn't help noticing the grass and moss stuck to the rear of Willow's dress. She knew all along the reason for their disappearance, but seeing it blatantly before her made her feel sad once more. She felt really lonely now and just needed someone to hold her and make her feel special too. Looking at Willow she couldn't really find it in her heart to condemn or criticise her. However, she did feel envious.

Blinking back her tears Alice hugged her brother, holding on to him a little longer than usual. She cuddled Willow too and whispered in her tiny ear.

'Please bear with me. I'm finding it so hard here, but I am genuinely happy for you and Rory.'

Willow returned the embrace and smiled. Her beautiful blue eyes bored into Alice's and the human woman knew she understood her strange mood. When they parted Alice entered her bed chamber without another word, whilst oblivious to his sister's pain, Rory and the woman he loved beyond words headed off together.

The following morning they took breakfast in the same woodland hall as the day before. Today, Willow's father Oak joined them, already sitting beside his daughter when Alice entered the hall. Rory graced her other side and offered her a piece of bread spread with peanut butter as his sister joined them. Despite still feeling rather low Alice couldn't help smiling when she saw Willow with the 'nut butter'. The memory of the little woman's excitement at the strange spread gave her quite a lift. Deciding to at least try to be positive she sat down and helped herself to a small loaf and some soft sheep's cheese. As she began to eat, Mel, Hazel and Barleycorn all arrived and sat around her. There was no sign of Cinder. Hazel appeared a little strained, but still managed to smile a greeting. The old lady took some porridge and made a great play of eating, but Alice noticed that she actually ate very little. Barleycorn seemed quiet too and unusually for him, said almost nothing. Mel sat silent, staring into space, the friendly and open chatter of the day before gone. Desperate to change the mood Alice addressed Oak.

'How are you feeling today Sir?' she enquired loudly.

Thoughtfully Oak set down his bread and answered her. His voice sounded soft and quiet and he still looked unwell. However, he seemed keen to talk.

'I feel a little better than yesterday, but not as well as I shall feel tomorrow,' he said, using the same phrase that

Willow had once used before the King. He smiled as he spoke and Alice detected a wicked sense of humour behind his words. Encouraged, she persevered, desperate for a decent conversation.

'You have more colour than the last time I saw you. Did you sleep well?'

'Yes, I did thank you. Knowing that my daughter is alive has made such a difference. Last night I slept my first night in a considerable time without being tormented by bad dreams. She is the best tonic of all for me.'

Willow squeezed her father's arm. She smiled at him in a way that melted Alice's heart. Patting his daughters hand he returned to Alice.

'I sense a troubled mind in you young lady,' he said. 'You are finding it difficult to adapt to our world?'

Alice nodded. She felt a lump forming in her throat, but she refused to shed tears. She remained silent. Oak spoke again.

'Give it time,' he said softly. 'You will come to love it here. With my brother now gone the countryside will be a better place. His evil is over and I am not sorry to see him receive the punishment he so richly deserved.'

The subject of Flint and his demise became the topic of conversation around the table until Rory, ever the optimist abruptly changed the subject.

'I've been thinking. Where do we all go from here? We can't stay in this castle forever. What happens now?'

'What would you like to happen Rory?' asked Oak.

'To handfast your daughter and find somewhere to live. To have babies and grow old together...'
Oak laughed aloud and slapping the table gave his own response.

'Well you don't waste any time do you boy!' he chuckled. 'Daughter, you've a keen one there. Perhaps we should make arrangements sooner rather than later.'

Willow actually reddened. Her embarrassment surprised Alice for she always thought of Willow as quite shameless. Finding Oak's conversation rather warming she responded by making a little dig of her own.

'Best you get a move on Willow. I don't think you'll be able to put him off much longer!'

Willow's smile said it all.

'I do not want to put him off,' she stated. 'The sooner the better as far as I am concerned.'

Hazel spoke up next. Alice had forgotten her amidst the banter and felt heartened to see her join in. She still looked drawn and tired, but she managed to smile as she said,

'I think we needs a good 'andfastin'. There's been far too much sadness round 'ere of late. What say you Barleycorn? Be a good excuse to get your mead out!'

As usual her mouth was full of food and some of it found its way onto the table, but the humans were getting used to this now. Glad to see the old lady talking at last Alice encouraged her.

'Yes indeed Hazel,' she said, 'but I might need a new frock though!'

The conversation continued in this vein for some time before Alice realised that Mel had not said one word since coming down to breakfast. Seeing her friend looking so glum she sidled across the bench to her and as the main conversation continued, whispered in her ear.

'Are you okay Mel? Where's Cinder? You look a little down this morning.'

Mel shrugged, her response sounding flat.

'I just feel a little low. They,' here she gestured to Willow and Rory, 'are talking about a wedding, but Cinder will be leaving me for a whole year. We've argued over it again this morning. It's just so bloody unfair...'

'I'm so sorry Mel,' whispered Alice. 'But he'll be coming back for you. He really cares about you - you do know that don't you?'

'Yes I know, but I mean... A whole year? What if he meets someone else in that time? I couldn't cope with that I really couldn't...'

Overhearing the conversation Willow and Hazel both came and joined the two human women and began adding their own words of comfort. Hazel made the greatest difference.

'Now come on littl'un,' she said sternly, but not unkindly. 'You makin' all that fuss'll turn the milk sour! It ain't that bad. You come an' stay with ol' Barleycorn an' me. We'll care for you. Those four seasons'll be gone in no time – you mark my words. And it ain't no easier for 'im goin' away like that neither. 'E loves you more than you can know. I ain't never seen 'im look at no one like the way 'e looks at you. Now stop that flippin' whinin'. If you're gonna carry on like this for the next twelve moons I ain't sure I wants you in my 'ouse! Come 'ere you silly thing!'

Hazel took Mel from Alice's arms and hugged her until she thought she would be smothered. The old woman trembled and as she squeezed the young girl to her breast her manner changed from stern to motherly.

'Don' fret no more precious girl. You're breakin' my 'eart – don't you think it's been 'urt enough already? Barleycorn, you tell 'er! We love you too you silly thing! Cinder 'as spoken to us both an' made us promise to keep you safe 'til 'e gets back.'

Barleycorn said nothing, but simply embraced her, and Mel felt more loved than ever before. Eventually after much coaxing, her friends convinced her to tell them the full story. It seemed that Cinder and Mel's argument that morning had been hurtful to both. She'd begged him not to leave her, but he'd said his magical studies must come first. Put out by that Mel had stormed off and now felt terrible about it. Willow decided to intervene. Quietly slipping away she sought out Cinder. He remained in the tiny sleeping cell, packing his few possessions into his bag when Willow found him.

'What are you doing Cinder?'

'Preparing to set off. Mel has made it quite clear that I should just go...'

Pausing, he put his bag down and glanced up. His eyes were moist.

'Mel is distraught,' Willow began. 'You cannot just leave her Cinder it would hurt her beyond measure. Go and find her and make your peace. We have already spoken with her. She is so frightened that you may not come back from your studies. If you just leave, then you will shatter her soul and I wager you would be full of remorse too. She is still in the feasting hall with Hazel and the others...'

Looking down Cinder began fiddling with the fastening of his bag saying nothing.

'YOU FOOL!' Willow hissed. 'You are regarded by so many as a wise man. Show some wisdom now and go and make your peace with her before you leave. If you do not you may well lose her for good!'

Cinder hung his head in shame at that. Letting out a sigh he rubbed his hand across his face.

'I may be skilled in many things,' he said defeated, 'but I will never, ever understand women. Where did you say she is?'

Mel and her friends were still sitting in the great hall when Willow returned with Cinder in tow and as he entered the hall Hazel glared at him so harshly that he almost went back out the door. Sitting beside Mel he just took her hand and looked at her with his great blue eyes. The others took this as a convenient moment to leave. Making their excuses they all rapidly departed from the hall leaving the two lovers together.

Mel sat silent, staring at the floor. Cinder stood beside her. Reaching out his hand he gripped hers and spoke softly.

'My love. Please forgive me for any offence I've caused. You must know how much I love you and want to be with you.'

'Then why must you leave me?' Her words were full of hurt.

'All my life I've studied the ancient mysteries. Healing, seeking, scrying, divining… It's a calling. I'm born to do this. Don't ask me how I know – it just is… I also know that we were meant to be together – and we shall. Hazel and Barleycorn will…'

'A WHOLE YEAR! You want to leave me for a year Cinder. Do you have any idea how that makes me feel? I returned to Eyedore expecting to be with you and now you want to desert me. I hear your words of love and how you will return, but will you? What if you meet someone else in that time? Some Fae girl – like Willow who steals you from me? That would destroy me…'

Trembling, she pulled her hand away. Cinder shook his head.

'I told you I want no other. My heart burns for you Mel. You accuse me of wanting to leave… I want to stay. Every piece of my being yearns to remain at your side, but I have a duty to the Gods, to my teachers and to myself. To not go would be to waste my life thus far. To not go would deprive me of an ancient knowledge which I know is my destiny to seek out. Everything happens for a reason. Without the additional skills I am bound to learn I know that our future will be compromised. I have to go, but by the Moon, the Stars and the Sun and all of the Gods and Goddesses I swear to you that I *will* return and handfast you at the first opportunity. Mel, I want you as my woman – my wife as you would say. Cease you tears and look at me. Give me your heart along with your hand. Give me your blessing to go and complete my training. Afterwards we'll never be parted again. I swear this to you by everything that is and everything that has ever been. I give you my word and my undying love…'

She stood then and faced him. Reaching out she took Cinder in her arms and pulled him to her.

'I fear losing you. Once I wanted Rory and I lost him to Willow. I never want to feel that pain again. Promise me something.'

'Anything.'

'You must think of me every day. Think of my face as you fall asleep and as you wake. Keep me in your heart and don't stop loving me.'

'That'll be the easiest promise I'll ever have to keep Mel. Yes, I promise.' He kissed her then, slowly and tenderly. She withdrew, still looking downcast.

'Then I give you my blessing to leave Cinder. I don't like it, but I can see why you must go. I'll wait for you at Hazel and Barleycorn's home. Don't let me down.'

'I'll never let you down. Thank you. It means much to go with your blessing. I value your trust and your consent. I can stay for a few more moons at the farm if you wish...' He kissed her a second time and when they parted she surprised him by smiling.

'We should tell the others,' she said. 'They will be waiting for us.'

Hand in hand they walked to the door. Despite her smile Mel felt anguish inside, but she resolved herself to be strong – for Cinder. She understood now his need to complete his studies, but she could not shake off the sense of impending doom which permeated her thoughts. Something would go wrong, she knew, but she would deal with that when the time came...

Willow and her friends hung around in the dank corridor for what seemed like an age before the door creaked open. Both Mel and Cinder were red faced, and moisture from fresh tears still stained Mel's cheeks. However, it seemed that some common ground had been made. They turned to Cinder for an explanation. He gave it nobly.

'Mel has accepted that I have to go away. She doesn't like it, but then neither do I. You may not all understand why she may not come with me, but it's simply impossible. I'll leave in three moons. Hazel - you and Barleycorn have kindly offered to look after her for me. We both accept that generous offer. Please love her and protect her for me whilst I'm gone. I'll think of her every day that we're parted as I look forward to my return.'

'Are you sure about this Mel?' Alice sounded aghast, but Mel put her hand on her friends arm and said,

'It's alright Alice, I understand now. It just seems such a long time. It's hard for him too. Cinder will depart at the appointed time, but first he'll stay with me at Hazel and Barleycorn's place. She turned to Hazel. 'Can we set off now for your home? I'd like that.'

Hazel and Barleycorn nodded their assent. It all seemed so surreal today after the drama and excitement of the day before. To be standing in a corridor discussing their futures seemed so wrong, but it could not be helped. The Stag King and his Queen seemed to have departed the castle altogether leaving the group of friends to make their own plans. Collectively they decided that they would set off as soon as possible. In less than an hour they were all assembled back in the corridor and were ready to leave the castle behind them. Their plans were simple. Mel and Cinder would reside with Tansy's parents whilst Alice, Rory and Willow would all walk back to Oak Hall. The only problem lay with Willow's father. Still weak and sickly, they all knew that the walk would be too much for him. Cinder, trying to redeem his previous status a little further made a suggestion.

'I have a little gold with me. I'll find a solution to get Lord Oak back home safely.'

'Thank you Cinder,' Willow said gratefully. 'I would appreciate that very much and so would my father.'

Cinder left the gathering without another word. An air of tension remained between him and Mel, but hopefully that would resolve itself soon enough. For the time being the group made their way down to the front entrance of the Castle where they had first entered two days before, but this time they seemed to bypass the mysterious 'Hall of Temptations' much to the relief of Alice. The thought of running the gauntlet a second time through the revelling Fae folk filled her with trepidation. The feel of real fresh air on her face as she emerged into the sunlight gave Alice such a lift that she felt as though she were floating. If this was how the sun affected the spirit in Eyedore, Alice could fully understand how Willow almost perished when starved of its warm sustenance. With her eyes closed she breathed in the scents of earth, flora and fauna. The sounds of her friend's voices brought her back down to earth. Willow squealed loudly and when Alice opened her eyes she observed the little woman jumping up and down excitedly and clapping her hands with joy. Beside her stood Cinder with a Fae pony. The animal, like everything else here was quite diminutive in size, but perfectly formed. Cinder assisted Oak up onto the creatures back whilst it stood patiently nuzzling around in a clump of fresh grass. Cinder beamed proudly and Mel, forgetting her fears smiled along with him and cooed affectionately over the beautiful steed. Somehow, with the introduction of the sunlight happiness returned to the group once more. Hazel and Barleycorn were still rather subdued after the events of the previous day, but even they had regained a little colour and happiness now.

Despite the morning rapidly disappearing they were all confident that they could be home before the sunset. As on their arrival the route took them through the market outside of the castle. Again they were assaulted by a battery of traders calling out to them and offering their wares as they tried to attract the attention of the humans. Two people asked to buy Copper and in a bid to keep her safe Alice handed her to Oak who cuddled her affectionately from the safety of the pony's back. This time everyone felt a little more confident and they exchanged banter and cheery waves with the Fae folk around them. However, despite the jollity, when they reached the edge of the tree line and stepped into the cover of the forest they all felt somewhat happier. The conversation turned to Flint and his incarceration, but Cinder brushed such thoughts aside.

'He took his chance and lost,' he stated. 'We've seen the last of him. Let's all now look to the future.'

The journey itself turned out to be rather good spirited. Once or twice they met others on the road and exchanged greetings and news and the omens were finally looking good. One old fellow they spoke to stated that the whole area now rejoiced at Flint's punishment, happy that his harsh rule had ended.

They walked until mid-afternoon when Cinder finally called a halt, for despite not having to walk, Oak still required rest. Gratefully he slid down from the pony and settled himself under a large tree with Copper at his side. It appeared that they were now firm friends. As Willow fussed over him he rested his head against the trunk and closed his eyes. It proved to be quite a tender scene and Alice felt quite moved watching the young woman and Rory caring for the older man. She continued to watch as Willow found a flask of ale amongst the pack the horse carried and she offered it to her father. Smiling, the ailing Oak took the vessel and drank. His smile broadened and Alice heard a contented giggle from Willow. Seeing the flask made Alice aware of her own thirst and she smiled gratefully as Cinder passed her a bottle of mead. There were no glasses or cups and they shared the bottle between them. Bread and fruit were also dispensed whilst Cinder foraged amongst the hedgerow. Dandelion leaves and a few blackberries added to the meal and after eating their fill everyone felt refreshed. Oak even regained a little colour and surprisingly it was he that urged them to end their rest and be on their way. Back astride the little pony he sat bolt upright looking far better than he had appeared for days. Willow, ever the loving daughter continued to fuss at his side as they walked on. It was a good day and by nightfall they should all be home. The final part of the journey promised to be a happy affair and with joy in their hearts they pressed on.

*

*He felt gratitude when the travellers decided to stop. Keeping track of them unseen amongst the trees proved to be difficult and tiring work. Sometimes his own path became blocked, forcing him to retrace his steps and catch up with his quarry. He too benefited from the welcome break. He guessed at the destination of the old man and his annoying daughter. That girl had been the cause of his own downfall – her and the yellow haired human bitch. At some point in the near future he would ensure that they both knew the full extent of his fury and frustration. Every night he lay awake for hours devising slow and agonising deaths for them both. Soon, his time would come, but patience being one of his greatest virtues, he knew in his heart that the outcome would be well worth the wait. First he would appease and make amends with the Master and he was already well down the road to achieving that end. Afterwards he would have his own retribution. The Master would not care what he did with the women once he owned the ring. They would be his reward. With ever more dreadful thoughts in his head he continued to follow the happy group at a discreet distance.*

*

They came upon the fork in the road quite suddenly. For a few moments they fell silent for here they would go their separate ways. The main road continued on and would eventually bypass Hazel and Barleycorn's farm whilst the left hand fork led on towards Oak Hall. Mel, Cinder and the elderly farming couple would press on whilst Alice, Rory, Willow, her father and Copper would branch off to the forest hall. The goodbyes became rather emotional. Mel in particular looked most distressed. Hugging each of her friends in turn she promised vehemently to see them soon. Hazel and Barleycorn proved to be more pragmatic, looking forward to being home once more, whilst Cinder seemed wistful, but eager to press on at the same time. The other party returned the hugs in equal measure but eventually the two groups separated and went their respective ways.

*

*His decision would not be difficult. The group with the sick old man would be going on to Oak Hall – that much he knew already. The other group however were another matter. He suspected where they were heading, but he needed to be sure - they would be the ones to continue following. It would also be easier with fewer of them. The threat of discovery was lessened now. Well, he would keep his distance; find out where they were going and then report back to the Master...*

*

It took the remainder of the afternoon for them to get home to the farm. In fact darkness already surrounded them when they reached their destination. For the last few miles Cinder quickened the pace, for to be caught outside in total darkness would be both foolhardy and dangerous. There were creatures out here who only ventured out after nightfall and some of them were far from friendly. To be home before the sun finally faded brought relief for them all.

At their homecoming Hazel retrieved the small guardian figure hidden on their departure. Lifting the small effigy from the ground she whispered up a prayer to the Great Mother in the old tongue before kissing the idol and slipping it into her pocket. It smelled stuffy inside the roundhouse and Hazel threw the door open and hunted for a candle. Cinder took out a piece of flint and a striker and soon made a small fire in the hearth. Within minutes the heat and light made the old place feel instantly homely. Exhausted the old couple flopped down onto one of their benches and just sat there. Mel, feeling a little uncomfortable broke the ice by saying,

'Does anyone want anything to eat or drink? I don't mind fixing something up... No, sit down Hazel – I'll do it – you looked totally whacked!'

'Whacked is it Dearie,' the old woman chuckled. 'Never 'eard that one before... But yes, I'd love some grub if you're askin'. 'Ow about you Barleycorn?'

The old fellow nodded his agreement. Since Tansy's celebration he remained uncharacteristically quiet and Mel continued to worry about him. The young girl began hunting around in the kitchen area for some food. Under Hazel's guidance she found some preserved fruit and nuts and some stale bread. Sticking the bread on a knife she held it over the fire and toasted it. As usual Barleycorn offered them ale and they washed their meal down with a couple of mugs each. It tasted sweet and Mel had certainly acquired a liking for it since coming to Eyedore.

However, after the stress of the last few days they were all exhausted and without even clearing up from their frugal meal the four of them closed the door, settled around the fire and fell into a welcome slumber.

\*

For Willow and her group the journey ended sooner. By the end of the afternoon they were safely home. As they approached Oak Hall there were a few locals hanging around outside collecting firewood and generally discussing the situation regarding Flint's departure. When they saw their old Lord approaching a great cheer went up and they gathered around Oak, giving him a tumultuous welcome home.

It took them some time to get inside the gates, but once through it became clear that Flint had left the old place the worse for wear. Rubbish lay scattered about the yard and the door to the kitchen block hung off of its hinges. The remains of a small fire were still smouldering in the centre of the yard too, but the still glowing embers gave no clue as to what had been so recently burned. As they helped Oak to dismount a shout went up from across the yard.

'Your Lordships! You're homes!'

In the kitchen doorway stood a Fae woman of huge proportions and if Mel were present she would have recognised her from the night she sneaked into the Hall and rifled through Flint's study.

'POPPY!' Oak's voice, despite his illness carried across the yard loudly. The woman set down the basket she carried and waddled across the yard. She was extremely fat, with a big red, round face and beaming smile. Coming over to Lord Oak she reached up to him on his pony and enveloped him in her vast bosom, hugging him for so long that Willow became quite concerned. Touching Poppy on the shoulder Willow said testily,

'Be careful with him Poppy. He is still rather sick at the moment... He needs to rest.'

Abashed Poppy pulled away and mumbled an apology and then setting eyes on Rory and Alice she squealed loudly.

'Stars and moon – humans! Who's this handsomes fellow?' she bellowed. 'Oooh, Isn't he long! Just looks at the sizes of him! Is he lookings for company Mistress Willow? I'd be more than happy to walk out with him...' So saying, Poppy whacked Rory playfully across the backside and beamed up at him. Alice started to laugh, but Willow petulantly intervened.

'Rory is with me Poppy and I would be grateful if you did not look at him in that way – and keep your hands to yourself too!'

Grinning, Poppy winked at Rory and replied,

'Oh well, if he changes his minds let me knows...'

Seeing his daughter beginning to bristle, Oak thought it prudent to intervene.

'Be a good lass Poppy and see my bed is made up and ready for me – and sort out a chamber for these two and another for Alice...'

Poppy frowned, but nodded her assent.

'Very well my Lord. Consider it dones. If you comes in and gets settled I'll sorts out some foods too.'

'That would be wonderful, thank you.'

The trio followed Poppy inside. It quickly became apparent that the inside of the hall had been left in a mess too, but Poppy had been attempting to clean the place up. In one corner were several pieces of broken furniture stacked neatly in a heap. In another, a mound of books leaned haphazardly against the wall, whilst the door to Flint's study lay on the floor. Oak frowned at the damage to his family home and addressed Poppy.

'What has happened here lass? Is this mess my brothers doing?'

'Somes,' she replied breezily. 'But the Stag King's mens added to it when they searched the place. They weren't too particulars about what they dids – and I swears some things have gone missing too. I've started clearing it all up as bests as I can, but with most of the servants gone it's not been easy.'

'Gone? Gone where?'

'Most wents back to the village whens Flint scarpered. We all thoughts you were deads my Lords so with Flint gones there seemed little points in them all remainings. I reckons if you sends words to the village they'd loves to come backs and serve you again...'

Willow interrupted the conversation.

'Poppy, my father really needs to rest. We appreciate you staying on and all you have done, but could you please make his bed ready? I really do not want him getting over tired. And Rory and I are exhausted and desperately want a bed too.'

Grinning mischievously Poppy winked at Rory and replied to Willow,

'I bet you do! He's a handsome one for sure...'

Poppy's attention to Rory clearly annoyed Willow. She glared at the forward speaking servant and snapped,

'Just get it done! And keep your eyes and your hands to yourself Poppy – Rory is with me'

'Steady on Willow, she meant no harm.' Rory sounded quite indignant.

Willow gave him a withering look and fortunately her father saved the day.

'Behave yourself Poppy! Things have become a little slack around here or so it seems. Get the beds made up and we can all get some sleep.'

Sheepishly, Poppy wandered off grumbling and then Rory began to laugh.

'She really upset you didn't she?' he said to Willow.

'Yes she did and so did you by sticking up for her. See you behave yourself around her Rory or you will get to see a side of me that you do not like!' Seeing that Willow took genuine offence by Poppy's behaviour Rory gave her comfort.

'Come on Willow, you know you are the only girl for me. Don't pull that face – it's just a bit of fun, and I promise, I'm not interested in Poppy or anyone else.'

Willow lowered her guard a little and nodded, accepting Rory's apology. To Oak she said,

'Come along father; let us get you to bed. I want you settled for the night.'

Oak made a great pretence of not wanting any fuss and winking at a grinning Rory he gave Willow his arm and allowed her to guide him to his bed chamber.

*

*At Barleycorn and Hazel's farm the first part of his plan was complete. The information he could now provide to the Master would be both valuable and well received. He could now withdraw and assist with the great scheme once more. As silently as he had tracked them to their home he began to retrace his steps back through the forest. Stealth would not be necessary now and he could move considerably faster. With any luck he would be delivering his news by daybreak and it should not be too difficult for the Master to continue with his original aims. The miserable peasants around here might be celebrating for now, but they had no idea of what was coming, no idea at all. Smiling he wrapped his green cloak tighter around his shoulders and plunged on into the darkness.*

***

# 20

# A PARTING AND A PLOT

*With the sun rising above the horizon he reached his destination. The journey through the forest had been long and harsh. However, the rewards would compensate for his exertions which now seemed a mere trifle. Patiently he waited inside the cave mouth. With his back against the wall and one hand on his dagger he settled down for some well-earned rest.*

*He slept for a considerable time before something wakened him. He sat up peering into the gloom of the cave and then he saw it. A small figure lurked within the shadows. Smaller even than most of the Fae people, in human terms this one reached only a metre high. It sported short hair, possessed a wrinkled and ancient looking face and pointed ears. Coarse, leathery looking breeches clad the legs which ended in cloven feet. Unsmiling, it observed the servant of the Master, then without a word the tiny faun beckoned before disappearing into the darkness. He followed, his hunter's instincts keeping him close behind his tiny guide. Eventually the tunnel opened out into a large cavern and there, seated before a fire and surrounded by piles of ancient books sat Flint. He looked tired and dishevelled and a black patch covered one of his eyes. He said nothing, but indicated his guest should sit opposite. Once seated, the faun passed him a steaming bowl of broth.*

*'You have news? What can you tell me?' Flint asked.*

*'I know where to find the wood nymph and her friends.'*

*'You think I do not know that already? Is that the best you can offer?'*

*'In three moons the cunning one will be departing for the Holy realm. He's to spend twelve moons there learning of the higher degrees and of the skills of second sight. Consequently his friends will be unprotected.'*

'And what of the Stag King? Where is he in all of this?'

'The Stag King has his own agenda. He's departed for talks with the Fenlanders on trade and their continued alliance with Eyedore. That will keep him busy for some considerable time.'

'I should thank you for releasing me from the tree. The fauns have performed well under your guidance and they have attended me admirably.'

Cobalt relaxed. His belly growled for the soup smelt good. However, he remained wary of Flint, but it seemed that the old man may be coming around. He dipped the wooden spoon into the thick broth and swallowed a few mouthfuls before going on.

'The human male and his sibling are with your brother and niece at Oak Hall and the yellow haired bitch has been taken in by a peasant couple. Their daughter helped Willow to escape – my men shot her down on the road.'

'Now that is news to me,' responded Flint. 'The yellow haired girl is another one who has a debt to settle. You do realise that I hold you responsible for the loss of my niece and the ring? At the moment you remain useful. Ensure that you continue so. One way or another I will obtain my brothers title and lands. If I kill the humans along the way then that would be a bonus. See that I am not disappointed a second time…'

Cobalt bowed his head. He dared one further question.

'The girl…your niece… When this is done what will happen to her?'

'I shall kill her.'

'A favour… In return for my continued loyalty… Could I have her? When I'm done with her I'll happily kill her myself…'.

'If you obtain my brother's property for me you can do whatever you wish with her – so long as she dies when you are done.'

'Thank you. With such a comely prize at stake I'll not let you down a second time My Lord.'

'Then in three moons from now when the cunning one departs I shall send you forth accompanied by a pack of my fauns. This is what you shall do…'

\*

The days following their excursion from the castle saw many changes in the human's lives. One of the first things that Hazel did for Mel was to make her a full set of Fae clothing. The peasant garb suited her and joyously she put the clothes on and showed them off to Cinder. With the animosity between them ended he looked on admiringly as Mel spun and twirled in her long green skirt, white linen tunic and a woollen shawl.

Similarly, over at Oak Hall, Alice and Rory found themselves kitted out in brand new Fae garments too. Oak commissioned a Fae tailor from the village of Nettlebed to measure them up and provide suitable clothing. The little man jumped at the chance to make something special for them both and he excelled in his work. Alice looked positively stunning. She now wore a close fitting dress similar to Willows although it hung a little longer on the hem. Hers was not made of leaves, but of a soft, natural fabric that clung to her figure without restricting her movements in any way. A bag, belt and pouch accessorised the beautiful plum coloured dress. A lace ran up the front and supported her ample bosom whilst remaining respectable. Normally a conservative dresser Alice had been sceptical about wearing the outfit when she first set eye upon it, but once on, she refused to go back to her human clothes saying,

'I never thought that I would possess anything as beautiful as this. I'm transformed!'

Rory also sported something a little more dashing than his usual style too. Bottle green breeches, a ruffled shirt and a wine coloured velvet jacket which almost reached his knees brought a smile to his face when he saw it. He felt like a pirate when he first donned the flamboyant outfit. Willow loved him in the clothes and on first seeing him she squealed and danced around the room with such merriment that Rory thought her quite mad. He knew she fully approved when finally calming down she advanced on him, wrapped herself around him with one of her enveloping hugs and whispered softly,

'I love you so much. Please do not leave me Rory, ever – promise me?'

'Of course I will never leave you, you silly little thing. I love you more than anything Willow – never, ever forget that.'

*

Three moons later a message arrived at Oak Hall. The message stated that Cinder would soon be leaving to complete his magical training and Oak, Willow, Rory and Alice were invited to the farm to see him off. Still rather weak after his long ordeal, Willow insisted that Oak would benefit far more by staying behind under the watchful and caring eye of Poppy. Despite her wandering eyes everyone knew she would take good care of him and he would want for nothing.

As the two humans and Willow prepared to depart Willow gave her final instructions to a grinning Poppy. Alice decided that Copper should stay behind too, much too Poppy's delight.

'Look after Copper well,' Willow said. 'Do not forget to feed her every day and do not see her lost or you will answer to me! And do not let father become over tired. He should rest Poppy – I mean it! He has been doing well in his recovery and I want no setbacks for him. If I find that you have been pestering him I will not be happy. He does not need you and all your high cockalorum! Feed him, wash him and help him with anything else that he wants, but that is all – do you understand?'

Poppy stood smirking back at Willow. Then, quite sweetly she said,

'Don't knows what you means Mistress Willow. Don't knows what you means at all. I have no ideas why you have such suspicions of me. Me? Well, I means if I...'

'Just behave Poppy or I *will* find out!'

Willow turned her back on the outrageous woman. She did not want to enter into an argument with her, for despite their sometimes frosty relationship Willow had known Poppy since childhood and loved her dearly. However, in Willow's view Poppy needed a little guidance in her behaviour sometimes, and a few well-placed words were all it normally took. Poppy would always give the impression that she did not care what Willow or anyone else said to her, but in her heart Willow knew that the message would have got through. Jabbing Rory in the ribs to distract him from Poppy's flirting she turned and set off huffily down the road with Alice and her sheepish looking brother following on.

For a time they walked in silence as Willow fumed over Poppy's blatant wantonness whilst Alice and Rory did their best not to laugh aloud. Eventually, still stifling his mirth Rory spoke.

'Good day for a walk...' Willow remained tight lipped and Rory tried again. 'Want some of these?'

Willow stopped and looked at him scathingly as he held out a handful of shelled cobnuts from his pocket. Still glaring frostily Willow said,

'Do not think that you can get round me like that. I saw you staring at Poppy! You could hardly keep your eyes off of her...'

Unable to contain his laughter any further Rory erupted into loud guffaws. Worse still, Alice joined in too. Placing her hands on her hips Willow scowled back at both of them, but after a few moments she began to crack. She found Poppy's behaviour quite amusing herself, but had no intention of letting on to Rory. Seeing him almost flirting with her made Willow decide to punish him. However, his laughter being rather infectious, Willow found herself joining in. The three of them stood there together giggling and then Willow struck out and cuffed Rory around the head.

'That is for flirting with Poppy!' she said loudly, 'and that,' she squealed, giving him another blow, 'is for laughing!' She aimed a third, but Rory saw it coming and caught her by the wrist.

'Listen woman,' he said jokingly, 'hit me again and I'd be forced to punish you...'
Willow smirked.

'And just how would you do that?' she whispered.

Rory said nothing, but just kissed her firmly. Alice made a vomiting sound and pretended to put her fingers down her throat, but her brother and Willow didn't even seem to notice her. When they parted Rory looked Willow firmly in the eye and said,

'I love you so much. I don't want anyone else, least of all Poppy – really I don't. Never think that of me...' He kissed her again and when he pulled away a second time saw that her eyes were moist with tears. 'What's the matter, he asked concernedly.

'Nothing, nothing at all. I love you too, so much so that sometimes it hurts. Now let us push on or we shall be late getting to the farm.'

They continued walking and holding hands whilst Alice followed on behind at a discreet distance, allowing them to talk until they all stopped around midday for a short break. The remainder of the walk during the afternoon took them through some rather beautiful countryside. Once or twice they met other travellers who greeted them and at one point as they walked Willow took out her flute and played a gentle tune as they strolled along. Rory could not remember anything ever being so perfect and soaked up the atmosphere of happiness and love that surrounded him. Alice joined in too, humming the tune as they went along. This wonderful world was far apart from the human version and both Rory and Alice now loved every moment of being there. Rory only snapped out of his daydreaming when Willow stopped playing and put her flute away.

Before them lay the farm where Hazel and Barleycorn lived and in the clearing just opposite the house stood Mel. With a basket over her arm she happily laboured below a dwarf plum tree, selecting the biggest fruits. With a twist and a flourish each one landed in her basket as she moved on to the next. She didn't see her friends advancing upon her until the last moment. Dropping the basket Mel threw herself across the last few feet and into Alice's arms.

'Oh thank you for coming! Thank you!'
Rory spoke first.

'Where's Cinder? We haven't missed him have we?
Mel shook her head.

'No,' she responded. 'He's inside packing. Hazel suggested I pick a few of these as he rather likes them.'

Together they trooped into the roundhouse and there they found Cinder sitting at the table sipping at a final mug of mead. Barleycorn offered the jug all round and in a few moments they were all surrounding Cinder and clinking their mugs together in greeting. Rory proposed a toast.

'Here's to Cinder,' he intoned. 'May the next twelve moons pass us by and bring him back safely. Here's to you mate!' Tipping up his mug Rory emptied the contents and placed the empty vessel on the table. Barleycorn topped it up without a word. Standing up Cinder raised his own mug and said,

'And here is to friends. I have made a few good ones here. To Willow, I say prosper and bless that man of yours with many children. To Barleycorn and Hazel, all I ask is that you stay safe and well and protect my girl there...' Here, he indicated to Mel. 'And to my own sweet love, Mel, keep a place for me in your heart. In the twelve moons I am gone please think of me every day, for I will be thinking of you. May the Goddess bless you all and grant me a speedy return.'

A silence fell for a few moments as Cinder began to pull his cloak about him and set his bag on his back. When ready he turned to Mel and bringing his hand from his pocket he showed her a small item. The amulet he held looked very similar to Willow's.

'I made this for you. Put it around your neck my sweet and it will always remind you of me. You are one of us now and should wear one at all times. It is made from Tansy flowers so that she will always be close to you and protect you. It will, I hope, make you closer to Hazel and Barleycorn too...'

Mel's hands shook as she took hold of the beautiful gift. As she touched it she felt it move in her hand as though the contact brought it to life. Cinder helped her to slip it around her neck and then kissed her. Choking back tears of joy Mel hugged him close.

'I said the old words over it; it knows it belongs to you now. It will bring you luck...'

'Come back to me safely Cinder. I will think of you every day... And thank you... Thank you so much for such a lovely gift. I cannot even begin to say what it means to me...'

Collectively the group fell silent except for a few stifled sniffs. As Cinder made to leave, Mel remembering her own gift called him back.

'I got these for you... They seem somewhat feeble now after the beautiful amulet you have given me, but Hazel said you liked them...' Her voice trailed off as she felt totally inadequate.

Cinder looked at the basket of freshly picked plums that Mel held in her hands. He looked at her solemnly before breaking into his dazzling smile. Taking the purple fruits he packed as many into his bag as would comfortably fit.

'They are gratefully received. I do indeed love these and will enjoy them on the road. Thank you, they are a thoughtful gift.'

It was time. Unable to delay further Cinder walked to the door followed by his friends.

'It's been a pleasure. I bid you all goodbye, but only for a short time. Keep safe and I'll return next summer.

You...' He addressed this to Willow, 'look after your father. He's a decent man. And try to keep out of trouble, for your uncle's followers would still do you harm if they could. I'll not be around for a while to protect you, so never go into the forest alone. Keep your dagger sharp and your wits sharper still. Make sure that you're here too when I return.'

Finally he shook Rory's hand, embraced Hazel and Barleycorn and hugged Mel one last time. Their parting kiss was drawn out and tender. Then he pulled away, turned and without a single glance back walked down the path that led into the forest.

*

After Cinder left the roundhouse the atmosphere at the farm felt rather tarnished. Mel became subdued and no one knew what to say to her. Hazel, seeing Mel's distress found her some chores to do to take her mind off things.

'Come on Dearie,' she intoned. 'I need some 'elp clearin' up from breakfast. You come and give ol' 'Azel an 'and.' Mel nodded. She stood up and began helping Hazel clear away in silence.

The day passed slowly, but eventually dusk came upon them. Hazel and Mel had prepared a fine dinner for the evening. They served a stew of root vegetables, steamed nettles and potatoes, all served up on large trencher breads. Mel added some wild garlic and it gave a lovely flavour to the meal. For the first time that day Mel spoke of Cinder as they ate. She appeared fine talking about him and everyone felt relieved to hear her mention his name so positively. They all contributed to the conversation and by the end of dinner Mel had been smiling and even laughed aloud a couple of times. They spent the remainder of the evening sitting out under the stars, drinking mead and discussing their futures. Willow and Rory already knew what they planned to do. Oak offered to assist them in arranging for a house to be built out in the woods. They would handfast in the autumn and have babies as soon as possible – lots of babies according to Willow. Mel spoke of Cinder's return the following year and of how she hoped he would still want to wed her too. Only Alice seemed a little vague for she could not even begin to imagine where her new life may take her. At first she had been so dubious about coming to live in Eyedore, but now, she felt that she really belonged here. They talked way into the night, but eventually Barleycorn stood up and stretching, announced he wanted his bed and one by one they all slipped inside.

They went to their beds that night with full bellies and a sense that despite her initial sadness Mel would be fine. Outwardly she seemed better and after the sociable evening with her friends she seemed almost back to her old self. No one however, saw her quietly crying herself to sleep. Cinder's departure had hit her hard. She felt no doubt that given a little time she would come to terms with his leaving, but for now at least she would continue to put on a brave face.

The following morning Willow rose early. By the time her friends had awoken she had washed, returned and now sat quietly by the fire. She looked pale and drawn, but when Rory questioned her she merely shrugged, stating that she had not slept well. When breakfast arrived Hazel did them proud as usual. Porridge, bread and butter spread with honey and fried eggs were all served up. Whilst most tucked in noisily, Willow ate frugally, merely picking at a piece of bread dipped in honey. No one noticed her reluctance to eat or her reflective mood and for that she was grateful.

The conversation turned to a discussion of their return to Oak Hall. Feeling a little better after eating her bread Willow expressed her concerns for her father – especially at having left him under the care of Poppy. She longed to get home as soon as possible. Alice decided however to stay on for a few days. She knew the route back to Oak Hall now and felt confident at making the return journey alone in a few days' time. Mel thoroughly approved her decision to stay on a little longer, but Rory objected to his sister making her own way back alone. Alice shouted him down though and even Willow sided with her saying,

'I used to spend all of my time alone in the woods around here – it is quite safe Rory. My uncle is gone and things have returned to how they used to be. Do not be such a curmudgeon! Alice will be fine, you shall see.'
Rory, being attacked from both sides surrendered.

'Okay, okay,' he laughed, 'you win. Just make sure you leave early enough to get home before it gets dark – promise?'

'Okay, I promise!'

*

Willow and Rory set off shortly after breakfast ended. It felt rather good, just the two of them together and the fresh air and exercise revived Willow further. An hour into their journey Rory reminded her of the time at the castle when they had walked together through the woods. Smiling, she laughed and kissed him passionately, but refused his advances.

'What's wrong,' he asked, irritation now emerging in his voice.

'Nothing is wrong,' she said. 'It is just that I worry about my father. I want to get home and know that he is safe. However, if you want to come into the forest with me - and just for a *short* time mind, I want to show you a special place – somewhere that I go when my spirit needs mending or when I need to reflect on some great thing. It is not far from here. Would you care to see it?'

Satisfied that Willow was not going off of him Rory accepted her reason for spurning him. But at her mention of a 'special place' his interest immediately piqued. As he nodded his agreement Willow took his hand and led him beneath the cover of the trees.

They walked for around ten minutes, dodging branches and having to skirt around clumps of brambles and nettles as they went. Rory questioned Willow's navigation, but she merely smiled, confidant in her local knowledge. Suddenly they were there as the trees parted and opened out into a forest glade. The place looked ancient and Rory stared around in sheer disbelief. Before him a clearing opened out to reveal a dip in the forest floor. Thick moss lay everywhere and the smell of damp earth and leaves became quite intoxicating. However, it was the monument that really caught his attention. Arranged in a circle around the glade were thirty or so standing stones. Some were leaning over a little and one had even fallen – most likely centuries before. More moss coated the stones in a thick green layer giving them an unearthly appearance. In the centre of the circle a shorter, cone shaped stone stood to about the height of Rory's waist. The atmosphere here felt peaceful and Rory looked on in wonderment at Willow as she closed her eyes and drank in the heady sensations of the place. He spoke in a whisper for he sensed that to talk loudly here would be wrong.

'What is this place? It's beautiful...'

Willow opened her eyes and whispered back.

'I know not,' she said. 'I discovered it one day as I played in the forest as a child. As soon as I found it I knew it held meaning for me although I have never understood why – I know I just belong – it always draws me back for I have some connection here that I cannot explain. Whenever I sit amongst these stones I feel both elated and sad at the same time, it is very strange. I know not why, but I often feel close to my mother here – perhaps she once knew of this place too... It is as though I know the place, although until I discovered it I swear I had never been here before...'

Tears welled up in her eyes and concerned, Rory embraced her.

'Whatever is it Willow?' he asked. 'You seemed so quiet this morning at breakfast and now you weep. Can't you tell me?'

She nodded, and indicating the fallen stone, she sat and beckoned him beside her.

'You are right. There is something we should speak of and this is the perfect place to do it…'

Something in her manner frightened him, but through her tears he could detect the hint of a smile and some hidden joy. When she took his hand and placed it on her belly he understood. He felt the blood rush to his head and then his own tears came too.

'Willow! You mean…? You…?'

'Yes Rory. The Goddess has blessed me and I am with child. That is why I felt unwell this morning. I have done so every morning for this past moon, but you never noticed…'

He looked abashed at that, but then hugged her close, holding her and feeling the love rampaging through his veins. He smothered her face in kisses and she laughed, enjoying the moment. When he finally withdrew she placed her finger to his lips and smiling, whispered,

'Sit quietly for a moment and I will show you something else…'

He fell silent as she bid and then Willow caught hold of his arm.

'There!' she hissed. 'On top of that stone! Do not move or speak; just watch…'

Perched upon the nearest of the standing stones sat a robin. The tiny bird seemed fully aware of their presence, but showed no sign of fear. Even as Rory looked on Willow held out her hand. Pursing her lips she whistled and perfect birdsong flowed from her sweet mouth. In a moment the robin flew down and landed upon her outstretched hand. Rory sat transfixed. Willow whistled away and the robin whistled back. It seemed as if they were talking to each other and she drew her hand close to her face. As though listening to her he cocked his head to one side and bounced up and down on his spindly legs. Willow turned to Rory and instinctively he knew what she expected of him. Holding out his own hand he gasped as the tiny creature hopped across the gap and settled on his finger. Like Willow he drew his hand to his face and smiled. But the robin only stayed a few moments and then quite suddenly took to the air and disappeared amongst the trees chattering frantically. Rory let out his breath.

'That's wonderful,' he stated. 'How did you do that?'
When he turned to Willow he saw sadness in her eyes.

'What is wrong now?' he asked.
Willow sniffed and wiped her face.

'The robin is so special to me,' she replied, 'although I do not understand his meaning either. If I come here he always seeks me out. When he flies away it makes me feel abandoned and tearful every time… It is as though I have lost something or someone very precious, although I know not what or who…'

Rory slipped a protective arm around her waist and pecked her cheek.

'Thank you for showing me this place and giving me such wonderful news,' he whispered. 'I can see just why you love it here so much. Have you shown anyone else?'

'No one, no one at all, you are the first…' Her mood changed. Standing up Willow looked about her. 'We should go now,' she said. 'The robin sensed danger.'

She started back along the path that had brought them to the glade, Rory following on behind. Her mood swing uneased him as a thousand questions ran through his head.

'What do you mean danger? Danger from what?
'I know not, but do not tarry. The robin always - *OW!*'
'WILLOW?'
'I have been stung…'

She turned her bare arm and flinched at the sight of a tiny dart embedded in her flesh. Made from a single feather with a sharpened and weighted quill, the tip had gone deep. She pulled it free and fresh blood ran down her arm. Alarm spread across her face.

'Oh Goddess *NO! Please... not that...*'

Her legs buckled beneath her as Rory reached her side. Catching her weight he gently lowered her to the ground. Her eyes rolled back into her head, showing just the whites and she began to twitch uncontrollably. Rory was devastated. Just moments before they had been so happy, sharing the news of her pregnancy. Now...

Rory looked about him frantically, clueless as to the danger that surrounded them both. A moment later he felt a sharp stinging pain in his neck and reaching there pulled out a similar dart. His vision began to blur. He sensed the weakening in his own legs and sat heavily beside the fallen Willow. His breathing became laboured and as he lay beside her the last thing he saw was a group of tiny, horned figures emerge from the undergrowth. He looked on helpless as they bent and surrounded his beloved Willow and then he knew no more...

\*\*\*

# ACKNOWLEDGMENTS

Thank you to Sarah E Smith and Kelly Lewis. Your advice, editing and overall support proved to be invaluable. I couldn't have completed this work without your input, advice and encouragement. Gratitude to you both.

Printed in Poland
by Amazon Fulfillment
Poland Sp. z o.o., Wrocław